Rogue's Lady

Robyn Carr

Jacket design by Natanya Wheeler
Interior design by Judith Engracia

This novel is a work of historical fiction. Names, characters, places and
incidents relating to non-historical figures are either the product of the
author's imagination or are used fictitiously. Any resemblance of such non-
historical incidents, places or figures to actual events or locales or persons,
living or dead, is entirely coincidental.

For more information, please visit http://www.RobynCarr.com

Other Works by Robyn Carr

Historical Novels
Chelynne
The Blue Falcon
The Bellerose Bargain
The Braeswood Tapestry
The Troubadour's Romance
By Right of Arms
The Everlasting Covenant
Woman's Own

Virgin River Series
Virgin River
Shelter Mountain
Whispering Rock
A Virgin River Christmas
Second Chance Pass
Temptation Ridge
Paradise Valley
Forbidden Falls
Angel's Peak
Moonlight Road
Promise Canyon
Wild Man Creek
Harvest Moon
Bring Me Home for Christmas
Hidden Summit
Redwood Bend
Sunrise Point
My Kind of Christmas

Thunder Point Series
The Wanderer
The Newcomer
The Hero

Grace Valley Series
Down by the River
Just Over the Mountain
Deep in the Valley

Contemporary Single Titles
Tempted
Informed Risk
Mind Tryst
The House on Olive Street
The Wedding Party
Blue Skies
Runaway Mistress
Never Too Late
A Summer in Sonoma

Novellas
Under the Christmas Tree
Midnight Confessions

For Sherrie Clark Jessup,
with thanks for your support and friendship.

One

Virginia, March 2, 1794

S ix men anxiously waited for the early morning fog to thin over a flat patch of ground alongside the James River. The dawn mists were too thick for a duel. The opponents, Tyson Gervais and Michael Everly, kept a discreet distance from each other. Alexander Gervais, Tyson's younger brother, was his second, and Peter Dunsby, Everly's manservant, was his. The other observers were the sheriff and the surgeon, both so distressed by the prospect of what was taking place that they passed a flask between them to gather courage.

As the sun rose, the fog lifted. A landau rattled down the road toward the river field, and Tyson Gervais scowled as he recognized Lenore Fenton, the antagonist in the midst of this battle. Alexander leaned toward his brother. "What is she doing here? She should have stayed away."

Lenore allowed the sheriff to help her out of the carriage. Her cape, clasped at her throat, was spread back over her shoulders to display her enticing décolletage, tight waist and abundant bosom. She was unmindful of the chill, dressed as if prepared to strut along the Richmond boardwalk in the afternoon sun rather than witness a duel between her lovers.

"Then you don't know Lenore Fenton," Tyson replied. "She has lived her whole life for this—to see two men do damage to each other...as if this duel were really over her."

"Don't go through with it, Ty," Alexander said. "Let us both walk away now."

Tyson's dark brows drew together broodingly, his gray eyes glittering silver in the early morning light. "Do you think he will cease? You know I don't want Lenore, and you have heard

Everly's demands. I am going through with this at his insistence. He has pushed too hard and it must be finished."

"Tyson, it is not worth it—"

"I could ignore the rumors he started," Tyson said lowly, cutting his brother off. "Telling Richmond at large that I raped his fiancée was amusing, since almost everyone assumes I'd visited Lenore's bed for some five years. Following me to my banking and business appointments to hurl insults at my back, calling me a coward and a fool—that, too, I could abide. But when he could not intimidate me and began to harass my family, I found the limit to my patience. He needs to be chastened and sent away from this country." Tyson took a deep, stabilizing breath and looked to the north end of the field, where he saw Lenore in conversation with Everly. "If I am quick and good, he will have enough blood left in his veins to take the presumptuous whore out of Virginia."

Alexander, too, observed the couple. Tyson had ended a liaison with Lenore after many years of casual intimacies. There had never been any commitment between the two, and Lenore had entertained a number of men. Tyson had urged his ex-lover to find a worthy man with whom she could settle into marriage, and she had quickly developed the relationship with Everly, the visiting Englishman. Her new courtship with Everly had been only two months old when Lenore called Tyson to her bed and Everly found them thus. Tyson had crawled between her sheets almost out of habit. Tyson's mistake had come when he apologized to Everly, who claimed to be Lenore's fiancé. Everly took the apology as an admission of Tyson's guilt.

"He is a pompous ass," Alexander breathed. "Look at him."

Tyson observed the British dandy dressed for an early morning duel in a ruffled shirt, a lavender coat, and wearing sparkling buckles on his shoes. Tyson, garbed only in britches and a linen shirt open at the neck, shook his head in bemusement. "Either the two of them have an appointment at a formal soiree following this contest, or he plans to stop a lead ball with his satin and lace."

"Damn," Alex cursed. "Here she comes." Both men watched Lenore swirl away from Everly and begin the long trek across the field toward Tyson and his brother. She held her dress above her ankles, picking her way through the damp field grass. When she stood before them, Tyson felt an urge to squeeze the life out of her.

"I'm sorry," she said. "He will not change his mind."

Tyson looked down into her green eyes, a cynical smile twisting his hips. "Where do you stand for the duel, *cherie*? In the north field, or the south?"

Lenore looked between Alex and Tyson, her lips quivering with the strain of confusion. "How can I make you understand? I love you both. Michael came to me with honorable intentions after you threw me down. After all the years you and I had...could you think I want your blood? Good God, Tyson, all I ever wanted was your love."

A muscle twitched in his cheek. This woman, whose experienced affections he had sampled over the years, had, until now, deceived only to play at courtship games. But the lies that led up to this occasion were too much. "You told him you were a virgin when he laid with you. You should have corrected the poor young rooster. You were not a virgin the first time I had you, some five years ago, and you were little more than a girl then."

The color rose to Lenore's cheeks, and Alexander looked away. "Would you strip me of my last ounce of dignity before the only man to offer me decency through marriage?" she asked, her mouth pinched in a furious line. "You played as if no price whatever accompanied your roving. You used me at your leisure, and would you save your own reputation with some public statement from me that I am fallen from any virtue? Do you draw yourself some sweet lad debauched by a wicked woman? I am twenty-four years old...you are five and thirty. You can take care of the largest family enterprise in Virginia, but you cannot be responsible for your own manly acts."

"Come, coward," Everly shouted from across the field. "Does the field give you favorable enough view, knave?"

Lenore's head snapped around to look at the man she had claimed as a fiancé. "You have ruined me in my own city," she whispered furiously at Tyson. "And you won't be happy until you have ruined my whole life."

She spun away from him and took angry strides back to her landau. She stood there with her driver while the sheriff, a bit wobbly on his feet from too much of the flask, signaled for the men to come together. The six met in the center of the field.

Everly sneered at Tyson. "So, at last you find the courage to fight as honorably as you should."

The sheriff spread a cloth on the ground, laying it open to expose two pistols. "They have been shot and reloaded. You are allowed one shot each at the end of the ten count."

"I warn you once more, Everly," Tyson said slowly. "I have never missed my mark. If you walk away from this now, there will be no injury. I pose no threat to your future with the woman. It was a passing affair, at her will, no more."

"Ha. Passing affair? Even now you malign her reputation, making it seem that I take a common whore to wife. There will be no injury, Gervais. I mean to kill you."

Tyson's mouth was set in a grim line. "Don't be a fool. Take this one last chance to leave the field."

"You are brave enough to bed another man's woman, Gervais. Is that the limit of your courage?"

The sheriff belched and turned away to cover his mouth. "Tyson...Tyson speaks true, sir, he will not miss. He is the best aim in the country. Heed his advice... take your fiancée away."

"Never," Everly shouted. "When a gentleman beds a woman, he weds her, and when a gentleman beds another man's woman, he answers his actions in the duel. To the death."

Tyson growled low in his throat, his ire stretched to the snapping point by the slight, fair-skinned dandy. Take your pistol."

Everly made a quick dip to pick up a pistol, looked at it briefly, held it before his chest, and turned his back, ready for the count. Tyson slowly did the same, each man waiting for the sheriff to back away from the line of fire and begin. They took their paces, and as they marked space between them, Tyson tried to steady his nerves. He doubted Everly could shoot, but hoped to hit Everly's pistol arm before the Englishman fired. Tyson did not intend to dodge a lead ball.

They turned. Tyson took quick aim, fired, and heard the explosion mingle with Lenore's scream. Everly's hands clutched his chest as his legs crumpled beneath him. Tyson was paralyzed for a moment, amazed at his poor marksmanship. He had meant to hit Everly's right arm, yet if he wasn't mistaken, the man's left chest had taken the ball.

Lenore shrieked in horror and ran across the field toward Michael Everly. His servant was already there, cradling his head, while the sheriff and surgeon stood in shock with the others. Tyson exchanged puzzled glances with his brother. Both had been wary of the Englishman, worried that by some freak accident he might injure Tyson with a chance shot, but no one had been prepared for Tyson actually killing the man.

Tyson was here only because he had been ruthlessly goaded into the duel. In spite of Everly's threat to use his one shot to kill, Tyson had meant only to stop the Englishman from firing and, he had hoped, silence him with the shame of losing. Tyson had hoped his anger would not compromise his ability to hit his mark to such an extent that Everly would be maimed, but he had never even considered that he might accidentally kill the man.

Tyson's hand was damp as he gripped the pistol and slowly walked toward Everly. Lenore looked up as he approached, tears streaking her cheeks. "You've killed him. My God, you've killed him. And you, the better aim, you could have spared him." She let her head drop over Everly's face as she sobbed. Tyson looked at the man's chest in total amazement. There was a black smudge where the ball had hit, and the crimson stain of his blood had spread over his chest. He was still and ashen, his eyes staring blankly ahead.

Tyson felt his stomach lurch. The surgeon knelt to look at the man, but Lenore hysterically pushed him away. "Leave him be, you drunken fool. You were called here to attend to any injuries. There is nothing you can do for him now." The surgeon remained a moment beside the dead man, but finding no usefulness in that, he finally rose and turned forlorn, glassy eyes toward Tyson. He slowly shook his head.

The sheriff looked at Tyson. "It was a fair contest, Tyson. You've got nothin' to fear from me. He wouldn't give it up before this." The men all stood looking down at Everly, but Tyson handed the sheriff the hot pistol and turned away. He walked briskly toward his horse and once there, donned the jacket he'd brought. Alexander ran behind him. "You couldn't help it, Ty," Alexander said.

"He's dead," Tyson said bitterly.

"You had to defend yourself."

"He didn't fire."

"You warned him to give up his idiocy, Tyson. Leave it be."

Both men turned as Lenore came running toward them, gasping and panting in near panic. Her cheeks were streaked with tears, her gown stained with the man's blood. "Tyson, what will you do?" she demanded.

His head gestured toward Michael Everly, who was being carried toward Lenore's carriage by her driver and his servant. "I have done my part, madam. It was a pitiful waste."

"Will you marry me?" she asked.

He looked down at her, his eyes glittering with carefully subdued rage. "Did you think to back me into marriage through a duel, madam? I warned you it was useless. No doubt you urged him on, but your scheming cost him his life." He put his foot in the stirrup, swinging into the saddle. "Pray for forgiveness, madam. I shall pray for greater wisdom."

She grabbed at his ankle. "If you don't marry me now, I will be worth nothing here," she screamed. "It was all because of you that this has happened. Will you end two lives?"

"Let go of me, woman," he growled. "I have made one serious mistake; I will not couple it with a second. Go bury your man."

She backed away from his steed. "Will you cast me off again and again, to be fed upon by the hungry wolves in their gossip circles? Now that everyone knows about us?"

Tyson looked at his brother, who still stood by his own horse, having not yet mounted. "Alex, see if there's anything you can do here. I am going home. I will be packing."

"Packing?" Alex said. "You have no reason to flee from this. There will be no charge."

"I do not flee," he said evenly. "If the stench of lies and death will not leave me be, I will leave it." He gave his horse a sharp heel, and the stallion reared and carried him away from the site. He rode the horse hard, not slowing until Lenore's wails failed to vibrate inside his skull.

Two

The gelding's hooves threw back huge clods of dirt as the animal tore up the rain-softened country road. Vieve leaned into Tristan's mane, her hands loose on the reins and her heels shoved hard into the stirrups. The horse did not respond to her control with his usual obedience, perhaps confused by his mistress's tension. Her heart was pounding. She lacked courage for this nighttime ride; she had always been afraid of the dark.

Her hood was pulled over her golden hair, and her long black cape rippled in the wind behind her. She knew she should slow the horse. It was most unwise to indulge in such speed along these winding country roads, especially at night. But it was the half-covered moon, which seemed so haunting, the oppressive darkness all around her, and the black, claw-like branches that loomed threateningly above her that caused her to mistreat the horse.

Trembling as she did, she couldn't imagine what had prompted her to agree to this late night meeting. But Andrew had been so insistent; the longing he expressed was so contagious. He simply wished to be alone with her, to hold her, just for a while. And she had come to desire the same. Their romance had been so awkward, their merest embrace or slightest kiss interrupted by family members, friends, or servants. They were never allowed any privacy, and she chafed as much as he against their interfering chaperones. How were they ever to discover their love under such conditions of restraint? And how could they marry without first letting love find a way?

Yet, was the answer a secret meeting in the old abandoned keep on her father's property? She had never thought she would be convinced to participate in such a hoyden antic, such a scandalous escapade. However, she had begun to think Andrew was right. They had a right to some time together, away from the prying eyes and the cold, calculating business propositions that accompanied marriage contracts. No one would ever know...

As she rounded the curve in the road less than a mile from the site of the old keep, Tristan reared in sudden panic, causing her to drop the left rein. A coach approached them on the curve. The driver might not see her at all, completely covered as she was in her black cape.

As she grabbed for the rein futilely, her fingers slipped through the gelding's mane and her left heel came out of the stirrup. The driver veered the coach sharply to the right, a shout of surprise accompanying his action. The wheels made a loud screeching sound as they swerved to the shoulder of the road and into the tall grass. The coach did not topple, but Vieve did. She grabbed for the mane, the saddle, the glistening flank, but caught nothing to break her fall. Her rump hit the ground first, knocking the breath out of her, with only her petticoats cushioning her landing. She lay stunned for a moment, listening to her horse gallop away.

"What the hell..."

A man's voice and the sound of a coach door opening came simultaneously. Vieve struggled to sit up and had a difficult time breathing. She felt as though her hips had been pushed into her chest. She was too dazed to take note that had the driver of the coach been any less skilled, she would probably be dead. Never... she never should have agreed to this madness.

She finally managed a gasp of clear air and looked up into the eyes of the man who crouched over her.

"My...horse..." she whispered weakly.

"Are you hurt?" the passenger from the coach asked.

"I... I..."

"Can you stand?"

"I think so."

His hands were under her arms, and her legs trembled with the effort of getting to her feet. Once standing, she let out a long, slow breath. She wasn't maimed, which was a miracle. She looked up into the face of the man who supported her shaky stance. He towered above her, and over his shoulder she could see that the driver still stood atop the coach with the reins in his hands.

"Nothing broken?" he asked.

"I... I think not," she replied. She looked into his eyes, hoping she would not cry for sheer fright. Her chin quivered, but only slightly. "My horse..."

The man released his hold on her arms and seemed to stand even taller as his expression changed from concern to irritation. "You nearly caused a bad accident, little one. Is it the custom in this country for a woman to be out riding alone at night, or are you fleeing from the law?"

Once he had spoken more than a few words, she was conscious of a foreign accent, but uncertain as to the origin. She was immediately relieved to find that he was not an Englishman. She would die of humiliation if a neighbor had found her and reported this escapade to her father. Lord Ridgley was impossible when he was angry with her. She sighed heavily, thinking ahead to getting back into her bedroom, having retired there earlier with a feigned headache. Not being caught was the only thing she yearned for now.

"I'm sorry," she said haltingly. "It was entirely my fault."

"Indeed it was, miss. Where the hell are you bound in the dark and at such speed?"

She winced slightly at his harsh, parental tone, but she was still more willing to be berated by a stranger than by her father, brother, or maid. She lifted her chin a bit. "Of course I should not be out alone, unescorted, which is my only excuse for my reckless speed. I see my error quite clearly now." She looked at his coach, noticing the lack of a blazon or displayed arms of an English family. There was a handsome dark riding horse tethered to the rear, and atop the coach there were traveling bags tied. She hoped he was just passing through. "I apologize for my carelessness. If there is any damage, I have a little money."

His white teeth gleamed in the dark as he smiled. "Well, now, I can hardly scold you any longer when you so willingly accept responsibility. I suppose you should sit down for a moment, to collect yourself. You shouldn't venture on to your assignation in such a flustered state of mind."

She flinched at the comment, but reminded herself that he was speaking from assumption and not knowledge. At that precise moment she'd rather have been bound anywhere but to a lovers' tryst. Her cheeks flamed. "Sir, I appeal to your honorable nature. Of course you must know that if I am discovered by my...ah...my master, I will be severely punished."

He smiled down on her and touched her cheek with a finger. "Your master should be advised, little vixen, so that he can bolt the door at night. Surely even you would agree that some discipline seems in order." He looked over his shoulder at his driver. "Pull the horses a safe distance off the road, Bevis. The lady and I will sit in the coach for a moment."

"Thank you, but I'd better be on my way."

"On your way where, miss? Your horse is gone and you are in need of a ride. I can take you where you're bound on the way to my appointment. I have business with the baron of Chappington at his home. I assume this is his estate."

The color drained from her face and her mouth opened, but she caught herself before she gasped aloud. Dear God, the man was on his way to see her father. Her knees became weak and she wobbled slightly, trying to seize both balance and wits.

"Oh...my...perhaps I will sit for a moment— just a moment."

His hand was firm on her arm, leading her to the open door of his coach. As he handed her in, he spoke to his man again. "Tie these horses and take the stallion back down the road a bit. See if you spot the girl's horse."

Once inside his coach, Vieve tried to take a quick accounting of her situation, seeking first to determine which threat was worse. Should she fear this stranger, her father's wrath, or a long, lonely walk home alone? He sat down opposite her. Outside, she could hear the driver softly coo to his horses as he tied them to a nearby tree, followed by the sound of his gentle murmurs to the saddleless stallion as he mounted; and then, all too soon, there was only the quiet spring night again.

"Are you going to tell me where you were going?" the man asked her.

"It... it is of no consequence, surely."

"I am only curious, miss. Does a lover await you nearby?"

A small lantern lit the inside of the coach, and though it cast only modest light, her view of him was better than it had been on the road. She eyed him cautiously. He had a strong chin, deep gray eyes beneath thick dark brows, and since he had removed his hat, she could see an abundance of thick, black hair. She could not judge his age; he was younger than her father and older than Andrew.

"The man I am to marry," she said evenly. Admitting that a lover waited nearby was embarrassing, but far safer than telling him there was no other man within earshot if she was forced to scream for help.

"Do not marry him, mademoiselle," he said with a chuckle in his voice. "He has too little regard for your safety. Any man who would coerce one so young into a late night ride, all alone, is only interested in himself."

She took a breath and pulled her cloak more tightly around herself, wishing to disappear into the folds. She did not know where this man came from or what his business with her father might be, but she desperately hoped that a little lie, if well executed, would preclude a worse predicament.

"Please understand, sir. I am a servant of Chappington Hall, and Lord Ridgley is a hard master. I am not allowed to see my betrothed, and the baron refuses to let us marry. He'd rather have an unhappy servant than a contented wife who would leave his employ. We are hard pressed even to speak to each other and are driven to dangerous lengths for just a few private words. I am sorry you were endangered by the risks we have taken, but if Lord Ridgley finds out what I have done, he will surely beat me."

The man watched her face closely. He slowly reached across the short space that separated them and pushed back the hood of her cape to reveal her thick tresses of golden hair. His fingers touched the frogs that held her cape at her throat, and he gently opened the wrap to expose the rich, cream-colored velvet riding habit and the diamond brooch she wore. Again, she saw the gleam of his smile. "Lord Ridgley dresses his servants well," he observed.

Vieve pulled her cloak back together. "The dress is borrowed, sir. I do not own such fine clothes."

"And what work do you do, miss? A scullery? Laundress?" He reached for her hand and turned it over in his palm. "A governess, perhaps? Your hands do not labor with anything more abusive than a quill or a book. Do you teach the baron's small children to read and write?"

She was tempted to assume that role, but something cautioned her. She had no idea how much this man knew about her father or the rest of her family. "No, messire, I am an attendant and companion to the baron's daughter. This is her gown and jewelry. She is the only one who knows that I am on my way to meet my fiancé."

He laughed at her then, as if amused by her story. "And how old is this daughter of the baron's?"

"We are the same age, seven and ten. We were raised together. My mother once served in the manor."

"I see. How convenient for you to have a good friend in the heiress, and one who can lend you decent clothes, too. But, miss, if she were truly your friend, she'd have loaned you an escort along with her gown and jewels. I think perhaps I should take you back to Chappington. The baron needs to caution his daughter not to become involved in such romantic dramas with a servant."

"Oh please, sir, I beg you, do not. He's a mean-tempered man and would whip his daughter as well. And my fiancé would be banished forever. Lord Ridgley has warned me against seeing him and has threatened to separate us." This was as much a lie as the other things she had said. Boris Ridgley did not really dislike Andrew and had never threatened to separate them. Vieve had never been whipped in her life, but her father would be in a fit of pique for an indeterminate length of time if he ever heard of this. Whippings, she fantasized, would be easier to bear.

The man crossed his arms over his broad chest. "You should not have to earn your sustenance under such horrid conditions, my pet. I could offer you employment with conditions not nearly so brutal."

"Oh, I could not. I am very happy where I am...except for his lordship. I do love the mistress...and my betrothed is here."

"Perhaps I could take you both," he generously offered, but his eyes twinkled and he smiled in such a way that Vieve suspected he was mocking her. "It would be better for you than being forced to steal away from the manor house at night to see your lover. Think of the many perils on the road."

"I shan't do so again," she said in a burst of honesty. And then she added, "These roads have always been safe. It is just that I... ah...I am afraid of the dark."

"Young woman, there is good reason to be afraid of the dark," he replied, sliding toward her and reaching again to open her cloak. She raised a hand to stop him, but he gently grasped her wrist, preventing her protest. As one hand held her, the other slipped inside her cloak until his long fingers circled her slim waist. His eyes glittered almost silver in the lantern light, and her breath caught in her throat. Was his rescue at an end? Could he abuse her and then casually travel to a meeting with her father? She opened her mouth to blurt out the truth, that she was the baron's daughter. Her father's anger seemed preferable to what she feared this man might do to her.

"Hush," he said before she spoke. "I have never treated a lady unkindly. I am just a little curious about you, that is all."

She sat stone still as he moved closer to the edge of his seat, his knees spread and pinning her legs between them. "Please, don't..." she whispered.

"I will not hurt you," he said, caressing her waist and looking into her eyes. "The light is not good, but it is easy to see that you are lovely. And young. You must be made aware, little damoiselle, that it is not necessary to sell yourself for such a low price as love. Tell your selfish lover that there are men who will pay a king's ransom for what you have to offer. They will clothe you so that you need not borrow your mistress's gowns, and they will carry you abroad in jeweled coaches, never asking you to brave the dark night alone for want of a tryst." He shrugged. "It will not matter much that you are not a virgin. You are still young and sweet."

"But... but, you misunderstand," she argued, not only frightened now, but annoyed by his assumption. "I care nothing for riches. I am not a harlot."

He laughed in genuine amusement. "At least not a very successful one. Prostitutes have the sense to take a good return for their virtue. You, on the other hand, are prepared to trade your decency for some promise of love... in a borrowed gown, yet."

"Please, just let me go," she begged.

From outside she heard the faint sound of an approaching horse and the whistling of a tune. As the man cocked his head to listen, he withdrew his hand and she tugged her cloak closed. When he opened the door of the coach and stepped out, she was right behind him. Coming down the road toward the coach was the driver, pulling Tristan alongside him. Her rescuer looked over his shoulder at her, smiling as if he harbored some secret "You're in luck, miss, for Bevis has recovered your mount... a fine-looking horse." He raised an eyebrow. "Borrowed, no doubt, from your mistress."

She held her tongue and checked her anger, but on whom she wished to vent this emotion was still uncertain. Her father, for failing in her remedy of a quick and decent marriage? Andrew, for convincing her to partake in this foolish escapade? This stranger, for his cocky intervention and advice? Or herself...?

The driver dismounted and handed Tristan's reins to his master. He then tethered the stallion to the coach. "He'd not gone far, Cap'n," he said as he stroked Tristan's handsome white head. "'At's a good lad, now."

Vieve had no wish now but to find Andrew at the old keep and bring this adventure to an abrupt halt. He might have set his mood for some lovers' tryst, some passionate kissing and murmuring, but she'd been through quite enough. It was her intention to go on to the old keep solely because it was closer to where she now stood than was Chappington Hall. She would insist that Andrew escort her back until her home was in sight. There would be no dawdling in the dark tonight.

"Thank you for your gallantry, sir," she said, reaching toward Tristan and getting his reins in hand. "Would you be so kind as to give me a hand up?"

"With pleasure, my sweet," he said in a teasing tone. She grasped Tristan's mane, placed her foot in the gentleman's hand, and was in the saddle again. She felt completely safe when in her saddle, for despite her poor judgment, she was a skilled equestrienne and the distance yet to travel was fairly short. She would be easy on Tristan and, after giving Andrew a piece of her mind, get on the road home. But one thing detained her: the stranger's hand was wrapped tightly around her ankle. "Heed my words, ma petite...do not sell your virtue at such a low price. There are men who will honor you with a great deal more than this boy offers." He smiled meaningfully. "They may even sweeten the pot with this great love for which you long."

She lifted her chin indignantly. "Is there a better price than marriage?" she asked.

"My mistake, mademoiselle. I thought you said it was your betrothed, not your husband, who asked you to ride out in the night for a rendezvous."

"And so he is my intended, but he will be my husband soon."

He chuckled and stepped away from her horse, giving her the freedom to leave. "Ah, but you ride to him now, before the wedding. Have a care, pet, that no part of the dowry is lost before the priest is met."

"Worry not, sir," she said. "He is an honorable man and desires marriage with a virtuous woman."

He tipped his hat. "I rest easier knowing so, mademoiselle. But should he disappoint you, I am at your service. A mistress should be better kept than you are. Send your petition to the Lady Lillian in London port and ask for Captain Gervais. Try to keep it quiet around the wharves that you seek an American."

So, he was a colonial sea captain. That explained the accent and his business with Lord Ridgley, who owned his own fleet of merchantmen. She was confounded, though, by his courteous nature. Since her father was engaged in foreign trade, she had often been warned about the long-starved and ruthless passions of sailors in port. And as to colonials, she had been a baby when the war between England and the American colony had begun. Now a mutual mercantile interest between these separated nations was just forming, but very slyly and without a formal treaty or any approval by Parliament. Vieve's countrymen did not speak well of Yankees, but Lord Ridgley had told her many times that traders were more impossible to stop than soldiers. What she had heard about Yankee seamen and colonials implied that they would rape, brutalize and then abandon her by the side of the road if she were ever at their mercy.

There was a delighted expression on his handsome face as he added in a hushed tone, "Your secret is safe with me, ma *cherie*."

"Please," she whispered. "I beg your discretion."

"Certainly, maid. Only a cruel rogue would damage your reputation to your... ah...master. Good evening." He turned and entered his coach while his driver climbed back up to take the reins. He leaned out the window of the coach and looked at her one more time. "Do use caution, petite—both on the road and in your young lover's arms."

Vieve turned Tristan abruptly and gave him a gentle heel, urging him into an easy canter down the road and away from the coach. Though she could hear no sound but that of her horse's hooves, it was as if she could feel the man's laughter at her back. He was terribly confident for a visitor in a country that would unkindly welcome him. The English hated those citizens of the rebel nation. The remarks she had heard all of her life left her with unpleasant notions, and yet he was so well dressed, leading her to wonder if some of the rebels had acquired wealth. The pictures of Americans that she had formed in her imagination had them resembling savage pirates in cheap, torn, and dirty clothing.

Tristan's slow pace was hard to endure. The darkness still frightened her, which was the paradox in her action. She had always fancied herself a daring maid. Tonight she braved a ruined reputation and endless trouble if caught, but it was the darkness of the night that held the greatest terror.

She went off the road and down a firm and often-traveled path toward the old keep, and to her great relief, Andrew stood beside his tethered horse.

He rushed toward her as she neared, reached up, and grasped her by the waist to lift her down. "You came," he said in a breath, his lips instantly proclaiming his delight as he held her face in his hands and covered her cheeks with kisses. "I was so afraid you wouldn't..."

Vieve was almost as unprepared for her fury as he was. "Stop it," she snapped, causing him to back away a bit. "You should never have insisted that I do this," she stormed. "If my father ever finds out, it will be over for us, and you know that. I want you to ride back with me right now."

"Vieve," he began.

"For all the love you claim to feel for me, you ask me to ride out in the dark of night and meet you in some dilapidated old building on my father's property, risking my hide and my reputation. I must have been crazy to accept your challenge."

"I thought you..." He released her abruptly. "You seemed willing enough this morning. This part of the country is safe. It's not as if you met some angry bear along the road."

"I did, in fact. Some foreign sea merchant who was traveling to an appointment with my father. I nearly collided with his coach. He says he won't tell that he's seen me out alone, but if he does..." She deliberately neglected to mention that the stranger did not know her true identity. She wanted Andrew to become as frightened as she had been.

"Good God. Who?"

"I don't know who the devil he is," she shouted. She had not actually forgotten his name so soon, but who he was had nothing to do with her anger. Her voice cracked slightly and tears threatened. She did not consider that the stranger had planted the idea that Andrew was less than chivalrous, changing her entire view of the situation. Earlier in the day, when she'd given in to Andrew's pleading and promised to meet him, she had pitied his desperate longing and had agreed they deserved some moments alone. Now, however, she saw him as a selfish opportunist. "If you cared anything at all for me, you'd be protecting my virtue rather than begging me to yield it. Give me a hand up, please, and ride back with me."

Andrew gave a low whistle. "I can see your mood has changed quite a lot since this morning." He locked his fingers together for her foot. "I was not the only one who spoke of love and a brief chance to be alone, Vieve. You act as if this is my fault."

She settled into her saddle again. "It was your idea. I want to go home, now, before you get any more ideas."

"So, you've changed your mind about me altogether? You no longer care for me?"

She rolled her eyes in exasperation. "You don't seem to understand, Andrew. If you truly loved me, you wouldn't ask me to do anything foolish or dangerous. And this is both."

"I hadn't thought you'd be in any danger. You know I wouldn't risk your safety for anything. I want to marry you, for God's sake."

"Marriage is decent. This is idiotic."

He touched her hand, looking up at her with his warm brown eyes aglow. "You should have told me you didn't want to come."

"I believe I did," she said, anger still ringing in her voice. She remembered the morning quite clearly. They had been left in the parlor, and the moment the door had closed, they had come together in a heated rush. His lips were hot and insistent, lingering on her neck, shoulder, ear...begging, wanting, complaining of the constant ache in his heart, and other unmentionable areas, caused by ceaseless desire without so much as a private moment. The lack of privacy and her father's resistance were driving him crazy. And her voice was continually chanting no, no, no...I cannot, while she clung to him in the same fever.

Then, as on every occasion they had stolen to be alone, the parlor door had opened. This morning it had been her older brother, Paul, who had deemed it time for them to be chaperoned. It was when she saw Andrew to the door that she relented, to his passionate relief, and said that she would meet him.

"It was only because I felt so sorry for you this morning that I gave in imprudently."

"That isn't what I wanted, Vieve," he said in a slightly injured voice. "I thought you wanted to be with me as well."

"Oh, Andrew," she sighed. "Just take me home before we're in so much trouble that Papa won't let us even speak, much less marry."

Andrew left her to mount his own horse, and they rode single file down the path to the Chappington road. Then, when they were side by side on the road, they conversed again. "Your father is no closer to letting me have you than he ever was. The size of my purse does not suit him."

"It isn't that, Andrew. He is just not quite ready, that's all."

"You're seventeen. What is he waiting for, if not a better offer?"

"He'll come around," she said quietly, looking straight ahead.

"There's a way to hurry him along," Andrew suggested, his voice low and grave.

She felt the swell of tears in her eyes, and her vision clouded. She would not respond to him. She rode beside him, silent and hurt. It was not the first time he had so spoken, but it was the first time that the suggestion tore at her heart.

"No one would know. I wouldn't get you caught with child. I know what I'm doing."

She laughed ruefully. "How lucky I am that you are so experienced."

"I am not a child, Vieve, but a man who has been about this world a few years longer than you. We want each other, and all that stands in our way is a stubborn old man. With a word from you, we could be as one now, and he would have little choice."

"He could shoot you instead of gifting you with a bride."

Andrew chuckled. "I may be a trifle light of coin, but I am not without some influence in this country. Mine is an old and respected name. And I do love you; you cannot doubt that."

Strangely, she doubted it this night for the very first time. She hurried Tristan a bit. Home, with her father's surly mood, her older brother's concerned presence, her maid's fussing—all seemed to be a better place for her right now.

"Dear Andrew, I would perhaps hold you in higher regard if you wished to prove your concern for my welfare rather than your great experience in lovemaking. I intend to be a pure bride with my father's blessing, and if you pressure me again, I shall have to believe that you do not love me at all."

"Vieve, I love you desperately."

"Good. Then we are agreed: you will try harder to show it."

"But Vieve, I—"

She did not hear what more he had to say. She slowed Tristan to a stop and listened. By the sound of galloping horse hooves, she knew she was not the only person to ride at an unsuitable pace for these dark country roads. It never occurred to her to try to flee from the person who ventured down the road, but after her near collision with the Yankee, she cautioned Andrew to clear the path. They withdrew to the edge of the road, and she recognized the horse and rider. "Paul," she called.

Her brother slowed his horse with a little difficulty, leaving the poor beast to prance a bit, and Paul closely considered the twosome. His frown bore down on them both as if they were little more than naughty children. Paul and Andrew were the same age, close in size, and had been friends for a long while. But the friendship, by the look in Paul's eyes, might be ended here.

"I will see that my sister gets home safely, Andrew."

"Paul, I..."

"The less you say, the better, Andrew. Come along, Vieve."

With a resigned sigh, she urged Tristan onto the road and went along quietly beside her brother. Even a spirited and determined lass knows when to forgo comment; she did not bid Andrew good night, part with a kiss, or even offer him a wave. She heard his departure behind her as he rode in the opposite direction. And her brother's furious silence was oppressive. He held his tongue for so long that when he did speak, she jumped in surprise.

"You little idiot. What the devil were you thinking of?"

She winced, but the darkness concealed her flaming cheeks. "I trust this means that the Yankee guest gave me away?"

"I don't know how you managed to fool Captain Gervais, but he took me aside before going into the study with Father to ask me if I was aware that my sister's maid had left the manor and was sighted along the road on her way to an appointment with her lover." He shook his head irritably. "I immediately doubted that your maid was capable of such foolishness. The captain said simply that he thought it better to let you go on than to force you to ride to Chappington with him and face your master's fury. He suggested I might send someone out to find you before you got into worse trouble." He cleared his throat. "I assured him I would do that."

Vieve felt a surge of relief. Paul's anger was easy enough to bear. Even though he often nagged her, her brother's loyalty was unquestionable.

"I'm sorry I worried you," she said quietly. "I won't do anything like this again, I promise."

"I don't think you know the half of it. You and your damned nitwit ideas about what you want seem to get in the way of any good sense. Look, Andrew seems to be a decent man, all things considered, but there is much more at stake here than some love poem or romantic moonlight meeting."

"Papa would be upset, but..."

"Upset? Ha." Paul stopped his horse suddenly. "You've been so concerned with petting in the garden with your young stag that you haven't listened to anything that's been said around you for the past two years. Why do you think Father has not consented to this betrothal? Do you think he dislikes your young man? Or wishes you unhappiness? Andrew is dead broke, Vieve. He has a little money for ale and gambling. How the hell do you think he's going to take care of you?"

Vieve stared at her brother, her mouth agape. "But... but Father has ships..."

Paul laughed bitterly. "Aye, the ships. Since the estate has failed, the merchantmen were intended to bolster our family funds. But we have had two warehouse fires this year and lost a hundred-and-fifty-ton frigate in a storm last year. We owe more for our cargo than we've collected in ten years. I can work until I drop, but all you can do is marry. And I doubt we're rich enough to take on the support of another family member."

"Isn't there...surely there is someone who would...I don't know...help?"

"Aye, we have a standing offer of loans from Uncle Charles, who wants nothing more than Father's entire estate in return, stricken as it is."

Vieve said nothing more. The strained relationship between her father and his younger half-brother was a matter of fact. Each seemed to want most what the other had. Lord Boris Ridgley had titled land and a position in government, but his financial troubles were many. Charles Latimer hungered for prestige and importance in the realm, but had somehow managed to gather an impressive fortune. Their differences had produced a constant undercurrent of jealousy and antagonism since childhood.

"Only Uncle Charles?" she asked softly.

Paul urged his horse to resume the ride to Chappington. "Perhaps it is too much to expect a young girl to worry herself with management affairs. Perhaps the color of your dress and the location of your next interlude with Andrew should take precedence. If so, Vieve, I can ask only one thing of you. Try to control your hot-blooded tendencies and allow Father to salvage his pride, if not his fortune. At least do not lose your virtue before he has had an opportunity to approve your husband. We are not so rich as it appears."

"But Andrew's family name is of some major influence in England..."

Paul laughed suddenly. "Good God, you actually believe that, do you? Aye, he has plenty of name, but how in the world do you imagine he's going to turn it into money? A man has to have property as well, and Andrew's estate is a total ruin, providing almost no income. Do you take your name to the clothier and buy dresses? Does the jeweler exchange a name for a diamond pendant?" He laughed again. "Name. Good God. That Yankee merchant's name would likely be spit on in England, the way everyone feels about Americans, but you can be damned sure he can afford the finest linen to wipe away the insult. Name."

He raved on and she listened to his tirade, hearing him for the first time. Her mother had died two years ago. Her own grief, her father's pain, and her ripening age, along with Andrew's hot pursuit, had distorted the situation her family faced. Since nothing much had ever changed, she never considered that it would. They still lived in a richly furnished country mansion, though it needed refurbishing. They employed many servants. There were fewer horses and parties...but she assumed that was because they had been grieving Lady Ridgley's death. She had understood their worry over two warehouse fires in London, but she had not thought the damage that devastating.

"Is it as bad as all that?" she hesitantly asked him.

"Vieve," he said with a long, exasperated sigh. "Father is proud. His estate appears richer than it is, but if I were you, I wouldn't count on your inheritance to keep you in parties and fancy gowns. When you do marry, you had best be sure that it is to a man who can support you. If Andrew cared one whit about you, he would put as much energy toward building his fortune as seducing you. For now, at least, refrain from such stupid adventures."

Vieve felt her throat constrict, and her eyes began to tear. She shook her head in disbelief; she did not know whether she had been completely selfish or whether her father and brother had neglected to explain their almost desperate situation. True, she had not paid close attention to dinner conversation. She had not eavesdropped when they closeted themselves with their accounting ledgers. There had been little change in her father's grim expression since the death of his wife, but she had not thought his problems with money any worse than usual.

"I suppose you can't help it if you're in love with him," Paul said in a softened tone. "Look, Vieve, I'm sorry to go on so sourly about Andrew's lack of wealth, as if it's the only consideration. Even if he wasn't a friend, I'd be the last person to ask you to sacrifice your life for the sake of money. But on your own behalf, understand Father's position and lend him obedience, if nothing else. You must not let Andrew convince you that there is any wisdom in these secret meetings." Paul's expression was full of pained sympathy. "Please do not worsen Father's dilemma by going to the priest with a round belly."

"I would not, Paul," she said meekly.

"As much as I like Andrew Shelby," he went on as if he had not heard her, "I know him quite well. He has quite a hand with the wenches, and the smooth-tongued devil might sound very convincing. I'm certain his intentions are good, but..."

"I said I would not, Paul."

"Yes, well, if you go on with these passionate little displays, you may find you have tempted him to the breaking point. Marry a paupered aristocrat if you must, but at least get to the altar intact. I suggest you put some distance in your, ah, courtship." He turned his head and looked at her through narrowed eyes. "If it is not too late."

"It is not," she said quietly. Her shame was so great that she trembled inside. She regretted that she had to be pushed to this degree to see her own insensitivity. She was chagrined, a spoiled and ignorant noble heiress, thinking her family wealthy beyond doubt since she was never denied new gowns. And her anxiety and embarrassment only heightened as she thought now of having to sneak into her house under cover of night. She did not look forward to facing her father or her servant, Harriet. "Please don't tell Papa," she asked.

"Don't worry, minx. Even I do not want to see just how red his face can get."

"And please don't tell Captain Gervais that it was I. Let him think one of the servants was..."

"I doubt you or your 'servant' will come up in conversation. However, he is staying a day or two, and if he sees you, he will know whom he met and it will be out."

"Oh," she sighed. "I think I feel an attack of the ague coming on. I shall most certainly be confined for a day or two."

"So long as there is not a ladder to your bedroom window, I believe that would be just as well. Perhaps you will take some time to consider your future."

"I think," she said very quietly, "that perhaps I should not see even Andrew for a few days."

"Yes, well, take special care that you do not shock us all with an act of good sense. Father's constitution may not be strong enough to bear the burden of surprise if you should suddenly behave with some maturity."

She grimaced at the slur. She had thought that her family had refused to consider her desires, not that she had been childish in her behavior. She said not another word, and Paul silently took the horses to be stabled. She tiptoed up the back stairs and noiselessly entered her bedroom. She had doffed her cloak before she noticed that the quilt was pulled down, exposing the rolled blankets she had hoped would be taken for her sleeping form. And in the far corner sat the generous silhouette of Harriet, arms crossed over her ample chest and her foot tapping.

"Aha," was all the woman said.

Vieve, in a gesture of impatience that would do credit to any four-year-old, placed her hands over her ears and flounced down on her bed. "I don't even want to hear it. I'm in enough trouble."

"Not yet, ye're not," the stout woman said, rising from her chair and walking around to pull off her mistress's boots. "But sure ye will be soon." And true to her word, it was a long while before Harriet felt that Vieve had had enough of her scolding.

Three

A few days of feigned ague and bed rest accomplished exactly what Vieve had intended: she was out of sight. But the time dragged as she took her meals in her room and suffered Harriet's ever-reproving tongue. "Ague, is it? And a wonder it's not a good deal more, what with the sneakin' about and carryin' on. Humph!"

"I am not sick," Vieve said slowly, emphasizing each word. "I am simply making myself scarce."

"Make yerself behave, and ye've done a day's work," the old woman advised.

Andrew visited the manor and Vieve sent her regrets. Lord Ridgley went to his daughter's rooms and mistook her flushed cheeks and docile temperament for symptoms of fever. Paul checked on her now and again, frowning with his eyes and smiling with his mouth. And four very long, very boring days passed. But the Yankee sea captain did not depart.

"What the devil does he want here?" Vieve demanded of her brother. "Has he decided to move in permanently?"

Paul laughed at her impatience, finding it justice, indeed, that she had to suffer through a melodrama of her own creation. It was the very least she deserved. Some of her behavior might be juvenile and impetuous, but it was the driving force of womanhood that was edging her toward trouble. Until forced to dash out into the night to her rescue, Paul had never suspected their romance was so serious and now hoped it was not too late for Vieve to still claim her virginity on her wedding day. Paul had not considered the desire that Andrew must have stimulated in her.

Paul knew it would be best if Vieve did not have to wait much longer to be wed. Vieve's eagerness to be a bride was almost alarming. And by way of an older brother's wisdom, he decided that to forbid them to see each other at all might do more harm than good.

"You might as well recover, Vieve, and join us for dinner, unless you intend to lie abed all summer."

"Good Lord, will he never leave?" she moaned.

"He has found some common topics of conversation with Father, and the two of them are quite enjoying themselves. There may even be a business venture in this."

"I had always heard that colonials were not equipped with manners. He must be a boorish clod."

"He's quite mannerly, actually."

"Doesn't Papa hate even to be in the same room with him? After all, they fought against each other."

"In a manner of speaking, they did. Of course, they avoid the issue very cleverly, both of them, and I have only heard it mentioned once, and that was to agree that now that it's over, ambitious traders must find a common objective in making money, regardless of politics." He smiled down at her. "Don't pout so, Vieve, you'll wrinkle early. And be glad that Father is pleased for once."

On the fifth day she realized there was little point in suffering through such loneliness and boredom any longer. Obviously, the Yankee merchant was not inclined toward common courtesies, since he did not limit his visit to an appropriate length of time. And Andrew had been invited to dinner to meet their guest.

The gown she chose was fashioned of a rich lavender silk, and silver braid trimmed the provocatively low neckline. She didn't worry that the spring chill, quite common for early May, might be uncomfortable. The important thing was the way the gown hugged her slim waist and emphasized her developed bosom. She turned and posed before her mirror, twisting a blond curl around her finger. She had no intention of being alone with Andrew for even a moment. She hoped he would faint in a misery of longing. And as that final thought came, she giggled.

A low whistle caused her to turn and face her bedroom door. She smiled at her brother. "What do you think?" she asked coyly, turning before him.

"I think there will be trouble."

She went to him and gave him an affectionate kiss on the cheek. Paul, at five and twenty, was both handsome and intelligent. He, too, had inherited the fair skin, blond hair, and bright blue eyes of their mother. Even though he had shown a rather fatherly attitude toward Vieve for the last five years, she still felt very close to him.

He placed a finger under her chin. "Do you think it wise, Vieve, to wear so shocking a gown while you dine with two handsome bachelors?"

She gave the neckline a slight tug to assure herself that she was covered. "You will be there, will you not?"

"Of course," he said.

"I think it's the least of what they both deserve." Vieve tightened her mouth in emphasis, although she didn't bother to explain any further. She was more than a little angry with Andrew trying to get her into marriage as quickly as possible with little regard for what humiliation she might suffer. She thought he might be a victim of the same misassumption she had suffered: because her family was so rich, the monetary contribution of a husband was irrelevant. But, she had stubbornly decided, that was no excuse for his behavior. Although she was a bit tardy in realizing it, Andrew could have done much to bend her father toward a more accommodating mood by gathering up some money rather than begging her to yield her virtue. She hoped he would stare at her all through the evening. She had heard quite enough about his suffering; she wished to see it in his eyes.

As for the Yankee, she was no longer afraid that he would betray her to her father. If he was so moved, she would apologize profusely. She was dreadfully sorry. And she thought Lord Ridgley might be impressed with a lavish apology and a new and mature understanding of their family's needs. She had not known why there was resistance to a betrothal with Andrew. Let the Yankee smirk. The rogue had offered her employment, promising that her virtue need not be sacrificed for want of a decent dress and an escort to her assignations. The captain would no doubt be most intrigued to see that it was the baron's daughter, not some common maidservant, to whom he had addressed such audacious suggestions.

"Well, you look divine, as always," Paul told her. "If you can endure all their stares, I can keep my amusement to myself."

She looped her arm into his. "All their stares. Where's your mettle, Paul? Surely you can defend me against two of them."

He laughed. "I'm certain that Andrew and our American guest will be manageable, but I wonder if I'll be able to protect you against Aunt Elizabeth, Uncle Charles, and our formidable cousins, Robert, Faye, and Beth."

Vieve moaned as her hand touched her brow. "I think I've risen from my bed too soon."

"No you don't. You've avoided this long enough. If I have to endure their haughty disdain, you can at least keep me company." He gave her hand a pat. "Evelyn is here, too."

Her eyes instantly brightened. Evelyn Dumere would be her sister-in-law when she and Paul could finally marry. Lords Ridgley and Dumere had been friends and neighbors for many years, and Vieve considered Evelyn her closest female friend. Although as different as night and day, they were completely loyal to each other. In fact, their contrasts brought them closer together, each envying certain characteristics in the other. Evelyn was demure and often coveted Vieve's boldness, while Vieve wished she had Evelyn's natural quiet grace. Evelyn adhered strictly to protocol, while Vieve was more inclined to challenge its limits.

But Evelyn was a bit older and closer to being a bride. This, in Vieve's mind, gave her a greater status. "Perhaps I should change," she said in an attack of conscience.

Paul chuckled as he led her down the stairs. "You won't shock Evelyn, who knows you only too well. You will certainly upset the relatives, but that has always been a favorite pastime of yours. As for our handsome bachelors, I imagine you intend to cause them no small amount of pain."

She held the banister with one gloved hand and looked up into Paul's twinkling eyes. There was nothing quite so secure as being understood and accepted just as she was. "I love you," she said. "But I think you know me too well."

At the bottom of the elaborate staircase he paused to touch her nose. "You be careful, Vieve." And then without further comment he led her through the drawing room doors to greet their guests.

The dress was perhaps a bit daring, but it was the height of fashion nonetheless. And all young women were wearing gowns with a more provocative décolletage. It did not cinch her waist to the point of pain, nor did she risk undue exposure when she curtsied, but she might as well have entered the drawing room in her chemise for the way she was received.

Lord Ridgley, who seemed inclined to show the same expression for both disapproval and amusement, gave a turn of his lip that caused his thick gray moustache to tilt across his face. One bushy gray brow rose in surprise, while the other plunged over a squinting eye. He was the first to approach her, kiss her hand, and in his gruff, scratchy voice, greet her. "Good evening, daughter. You look well. All of you."

Andrew followed right on her father's heels, letting the room at large know that he intended possession here. As he bowed over her hand to kiss it, his eyes lingered for an indelicate length of time on her swelling bosom. "You mean to drive me mad, madam?" he asked. She declined to answer, but her eyes brightened slightly at the prospect of his discomfort. He took his place at her side, where he was obviously determined to stay.

She curtsied toward Aunt Elizabeth, whom she could count on to smile sweetly, if blandly. However, her female cousins lifted long, slender noses. Elizabeth had always been staunch in her adherence to polite public behavior and conservative dress, but Faye and Beth, Vieve thought scornfully, were too young to be so old. At fifteen and thirteen, respectively, they clucked in judgmental quips like two little old ladies. Vieve had never known them to have fun or tempt the daring limits that young people usually sought. They seemed to have inherited their mother's rigid manners and their father's haughty superiority.

The three Latimer women were all buttoned up to their chins and sank in unison in a perfectly coordinated curtsy. The girls, a trifle thick around their waists, frowned at Vieve's gown, while Elizabeth pinkened slightly. Vieve lifted her chin a bit, hoping they were envious rather than disapproving, which indeed they should be.

Charles Latimer, who was tall and broad-shouldered, sauntered forward to greet her. He displayed the familiar, big-toothed, gleaming smile that was always the same whether in the most bitter of disagreements or at the funniest of jests. That peculiar, identical grin was so unchangeable it seemed as if etched by an artist's pen.

Charles's son, Robert, was a younger version of his father, except for the smile. Robert rarely showed his teeth. Rather, he wore a perpetually bored pout on his lips. At nineteen years of age, he had done little more than loll in the lather of his father's fortune. He did not even rise from the settee he occupied to greet Vieve, but lounged in complete disinterest until his mother tapped his knee sharply with her closed fan.

Evelyn had attached herself to Paul's arm. They were in love and therefore inseparable. Vieve's sparkling blue eyes and Evelyn's warm brown ones met across the room and spoke without words of their established, companionable sisterhood.

Captain Gervais was the last to approach, brought to her attention by her father. "Captain, I should like you to meet my daughter, Vivian Donnelle."

She had to admire the captain for his quick intelligence, for not an ounce of recognition or surprise showed on his face. He nodded amiably, took her extended hand to kiss it, and let his eyes rise to hers without any roguish or overlong attention to her low-cut gown.

"It's a pleasure, madam," he said. "And please, do not stand on formality. Call me Tyson."

She tried to convey with a gracious smile that she appreciated his discretion. She fluttered her lashes a bit, feeling Andrew stiffen at her side. "Thank you, Tyson. And I am most often called Vieve by friends and family."

He gave a slight nod of approval. "Your father said you were lovely, but his words pale in your presence. I've looked forward to meeting you." He glanced at Andrew and added, "And I have enjoyed chatting with your young man. He tells me that you are a very accomplished horsewoman."

So, she thought, he was clever enough to level her with an insult without giving her away. She responded with a startled grin, surprised by both his finesse and quick wit. "Not so skilled, I'm sure, as your colonial women. One must have need of good riding ability in the wilderness."

He laughed good-naturedly, looking over his shoulder at Boris. Her father cleared his throat and removed Tyson quickly from the piercing point of his daughter's sense of humor. "Ahem, come along to the dining room, Tyson. She knows better than that, I assure you."

As he moved away, Vieve heard him exclaim, "A little Tory pride is in order, I'm sure...."

"Yankees," Andrew whispered, ridicule seething from his tone. "Barely civilized creatures."

She cocked her head slightly in question and absently took Andrew's available arm. Andrew could not have known how his last remark had sparked her curiosity about the captain. Vieve watched Tyson's departing back and began to marvel at the different form he assumed in her imagination. She had a sudden vision of him in buckskin and a beaver cap, a rifle over one shoulder and a large hunting knife in his belt, like a drawing on a lampoon she had once seen. Yet for a frontiersman, he seemed to wear his dark surcoat and flawlessly white stock as though he was accustomed to formal wear. It was interesting that one who lived under what were often described as barbaric conditions in America could manage to conform to British style so elegantly.

Charles Latimer's smile was in place, but he did not seem to have much conversation to contribute. When he did speak, he had an unusually large number of bad omens to share. The future of shipping, he predicted, was grim. The forecast for crops was not good again this year. And he had a few uncomplimentary things to say about France, which Vieve assumed were directed toward the captain, whose name suggested French ancestry. As Vieve listened to her uncle's bleak contributions, she was not surprised, for Charles liked to dampen her father's mood. And tonight was no exception, even before a foreign guest.

It was Tyson's presence, of course, that lifted Lord Ridgley out of his usual despondent condition. The two men conversed affably about ships, foreign lands, and trade. Ships had long been her father's first love. Estate management, farming, and husbandry were not his greatest gifts; Paul was more inclined to that. Lord Ridgley's merchantmen had begun a good business until England had gone to war with her colony, causing his trade to suffer dreadfully.

"Do you have a family, Captain Gervais?" Elizabeth asked.

"Indeed. Quite a large family. I am the oldest of five children—four boys and one girl." His eyes darted once, very quickly, toward Vieve. "I am the only one tardy in marrying. My sister, Adele, the youngest at eighteen, wed last year. My mother died just a short time later."

"Surely there is a woman in the colonies who has cast her lot for you," Elizabeth said.

"I am not yet married," he repeated evenly, making it sound as though lots cast and other such dalliance were of no significance to him. "And in Virginia, long betrothals are less popular than they are here."

"I suppose there are fewer women," Charles observed dryly.

"There are a great many beautiful women in America—albeit, most of the truly desirable ones do not feel inclined to wait on the whim of a sailor."

"Sailor, bah," Lord Ridgley scoffed. "You are an able captain and your family owns an impressive fleet. You are too modest. I intend to plague you with many questions about your business."

"What?" Charles questioned with a laugh. "Are you trying to sell ships, Boris?"

Vieve could not mistake the embarrassed look on her father's face. Charles was infinitely more successful with money than Lord Ridgley, for over the years Charles seemed to have profited, while her father seemed to have suffered one loss after another. She looked askance at Tyson. He considered Charles from under lowered brows. The displeasure in his eyes was obvious. It interested her to find that even the Yankee could pick up on Charles's clear intent to demean her father. Her own cheeks felt hot as her anger rose. And Andrew, consistent in his pursuit, let his hand touch her knee in a poorly timed romantic gesture.

"Captain Gervais is not involved only in shipping, as it happens," Paul interceded. "His younger brothers manage a very prosperous plantation where tobacco, cotton, and soybeans are grown. It seems that the family has both cargo and the means for shipping it to foreign ports. We'd like to interest them in a larger fleet of cargo ships and a wider territory for trade."

"Well, I can certainly understand your desire for that," Charles said, his large, phony smile causing Vieve to grimace with distaste. His intention to laud over them his acclaimed prowess with money was so obvious, so determined.

She unconsciously brushed away Andrew's hand, suddenly irritated with such nonsense.

"What with all the terrible setbacks you've had, Boris," Charles went on, "it would be sheer genius to get this American merchant to back you in a few good hauls." Charles picked up his glass of wine and took a leisurely sip, contemplating Tyson as one would a side of pork ready for the spit. "God-awful bit of bad luck, the fires and all."

"You're speaking of the warehouse fires, of course," Tyson said.

"Yes, dreadful... and just when things were improving for my brother," Charles said, shaking his head as if saddened, while every tooth in the front of his mouth gleamed.

"Yes, dreadful, but hardly bad luck." All eyes turned to the Yankee, but he seemed not to look at anyone in particular. "I have looked at the ruined buildings. I think a fire was set on the ground floor at their common wall, destroying both structures. I heard some rubbish about lightning, but the fire burned hottest and longest on the lower level. Although there was supposedly a bad storm that night, a barely damaged, rain-soaked roof collapsed and thus extinguished the fire. The body of an unidentified man, perhaps using the warehouse as shelter, was found."

"You looked at the charred buildings?" Charles asked in surprise. "Whatever for?"

"I am interested in the warehouse property in this country," Tyson replied agreeably. "Soon it will become a rare commodity, and trade will be flourishing."

Charles coughed suddenly. "How--how in heaven does an American examine British property?"

Tyson peered askance at Lord Ridgley and smiled. Looking back at Charles, he answered. "Very cautiously, I assure you."

Charles laughed openly. "It's a pity that Boris can't help you. Unfortunately, the only space Boris has is nothing but a pile of ash."

Vieve grew more appalled at her uncle's behavior, but as she looked at her father she noticed that for once Lord Ridgley said nothing at all and only watched his brother with interest.

"That's where you're wrong, sir." Tyson looked around the table. "The cost to rebuild might be more appealing to my purse now than leasing another building at a higher price in the future. I plan for more than one voyage here. Despite the government, England is eager for our harvested goods, and we still need a great deal that England can provide. For example, we have timber aplenty, but very few of our people manufacture nails."

Charles snorted derisively. "You are quite brave, Captain, to plan for many visits to a country that would rather you stay away. You don't worry about your own safety?"

"Trade may be constricted for the time being, but visiting between our countries is not punishable."

"Well, I cannot imagine the cost of rebuilding two completely burned buildings. The cost would be phenomenal."

Tyson Gervais mimicked Charles Latimer's slow and deliberate act of raising the glass, taking a sip, and looking shrewdly over the rim. "I am not without the means," he said easily. "And I have cautioned Lord Ridgley to establish watchmen at the site, lest some criminal seek to do more damage."

"Watchmen?" Charles asked in surprise.

"Certainly," the captain explained. "The fire, sir, was one kind of crime, but remember that a body was found. Whether or not it was deliberate to kill that poor unknown soul is irrelevant. Murder was committed. Though I am not entirely familiar with your laws, I imagine that bears a weighty punishment."

Charles looked at Lord Ridgley and, for the first time in Vieve's recollection, seemed almost panicked. "But I thought you had concluded that it had to be lightning that caused the fire."

"No, Charles," Boris said. "If memory serves me, 'twas you who decided that must be the cause. I have always thought that perhaps the fire was purposely set."

"Surely your competitors profited," Charles suggested.

Boris shrugged. "There has been nothing to suggest that. In fact, my competitors are also friends, and I was even generously offered the use of a warehouse in port, free of rent for a few months, to temporarily ease my plight. But we continue to investigate, Charles. If I learn anything new, I will certainly let you know."

"There has been a good deal of trouble," Charles said meaningfully. "Especially around the wharves, since more and more colonials are presuming upon the establishment of open trading." Charles looked around the table slowly, hungry for a challenge to this statement, but none came.

"There is trouble around every port," Tyson said flatly. "I pride myself in sensing trouble in business even before it happens. Fortunately, the rebuilding is not too extensive and could begin immediately, and Lord Ridgley impresses me as a man with good ideas. He is crafty and entices me to yield a large sum to a future partnership."

"Partnership," Charles nearly choked. "See here, Boris, I have made plenty of offers..."

"Now, Charles, the captain and I have only begun to talk," Boris said with a laugh. "And I hope he will stay on for a while so that we might continue our discussion. Partnerships take a long time to settle."

Tyson touched his lips with his napkin and leaned away from the table. "Unfortunately, my lord, I cannot remain. I must return to London in just two days. I have been informed of cargo that I would like to inspect myself."

"I was not aware of any trade agreement. How is it you have cargo to take out of a British port, Captain?" Charles asked in a demanding tone.

Tyson frowned. "Lord Ridgley told me you were a merchant. Your business must be confined to this country or you would understand that shipping has more to do with fines, embargoes, and bribes than the simple buying, loading, unloading, and selling of goods. If the profit is good, the crew is better off paying fines than to forgo the venture. When there is an open treaty, England will simply exchange the fines for port tax. You may believe me, there is a good deal of trading going on."

Tyson turned to Lord Ridgley. "Although I have enjoyed myself much more than I expected, I still have a few duties." He chuckled. "When I informed my family of my plans to spend some time on the continent, I was warned that the reception to Americans was still very strained in England, but I have found Lord Ridgley's hospitality unsurpassed."

"Two days?"

To her own surprise, the question came from Vieve. She had spoken without even thinking, and instantly Andrew's hand was again on her knee. She could not lower even one of her own hands from view without bringing attention to herself.

"Aye, madam. But perhaps I will be invited to return."

"Of course you will return," Boris insisted. "And in the meantime, while you are at work in London, I will go to the city, where the base for our proposed partnership sits in a heap of ashes." He laughed loudly at what was not entirely funny.

"Of course you understand that I cannot make any agreement without sending word home to my brothers," Tyson said.

"We have plenty of time for agreements and letters," Boris told him. "The important thing is that you have a good visit, and if we can do a little business as well, all the better."

Vieve couldn't remember seeing her father quite so pleased, or her uncle so disgruntled. She smiled wryly. Charles derived far too much pleasure from her father's crises and suffered greatly when Lord Ridgley did well for himself. He ought to be ashamed, she thought.

Tyson looked around the table, and as he glanced at each face his brows rose with the corners of his lips, as if to thank each one personally for the hospitality, when only Boris had issued the invitation. "I'm flattered. I don't think I can ignore my duties or my ship completely, but I'm certain that something can be arranged. Perhaps I can return in a few months."

"You must have very light responsibilities in America," Charles observed with a touch of malice.

"I have a very capable family," Tyson corrected. He turned to Boris. "A little time abroad is good for me. I have worked too hard." Vieve watched as Tyson seemed to spy her uncle Charles out of the corner of his eye. She lowered her hand and removed Andrew's clinging grasp on her knee.

When the women rose to retire from the dining room, Vieve stayed in her chair. She wished to remain and listen to more of the men's conversation, but before she could do anything so improper, Aunt Elizabeth pointedly called each one of them by name to accompany her to the sitting room.

Although that was the last place Vieve desired to be, the only alternative offered was likewise unappealing. Andrew, having quickly extricated himself from the men's discourse over brandy, lightly tapped on the sitting room door, pushed it open, and smiled at Vieve. He already had her shawl draped over his arm, and his message was clear: he wished for a stroll in the garden. She found his presumption appalling.

Vieve entered the foyer, softly shutting the sitting room door behind her. It suddenly amazed her that she had endured this kind of behavior from Andrew for a year. She failed to remember that only a few days before she might have pranced out of the house with him, as eagerly as he.

"What do you want?" she whispered impatiently. "Why aren't you in the dining room, listening to their discussion?"

"I'd rather be with you," he said.

"Don't you think we've created enough of a stir? Paul is already very distressed about us, and I don't want to cause any more trouble for my father."

"What kind of behavior should your brother expect from two people who wish to marry?"

"He probably expects you to give as much diligence to the family business as you do to seducing me. I believe the conversation that should interest you most is taking place in the dining room."

"But I haven't seen you in days."

"I think the separation is a good deal safer than what we have been doing. And it's still cold outside. I wouldn't want to catch my death in the night air."

"I'll keep you warm, darling," he said, smiling down at her, gently running a finger over her bare shoulder.

"Go have a brandy with the men, Andrew. I don't want Harriet to have to replace another row of perfectly good buttons after you've tried to rip off my gown." She whirled about, opened the sitting room door, smiled sweetly at her aunt and cousins, and sat on the settee beside Evelyn.

"Are you not going for a walk with Andrew?" Evelyn asked in surprise.

"I've only just recovered from a mild bout of ague," she lied, smiling as convincingly as she could for the benefit of Aunt Elizabeth and her cousins. Faye glanced up from her book and actually glared at Vieve. "I don't think I should chance the night air."

Evelyn looked at her closely, first knitting her brow in a bit of confusion and then slowly breaking into a devilish smile meant only for Vieve. "I see," she said knowingly. "It is a little cool. But I was just thinking that it should soon be getting warmer."

"Indeed," Vieve replied. Evelyn might fool the rest of the room, but Vieve knew her dry humor and her ability to seize upon small clues and make correct assumptions. Evelyn had undoubtedly noticed Vieve's strong interest in the Yankee captain.

As she picked up the sampler and bent her eyes over her work, Evelyn murmured softly, "I wonder what the summers are like in America. I've heard they are deliciously hot."

Vieve reached for her own sampler, a pastime she made no secret of hating, and in the process managed to give Evelyn a nudge in the ribs as a warning.

"Wouldn't you love to visit?" Evelyn asked, keeping her eyes downcast and controlling the laughter in her voice.

"I've heard it's a barbarous place," Vieve responded.

"Oh, I doubt that, Vieve," Evelyn said gently. "Although I imagine it takes great strength and a strong character to build something out of an untamed land." She laughed lightly. "Surely some things from America can be tamed."

"That's not what I've heard," Vieve said slowly, glaring at Evelyn out of the corner of her eye.

"Well, we'll have to ask the captain."

This time Charles did not overstay his visit. He was a bit more tense than usual, which Vieve assumed had to do with the captain's presence. If Charles could not humiliate her father, he seemed not to enjoy himself. He called for the Latimer women after just a short time, and when the front door closed behind the Latimers, Vieve stood and let out a long, bored sigh, fluffing the wrinkles out of her skirt with a little shake.

This time it was Paul who appeared at the sitting room door with Evelyn's wrap already in hand. She greeted him warmly, rising on her toes to place a wifely kiss on his cheek.

"Has Andrew gone?" Vieve asked hesitantly.

"I believe so," Paul said as if only suddenly aware that Andrew was missing. "He was acting a little oddly when he returned to the dining room. Did you have a disagreement?"

"He is probably angry with me," she said absently. "Papa?"

"Retired," he said, placing Evelyn's wrap around her shoulders. "You're on your own, Vieve. We'll be in the garden."

Vieve wandered into the dining room to be certain Andrew was not there and then stepped out onto the veranda. She would not embarrass Paul and Evelyn by wandering into the garden, but she was too restless to go to bed. She almost laughed aloud as she thought about Evelyn's taunting and planned to give her a piece of her mind later. Because Evelyn was rather quiet, not many people recognized her wit and apt remarks.

Her movements onto and around the veranda had not been intentionally quiet, but apparently she had issued no sound, for she recognized Captain Gervais's back as he leaned over the rail at the far end of the veranda. "Good evening," she said.

He straightened and turned, as if startled, and then upon seeing who it was, casually walked toward her. He held a smoking pipe in one hand and a glass of brandy in the other. A slight shiver made her aware that she had not even taken her wrap. "I didn't hear you come out," he said. "I saw Paul and Evelyn pass, and I assumed you were already far from prying eyes with your young Andrew. After all, we wouldn't want your 'master' to beat you."

"You don't have to make fun of me," she informed him. "I was more concerned with protecting myself from you than whether or not I was telling a lie."

"Oh," he said. "I see."

She thrust out her lower lip in a pout. "I didn't really expect you to understand."

He chuckled lightly. "I am not such a stranger to young love, my dear. I understand perfectly."

She looked up at him, conscious for perhaps the first time of how handsome he was. He was over six feet tall, and his broad shoulders made him appear almost a giant compared to other men. She hadn't realized until now that he'd been the tallest man in the room that night. Her uncle was quite proud of his own height, but Tyson's trim and muscular physique had made Charles appear slouched and paunchy by comparison. Tyson's face was a healthy bronze, his hair as black as coal, and his eyes, which she had earlier noted were gray, seemed to burn a bright silver in the veranda's torchlight.

"I do appreciate the fact that you didn't tell my father. I should never have allowed Andrew to talk me into such a thing. It was very foolish."

"Love will find a way," he shrugged.

"It's not that... it's...oh, I don't know what it is."

Tyson laughed lightly and lifted her chin with his finger so he could look into her eyes. "Andrew seems to be a good fellow. I'm certain he'll marry you."

She stiffened slightly. "Of course he will. The question is whether I will marry him."

"Oh, I see," he laughed. "Well, then you have every right to insist that he mind his manners. Should you reject him, the next man might be offended by the liberties Andrew has already taken."

The veranda thankfully was not light enough to betray her bright cheeks. She was beginning to regret that Andrew had been allowed any return of affection at all. She cooled her embarrassment as quickly as she could by turning her face away, reminding herself that she was still a virgin, and changed the subject.

"You seem to be very comfortable here," Vieve murmured.

"Your father is a very good host."

"I mean in England," she said, turning back to him.

"My roots are here as well, madam. My mother was English and was born in this country."

"But you must have fought against England...."

"My family considered themselves Americans. But some of my mother's family still lives in England. I have a rather distant cousin in London, and I hope to find him receptive to a new family acquaintance."

"Was your mother a bondswoman?" she asked boldly. Vieve had heard of only two ways of settling in the colonies: either by a large and lucrative land grant or as a slave. Impulsively, she had asked if his family's background was modest rather than prosperous, without realizing how insulting it sounded.

"No, she was the daughter of an earl, as a matter of fact. But I'm afraid she was not only the fourth daughter, which left her quite far from the lineage of title, but also a traitor. She cast her lot with her American husband and refused to support England in the war." He took a sip from his drink. "Have I disappointed you, petite? Did you hope to learn that all Americans were raised by wolves in the wilderness?"

"Of course not. I'm...very...pleased for you. How do you have the time to visit this distant relation?"

He looked away from her immediately, an unmistakable frown of annoyance darkening his face. "I have worked hard for a good many years; my father died when I was fairly young. My brothers are all married and have children, and so when the time came for someone from our family to travel abroad to look at trade prospects, I was the best choice. They strongly encouraged me to add a little pleasure to my work."

She was caught in an almost instant giggle. He had sounded so glum, and more than that, so well rehearsed. Was he ashamed to be taking a little time away from hard work? "That's very nice," she said. "But you don't seem in the least happy about it."

"I don't like being so far from my work," he said grimly.

"And your family," she added.

"And my family," he confirmed in an impatient voice.

"Well, I hope that even under such dreadful circumstances, we can ease your loneliness and make your stay pleasant."

"And I hope my impatience with holidays does not upset my host."

"I highly doubt that," she laughed. "In fact, you're exactly the kind of man my father likes best: a man with a grave dislike for leisure and a true passion for hard work. If you are also stubborn and temperamental, you are exactly like him."

He turned toward her, and she cocked her head slightly to study his frowning countenance. If she were a bit bolder, she would smooth away the stern set of his jaw with her fingertips. No wonder he got on so well with Lord Ridgley. She couldn't suppress another giggle, and the grim lines on his face seemed to smooth.

He smiled in spite of himself. "It certainly isn't your fault that I dislike long spells in port." He took a sip from his glass. "And my brothers are right; since I've come so far, I must learn to take more time to view the rich beauty of this country... and all of its treasures."

Vieve felt a warm flush creep over her. His deep, resonant voice held a seductive quality that titillated her, and as she looked up into his mysterious silver eyes, she observed the color changing, darkening into an almost black, smoldering fire. He reached aside and placed his pipe on the rail, and then did the same with his glass, never breaking their mutual gaze. She began to tremble with anticipation. "Yes," she said softly, "do take some time."

His hand touched her waist and tentatively moved around to the small of her back. Vieve lowered her eyelids and tilted her chin upward, readying herself to be kissed. She was very adept at this, preparing for a kiss. Although there had been only Andrew, he had schooled her very well in the art of kissing, and she admitted she liked it a great deal. She might like it even more with this bold sea captain. The mere touch of his hand brought the most deliciously thrilling thoughts to mind, and she allowed him to pull her closer.

His other hand touched her shoulder, his strong fingers gently caressing her bare flesh and sliding her gown off her shoulder. She knew she was still demurely covered and so she allowed this, too. She could feel the hard press of his thighs against hers as he pulled her against him, his breath warm above her closed eyes. She sighed with pleasure. If he did not claim her lips soon, she thought she might faint from desire. Throughout the evening the captain's masculinity, his manners, and his uncanny support of her family had heightened his appeal for her. She wanted his lips to cover hers. The sweet scent of brandy on his lips nearly hypnotized her.

His lips lightly touched hers, a brush so delicate that she feared she imagined it, and his hand barely urged her closer. "I cannot do this, Vieve," he whispered. His fingers gently squeezed her shoulder, and then he released her. She stood stunned and shaken. He turned away from her, leaning on the banister, and let go with a laugh, shaking his head.

"But..."

He turned back to her, an almost embarrassed expression on his face. "I'm terribly sorry, mademoiselle. But I do not want Lord Ridgley to find me on his veranda, molesting his daughter."

"But..." She was almost too flustered to speak. "Surely you would not be flogged for a kiss."

"No, I don't think so," he said, laughing again. His finger was under her chin, his thumb testing the silky softness of her cheek. "And you are a tempting woman, I admit."

She let her eyes close again, giving him another opportunity.

"I know you wish to be kissed," he said matter-of-factly. Her eyes flew open. "Indeed, more. But that is not what I wish, petite.

It is clear that you have spent enough time on moonlit garden paths to have learned some of love's pleasures, but perhaps not enough. No, *cherie*, I do not wish to hold you, taste you, touch your sweet body, and then go alone to my bed."

"What?" she asked in shock.

He smiled lazily and reached for his glass. "I am not a young stallion, untried, prancing at the heels of my mare in wait for her father's blessing like your young Andrew. He may feel compelled to hold himself in painful restraint for the priest, in deference to your dowry and your father's permission, but I am not so inclined." He winked at her. "If I touch you like that again, I will make love to you." He leaned closer as if sharing a secret, and Vieve's eyes were so round and awestruck that she did not blink even once. "And there is no turning back, once a man has made up his mind. Take heed."

She didn't realize until he had straightened that her mouth was still standing open. She closed it, swallowed, and narrowed her eyes. "How dare you."

He chuckled. "Which insult angers you more, ma petite? Telling you that I wish only to touch you if we are to make love? Or is it the desire that I leave unsatisfied?'

"Ooooo. How...how..."

He turned away from her again, but this time he did not laugh. Instead he waved an impatient hand in what appeared to Vieve to be a gesture of dismissal. "I know, I know. How dare I. It might be wise to judge the temperament of your prey, my sweet, before you tempt so. It is a dangerous game you play."

"Oh, you...you beast."

He lifted his glass as if in a toast. "I suppose you'll be saying good night now?"

She whirled away from him and fled into the house, slamming the door. She stomped her feet on the marble floor of the foyer, groaning aloud in rage. She had invited him to sample an innocent kiss and he had turned it around to make her look like a teasing hoyden. The arrogant bastard.

Her temper fully aroused, she snatched open the door and stepped quickly onto the veranda. From the rail, he turned to face her, completely surprised to see her again. She took determined steps toward him, raised her hand, and slapped him so hard the night air was split with its sound. He did nothing but stare. She whirled around, storming back into the house and slamming the door. Without pause, she fled up the stairs to her room, slamming another door.

Tyson looked first at the closed door of the house and then casually glanced out into the garden, where his gaze met those of Paul and Evelyn. They were at the foot of the steps, having just approached when the angry Vieve had first left the captain. They were about to mount the four steps up to the veranda when she returned, in a fury, to slap his face. She apparently had not seen her brother, but then, she was in such a high-flown temper, she was blind to everything but the insult she felt. Tyson had a nagging curiosity about the point at which he would have been stopped had he proceeded with the maid and decided that it was a far better thing that Paul had seen only the angry slap. Paul came up to the veranda quickly, surprise more than anger showing on his face. "What the devil was that about?"

Tyson took a long pull on his pipe, sending swirling puffs of smoke into the clear night air. "Paul," he began in a concerned voice, "how long has it been since your mother died?"

"Nearly two years now. Why?"

"I think perhaps your sister could use the wisdom of an older woman, that's all. Somehow, I don't think her aunt Elizabeth would be the appropriate one, but perhaps Evelyn could gain her confidence and offer her some advice."

"Advice about what?" Paul demanded. "Why did she slap you? What did you do?"

Tyson laughed a bit uncomfortably, and if the lighting on the veranda had been better, Paul might have discerned a slight blush on his cheeks. Tyson had met with an angry father or two, and even a possessive brother or husband. Although Paul was considerably younger than Tyson, the situation was no less tense. "I'm afraid, Paul, that she slapped me not for what I did...but for what I didn't do." He moved past them to the door and turned to look back at the couple before going inside. "I think a little guidance is in order, but please be careful not to hurt her. I'm certain she does not fully understand her error." He smiled sympathetically. "She is a perfectly normal young woman and it is time for her to have a husband."

Four

When Vieve opened her eyes in the morning, her very first reaction to the new day was to flush scarlet equally in embarrassment and outrage. The Yankee was staying for two more days, and while that length of time had originally disappointed her, she now thought it an eternity. She was not willing to face his superior smile after the events of the previous night.

Before her breakfast was delivered, everything changed abruptly. Since Lord Dumere and Lord Ridgley were on the best of terms, Evelyn regularly stayed overnight at Chappington when some family affair required her presence. And Lord Dumere, elderly and less given to social invitations than he once had been, seldom accompanied his daughter, for Harriet and the other female servants provided adequate chaperones. On this morning as Evelyn prepared to return to the Dumere estate, her carriage arrived with sad news. During the night her father, her only relative, had quietly passed into death.

Now hiding away in her rooms to avoid Tyson's taunting grin or sparkling, knowledgeable eyes was no longer even a consideration for Vieve. In fact, upon hearing the sad news, Tyson himself quickly packed his things and hailed Bevis with his coach to make a hasty departure. He was shaking hands with the baron on the manor's portico just as Vieve came out of the house.

"You needn't leave so abruptly, Captain," Lord Ridgley said.

"I think it is best, my lord. Your family must not concern themselves with my entertainment now. You know where I can be found." He spied Vieve and turned toward her, bowing. His eyes did not tease. "Madam, I have given my condolences to Evelyn, but I'm sure you feel the loss as well. I am sorry for the sad event."

She pulled her shawl more tightly around her shoulders. "Thank you, sir. We will all miss Lord Dumere."

He took her hand and gave it a light squeeze. "You will surely be called upon to help Evelyn through this period of grief. The young woman is sweet and kind. I'm glad for her that she has a good friend in you."

Vieve was speechless. His sensitivity warmed her; she nearly forgot that a few hours before she was so furious that she had decided never to speak to him again. "I'll do what I can," she told him.

Tyson put his hat on his head. "I'll delay you no longer. Thank you again for your extended hospitality; I will await a message that you will be coming to London to continue our discussion."

Boris nodded. Tyson entered his coach and left without further ado. Vieve stood with her father and watched the departing coach. Then she turned toward him. "What do we do now, Papa?"

Lord Ridgley put an arm around his daughter's shoulders, walking with her back into the house. "Paul has taken Evelyn home and will stay with her through the next few days. She has plenty of chaperones in those servants."

"Did the death come as a surprise to you?" she asked him.

"None of us could have expected many more years with Lord Dumere," Boris said solemnly. "For that matter, I have not so many either."

"But, Papa, you're in the best of health."

"I am sixty years old. I have overstayed my welcome on this earth as it is." He stroked his thick moustache in contemplation of this, and she could not mistake the watering of his eyes. "I had better get this family settled. There is a great deal undone."

"Papa, just because Lord Dumere has died, you needn't be so discouraged about your own..."

"Both my parents were dead before I was your age. My father died when I was only twelve, and my mother married a commoner two years later. She never recovered from complications that arose when she gave birth to your Uncle Charles. When she died, my stepfather did not even remain long enough to see her buried. I was left with a large estate to manage alone and that self-centered young whelp to try to raise. You young people—you think things go on forever. They don't. We don't. I had best get my own affairs in order before the dark angel makes his call."

"Oh, Papa," Vieve sighed, hating this kind of talk from him.

"You will be busy for the next few weeks, my dear. I think you should pack for an extended stay with Evelyn. However much snickering there is at our lack of etiquette, a wedding had best follow the old lord's burial. She cannot be left to fend for herself on that dwindling acreage. She will need Paul now."

"Of course I'll go," Vieve said.

"You'll have precious little time for courtship games, daughter. You'll have to put all frivolity aside until Paul and Evelyn are settled. Tell that young buck who's prancing at your heels to cool his."

"I already have," she said quietly.

"Hm, well, that's good, daughter. There are more important things just now than his relentless petitions for your hand."

She almost told her father that he was not alone in that complaint, but instead she asked, "Papa, about Andrew, do you find him completely unsuitable?"

"For marriage with you?" Boris snorted. "I had higher hopes for you, but if he is your final choice, I will not argue. I only ask that you consider the prospect carefully. There may be better for you than young Shelby. For all his arguments to the contrary, he does not seem quite ready to take a woman to wife."

"He is the same age as Paul," she said.

"Aye," Boris returned. "That is what concerns me." Boris gave her hand a pat. They stood in the foyer. "I will see to my accounts. There will be some adjustments to be made for my friend's passing. I must prepare my ledgers for Evelyn's dowry."

"Papa, do you begin to add her estate to ours already?"

Boris gave a short, rueful chuckle. "In a manner, child. Go ahead with your packing. Tell me before you leave."

Weeks passed before Vieve was again made aware of the issue of Evelyn's dowry. Lord Dumere had been quietly buried, and Evelyn and Paul had sent around invitations for a wedding to follow her father's death by only a month. Vieve conceded that there was good reason for sadness, but hoped that the bride, who was strong and sensible, would manage to set aside her grief for this one special day.

On the morning of her wedding, Evelyn's mood was melancholy. As Vieve spread out the long French lace veil, she noticed that Evelyn's eyes misted again, and it was not with the sentimental tears of joy common for brides. "Your father would not have wished your wedding day to be marked with sadness. Happiness is what he always wanted for you."

Evelyn nodded. "Do you know, Vieve, that when my father and Lord Ridgley agreed on our betrothal, this estate was four times its present size?"

"It is still large," Vieve said with a shrug. "I doubt that the size of the Dumere estate has much to do with Paul's interest in you."

Evelyn looked away and her lips trembled. "Oh, no. My dowry is the furthest thing from his mind." She looked back at Vieve with eyes brightened by some tender reminiscence. "I recall the first moment that something of love grew between Paul and me. Even though we were promised as small children, I was fifteen— five years ago now—when we first spoke of love. By the end of that summer he was impatient to be married. My father cautioned us that we would be much happier if we waited just a little longer. But I think that what Father wished for was a little time to try to bolster the dowry. You know there is nothing of love lacking between us. Yet there is something lacking."

"Don't be ridiculous, Evelyn. Enough of this. Paul adores you and you are everything he has always wanted."

"Oh, my dear, sweet Vieve," Evelyn sighed. "I am not sad because of my father, or for any lack of love for Paul. Paul is the most wonderful man in the whole world. But he has needs beyond a willing wife. And if he would but look elsewhere, he could find a woman with so much more to give him."

"That's absurd," Vieve scoffed. "He could never find anyone better than you."

"He could find a bride with wealth."

Vieve laughed and took Evelyn's hands. "It is so unlike you to bemoan your condition. Your estate is not the richest in England, but it is still valuable...."

Evelyn shook her head. "I'm afraid it has very little value. Father was much in debt. I only bring your family more problems. What was once a proud dowry is little more than a burden now."

Vieve was shocked. "I didn't realize...."

Evelyn dropped her gaze, and Vieve saw that her cheeks were slightly flushed. "Of course you didn't, darling. Father would not have boasted of the fact, and Lord Ridgley is too much of a gentleman to turn me away with a forfeited contract for marriage. As for Paul, he is just a poor fool in love."

"He is not a fool," Vieve said, seizing a brighter attitude. "To the contrary, I have heard Father say that in estate management he is brilliant. Much more so than he is in the merchant businesses. I'm certain that he intends to build up this estate and make it useful and strong."

"Yes, that is what he says."

"You have only one choice, then," Vieve said in an almost admonishing tone. "You must not appear a sour, discontented bride. You must be happy for Paul's sake."

"Yes," she said, smiling tremulously. "Yes, it is too late for anyone to change their minds now."

"Evelyn, you mustn't worry. You will make do. Wealth is not the most important thing."

Evelyn's hand touched Vieve's cheek in a gentle stroke. She smiled tolerantly. "My dear, dear Vieve. Sometimes I forget how young you are."

Vieve shed a few tears during the ceremony, but not because Evelyn had succeeded in casting any doubt on the appropriateness of her marriage to Paul. As the couple clasped hands and repeated their vows, it was as if a shower of light fell on them.

Vieve considered Evelyn's worry over her modest dower lands, thinking how like Evelyn it was to put her own desires behind the needs of everyone else. So, the Ridgley family would not profit from this match, but it was easy to see that they had gained something more important than money. Evelyn and Paul had love, passion, devotion, loyalty, respect, and many common goals. Evelyn would be the perfect wife, having already proven she could gracefully endure Paul's proclivity for hard work. And likewise, Paul's insistence that they quickly marry demonstrated that he was a man who would try his hardest to anticipate Evelyn's every need.

The marriage had been arranged when they were mere children, but it was plain to see their elders' wisdom in matchmaking.

Vieve shed a tear of vicarious joy. A true love match was rare. She feared that she and Andrew did not share that kind of love. Aside from those very stirring romantic feelings that Andrew had recently inspired, she didn't know whether they shared anything at all.

She stood with her father as the bride and groom left the dais and walked down the garden path toward the house. Lord Ridgley looked down at her, his eyes sparkling under his fierce bushy brows. "Your day will be next, I imagine. I hope you will be as happy as they."

She sniffed a little. "I was just hoping for that very thing, Papa."

As he escorted Vieve behind the bridal couple, he leaned down so that his lips were close to her ear. He did not look at her when he spoke, and he kept his voice low so that only she would hear him. "If you will consider more than one suitor and use just a little patience and restraint, I am sure you will come to me with a worthy request when you're ready."

She looked at her father's profile with a softening in her heart for him. How late she was to realize that he wished for her happiness.

There was no shortage of wine for the wedding guests, yet Vieve drank very little. She stayed apart from the celebrating, partly because of the inner conflict that caused her to question her future, and partly because Captain Gervais was in attendance.

Vieve was only slightly surprised that he had come. When her father found it impossible to journey to London, an invitation for the wedding was sent to the captain. But if Tyson had made the journey on the pretense of discussing business, he had a strange way of showing it. He refused the offered hospitality of Chappington Hall and insisted upon a room in a country inn. She had glanced at him a few times and could still feel her cheeks grow pink at the thought of her experience on the veranda.

Her father did not remark on Vieve's reserved mood until the dancing began.

"Vieve," he instructed, "go see if that colonial merchant can dance."

She smiled, but demurred, and moved away to give her father a wide berth. The wine had livened his spirits, but she hoped to stay in the background and go unnoticed. She felt so confused by the course of events and their meaning in the past month that she felt a strong need to retreat into her private thoughts. Had she not met Captain Gervais on the road that night, this might be her own wedding. Her defiance now appalled her. And each time she looked askance at the handsome Yankee captain, she remembered that night and his clear proposal that he would lay out generous coinage for a young mistress. Her naïveté where men were concerned was a dangerous and suddenly frightening thing. On this day most especially, she was unwilling to tangle with either Andrew or the bold sea captain.

Tyson Gervais did not bother her, but Andrew did. She had avoided being alone with him since the night she had ridden to the old keep weeks ago. Many demands were being made on her. She had to lend support to her grieving friend while simultaneously trying to make quick but elaborate wedding plans. Such juggling of duties and emotions drained even the most resilient spirit, which even Andrew had finally begrudgingly understood. But his patience was not endless; the wedding was here, the celebrating had come, and yet Vieve did not cease in her evasion. Now he seemed determined to make an issue of his concern.

Vieve resisted his invitation to enter the deserted library for a few quiet moments. She refused when he tried to steer her toward the veranda doors, and she declined when he suggested a walk in the garden to watch the setting of the sun.

"Why are you ignoring me?" he finally demanded. "You're acting as if something is wrong between us."

"Something is wrong between us, Andrew," she said solemnly. "I'm not exactly sure what it is, though."

"This all started when that damned colonial visited Chappington. I've told myself you couldn't possibly be thinking of striking up an affair with a common foreigner, but now I'm beginning to think you already have."

"An affair?" she repeated.

"Well, what else could it be? You won't even come into the garden with me. Are you no longer interested in the promises we've made to each other? I thought you loved me."

Vieve felt her cheeks become warm. There were people all around them. Although their voices were hushed, she did not wish to be overheard in such a provocative conversation. Conjecture over affairs and promises would provide irresistible gossip.

"Please, Andrew..."

"I demand to know what's going on."

"Will you hush?"

"If you don't explain the sudden change in your behavior toward me, I shall have to speak to Lord Ridgley about—"

She couldn't bear to hear another word. She took his hand and walked with him out into the quiet dusk of the garden.

"You're right, I must try to explain. But I warn you, Andrew, if you try to take advantage of me, I'll scream loud enough to bring the whole party outside."

"You'll what? Good Lord, what's gotten into you?"

"I'll tell you, if you'll only listen to me. The problem is that you seldom do listen, you are so anxious to get me locked into your arms."

"Your tastes have greatly changed. I remember when you welcomed my embrace. Now you behave as though I've committed some scandalous offense, when I've loved you so desperately that I've been...oh, hell, you've fallen for the Yankee clod. It's perfectly clear. You shared my desires willingly enough before he came along."

Vieve's cheeks were no longer flushed from embarrassment. She was slowly burning into a rage. She clenched her fists, trying to keep control. "Do you see? You never let me speak."

Andrew pursed his lips and plunged his hands into his pockets, the gesture making him appear more as a small boy in a snit than a man in love. "Say what you have to say. I'm listening."

"I think we have gone too far without my father's approval. I am sorry."

"I see," he said angrily. "And what exactly does that mean?"

"I am very fond of you, Andrew. My father has not asked me to refuse your company, nor has he finally denied your petition to marry me. All he asks of me is that I take a little time, use a little patience and restraint, to be sure that marriage with you is the best possible choice for me. I think that is a fair request. And I cannot offer my father that assurance when I am constantly in your company, continually struggling with your lustful demands."

"So, you expect me to sit idly by like some docile eunuch while you look over the other prospects?"

"No, no. I wish only to know more about our prospects for the future. You have never mentioned how you plan to support me."

"I have family lands, as do you. The fact that I am not as rich as you has never bothered you before."

"My father is not so wealthy as you think, Andrew. I must marry responsibly. There is a great deal you could do to that end. You might at least show some interest in the businesses in which my father is engaged."

"There is plenty of time for that," he told her tiredly. "I have my own family lands to manage right now."

Vieve laughed suddenly. "Good Lord, Andrew, when do you do that? I've never seen you work a day, unless you are working to get me alone."

"If that is your doubt, it comes too late, in my opinion."

"I thought I knew my own mind, Andrew, but when I saw how much I dared on your behalf, I... I'm sorry; it is only partially your fault. I have to take my share of the blame. I confess that I was brought to my senses the night I risked my safety, my reputation, and my father's respect by giving in to you. I think you have pushed me beyond all the proper limits."

"You risked no more than showing the limits your love would go. In time, even your father would have understood."

"You take far too much for granted. My father would have been furious."

"I am desperate for you," Andrew went on, undaunted, "and after all that has passed between us, you would have me look the other way while you thrash about in search.... Is it one with more wealth you wish, or a more virile man? Lord, what sort of scruples do you have?"

She stiffened, deeply hurt by his implication. Of all the people in the world, the man who had constantly sworn his love and begged for one taste of her body should not now question her morals. How could he claim devoted love in one breath, then doubt her integrity in the next?

"Do you think me indecent, Andrew?"

"Your intention lacks decency, madam," he countered.

She eyed him warily. "Would I be more decent if I went into the garden with you and yielded to you finally and irrevocably?"

"Do not turn my motives around," he said angrily. "I want to marry you; my intentions are most honorable."

"If you honor me at all, cease in your demands," she said hotly. "Show me your devotion without demanding my virtue in payment."

He grasped her suddenly by her upper arms, hurting her. His eyes blazed with fury. He spoke through lips whitened with tension and hostility. "This is not child's play, madam. Much of your virtue has already rested in my hands. It is too late for you to change your mind and go to another man."

"Another? I have said nothing to indicate there will ever be another man, but if I do accept your proposal, it must be with a clear conscience. How can you deny me that?" she finished, shaking her head with a new confusion. She had faced much of Andrew's impatience, but he had never seemed so selfish or cruel.

"We have shared tender moments. I have dared much with you," she said softly, "but I am still pure."

"Oh? If I tell your father each detail of our tender moments, will he agree?" he asked in a menacing tone. "If I describe the sweet flesh of your breasts, will your brother bid me step aside and give you time to set your mind to marriage with me? A decent woman is sure before she commits so much to a lover's caress."

Vieve was shaken by his ferocious grasp, by his threateningly ominous tone. She searched her memory for a time in the past when she might have realized his resistance to reason. But she had never before suggested that they would not be wed; she had answered his desire to be married with agreement.

"I think you had better let go of me, Andrew, unless it is your wish that I add fear to my other doubts."

It was as if what she said finally reached him, for his features softened and he slowly released her with an apologetic shrug. She rubbed her upper arms, and a shiver of apprehension ran through her. "You certainly have the option of shaming me before my family," she said with all the determination she could muster. "But I am confident of their trust, and I think it would not hurt my case as much as yours."

"I think you're making a big mistake," he warned her. "Do not expect me to wait quietly while you taste the passions of other men."

"I don't believe you really think that is my intention. You are angry, that's all."

"You came to me easily enough."

No slap in the face could have hurt as much. Vieve looked at him with shocked wonder that would cost her many sleepless nights. How could she have been so wrong about him? This man had cajoled, begged, manipulated, and pressured her. She had succumbed to a large degree, true, but she had not brazenly sought his affection. He had not only worked hard and long to gain her acquiescence, but had sworn his devotion and respect. All lies?

"Will you make me appear a hoyden and a tramp unless I yield yet more? Now, Andrew? Will you take me here, in the garden, at my brother's wedding party?"

His eyes were cold and implacable. "If you ask me to step aside and withdraw my proposal so that you may look over the available stock of men, you are little more than a common slattern in my eyes. I have, for more than a year, committed myself to only you, enduring no small amount of misery. You should have raised your doubts much sooner. My life has been promised to you; by right, you owe me your vows, your body, and your dower estate, just by what has already transpired."

Vieve stepped backward one step, then two, feeling a strong need to put distance between them. "Thank heavens we had this talk, Andrew," she said, still retreating. "It is very clear we are not right for each other. It is good that we know it now, before it is too late."

"You don't worry that I will soil your reputation among all the other suitors?" he asked with bitter sarcasm in his voice.

"Indeed, it worries me a great deal," she said with grave certainty. "If you do that, Andrew, it means I have been wrong about you from the beginning. And that would be so very unfortunate."

Before he could say another word, she turned quickly away and hurried back into the house. She went directly to where her father sat with some of his friends. Lord Ridgley rested a full tankard of ale on one knee and noticed her arrival, but not her distress. She was about to sit down beside him when she became aware of a great stir among the guests. Evelyn was being urged toward the stairs by her maids to be prepared for the nuptial bed; Paul was being raised atop the shoulders of his fellows with much chortling and crude jesting.

Evelyn wrestled herself away from the maids and struggled, laughing, through the throng of men who made a great show of detaining her spouse from his rightful place at her side. She came breathlessly toward Vieve, her eyes alight with excitement and joy, her cheeks flushed with happiness. She pressed the small prayer book encased in a bed of roses into Vieve's hand. "We are truly sisters now," Evelyn said. "For your own wedding, my dearest, which will be soon."

The single women in attendance pulled impatiently at Evelyn, eager for the fun of making her ready for her husband. The ritual was a bawdy and merry one, and the highlight of every noble wedding. Despite the laughter and tugging from behind her, Evelyn's eyes were only for Vieve as she passed the treasured book and bouquet on to the next bride. Tears wet Vieve's cheeks as she embraced Evelyn. "Be happy, my love," Vieve said with much emotion.

The maids succeeded in drawing the bride away toward the stairs, and the men became louder in their cheers and shouts as Evelyn disappeared from sight. An elaborate mockery of getting the groom too drunk to stand, much less to do his duty as a husband, was staged. The men held Paul and pushed full tankards toward him, but he pursed his lips and refused the brew. The laughter in the room was boisterous, and the wrestling among the men was wild, but even through the clamoring crowd Vieve could see Andrew glaring at her from across the room.

She raised the prayer book and flowers to her face, as if she would capture the sweet scent, hiding her angry tears. Within moments Paul had managed to make his escape from his friends and stood victoriously at the foot of the stairs. A round of cheers at his success filled the room, and Vieve turned away from the scene.

She felt a hand on her shoulder and whirled around, prepared to slap Andrew's face if he dared approach her. The raucous noise all around was deafening, and no one noticed that Tyson Gervais had singled her out. She knew from his frown that her tears were visible. "Can I be of some assistance, damoiselle?"

"Not at the moment, Captain."

"When, then?" he asked, his eyes burning bright.

"Not in the near future, sir."

"Do you tease me purposely?" he asked, smiling at her as if he only joked.

She gave a short, bitter laugh. "I have learned to play no games with you, Captain. Do not pester me. At the moment I think I hate all men."

He smiled down at her and lifted her chin with a finger. "Perhaps you have just tired of little boys, madam. If so, I am at your service."

He turned away from her and disappeared into the throng of well-wishers. She followed his departing form until he was out of sight, and then her gaze slowly moved toward Andrew. He stood red-faced and furious just inside the veranda doors. His fists were clenched at his sides as if he struggled with the urge to beat the Yankee senseless.

The warmth of London in July caused the city to steam, and every man on the street forecasted a good harvest and mild winter and thus a chance to recoup their losses from the two past rugged cold seasons. As Tyson Gervais waited in his coach beside the charred remains of Lord Ridgley's warehouses, he thought of Virginia and longed for the mild comfort of summer at his own home.

His family had conceded that he deserved a rest from his Richmond plantation. The duel with Michael Everly had taken its toll on the entire Gervais family. When Tyson said he was leaving the management to his brothers, no one balked at such responsibility, but when he said he was going to England, they thought him mad. They did not think visiting the homeland of a man he had recently killed showed any sense at all. But gathering some information about Michael Everly, who had claimed to be a British aristocrat, was Tyson's first priority.

Tyson was a rigid man and when his mind was made up, he stood firm on his decision, however much it rankled those around him. But so far he had had no success in finding any family

named Everly in London, and his pursuit of this man's kind
needed to be cautious. He hired a young solicitor named
Humphrey to continue the search on his behalf. He was not at all
surprised that Everly had not descended from royalty. Noble
names were very easy to trace.

Tyson prepared himself to become entrenched in business
while Mr. Humphrey continued investigating the young man
named Everly. As he looked in the direction of the warehouses,
he saw that Lord Ridgley was completing his conversation with a
building agent. As he walked toward the coach, Tyson smiled to
think how brisk his stride was for a man of sixty years.

"There is no disparity in the sum required to rebuild,
Captain," Lord Ridgley said as he settled himself into the coach.
"This man and the three before him have come up with like sums
that will not change. And though building through winter will be
difficult and expensive, it can be completed in time for shipments
as early as June."

Tyson nodded. "The price is a good one, my lord."

"It is horrendous, but then you expected as much, didn't
you?"

"I am aware of the cost of building, my lord. But I am certain
that the cost will only increase when trade between our countries
is supported by the government, which I perceive will happen
quite soon. Washington has already sent an emissary to London
to discuss the issue. I hope to make many shipments to England
in the future and I am therefore resistant to temporary
arrangements. However, I cannot pilot my own vessels for many
years. What of the future management?"

"At the risk of sounding like a prattling old man, I would
advise that we settle on a hired manager, from your own colony
of Virginia if it suits you. Paul is a good and determined young
man, but much better at farming, husbandry and estate
management. I watched him struggle to help me with the
merchant business, and I don't see any gift for trade in his blood.
Bless him, he has inherited more of his mother than his father."

"A hired manager would suit me fine."

"I don't think you should invest blindly and leave England. If
we can come to terms, I would suggest that you see through the
building, if at all possible."

Tyson smiled in sudden surprise. "Do you advise me to stay near and thereby protect my investment?"

Boris laughed shrewdly. "In a manner, young man. It is not that I think myself incapable, but at this precise time it is better that I remain in the country. We have a new family member, and I'm afraid my home needs my attention." He leaned forward in his seat as the coach jolted into action. "If you have any doubts that I intend a fair partnership with you, you can assure yourself by remaining on the site of building to see it through."

"If I doubt, my lord, I will not invest."

Lord Ridgley leaned back. "You make me miss my youth, Captain. I was much like you at your age. You are ambitious to a fault, coming to do business in the one country where you face the greatest risk, yet where the largest possible profit exists. I admire your courage."

"You amuse me," Tyson said. "As I watched you talk to the building agent I was thinking I would be a lucky man to have your strength and energy at sixty."

"From what you've told me about your own life, being left a huge family property and siblings when you were but a lad, it strongly resembles my own. The fact is that I was so consumed with business that I did not marry until I was your age. Until half my life was gone I didn't have the time. And since I married a young woman, I expected I would leave her a widow."

Tyson looked out the window as they passed through the wharves and into the city, but said nothing.

"When do you expect to hear from your family?" Lord Ridgley asked with obvious impatience.

Tyson looked back at the baron. "They will respond at their earliest opportunity, I'm sure. Be patient, my lord. An ocean keeps us from making a final commitment."

"I must warn you, Captain, I have had another offer."

"A good one?" Tyson asked, lifting a brow.

"Extremely good, but there was a definite drawback. A local merchant sent an agent to me with a large sum available, but unfortunately the man does not have a shipping concern with a line of plantation goods. That possibility still entices me more toward your offer. But a long wait is not good for my purse. If we can't make a final decision soon, I shall be forced to take the sum."

Tyson smiled at the baron. "Either you have a devious plan to rook me in the deal, or you expose too much of your poverty, my lord. Knowing you are hungry for my money...I could lower my price."

"You could," the baron replied, "but it is a partnership you plan. I cannot see the advantage in lying to you. Surely you would guess, despite any craftiness from me, that I would rebuild myself if I could afford the cost."

Tyson leaned back and crossed his arms over his chest. "I made many inquiries about warehouse space myself, and one of those owners I had earlier sought returned to me with an irresistible offer of leased property." Tyson watched as the baron's eyes widened in surprise and then he scowled.

"Did you accept?"

"If he had been quicker with the offer, I would have. But I found the sum to be suspiciously low, and I have come to the conclusion that no matter what the price, owning is far better than leasing. I have a large family—there are many heirs."

"At least we both have options, should we fail to reach a final agreement," the baron said, but the look in his eye indicated that he was very displeased.

"I am optimistic, my lord. We wait approval from my brothers, but they often trust my judgment in such things."

"Come back to Chappington while you wait," the baron urged. "London must be a dreary place for an American."

"It is not without its diversions," Tyson replied.

"Soon, then," Lord Ridgley pressed. "Our life is dull. You liven the place considerably."

"Dull?" Tyson laughed. "You lie like any good merchant. I have met your family. Some of them are stuffy, some of them a bit too bold, but none of them is dull."

"My family," Boris said. "How they test a man's patience. Never mind the righteous Latimers, the rest of us make good company. We want you to visit."

"I have some business in the city, my lord. It is of a personal nature."

"Is there anything that I can do to hurry your final decision?" Lord Ridgley asked. "If so, I will stay in London."

Tyson smiled at the man's eagerness. "I think not. But if you choose to take the other offer, I will understand."

"I think I have made my preference clear enough, short of begging. May we say September? The first week?"

Tyson thought about seeing Vieve again, but he was not aware of the frown that betrayed his inner conflict. Vieve, the golden flower from the baron's garden, had awakened that part of him that he thought Lenore had killed. The business venture appeared perfect. But he was quite upset by the way the memory of her moist lips and soft scent of lavender haunted him still. He had barely touched her, yet he had not enjoyed a peaceful night's sleep since.

"September," he finally agreed. "The first week."

"Good. Paul and Evelyn will welcome you and Vieve will be delighted to see you."

Tyson sighed ruefully. The baron did not know what he asked. Tyson needed the month between this business discussion and seeing Vieve again to bolster himself and make a few resolutions. He had already killed a man because of a woman. He hated to think what form of violence the little seductress at Chappington might inspire.

Five

Lord Ridgley remembered with clarity that as the first buds had appeared on the trees last spring, he had been despondent. He had feared that after many years of struggling with his properties, he would be forced to admit defeat. Though he held no grudge against either Evelyn or Lord Dumere, it did not help his estate to take a heavily indebted dower farm and manse into his accounts. His warehouse and shipping losses had forced him to borrow against Chappington Hall. And Vieve, it had seemed, was destined in marriage to a useless and poor young noble.

Over the summer the captain had come closer to making his generous investment, which would not only bolster the shipping business but allow the baron to remove the debt from his family lands. And his daughter had somehow come to her senses and relented to consider other suitors.

The approach of fall cooled the land, and Lord Ridgley felt robust and strong. He was fully cognizant of the fact that there would not be many more such profitable summers. He was driven to set many troubles aright before his own death. He would not leave his children problems and debt, but a secure base from which they could do well if they were willing to give the effort.

Lord Ridgley took great pride in the attributes of the suitors he funneled into Vieve's life. After she had nodded her head in agreement that she should widen her prospects, Boris had contacted friends and acquaintances to send suitors to her stoop. Although the Ridgleys had lived in a quiet and retired country style, his daughter's comeliness was not unknown. It proved a very simple task to recall those men she had earlier discouraged and even to provide new ones.

And then he watched, from a distance, with great amusement.

Vieve kept company with Lester Bryfellows, the son of a neighboring baron, for only a fortnight. The tall, lanky heir apparent would likely prove a good manager of money, but he was a gawky lad with no sense of humor. When he visited Chappington, his clumsiness saw the staining of good imported Irish linen and cast more than one china cup into the trash heap.

"He may be wealthy one day, Papa, but his money will be fast diminished as he replaces his wreckage."

"Perhaps it is only his youth, and he will outgrow it," Lord Ridgley replied consolingly.

"Good Lord, Father, I am to marry the man, not raise him."

Samuel Trenner, who would one day aspire to an earldom in the south of England, graced their parlor and dining room for a time. His manners were rigid and impeccable, and his appetite tremendous. His chubby appearance and unabashed gluttony caused Vieve to grimace as they shared a table. Poor Samuel was not rejected for this reason, however, but the fellow departed, shamefaced and guilty, after a shriek of outrage and a ringing slap were heard from the sitting room.

There were a few others whom Vieve found too dull, too unsightly, too foppish, or too poor.

Lord Ridgley brought one more to her attention. Sir Wayne could not be said to have any of these faults, for he was a fine figure of a man. He also had a generous stipend from a flourishing estate, was successful with money, was mannerly, humorous, and held a position of some influence in government. He was quite handsome. But...

"My God, Father, he is fifty years old."

"A bit too mature?" Lord Ridgley asked.

"He has buried three wives and has a son older than me."

"Ah, you worry about the inheritance of your offspring. Good point, daughter."

"Please," she begged, "teach me the accounting of these ledgers and take me to London to see the ships. I would rather die an old, unused virgin than settle for any of these men."

"Now, Vieve, you are too impatient. It is only one summer; you haven't seen them all."

"It does not look good," she insisted, crossing her arms over her chest and tapping her foot.

"Perhaps you are too fussy."

Her eyes glittered with anger. "Your complaint about Andrew was that I was not fussy enough."

"Ah, yes, it was, wasn't it? Well then, perhaps you are missing your mark by looking for the obvious. Learn to trust your instincts. That is what I do in trade, and it never fails me."

Lord Ridgley ciphered his sums, and his daughter's disappointment increased as August aged. But the baron was not discouraged. His children thought he was crusty and old, given only to work and blind to all other matters of living. They would be shocked to learn that he had a strong sense of the romantic and that there was very little he missed. He had seen how Captain Gervais regarded his daughter, and he had noticed, as well, how Vieve's manner changed in the company of the captain.

Lord Ridgley was hungry for the Yankee's money, but he was not blind to other concerns. There were a few other things he needed as well, and he had come to believe that Captain Gervais was the perfect man to oblige him. He saw stubbornness and pride in Tyson, and the appearance of ruthless loyalty to Tyson's own family and possessions. In this Lord Ridgley found hope. Like his daughter, Lord Ridgley knew how limited the possibilities were for finding a good, handsome, and rich man. What Lord Ridgley alone realized was the requirement for such qualities as ingenuity, craftiness, plotting, and devising of plans. There were family troubles that Lord Ridgley feared he would not live long enough to finally settle.

He found Vieve alone in the parlor, lounging on the settee with her feet raised on the arm. She wiggled her toes and her gown was hoisted up, petticoats ruffling around her knees. There was still so much of the child left in her, but it was quickly giving way to complete womanhood. As he entered, she jumped in surprise and quickly assumed a more demure posture. "No young man calling today?" he asked her.

"Truly, Father, even I deserve a rest from this nonsense."

"Nonsense? No wonder you find no suitable man. You must be a bit more serious in this quest."

"You may believe me when I say that I am more than serious. Thus my disappointment."

"Patience, Vieve. It is only the last week in August. You are fairly new at this venture."

"And the sooner it is a memory, the better."

"I have found," Lord Ridgley said philosophically, "that when things seem the darkest, there is a bright dawn ahead."

"I'm telling you, she won't let me near her." Andrew Shelby raised a closed fist in emphasis, and his face reddened in an effort to convince the man. He paced in the small study and rubbed the back of his neck with his hand. Charles Latimer did not reply. Andrew turned to face him again. "It has been almost four months since I've been alone in her company. And nothing I say will change her mind."

Charles leaned his elbows on his desk and looked at Andrew. "And her complaint is that you demanded too much?"

Andrew nodded. "She says she cannot believe that I truly love her, since I have asked her to forfeit her virtue to hurry her father toward our marriage."

Charles shook his head in disbelief. His teeth gleamed. "So unlike a woman," he said. "I assure you this is rare, Andrew. Once you've touched them, raved about your agony and desire, they come panting to you."

"Well, you were wrong this time," Andrew said with disappointment.

"You sampled a little of her, eh? How did she seem? Reluctant?"

"No. Not until the Yankee arrived. Perhaps he's her lover now."

"Not hardly. He was only here for a few days after you failed with the maid. His interests, it seems, are more wisely placed to business than wenching."

"How do you know that?"

"Why, Andrew, do I appear to be so foolish as to let my brother blindly enter some agreement with a foreigner without inquiries of my own? Poor Boris has failed so miserably and so often that I feel it is my duty to take a look at Captain Gervais's credibility...for Boris's sake, of course. However, I think you had better get to Vieve before the captain returns to Chappington with business settled and diversion on his mind."

"What am I supposed to do? She will not even speak to me privately. She prattles about thinking with a clear conscience and about her family troubles. Money, and all that."

"We already know that Lord Ridgley has problems with money. That has been my major concern. Have you tried taking a different approach to the wench?"

Andrew frowned in frustration. "I have been on my best behavior. She is unmoved."

"All right, then you had best remain so. I think we should prepare a new plan immediately. We'll arrange for the sudden death of one of your distant relatives."

Andrew laughed bitterly. "And who shall that be?"

Charles licked his lips in thought. "You must look into your ancestry quickly, young man, and come up with a name. It will afford you a small fortune and you can step in to save the day for Lord Ridgley. Behave yourself with the girl, for now."

"This isn't working out the way you said it would," Andrew said sullenly. "I'm beginning to think it was a mistake from the start."

"Here now," Charles cautioned. "It is too soon to be discouraged. She's a little more skittish than we expected, but do not lose heart. If Gervais had not startled her on the road, it would be done now. I think it's a simple matter that the girl got frightened by the Yankee, but she'll come around. How far have you gone with her?"

"Not very far, actually. It's not been easy to endure, I'll have you know."

"Come, come, you young people are so impatient. There are plenty of village wenches upon whom to ease yourself. I've given you enough silver to buy your whores. Tell me what you've done. Have you taken enough liberties to move her father?"

"As I told you, it is different with Vieve. Something in her manner suggests she is ready for a man, but she allows me little. The minute my hand begins to move, she pushes me away. She is not like other women; she carries on as if one simple kiss is a passionate compromise."

"Well, even though she doesn't admit it, by now she's probably aching for a man. You've stirred her up a mite, eh, boy?"

Andrew shrugged. Things had become too complicated for him. He had begun this alliance with Charles Latimer with money as an incentive, but he wanted only Vieve now. He couldn't take another to his bed without having visions of her. He might have intended to arouse her, but now it was mostly the other way around. She seemed to be managing too well without him, while he was having torrid dreams that were driving him crazy. He looked at Charles. "I think I actually love her."

"Nonsense, Andrew. That is how every man feels about a woman who won't give in to temptation. If you let feelings like that upset you, you're likely to act without thinking. And believe me, this requires some thought."

Andrew sighed. "What do you want me to do?"

"Well," Charles began, rising from behind his desk, rubbing his chin pensively. "I can provide you with money to take to Lord Ridgley. If you're even a little clever when you talk to him, you can convince him that you adore his daughter, that you're more than willing to combine your wealth with hers for the betterment of the entire Ridgley family, and get his permission for the marriage. He was never very concerned that you didn't come from good enough noble stock. It was your conspicuous lack of money that distressed him."

"Perhaps money was an issue," Andrew relented.

"Of course it was. Boris needs money. Badly, in fact. But money has never been quite as important to him as his bloody nobility. He'd have taken you over an untitled rich man in a moment."

Andrew raised both his eyebrows questioningly. "Are you absolutely sure about that?"

"I can give him plenty of money, but he refuses to accept my help." Charles's shrewd, narrow eyes mocked his attested concern for his brother.

Andrew had mismanaged his inherited estate, and through his inexperience and lack of effort, the Shelby lands had gone to ruin. A year before, Charles had taken advantage of Andrew's desire for Vieve and his need of money and cleared the debt from the Shelby lands. Charles now held a contract signed by Andrew. Upon Andrew's marriage to Vieve, Charles would take possession of the estate that Andrew had inherited, beleaguered though it was. Andrew was pleased, since Chappington appealed to him much more.

Charles's only requirement of Andrew was that the Ridgley family never be told there was any monetary help from Charles Latimer. Charles wished to help his brother settle Vieve with a good noble name, anonymously. Since all Andrew wanted was

Vieve, he did not doubt Charles's charity, nor did he question the fact that he had all but gifted the crafty merchant with everything he could claim as his own.

A year ago, Andrew had been excited and hopeful, for how could such a plan fail? Without help from Charles, Andrew could not even afford to court the woman of his dreams. But now, with things going much awry, Andrew was not only disappointed, he was frankly a little frightened. He did not know how he would survive as an esteemed noble without Chappington by marriage or his own family lands. He had nowhere to turn but to Charles Latimer.

"Listen to this, Andrew," Charles said, after a few moments of quiet deliberation. "I think you should go first to Lord Ridgley and offer to help him out of the financial trouble he is experiencing. Tell him...no, convince him that it is because you love his daughter that you are willing to make your money available to him She should come to your marriage free of worry; her father's problems should not interfere with her happiness. And then, when you have saved her father from ruin, you must go to the young woman and plead for a chance to change her mind. But mind you, do not frighten her, or she will refuse to give you the merest portion of her time."

Andrew shook his head in confusion. "I admit, Charles, that I do not fully understand why you go to such lengths to aid me."

"Of course you do, Andrew. When you marry her, I shall own the Shelby estate. My niece will marry a good old English name, I will make money, and my brother will have the help he needs."

"My estate is not worth as much as you've invested already."

"But I like you so well, and surely you've gone too far with my niece for me to consider another for her hand in marriage."

"But," Andrew interrupted, "if Lord Ridgley accepts help from me, he will actually be accepting it from you."

"True," Charles admitted. "But he won't know it."

"Why does he refuse help from his own family?"

Charles shrugged. "Our mother, you see, was nobly born, but we were sired by different fathers. My father was a commoner, and for all the years of my rearing I was dependent on my brother for everything. Lord Ridgley is stubborn and proud. It does not sit well with him that I have attained so much more than he has. It was easier for him to dole out money to me for all those years than for him to accept my charity. He feels that as a baron, born to so much responsibility, he should not be forced to admit defeat... especially to a younger brother he has always resented."

Andrew frowned in confusion. He had been in the company of the two families many times, and it had always seemed to him that Charles resented Boris, and not the other way around.

He shrugged off his suspicions. "I suppose that when all is said and done, everyone will be content with a better state of affairs."

"Exactly, Shelby. Do as I say now and present Lord Ridgley with an improved offer. The sum is unimportant, for certainly it will endear my niece to you." Charles rushed Andrew toward the study door. "I know you think of yourself as a very good lover, young man, but if you are clever you will humble yourself to my niece and promise to show deep respect for her virtuous conduct. Admit you were wrong to demand so much, if it should come to that. If you give her the impression that you are in rut and charging like a wild boar toward her maidenhead, she will fear to be alone in your company."

Charles's hand was on the door when Andrew asked, "And if she consents to be alone with me again?"

"Good Lord, boy," Charles laughed. "Don't let the moment get away from you. She can only tease you so much before you lose control. She has tortured you for a year, who would not understand? You want her, do you not?"

"I want her desperately. I have wanted her more with each passing day."

"And though she hesitates, it is all for the sake of propriety," Latimer told him. "She wants you as well, or she would have denied you long ago. The lass is frightened, poor thing. It is better that you make the decision for her. Believe me, Andrew, when you are married and Vieve is expecting your first son, you will barely remember these hard times." Charles gave Andrew an affectionate, fatherly pat on the back. "But if you delay, she may find another, and we cannot let that happen."

Andrew nodded. "You are probably right. I think perhaps she is exercising great will for the sake of good conduct. I will try my best."

"Good, good," Charles said, opening the study door and virtually pushing him out. "Come and see me when you have some good news. I will leave it to you until then."

Andrew left the study feeling as if some unfinished business still nagged at him. Before he could give consideration to his doubts, he heard his name urgently whispered. He turned and looked up and down the long hall several times before he saw young Faye Latimer. She stuck her head out of the parlor doors, her eyes alive with mischief and her cheeks rosy with desire.

"Andrew, in here," she whispered.

He frowned slightly. He would rather have gotten out of the house without a confrontation with this girl. Faye was too well endowed for a fifteen-year-old; she was too forthright and too brave. Each time he visited the Latimer house, this troublesome girl hid in waiting for him, tempting him to tarry with her before he left.

"Go away, Faye," he warned. "You'll get into trouble."

"Come here," she demanded.

Andrew sighed heavily, stepping into the parlor. Faye was outrageous in her pursuit of him. While Vieve had pushed his hands away, Faye pressed against him. Vieve refused to yield her virginity, while Faye begged him to take hers.

Faye closed the parlor door and looped her arms around his neck.

"This is dangerous, Faye. You shouldn't be doing this."

"Just kiss me," she begged, lifting her chin and closing her eyes.

"It's not easy for a man to 'just kiss.'"

"Andrew..."

"You little tease...you ought to be spanked."

He covered her mouth in a searing kiss. She strained toward him. It was impossible for Andrew to believe the girl was inexperienced, she moved her lips so convincingly.

"Someone might come," he warned her.

"Father is the only one at home. And the door locks."

"I'm warning you, minx, if I start kissing you, I'll want more. I have been a long time without a woman."

"Oh, Andrew, why do you try to frighten me?"

"Because you should be frightened, Faye. You tempt me more than is wise."

Her-eyes lit up with excitement. "Do I? Do I really?"

"Of course you do. Now stop moving so. I am not a eunuch."

"I know, Andrew. Oh, I know. Just kiss me."

"But..."

"Don't worry. Just kiss me."

He looked down into her eyes and frowned his displeasure. She was plump and pale; she was really only a child. In fact, of all the women Andrew knew, from noble dame to peasant wench, Faye was undoubtedly the least attractive to him. But she was the most eager for him. While Vieve had a way of making him feel like a foolish boy, Faye made him feel like a man.

He touched her cheek with a finger. "You are not prudent, dear. Surely you know that you can only tease a man for so long before he loses control," Andrew warned, knowing full well he echoed Charles Latimer's very words.

"I know," she said in a passionate breath.

He relented then and kissed her in a way that satisfied her wildest expectations. She took his hand and pressed it to her large, round breast. She writhed in wanton pleasure, and it was far too late by the time Andrew felt in control again.

Vieve sat in the sitting room beside her bedchamber with her eyes turned toward the window. The summer of her seventeenth year had not been much fun. Her decision to follow her father's advice had certainly not increased her prospects for a husband. In number, perhaps, but not in quality.

Her brother sat nearby and leaned the chair he occupied back on its two rear legs. "Do you worry that you can't trust me?" he asked in a tender voice.

She would not look at him, but continued to gaze out the window.

"Perhaps I should have sent Evelyn to speak to you." As he leaned forward the front legs of the chair banged on the floor. "Simply tell me the truth."

"But I have," she sighed. "I have not been compromised by any man. Andrew did not steal my virtue, although he wanted my virginity. He did not mince words; he said that Father would approve if we had lain together."

"That is not a very chivalrous request, but I doubt that Andrew is the first man to make such a suggestion. You seemed much in love with him," Paul said. "Now, why do you refuse to see him?"

"Refuse?" she repeated. "Oh, no, he is welcome here, but I will not be alone in his company, and he is very angry about that."

Paul frowned. "That is not exactly what he told me. However, if Andrew's demands are as excessive as you claim, you must maintain a proper chaperone."

"What exactly did he tell you?" she asked hotly.

Paul shrugged. "He said you have been extremely close, that you had exchanged many promises and words of love. He was not more explicit than that, but he implied..."

"Oh, that blackguard," she stormed. "He threatened to cheapen me before my own family to get Father to approve our marriage. I see it was not an idle threat."

"Perhaps that was not his intention. My reason for bringing this to your attention is because Andrew has approached Father again and also came to me. His estate has apparently improved, and yet Father is not moved to accept his offer of marriage. And neither are you, it would seem."

"Good for Father," Vieve said smugly. When she was first made aware of Andrew's poor estate, it gave her reason to pause, and she had fantasized some instant relief if Andrew could quickly rectify the situation by coming into some money. Now Andrew's money or even lack of it had nothing to do with her decision.

"Does that mean that regardless of Andrew's improved estate, you are no longer interested in marriage with him?"

"I'm afraid that is what it means."

"Has some other suitor caught your eye?"

"No. Paul, do you support Andrew? Is that it?"

"Well, he is my friend, though you must not be influenced by that. I came because he asked for my help. He says he loves you desperately, and I believe him. I could say nothing more to him until I heard your explanation."

"I don't think I quite understand his great longing."

Paul laughed indulgently. "You are proud of your good looks. Is this an attack of humility?"

"No... but... he is fine-looking, noble, and has the ability to be charming, yet over this past year he has become angrier, more desperate and less chivalrous. I feel as if he is a different person from the man with whom I once kept company."

"I will have a word with him about that," Paul said. "He needs to mind his manners with you."

"You may tell him that courtesy is the first thing he must learn, and if he truly wishes to endear himself to me and to Father, he should begin by acting the gentleman in our presence."

Paul put his hands in his pockets, and his shoulders rose in a shrug. "That is fair enough. I will ask only one thing of you."

"Anything," she sighed with relief.

"I would have you shed some small bit of understanding on Andrew's blighted case. I do not ask you to fall in love with him," Paul assured her when he saw her angry expression. "I do not ask you to go alone with him, nor do I ask you to marry him. Just try to understand that he is a lover scorned and his behavior may not be at its best."

She shook her head. "You were the first to caution me about Andrew, and now you urge me toward greater patience."

Paul took her by the hands. "That is exactly why. It was because of Andrew's lack of money that I worried about your marriage to him, but that is remedied. And, you see, darling, I am sympathetic because I know what it feels like to love a woman. Evelyn tried to withdraw from our betrothal because of her estate problems, and I was in a fit. Andrew's whims need not be indulged, Vieve, but we can make an effort to understand his hurt."

Vieve gazed into her brother's eyes. She would not try to explain to Paul that her romance with Andrew was quite different from anything that had passed between him and Evelyn. Paul, she was certain, had always loved Evelyn far too selflessly to ever ask her to demean herself for him. But she could see that Paul had some sympathy for Andrew, so she smiled instead.

"I will try to understand him, Paul. But you will be doing Andrew a grave disservice if you lead him to believe he might expect any more than that from me."

They walked arm in arm down the stairs, and by the time they reached the lower floor, they were laughing together. As they crossed the foyer, Vieve was halted by the sound of two men's laughter. She stopped suddenly and clung more tightly to Paul's arm. Within a moment both her worst fears and greatest hopes were realized, for her father came into the great hall with Captain Gervais.

Lord Ridgley stopped when he spied his offspring, and his thick moustache rose to expose a wide grin. "I couldn't have planned it better myself. These are the two finest children, Tyson. They are ever around when you call for them. Come, you two, well have a toast. Captain Gervais and I have just this moment had a handshake that will begin a very long and prosperous partnership."

"Father," Paul said, breaking into a wide smile. "At last? The warehouses? By God, I knew it would work out."

Paul abandoned Vieve, grasped his father's hand, and gave it a hearty shake. Then he turned to the visiting captain and shook his hand. Vieve watched, her eyes wide with surprise, her heart beating rapidly. *He is back.*

"More than the warehouses. Tyson sent a letter on a packet bound for the Americas last May, and his brothers answered him with both hearty approval and money. It will be both warehouses, and Tyson would like to consign all four of our ships to bring cargo from their family plantation to England. It is better and bigger than we even anticipated."

Paul slapped his thigh and gave a wild hoot of enthusiasm. "You won't be sorry, Tyson. We have the best ships and crews in London port."

Vieve watched Tyson and he watched her. His attention was drawn away from the happy exclamations of Paul and Lord Ridgley.

"Daughter," Lord Ridgley said, startling her out of her stare, "come along, this calls for a brandy." He held his arm out to include her.

"Urn, no thank you, Papa," she said softly, looking back at Tyson. "Go ahead. This celebration is more for the three of you."

She turned toward the steps. Paul had forgotten all about her problems with Andrew, but it was understandable. After the years of hard work he had endured to try to help heal their ailing business, he was entitled to this happy distraction. The Yankee had brought them trade and money. Perhaps Paul could rest easier now, and her father would not be so beset by worries.

"Come, Vieve," she heard Tyson say. A shiver went up her spine at the slow, seductive drawl. Without even thinking about the action, she turned back to him. It was natural to respond to the sound of his voice. "Don't disappoint us. This is a family agreement... and you are family."

He stood, holding his hat in his hand, his eyes seeming to call her with their amorous glitter. She knew at once that the summer had been wasted, for no man could ever interest her now that the Yankee had returned. "It is better that I decline," she said softly. "I am no less pleased than the rest of you, but I think you should celebrate without me."

"It won't be the same without you," he said.

Her brother and father continued to laugh and talk and slap each other on the shoulders in profound relief and excitement, but Vieve felt as if she were alone with Tyson.

"You will be staying on for a while, won't you, Captain?"

"For a while."

"Then we will see each other again."

His eyes burned an intense message into her. She could not tear her gaze away. Though no words were spoken, she thought they both understood their attraction mutual and confirmed. She was surprised her father and brother did not feel the sudden heat in the room. She trembled slightly, but it did not show. All that could be seen was a new apprehension that put color in her cheeks and caused her eyes to widen, for his expression had promised he had returned to Chappington for more than business. Then she turned to mount the stairs, listening to their voices behind her.

"What?" Lord Ridgley asked. "She's not coming? What the hell, she complains I don't include her in business, then she won't be included. Well, come along and let's get a drink."

"Your daughter seems different somehow," she heard Tyson say. "Older."

"A few months makes a world of difference in a girl her age," Paul laughed.

"Bah," Lord Ridgley scoffed. "She's too young for one thing, too old for another. I need a husband for her, that's what."

"I'm sure you'll find one, my lord. She shouldn't be that hard to match."

Vieve slowly opened her bedroom door, entered the quiet of her room, and shut out their voices from below. She leaned against the door with her hands behind her back and closed her eyes. An almost imperceptible smile formed on her slightly trembling lips.

Elizabeth Latimer was just coming down the stairs to attend to a housekeeping matter in the parlor when the sound of crashing glass caused her to halt in surprise. She took two cautious steps, and then the sound of her husband's angry voice brought her up short again.

"Get out. Just get the hell out."

Elizabeth stood in the foyer in wait to see who was being so chastened. Will Tetcher, one of her husband's hired agents from London, walked briskly toward the door, not exchanging words or even glances with her.

Elizabeth went directly to the study. Charles paced behind his desk. She stepped over the broken remnants of a pitcher that lay smashed on the floor. "Charles, what is it?"

"That damned colonial bastard," he growled. "He's done it. He's given my brother money even though I had agents offer both Gervais and Boris better agreements for what they need."

Elizabeth twisted her hands with worry. "What does it mean?"

"It means, you imbecile, that he no longer needs money."

"Will he...ever?" she asked haltingly.

Charles glared at her. "Ever? The man is sixty years old. There is precious little title left before he dies. And that blasted Yankee has given him enough money to see him through at least a few years."

Elizabeth felt her heart begin to beat wildly. She had lived through this obsession of her husband's for so many years. Could it truly be over so easily? "Charles, we have so much—"

"I don't have what I want."

"You are rich and respected and..."

"I am respected by tailors and printers and farmers. My brother is asked to devise the laws that govern the land when I hold more property than he. Yet he refuses to grant me the slightest respectability through title. Our mother was noble, but I have been separated from her property and title because my father was a tradesman. I won't stand for it."

Elizabeth felt tears in her eyes. "You could have found a noble dame to wed."

"Ha. And be the consort of some old duchess? Chappington and all the prestige of that title is as much mine as his. And I have worked for twenty-five years to show him so."

"But Charles, if it is hopeless..."

"I will find a way," he shouted. "By damn, I will roust him yet."

"Charles," she entreated. "Please give this up. Think of your family."

"My family will be better off when I finally succeed. Robert will be a baron and my daughters will marry nobility."

"It doesn't matter," she insisted. "We don't care about titles and nobility."

"Of course you don't. You are common yourself, offspring of a simple merchant."

"My father was the most successful man in his—"

"Why the hell do you think I married you? For passion? I needed your father's money to get the title I deserve. I almost had it, too. My brother was ready to name me his heir in exchange for money...until that Yankee—"

"You delude yourself, Charles," she interrupted stiffly. "He has never been ready and he never will be."

"He will. He will have to."

"He won't. Not ever. Why don't you see that you risk everything that matters in a futile attempt to overthrow your brother?"

"What matters more?" He laughed suddenly. "If that is how I choose to spend my money, if my family profits in the end, why would you care?"

"You fail as a husband and a father in this pursuit," she said courageously.

"I fail? You have two fine houses, three children, plenty of dresses and jewels and servants."

"The London house was my father's. The country manor that I inherited was sold for this, so you could be near Chappington. You barely know your own children, and you have not been a husband to me for ten years. I won't allow you to go any further with this horrid scheme of yours."

"You will be quiet and stay out of my business. All I have ever done is to buy property and lend money through agents."

"Oh, Charles, I think you have done much worse than that."

"It's none of your damn business."

"If you do not cease, I will go to Lord Ridgley myself and—"

Her threat, the first she had ever leveled in twenty years, was cut short as he took two quick strides toward her and slapped her so hard across the face that she fell backward against the bookcase. Her trembling hand rose to touch her bloodied lip. She looked up into his enraged eyes, seeing that his fists were clenched at his sides as he struggled to control himself.

"Don't you ever suggest such a thing again. If you take the slightest action against me, I will see you and your precious children stripped to naked flesh and cast out into the gutter. And don't for a moment delude yourself that my brother will grant you some charity. He won't give anything to any of my family."

She shook her head in pained realization that he spoke the truth. "Charles, how can you be so cruel to those who love you?"

She saw his eyes glitter as if they welled with tears. His voice was a strained whisper. "Don't you know how important this is to me, Elizabeth?"

He held out a hand to help her to her feet. She hesitated a moment, frightened that he might strike her again. Finally, putting her hand in his, she rose to her feet.

"You are my wife, whether content or not," he said sternly. "Do not threaten to betray me again."

She moved toward his study door with eyes downcast. Once there, she turned back to him. "I only wonder what will become of us when you are finished with this great effort."

"I have kept you for many years past my need for your money, Elizabeth. As long as you act properly, you have no reason to fear for your future. Just take special care not to question me again. Remember that I am your only route to any decent kind of life."

She looked at him with pity. "Unfortunately, Charles, I know that to be true."

She left him alone in his study, and she went about her daily duties as if nothing had happened.

Something about the girl had changed. Tyson found her to be even more captivating than she had been four months earlier. He had been watching Vieve for a week since his return to Chappington Hall.

During their very first encounter she had seemed to have poor control over her youthful sensuality. He had reckoned that those early stirrings were both exciting and confusing for her; he was far past that time in life, but his memory of that period was clear. Typical of a flighty, blushing virgin, she had appeared to be romanced by the notion of marriage and seduced by the concept of true love.

However, over the summer of her seventeenth year she had become calmer of spirit. She was apparently done with adolescent games. She no longer appeared at the dinner table in teasing frocks, although her more conservative choice of gowns did little to hide her elemental beauty. Whether she realized it or not, her lace-covered décolletage, which alluded to rather than exposed her bosom, was much more alluring. In addition, her disposition was quieter. She was poised, but not solemn; reserved, but not dull. She behaved, he realized, like a woman.

Tyson kept a careful eye turned to Vieve, judging these changes in her behavior. He decided that her new temperament must be due to her having taken the persistent Andrew Shelby as her lover. But her young beau was conspicuously missing, which left Tyson confused.

Maintaining such an observant vigil had a curious effect on him. Although he believed himself capable of gentlemanly behavior, a recurring ache in his loins warned him that his resolve could fail if she appeared willing. He slowly grew accustomed to the idea that if they did finally come together, it would not be in some childish display of temporarily unbridled emotion. He wanted more from her. It came as a pleasurable jolt to realize he wanted her as he'd never wanted a woman before.

"Young Andrew does not seem to be calling quite so much," Tyson observed while they dined one evening.

"No," she replied, barely looking up from her plate. "He does not."

"The boy seems discouraged by something or other," Boris grumbled. He peered suspiciously at his daughter, but she did not return his gaze. "I can't imagine what happened. I gave him credit for a great deal more stamina."

The corners of Vieve's mouth turned up slightly, but she declined comment and did not look at either Tyson or her father.

One afternoon Tyson found her in the sitting room with a book in her lap, although she appeared to be staring out the window, lost in a pensive daydream. Had she begun to regret some hasty decision to send her young man on his way?

"The house is very quiet today," he said.

She looked toward him and smiled. "It is, isn't it?"

"It is not at all what I expected. I had prepared myself to be stumbling over your ardent suitor. And if he has been chastised and sent from your stoop, where are all the young men who should be taking advantage of his absence?"

"There have been a few. They have not interested me."

"You've had a disagreement with your young man, haven't you?" he asked pointedly. "You were most determined to marry when I last visited."

"Yes...I was."

"You must be lonely," he stated frankly.

"I assure you, I am not. Father seems to require more of me these days, and Paul and Evelyn are close enough that we visit often. I am quite content."

"Yes," he said. "I have noticed that as well."

He troubled with his appearance every day, but cautiously kept himself from being disarmed by her charm. He had always prided himself on his ability to intrigue reluctant women with his straightforward manner and smooth control. This time he feared he had met his match. He quivered in his boots at the thought of her most innocent and unintentional touch. When she passed him in the foyer, the sweet fragrance of her soaps teased his nostrils and the sight of her gently swinging skirts gave his manhood cause to rise. He felt like a lad embarking on his first intimate experience, a condition that began to amuse as much as frustrate him.

Tyson was stunned when he realized the permanence of his emotions toward Vieve. He cursed the fact that he had not seduced her, or bent to her seduction, on his visit the previous spring. He might have become her lover before she had submitted to Andrew. But that was not the most important issue, since chaste women were rare in Tyson's experience. He was feeling a rare possessive spirit where Vieve was concerned and became determined that no one must ever come after him. He believed, of course, that he would make her a better lover.

On the seventh morning of his visit he rose with a firm decision that he would wait no longer to begin his slow seduction of Vieve. He was as yet uncertain about the ends to which he was bound and understood the ramifications of acting improperly. He was an American in a noble British household and bolstered himself for the agony of arousal without satisfaction. He believed he read desire in her glistening blue eyes, but he expected her to show hesitancy. It was the way of young dames.

He bathed with the fresh scent of sandalwood, cautiously removed the last stubble from his chin, and donned his riding clothes. His single apprehension came from the notion that she would expect to be courted as a young virgin would, and his ability to comply. It was not as if all the women he had known were promiscuous, but he had always been put off by the skittish nature of the very young. Their bodies and manners invariably invited while their declarations forbade. He was thirty-five years old. It had been a long time since he had embarked on this kind of adventure.

Wearing his leather boots and velvet riding jacket, and with his crop in hand, he went to the stables to be assured that his stallion would be saddled before he asked Vieve to join him for a ride. He was en route when he saw two riders disappearing over the hill. There was no mistaking Tristan's light color and the golden tresses that bounced down Vieve's back. And even though he saw them for only a moment, he knew the man with her was Andrew Shelby.

Without any clear intention, he saddled his own horse and rode out after them. He had no plan, but felt anger throbbing in his temples. He had not even spoken his intent, but still he felt betrayed. He did not take the time he should have to think about the dangerous implications of assuming such possession.

Vieve gave a critical eye to her reflection in the mirror, judging the conservative style of her gown. She smiled in appreciation, finding that it suited her mood very well.

She went to her father's study and tapped on the door. She was relieved to find he was still alone. On every previous day he had been involved in deep discussions with Tyson and it had been impossible to beg a moment of his time for a private conversation.

"What is it, daughter?"

"If you have a moment?" she requested almost shyly.

"Certainly, child. Come in, come in."

She perched on the edge of a chair in front of his huge oak desk, her hands folded in her lap. "I don't mean to pry, Papa, but I am wondering what this business with the captain means to our family wealth. Are your worries over?"

"Over? I think not. But I admit, his invested money is a tremendous help."

"But Father, I..." She seemed to lose the words she had so ably rehearsed.

"Speak up, lass. I don't think I follow you."

"I have worried about money. Paul said there were problems and you said more than once that Andrew did not seem well suited to care for me."

"Ah," Lord Ridgley said, leaning back in his chair and looking at her shrewdly. "You wish to know how this improved state affects you?"

"In a manner, Papa. It is just that there has been no one...I mean I have kept company with many... my lord, I have not liked any of the men of able means who have called."

He did not even attempt to conceal his grin. "You would like to be relieved, daughter? You do not wish this burden of finding a well-endowed husband to save me from ruin?"

"Oh, Papa, I didn't mean..."

"It's all right," he coughed. "Your worries over that issue were of your own making; I did not ask you to find a wealthy husband on my account. You have my leave to relax your pursuit, if it pleases you. But heed my advice, daughter. Do not be so foolish as to fall in love with the first handsome swain who looks your way. Even with the captain's investment, our wealth has a bottom, and a poorly sought groom will find the end of your fortune quickly."

Her face instantly brightened. "No, Papa," she said with a beaming smile. "I assure you, I wouldn't do that."

She left her father's study with a lighter heart. She did not wish to be distracted by suitors. She had always been both bold and romantic; she wanted to fall in love and with a bit of good fortune, have him be a worthy man. She began to believe Tyson Gervais was the man.

She tried to dispel illusion about Tyson, but it was difficult, for she desired him. He had displayed himself well: handsome, mature, and masculine. He was an erotic figure of a man, but she remembered the night she had invited him to kiss her and knew better, this time, than to put herself boldly in his path. She tried to linger in the background of his visit, for she doubted him capable of an innocent courtship. She could only hope that if she carefully crafted her manners around him and did not attempt to undermine him with teasing and adolescent behavior, he would find her a worthy woman. But, she prayed, let him find her soon.

Luncheon was just past when Andrew called. Vieve was surprised that he came to Chappington and a little reluctant to see him at all. Realizing she could not avoid him forever and judging his humble and contrite expression, she invited him inside.

Andrew did not live in the Chappington town, and his own family lands were far northeast of London. He kept apartments in London, but when he came to the country he imposed himself on those neighbors who would feel obliged to house anyone of noble stature. To Vieve's recollection, he had never rented rooms of his own, and on this trip he had presumed upon the hospitality of Paul and Evelyn in the Dumere manse. This was partially the reason that Vieve felt obligated to allow him within. She had told Paul she would try to understand his hurt as well as her own.

She called him into the parlor, deciding that if Andrew was of the same bent, to attack her the moment they were alone, she would prefer to find out in a safe environment where her protests could be heard.

"Paul had a serious talk with me and I understand why you are reluctant to be in my company," he said quietly, coming straight to the point. "I bring apologies."

"Accepted," she said simply.

"I am sorry, Vieve." A look of complete embarrassment marked his handsome cheeks with bright, pink blotches.

"Before you die of shame, I admit that I did not discourage you soon enough."

"Thank goodness you showed some good sense," he muttered.

"Andrew? Do you mean that?"

"Vieve...I... truly do mean it. Thinking back on the whole past year, I hardly recognize my own behavior. Everything I said and did goes completely against my nature. I respect your father and Paul." He hung his head in shame. "Vieve, you saved me; I would not have been able to look any member of your family in the eye, had you obliged my indecent request."

She cocked her head slightly, peering at him. She wondered if she dared hope he was sincere. "You seem to see the error of your ways."

"But... I wonder..." He seemed to falter, not able either to look at her or to formulate the right words. She was suddenly torn with pity for him, for clearly she had broken his heart.

"You wonder what, Andrew?"

"I'm afraid of your answer, Vieve, but I must know: is there any hope that we will ever be as..."

"As we once were?" she finished for him as his query failed him.

"Yes."

She frowned slightly, knowing how cruel it would be to mislead him. "Andrew," she said with a strong voice, "I don't think that I can accurately explain all the changes in my feelings, nor can I honestly tell you that you are the only cause. But I cannot lie; I do not feel as I once did. It will not be the same for us. I am sorry if I hurt you. Perhaps you will find the truth less painful than some charitable lie and my continued avoidance."

He gave a long, heavy sigh that almost sounded like relief. "Even so, I can't abide the thought that you will forever suspect me of being nothing more than a crude and selfish rogue." He shrugged. "I really did care for you, though I showed it poorly. I want to regain your trust enough so that we can be friends."

He smiled, though she could see sadness in his eyes. For the first time in months she had lightened her opinion of him. "Your brother," he went on quietly. "He is my friend. I'd like it best if I have not destroyed that through my bad manners with you."

Vieve smiled very tolerantly. "Paul is not angry with you, Andrew. In fact, he urged me to try to understand that you were hurt, too."

"I must remember to thank him, though I don't think I deserve much understanding. I behaved as only a vulgar beast would."

She frowned at the recollection, but it was a beginning that he had the presence of mind to admit his mistake. Her anger with him had provided her with a dilemma: she was the only one he had wronged, and he was a family friend. She wished for him to occupy a tender place in her memory. After all, he was her first love.

"Your friendship is accepted. So long as you don't attempt to compromise me, I have no cause to dislike you or be angry with you."

He smiled brightly. "You know, Vieve, I've missed you. You complained all I ever wished was to have you in my arms. But while you were avoiding me, and I have been much alone to consider my actions, I've been quite lonely. It has not been for want of kissing that I've hungered most. I've missed your company."

"Really?" she asked. She remembered when he began to court her, over a year ago. She recalled that walking with him, riding with him, and sitting in the parlor over tea cakes and sherry had been pleasant and easy.

He seemed to relax a great deal, unburdened as he was, and leaned back in his chair to begin a series of entertaining stories about pranks and pastimes of his youth. Within an hour Vieve was laughing and having a good time. She knew it was impossible for them to ever resume their romance, for reasons that went far beyond his conduct—reasons that had only recently become clear to her. However, she discovered that when Andrew was well behaved she was not bored in his company. It took very little time for her to form the hope that a family friendship could be rekindled.

As the afternoon passed she doubted her own memory and started to wonder if she had made the crisis larger in her mind. It was nearly three o'clock and the day at its warmest when he stood and said that he had to leave. When she was at the front door with him, he issued an invitation that was so light and innocent, she did not think of it as any conspiracy against her. "God, it's a beautiful day. When have you known it to ever be so pleasant in September? Vieve, change clothes and let's go for a quick ride. I don't have much time if I'm to return to Paul's home before dark."

"All right," she said, all worry gone. Andrew could not comport himself poorly and then go innocently to her own brother's house to dine. "But I can't go far."

"I'll see that Tristan is saddled for you while you tell your father that we're out for a very short ride. Tell him it will not be more than an hour."

She was not unduly concerned when there happened to be no groom to attend them, and she had only a slight hesitation when Andrew suggested they go off the road near the old keep. "Come on, goose. I gave you my word, didn't I? I want to show you where Paul and I camped when we'd both decided our parents were too severe and we'd have to run away and become soldiers of fortune."

"When was that?" she asked with a laugh.

"Let's see, I think we were both twelve...maybe younger. It took Lord Ridgley about an hour to find us, but we'd built quite a home for ourselves in that short time."

The old keep, built by some Norman warlord centuries before, had not been lived in for over two hundred years. Chappington Hall was constructed by a Ridgley ancestor during the reign of Queen Elizabeth, and much of the ironwork and stone from the original keep was used on the new structure. The keep could be reached in a short ride, and though bereft of doors, windows, and safe stairs, it was used for storage and occasionally as a winter shelter for the village stock. And it was far out of sight of the Chappington road.

"It was in here," he said as they dismounted and tethered their horses. "I imagine this was once the common room. We built a fire, had pallets laid out and had rummaged around long enough to even find old, abandoned cookware to use on our fire. Did you play in here as a child?" he asked in a bright and carefree tone.

"We were told it was unsafe for all children and risked a beating if we used it as a playhouse."

"And so it is unsafe for children," he said. "But we are not children."

"Andrew," she warned, backing away.

"Will you not kiss me? Not once?"

"No. I will not. Now stop; you frighten me."

"There is no cause for you to be frightened, Vieve. I mean you no harm; I love you."

"We agreed...we are to be friends..."

"I cannot endure friendship with you when I am cursed with this painful hunger. I want you!" He grabbed her suddenly, crushing her lips with his, his hand covering her breast in a quick and rough caress. She pushed against him frantically, but he held on fiercely. She resisted his kiss, turning her lips away from his. He released her suddenly and she stumbled away from him.

The true nature of his character came back to her instantly, but the shock of his intentional, methodical deception would be a long time in settling. "You...you lied to me," she accused, her cheeks hot with rage. "You brought me here on purpose. You pretended to be sorry, to want my friendship. I never should have let myself be fooled by you."

There was a cruel gleam in his eyes. "It is time you realized that you are my betrothed—soon to be my wife."

"I am not," she screamed. "You dare too much."

He seized her arm and held her so tightly against his chest that she could only gasp for breath. Her hat fell away and quick movements were impossible because of the heavy, restraining folds of her velvet skirt.

"I am through playing games with you, Vieve. You accepted me once and you will again. You may struggle if you like, but the decision has been made."

"Release me at once, Andrew."

He smiled at her rage, and she began to tremble from genuine fear. His hand locked into the fabric of her riding habit, and with a quick motion, he rent the cloth to expose her breast. She gasped in stunned disbelief.

"Andrew," she said beseechingly. "Do I mean so little to you that you would do something to hurt me?"

"Hurt you?" he said in a fury. "Have you had any regard for the way you've hurt me? No, my vixen, you have given little thought to your promises, your sworn intention. You prance around me and speak of friendship when a mere four months ago you were destined to this very place to sacrifice your maidenhood for love."

This very place? The words rang in her mind as she shook her head in confusion. She had been a fool. He lured her here not once, but twice, to claim her body, while he had sworn other motives both times.

"Do you really believe that my father will bless your rape?" she asked him.

"His blessing no longer matters, wench. You may say what you please about me; Lord Ridgley must see you properly wed once you are defiled. We will finally have this my way. You have held yourself as some grand prize for long enough."

"No!" she screamed, but the sound was muffled by his mouth as he covered hers. She fought in earnest then, kicking, scratching, and writhing with all of her strength, managing to throw them both off balance. Her struggle only aided him, though, as he landed atop her on the ground. Still, she would have some proud bruises to display when her father heard of her low virtue, for she refused to give in to his demented plan.

Her knee found a tender target and he grunted in pain, but wrath only made his attack more violent. He managed to pin her hands over her head and raise her dress with his other hand. She felt his hand on her thigh, and she screamed at the top of her lungs.

He did not even attempt to quiet her. Instead she was aware that he fumbled to unfasten his trousers.

Suddenly, he was lifted from her so abruptly that her scream was cut short. Tyson Gervais held him by his collar and the seat of his pants and flung him so far across the room that he might have been a bale of hay rather than a good-sized man.

Andrew hit the floor with a thump, coming to rest a good ten paces from where Vieve lay. He groaned in pain, shook his head as if to clear the image, and then with a snarl of outrage was on his feet, charging toward Tyson.

Tyson did not even brace himself for the attack. He merely extended a fist into Andrew's jaw and sent him sprawling once more into the dust. Vieve could see the network of muscles under Tyson's jacket as he took two large steps, gathered Andrew up by the front of his shirt, and delivered another powerful blow to his jaw. A cloud of dust rose around Andrew as he sprawled in the dirt a third time. This time when he looked up, blood trickled from his nose and lip.

Vieve watched the tension in Tyson's back as he clenched his fists in an effort to control an urge to damage Andrew further. "Get out of here," he growled. "You disgust the dirt with your presence."

Andrew needed no further prompting. He rose to stand on shaky legs, gingerly touching his bruised and bloody face, and fled. Tyson did not turn toward Vieve until the sound of the departing charge of Andrew's horse was no longer heard. It seemed an eternity that she stared at his rigid back.

Then she saw that his face was carved out of stone, and the smile of thanks on her lips froze. His eyes traced the length of her body, reminding her of her exposed state. Self-consciously, she pushed down her skirt and sat upright, attempting to tuck in the torn flap of her habit that exposed her bosom. Still glaring at her, he reached out a hand to help her to her feet.

"Thank you," she said weakly. Her hat lay several feet away, and she took the opportunity to retrieve it. "I... I... don't know why...I'd never have left the house with him had I known...." She glanced at Tyson uncertainly, forgetting the hat now that she had achieved a safer distance. She could still see the anger in his expression. "I am grateful, but I am sorry that you were called upon to rescue me."

"Are you? Or do you like the game, damsel?'

"You can't possibly think that I...? Oh, please," she said with a quivering chin. "If I were nothing but a whore, would I allow my clothing to be destroyed?"

"I think you have dallied with the boy too much. He seems to think he has acquired some special rights with you. What did you expect?"

"I expected too much," she admitted. "He swore he was sorry for his effrontery and intended to mend his ways. That is why I agreed to go out for a ride with him."

Tyson laughed, but it was clear he was not in the least amused. "Madam, are you truly so naive, or is this another game you play?'

She closed her eyes and took a deep breath. Her fists tensed at her sides. The anger within her was reborn. "I am a complete fool, for I believed him. I admit it. It should be clear to even you that he was about to take me much against my will."

"Plain enough," Tyson shot back. "But did you have no better sense than to place yourself alone with him? Do you deny that you have always known his intentions?"

"He tricked me," she shouted. Tears smarted in her eyes and ran down her cheeks. "He begged me to forgive his earlier behavior and be a friend for my brother's sake." She shook her head in disbelief, for Andrew's duplicity still astounded her. "Tyson, please understand," she entreated. "Andrew has lingered about our parlors and halls for as long as I can remember. He was first a friend of the family; my father was acquainted with his parents. And when he became my suitor he was not always so bold."

Tyson's expression eased slightly. The glitter of fury in his eyes ebbed as he stepped toward her. His voice was softer, though his words still bit deeply. "But you toyed with the boy," he said. "You have purposely tempted him."

"Oh, damn," she cursed. "A kiss or two? An embrace between two people who expect to be wed? Am I a fallen woman for that?"

His hand cupped her chin. "Oh, mademoiselle, I am sure there was more than that."

She straightened her posture proudly. "I will admit even to you, Captain, that I did not discourage him soon enough. I did not see the ends to which he was bound. And I will not be blamed for his conduct."

"One moment you play the temptress as if you invented the part, and the next you are nothing more than an innocent child."

"I am neither, Captain," Vieve said through her tears. "Not temptress, or innocent, or schemer, or child. I am only a victim. I had no part in what he dared."

"He was so very foolish," Tyson said gently. "Had he led you rather than pushed you, he might have met with more warmth."

She looked up into Tyson's eyes and was touched by what seemed to be understanding in his softened expression. "I will never forgive him." In spite of her wish to be strong, she began to weep, and Tyson's arms went around her to give comfort.

There was a feeling of security in the circle of his arms. He gently stroked her hair and held her for a long, tender spell. But as her tears gave way, she was conscious of another, more stirring emotion. She felt the hard press of his solid chest against her breasts. The soothing caress of his hand along her back began to tease her longing. She was not in the least surprised when he lifted her chin and touched her lips with his.

She was caught in a quandary that made her gasp both from fright and desire as he tasted her mouth for some response. She did not question that she wanted desperately for the moment to go on forever, but she knew this was but a sample of the deeper passion he possessed. He had warned her once; he was not a man to begin such an interlude and be halted. She tried to voice her protest, but even she was aware that the quality of her voice held more of a rapturous sigh than determination.

"Please . . . don't..."

"I have wanted you," he whispered. "And you have known."

"Will you remove Andrew only to take his place?" she asked in a faint, trembling voice.

"You know better than that," he murmured. His hand traveled up the line of her ribs toward her breast. "I intend no force, as you are well aware. You have played your vixen games with a boy, but now you are in the arms of a man."

His lips covered hers in a searing kiss. Her will was instantly weakened, and she shook with longing. His weapon was gentleness, and he slowly awakened in her a fierce desire. He titillated her yearning with sure finesse and deliberately paced his caresses until she was disarmed.

"If you are to have a lover, *cherie*, let him at least be a man of suitable experience. You will find me more reliable than Andrew."

He lifted her into his arms without releasing her mouth and lowered her gently to the floor.

"Have mercy, Tyson," she said softly. "I cannot fight you."

"Tell me you do not want me," he demanded hoarsely.

"I cannot," she sighed. "But you know it is wrong."

His lips touched her cheeks, her eyes, her ears and traveled in a fiery path down her neck to her shoulder. "It was wrong with him, my sweet, but I will not disappoint you."

His lips occupied hers so deliciously that she was unaware of the way his hand had traveled over her hip to pull up her heavy velvet skirt. The warmth of his fingers on her thigh blinded all other thoughts, and she embraced him in a frenzy of desire. He touched where no one else had ever touched her, and she softly moaned with pleasure as a soft glow of warmth spread through her. It did not matter anymore that he came to her without benefit of a priest or a blessing from her father. She had already accepted the fact that she belonged to only him. She was in love with him. In a blur of bewilderment, she began to think it was better done.

She was so lost in his careful manipulations that she was not aware of how he managed to free himself from his trousers. When she realized the fact she distractedly thought about the lack of fumbling with this experienced man. He was so skilled that when she felt him urging his way within her, her brief rally to save her virginity only aided him, and he plunged himself into her.

Through eyes widened by the abrupt pain she could see his expression of surprise. She had seen a great many emotions etched into the fine, handsome lines of his face, but never surprise. When he encountered the natural resistance of her body—her purity—he was totally amazed.

She turned away from his perusal. Had he truly believed that she was already soiled? A woman he could lay with because he believed she'd lain with others?

He was motionless for a long moment, but soon he moved within her again, whispering in her ear, "Easy, my Vieve, my love...

A low moan escaped her and she kept her face averted from his, not looking at him again until he turned her gaze toward him with a hand on her chin. He held himself still and stared into her eyes. She read confusion, and if she was not mistaken, betrayal. Then his eyes darkened again to the passion she had earlier seen. He touched her mouth, traced her lips with his tongue, nibbled gently at her lips.

"Put your arms around me," he instructed in a whisper. "Come, my sweet vixen, hold me...love me..."

She wrapped her arms around him and gave her lips to his in a deep kiss. The burning ache began to subside as he began a slow, temperate movement. His hands and the gentle thrusting of his hips caused a warmth that was deep and glowing to spread through her, until she forgot herself again and moved with him, meeting him in each movement, receiving, giving, taking. There was an ecstasy alluded to, and she found herself not knowing it, but reaching and yearning, just the same.

He was suddenly possessed of a wild, shuddering spasm, pressing deeply within her and holding her desperately for a long moment. When he was so motionless, she was left to listen to his rapid breathing, wondering vaguely what joy she had missed and he had felt. Finally, he gave her cheek a light kiss and carefully withdrew.

She didn't watch as he pulled back to sit on his heels. She could hear him arrange his clothing and felt him gently pull her skirt down. She felt a strange emptiness, already missing that helpless longing she had felt moments ago. It felt cool and lonely to be out of his arms. She bit the knuckle on her index finger, hoping she would not cry the predictable and forlorn tears of a defiled maiden. That struggle occupied her for a generous length of time.

"You didn't tell me in time," he finally said, his voice subdued by unmistakable displeasure. It had never occurred to her that should she engage in such intimacy, she might find the man disappointed by her purity. "I hope you're not hurt; it is rarely pleasant for a maid the first time."

She pulled herself to a sitting position, ready to tell him that there was great joy in being so close to him, taking him as a part of her body. But the angry look on his face halted her endearments. Was it not a beautiful moment for him, too?

"I'm all right, Tyson," she said very softly.

He stood, sighed deeply, and held out a hand to her. She found it difficult to look at him now, but it was not shyness that deterred her. Rather, she feared the expression she might read on his face.

"One question," he said, his tone quiet but demanding. "And have a care, petite, do not lie. Deception has a way of coming to the surface sooner or later. Did your father ask you to do this?"

"My father?" she repeated, aghast. "My God, my father may well wash his hands of me when..."

"Did you enter into some plot with your family to see me trapped?"

She shook her head in disbelief. "Could you think it?" she whispered in a new agony. "Would my own family use my virtue as a pawn?"

"I did just commit myself to a huge sum of money in partnership with your father and brother. Had you offered yourself before the contracts were drawn, there would still have been time for me to flee."

She looked away from him. Her shoulders shook slightly with misery. "Oh, flee, Captain, if that is your wont. I assure you, I will not try to hold you."

She felt his knuckle gently brush a tear from her cheek. With his hands on her shoulders he turned her to face him. "It was your own notion then? That I would be the one to claim your virtue? Was it for profit?"

"Notion?" she queried, numbed by this inquisition. "Profit? My lord." She shook her head in wonder.

"Your family needs money," he said. "I would not fare well in England, charged with a crime against a noblewoman. An American would have no chance in your British courts. My influence and wealth will matter very little in this country."

"And you think that I will fare well, sir, debauched by a colonial seaman?"

"Though you have been coy, you will gain more than I. And you knew I wanted you."

"You wanted me," she cried. "And that is my fault. Good Lord above us, my worst offense is that I am intolerably stupid."

"You barely resisted—"

"You would not cease."

"Many women have tried to trap my wealth," he told her. "It is not the first time such a ploy has been used to capture a man."

Her hand rose to her mouth as she felt hysteria threaten. Her pain was never more intense. "And none of them virgins?" she cruelly mocked. "And you called me an unsuccessful harlot" She began to walk away from him, but he quickly grabbed her wrist and drew her back. "Just let me go," she said. "The mark of my passing will not show on you. I am the one changed."

"If not for gain, then why?" he demanded.

She was speechless for a moment, staring at him. Was she to humble herself now and admit that she could not resist him because she adored him? She glared at him. "You horrible wretch. Leave me be and cease in your demands."

"You must live with this quietly, my love," he warned. "You may not speak of your stolen virtue unless it is your wish to see me gelded and nailed to the wall of this old keep."

"At the moment, Captain, that is a very promising idea."

"You will be still about what has passed between us."

Although she wished to crumble into sobbing grief, she lifted her chin and smiled scornfully. "You once said a king's ransom could be mine for what I would yield to love. Have you changed your mind about that?"

"Vieve," he warned, the anger seeping back into his eyes. "It is done. The secret is not mine, but ours. Do not defy me."

"Your secret is safe with me, *mon cher*," she said with no small amount of sarcasm.

"You test my temper, wench..."

"Good God," she whispered. "As if my humiliation is not enough, do you think I would boast about the fact?"

"If you speak you know what will happen. I don't think it will be pleasant for you to live with my blood on your conscience."

She gave her head an angry toss. "How will it be for you, Captain, to live with my blood on yours?"

"I shall manage as best I can. I would have your word on your silence."

"Do not worry," she said wearily.

She tried to turn away from him again, but again he drew her back. He held her chin, forcing her to look into his eyes. "I did not intend to hurt you. I meant to give you pleasure. Come, I will take you home."

She shook her head in dismay. He obviously wished for a convenient lover, a woman whose purity was not an issue, or he would be on his knees begging for her forgiveness. How very nice it must have been for him to think of the pleasant affair he could engage in while visiting Chappington.

"Please," she implored, placing a firm hand against his chest. "Let me ride home alone. It will be better if we're not seen together now."

He hesitated, but finally nodded in agreement. "But I will be close behind, to be sure your journey is a safe one."

She wished privacy along the Chappington road so that he would not witness the tears she believed would consume her. She knew that once she was in her bedroom again, with Harriet's close perusal, any weeping that she might indulge in would not be ignored. There were few things one could hide from a close personal maid. Harriet would have many questions; Vieve thought she knew each one already.

Unfortunately, she could not think of one answer.

Six

As Vieve dismounted by the stable, the sun was sitting low in the sky. She entrusted Tristan's care to the groom, and in turning toward the hall, she noticed that her father had just emerged from the back of the manse. He stood there in wait for her, and she took a deep, bolstering breath, knowing better than to flee from his sight. The closer she came to him, the more suspicious was the narrowing of his eyes. By the time she paused before him he was frowning and his face had reddened.

She could read his mind. Although she had managed to tuck the torn corner of her jacket into the other side, the ripped seam was still obvious. Her hair was tangled with dirt and straw, her hat missing, and her cream-colored habit patterned with gray streaks from the ground. She might have passed off her disheveled appearance with some invented excuse if it were not for the way her tears had cut neat paths down her dusty cheeks.

Before Lord Ridgley said a word, he looked past her and stared. She followed his gaze and found that true to his word, Tyson had followed behind her. He was just about to dismount so that his stallion could be taken into the stable. She touched her father's arm to draw his eyes back to her face. "Papa, it was Andrew who would have dishonored me against my will, and it was Captain Gervais who intervened."

Her father's scowl deepened. "And he did not ride back with you?" he growled in question.

"Please, Papa," she implored. "Leave it alone."

"Go in, child," he told her.

"Papa, please promise me that you will not—"

He looked down at her, and she could read the pain in his eyes. She gave his arm a gentle squeeze. "I am not hurt, Papa. Please, let me..."

"I have left this to you long enough. I am not a fool."

"But, my lord—"

"You may stay or go. The choice is yours."

His focus settled on Tyson Gervais as he approached. Vieve could not bring herself to endure their meeting. She was afraid she would crumble into a heap of cowardly tears if she allowed herself to stand between them. These were the two men who could best pull unwanted emotion to the surface. She knew that if she remained she would betray everything, if only with her eyes.

She fled into the house, eager for the solace of Harriet's interference.

Boris kept his arms still at his sides as Tyson came closer to him. He tried to read the captain's face, but found that the younger man's features were as unyielding as his own. None of Boris's questions were answered by looking at Tyson. But Vieve's appearance burned in his mind, and he had learned more than he wished to know from one look at her. The baron's suspicion peaked. His spirited daughter, he reasoned, would have met him in a high-blown rage had she been attacked. But crying when she had been rescued? Tears were unusual for her; she was not given to sniveling and weeping over minor misfortunes or near scrapes.

Tyson stopped before the baron, his face an implacable visage that would tell nothing. He waited, his silver eyes glowing with either apprehension or anger.

"I wonder if you can even imagine my dilemma," Boris began. "My daughter rode out with one man, returned with another, and her condition is deplorable. She has been crying, although she says she is not hurt."

"I concede your predicament is a large one," Tyson agreed.

"The prospect of questioning my daughter further does not hold much appeal. I know more than I like by one look at her. You are a guest in my house, Captain. We are partners in business. Although you have comported yourself well, I am not too old to notice how you have regarded my daughter."

Tyson slowly nodded. "I know whose hospitality indulges me. I am fully aware of my disadvantage, regardless of what the lady would say upon questioning." He paused and clenched his fists at his sides. "I am willing to have a discussion of terms."

"For marriage?" Boris asked.

Tyson slowly nodded. "It is the lesser of many evils."

"Which evil will you name? My daughter's reputation? Your ability to withstand the angry reprisal of an English noble? The possible loss of your very large investment in a land that does not exactly welcome you?"

"Those carry great weight, my lord," Tyson said smoothly. "But considering your daughter's distress, perhaps it would be best to confine ourselves to a discussion of terms and let her accept an honorable proposal. It puts me in a better light, and prevents her further humiliation."

"That is nearly an admission," Boris stated.

"There will be none of that," Tyson angrily replied. "I know only too well what you can do to me, regardless of my guilt or innocence." He smiled cynically. "You could secure a fortune by putting me away, but I warn you, my family will not sit quietly for it."

"Is it to be a discussion of terms or a battle, Captain? Do not complicate your case by fighting with me. I, too, am aware of your disadvantage."

"Then unless you have an eye on a fast fortune, let us negotiate."

Boris struggled with the urge to go to Vieve, demand the details, and behave as an enraged father should. But with effort, he suppressed the temptation. "I will listen to your offer tonight. Consider your terms carefully, for my daughter's approval is among my requirements."

Tyson nodded and walked toward the rear door. His hand was on the latch when Boris halted him. "She told me that Shelby assaulted her." Slowly Tyson turned back toward the baron. "What did you do to him?"

The flare of new violence throbbed in his temples, though Tyson's features remained composed. "Rest easy, my lord. I somehow stopped myself before I killed him."

Without another word, Tyson entered the house and was out of sight. Lord Ridgley stood and considered his daughter's plea, Tyson's angry benevolence, and the vast amount of information he must just assume, without confirmation from either of them.

Curiosity gnawed at him, but if Tyson were to come forth with a proposal and Vieve were to accept it, he knew that it would be better for them to begin their life together without the added burden of having their secrets divulged. He had seen the way they looked at each other; he shrewdly deduced that they had been drawn together, and under these conditions, theirs would begin as a stormy alliance.

Captain Gervais considered himself a clever and worldly man. But had Lord Ridgley not already considered this marriage, the Captain would never have regained entrance to the house.

Evelyn sat in the drawing room in the Dumere manse, crafting small articles of clothing for a baby. Although she was not quite sure, she had already alerted Paul to the possibility that she had conceived. She set aside her sewing as he came into the room. This was the part of the day she treasured most. As the sun lowered and savory smells from the cookery filled the house, Paul left his chores to join her before dinner.

He dropped a light, husbandly kiss on her brow. "My work goes well, darling," he said, making his way to the cabinet that held his decanter of brandy. "I see little reason for you to fret any further about our future."

"I don't fret," she claimed, but her embarrassed laugh gave her away. She had worried ceaselessly about the failing Dumere estate and the problems at Chappington. She was afraid the price of their love was too high.

"Fie on you, madam. I am the one to know best how little you slept during the first days of our marriage."

A light flush marked her cheeks, but her eyes were aglow. "Yes, I know you were aware. You, my love, were the one who most often denied me my sleep."

"I have checked and rechecked my figures, and my ciphering shows me that the harvest was a good one. One or two more generous plantings, then what is left of this stricken farm will be standing tall again."

"Wonderful. And Chappington?"

"By the profits of trade, the family demesne will survive. Captain Gervais was quick to put in his money for the rebuilding, which created an embarrassing situation. Father and I had no money to contribute our half. But Tyson relieved that discomfort quickly by paying the commission on four ships in advance to allow the building to begin."

"How does he dare so much? He enters into a partnership in which the investment is almost entirely his own, except for the land under the ruined warehouses?"

Paul shrugged. "There are few options for an American with money to advance in British trading; he could not come by property easily, and he was quick to see how the other merchants with warehouse space would cheat him. And putting in the money gives him a great advantage, for until the sum is repaid by ships returning to port with their bellies full of his tobacco and cotton, he actually can claim ownership of the warehouses. We all believe that the king will soon open up trade between our countries, and even now His Majesty tries to look the other way, for the trade goes on in spite of embargoes. Gervais has a mind for good business, even if it temporarily lightens his purse a bit."

"But Paul, doesn't he worry that Lord Ridgley might cheat him? If your father simply took the money and did not build as he promised to do, would the captain have a chance of claiming ownership of the warehouse property? Lord Ridgley has tremendous influence here. The risk is so great."

He gave her hand a pat. "Do not delude yourself that it is a matter of trust. The Gervaises and Ridgleys are bound by want of trade; to rob the captain of his investment would not help us with any future income. The captain is very rich, Evelyn. He did not amass a fortune by playing it safe. Rest assured, Father would be willing to take like risks in America."

"He seems an honest. .." Evelyn's words trailed off as she heard the front door open and close. "Andrew?"

"Yes," Paul said, rising from her side. "He went to Chappington to beg a moment of my sister's time. A long moment, it would seem," Paul laughed, going to the drawing room door to open it. "Although he said he would be back for dinner, I thought perhaps... Andrew?" Paul said as he looked into the foyer. Paul backed away from the drawing room door to allow Andrew to enter.

Evelyn gasped at the sight of him. A purplish lump had begun to rise on his cheek, and his lip was split and bleeding. He had his hat in his hand and a scowl on his battered face.

"That bloody colonial bastard," he growled.

"Tyson did this to you?" Paul asked. "At Chappington?"

"The son of a bitch came upon me while I was out with your sister, and he beat me half to death," Andrew declared. "The man is a raving lunatic."

Evelyn slowly rose, her brow furrowed in an angry frown. Anger was a rare emotion for her, but there was no mistaking the fury that grew in her brown eyes as she approached Andrew. She went to stand at her husband's side, looping her arm through his.

Andrew's features visibly softened in his effort to control his rage. He looked apologetically at Evelyn. "I'm sorry for my language, Evelyn, it's just that I'm so furious I could kill someone."

"No doubt," Paul agreed heartily. "I can't believe..."

"Where..." Evelyn said abruptly, cutting off her husband's speech. Even Paul looked at her strangely. Evelyn's manners were usually flawless. "Where exactly were you when Captain Gervais struck you?"

"We were at the old keep," Andrew said. "We'd gone for a short ride, and I was showing her where it was that Paul and I had hidden from our parents when we were boys."

"And he beat you for that?" Evelyn asked, her lips pinched in a white line. "I find that rather hard to believe."

"Oh, do you?" Andrew said, his anger blossoming anew. "Well, I assure you that the man is little more than a beast. What can be expected from a yeoman clod from the colonies? He's a presumptuous, blackhearted son of a—"

"And you were doing nothing to cause Captain Gervais to think his intervention was necessary?" she demanded, raising one finely arched brow.

"I was kissing my betrothed," Andrew shot back defensively.

Evelyn's anger was so great, and the effort it took to keep from adding to Andrew's already generous supply of bruises was so difficult to control, her arm tightened around Paul's. He looked down at his wife's fury in amazement.

"There has been no betrothal," Evelyn said very slowly.

"Vieve and I were working out our differences and—"

"I think you had better leave, Andrew," she said. "Get your things together. Cook will give you something to take with you."

"Evelyn?" Paul questioned.

She looked up at her husband. "If you think about this for just a moment, Paul, you will realize that it is not a good idea for us to extend our hospitality to Andrew any further. There is no question in my mind that Captain Gervais would not abuse him to this degree unless Andrew did something to deserve it." She looked back at Andrew. "I only hope that Vieve is all right."

"So," Andrew laughed. "You think you know him so well? His money is so damned precious to you all that you'd even throw an old friend to the dogs and take his side."

"It is not the captain we defend, but Vieve," Evelyn said with determination.

"Paul?" Andrew questioned. "I've been your friend for years. Has the man with the money come to remove me?"

"Family," Paul said slowly, "takes loyalty before friendship or money, Andrew. If you've wronged my sister, you are not my friend."

Andrew turned toward the stairs. "I can see of what the two of you are made," he said bitterly. "You'd have some bumpkin from the colonies in your kind regard rather than a friend of many years. Someday you'll regret this betrayal. It's a good thing I found out about your meager loyalty before I actually believed you had any honor."

"Andrew," Evelyn said, stopping him before he went upstairs. "Did you leave Vieve with the captain?"

He gave a short, bitter laugh. "Oh, yes, my dear. I'm certain they had a very pleasurable afternoon."

Evelyn slowly smiled. "Then I rest easier," she said with no small amount of sarcasm. She turned abruptly away from both men and went back into the drawing room.

Paul entered behind her, slowly closing the doors and looking at her in astonishment. "I don't believe I've ever seen you behave in such a way," he said.

"I don't know that I can contain myself long enough for Andrew to get safely out of my house," she said with a trembling tongue.

"Evelyn, are you so sure that Andrew is to blame?"

As she looked at her husband she had to shake her head in wonder of her own. "Do you really doubt it? Your sister told you about Andrew, yet you tried to dispel her worry, passing him off as some spurned young lover who'd temporarily lost his head.

She has rejected him. Andrew must have given her good cause. Vieve is not a skittish girl."

As he thought about what Evelyn was saying, there remained a certain confusion in his eyes. He did not have to form his next question, for she answered that as well. "Would an American sea captain trespass against a young noblewoman in her own country and take his chances in our courts? Would he flee Lord Ridgley's reprisal, leaving behind such grand sums of invested money? No, Paul, Andrew has abused our friendship. I imagine you owe the captain your thanks. Undoubtedly, he saved your sister from some dreadful circumstance." She sighed and looked away from Paul. "I hope he saved her. I hope the captain did not do his damage to Andrew when it was too late for Vieve."

Paul sank into the nearest available chair, considering his wife's conclusions very carefully. There was a great deal of emotion accompanying her statements, and Evelyn was not flighty or given to outbursts.

"Could I have misjudged my friend so thoroughly?"

"That you are honest, my love, encourages the frequent fault that you expect others to be." Evelyn shook her head sadly. "Paul, we should have given Vieve more credence. And we should not have sympathized with Andrew, trying a simple warning about good manners."

"If he's hurt her, I'll..."

"We had better show restraint, here and now, for we are too late to help Vieve."

"Perhaps we should ride to Chappington," he said, his own anger building as he began to realize his error.

"Tomorrow will be soon enough," she said firmly. "We cannot arrive before it is very late, and something tells me that our expression of alarm will do more harm than good."

"What if she is hurt?"

"If there is anything wrong, your father will send word to us and we will go. Otherwise, let her keep this difficulty to herself for now."

The sound of the front door slamming caused Paul to jump. It was the unmistakable sound of a longtime friend making an angry departure. He winced slightly at the thought that his show of loyalty for Andrew might have compromised his sister.

"We did not, either one of us, take her seriously enough," he said quietly. "She may need us now."

Evelyn looked up at her husband and braved a half smile. "I think it is dear by the color of Andrew's ravaged face that our Vieve has what she needs. Let her be."

Vieve's place at dinner was conspicuously empty. Tyson looked warily at Boris, but saw only his usual surly expression. This was one kind of bargain upon which Tyson had never before embarked, but he knew the same trader's ethics would suffice. They began to eat in silence, saving the discussion until after dinner. They both cautiously maintained the cool, confident pose necessary for negotiation.

"Will your daughter attend our discussion?" Tyson finally asked, midway through the meal.

"She does not know we are having a discussion. She has chosen a hot tub and private meal in lieu of our company." Lord Ridgley peered at Tyson, but the latter hid his displeasure by lowering his eyes to his plate.

Tyson could not believe the foolhardiness with which he had stepped into the trap. Worse, he recalled how his mind had been whirling with possessive thoughts; he had carried out a sharp determination to change her preference from a boy to a man, only to be forced to pay for the act. She had not bargained with him for a promise of marriage. She must have wanted a wealthy husband speedily delivered. By her own lips, marriage was her price. And who better to be forced than a man who stood no chance against their laws?

He forgot that he had intended to seduce her, for he had been seduced by her tearstained face, her mien of trust, and her less than willful resistance to his advances. And he was further incensed by the image of Shelby touching her. Even though he had not made her his by oath, act, or law, he could not abide the thought that another man would touch what he already considered his. He pushed past reason and put his mark on her.

He knew it unwise to yield to a softening, teasing sensation that threatened his posture for the bargaining. He fought against the knowledge that he had done exactly what he had accused Andrew of trying to do. He would not question whether she had tricked him or whether he was the fool. However, there was one fact that could not be dismissed: she belonged to him now. The moment he had taken her young body he was instantly aware of the trap that had closed around him, and the possibility that she had willed it so.

Tyson glanced suspiciously at Lord Ridgley. He did not consider the baron's fatherly pride. He did not think of Vieve's discomfort. He had been deceived, and he would assure himself that it was for the last time. She wanted a rich husband; she would have one. It might be more than she bargained for.

Tyson filled his glass when he had finished with his food. Knowing his disadvantage, Tyson opened the conversation. "Before I came here, I sent a message to my mother's cousin. We are planning to meet in London. It will no doubt relieve your entire family to know that my mother's cousin is the earl of Lemington."

"Ah," Lord Ridgley said, raising one brow and peering at Tyson with a smile twitching under his moustache. "How is it you have not mentioned that before?"

Tyson leaned back in his chair. "It is a presumptuous connection on my part. We disclaim such noble hierarchy in America, and the connection is a distant claim. But I assure you, Lord Ridgley, I am well aware of whose table I share."

"And your lineage is an issue? I am surprised at you, Captain."

"What other requirements do you have?" he asked, letting his eyes narrow to show that he disliked this aspect of the subject. Tyson was compulsively private.

"Has it seemed, even to you, that those are my priorities?"

"The British practice some rituals that are not common to me. Perhaps you will direct me. If we were in Richmond, at my table, I would invite you to examine my fields, my fleet, my horses."

"We could as well be there," Lord Ridgley offered. "I am convinced of your ability to keep my daughter. How could I ignore your achievements when a great deal of your money has already passed into my hands?"

"Then name your requirements," Tyson said.

"Only two," the baron said. "Although Chappington and the land on which it sits will belong to my daughter one day, I would suggest that you allow this English holding to pass to my son.

You may take a larger share of the shipping and warehouse venture, if you wish, by yielding a small income to Paul after I am gone."

"That is agreeable. I have an estate in America; I do not need another one."

"I have already laid bare my shipping accounts; you have seen the trouble that industry has suffered. I would consider it a personal favor if you would give a cursory look to these estate accounts before giving the property over to Paul for management."

Tyson frowned slightly. "How many other personal favors will you be adding to this still tenuous agreement?"

Lord Ridgley leaned his elbows on the table. "A few. My second request: you have said you have time to spend in England and have already indicated that overseeing the warehouse building appeals to you. Do not take my daughter out of the country for a year."

Tyson stiffened, and his frown grew into an insulted scowl. "You wish to have her wed, but you will continue to guard her?"

"I will not interfere with your marriage. Unless it becomes necessary."

Tyson tried to maintain his composure. "What will necessitate your interference, my lord? The slightest complaint from your daughter's lips? My failure to coddle her as she feels she deserves? What simple-minded fool would allow such—"

Lord Ridgley's fist hit the table with a loud crash. The dinnerware clattered on the table, but Tyson did not even flinch. "Enough. You may go and take your chances on my next action," he said threateningly. "I already have your money; I could give the lass to Shelby, though such a decision would stick in my gullet for a long while."

"How do I know that at the end of a year you won't press your advantage?"

Lord Ridgley leaned back in his chair. "You don't."

"You have said what it is you want," Tyson said slowly. "What is it you will give?"

"I give you my daughter," Lord Ridgley said slowly. "I do not consider that a meager gift."

Tyson gave a short, angry laugh. "One wily young virgin for the sum of fifty thousand pounds. Who would argue the fairness of such a deal of trade?"

"You feel the insult now, young man," Lord Ridgley said testily. "But if you are wise, hold your judgment until you are gray around the edges and short of time to settle your family accounts. I will have been gone a long time before you reach such a stage in your life." He paused and looked closely into Tyson's angry eyes. "I have seen how you look at my daughter. You will one day feel this father's bite."

Tyson lifted his glass and took a drink. "You wish to buy a manager for your warehouses, and you will guard your daughter's welfare past the wedding day. Is that all?"

"I would rest easier if in addition to that, you would give me your word that she will be loved and cherished."

"There has been enough dalliance. With all due respect, there are some things even your high-handed law cannot guarantee."

"The terms, then?" Lord Ridgley asked.

"To the terms of your advantage, I bend."

"You are angry now, Captain, but you are clever enough to find your own advantage in any wager. We need not draw out the hostility, if we understand each other."

Tyson stood from the table and downed the remainder of his wine. "I will leave your house as soon as the contracts for my marriage to your daughter have been drawn. I can be of more use to my investment in the city, but within a month the wedding will be done— unless you wish to imprison me here in fear that I may flee."

Lord Ridgley smiled shrewdly and looked up at Tyson. "I do not fear your escape, Captain. If you fly from here, do so with my blessing. I will keep your money and give my daughter to Shelby."

Tyson's temples began to pound. He placed both hands on the table and leaned close to the baron's face. "Do not push me too far, my lord. It meets my mood to accept your terms, but should I find it a better notion to fight, you will be astounded by the force of my dissension."

The baron looked into the captain's eyes and showed no fear. "Of that, my son, I am well aware."

Tyson leaned back from his threatening pose and watched with interest as the baron lifted his glass as if in a toast. Without another word, Tyson turned and left the baron alone in the dining room.

Lord Ridgley held up his glass in a solitary salute. "To my first grandchild," he said softly.

After a bath and a light meal taken in her room, Vieve requested a brandy. "A brandy is it?" Harriet scolded. "Aye, he'll love that, his lordship will."

"You needn't tell him."

"Aye, and we'll add that to the long list of things we needn't tell his lordship. That we shall."

In spite of Harriet's dubious scolding and her overbearing presence, there was little question of her loyalty. She had diapered Vieve's bottom, and now her constant, reproving tongue played havoc on Vieve's manners with all the affection of any mother hen.

As Harriet picked up the discarded clothing by the cooled tub, she hung up the velvet habit and cast a wary glance over her shoulder at her young ward when she spied the tear. Then, upon gathering up Vieve's chemise, she could not mistake the stains and dirt. She looked again at her young mistress. "Let it soak, Harriet, and it will be fine," Vieve said in a smooth, controlled voice.

Harriet dropped the chemise into the pile of laundry she had collected and quickly fetched the requested brandy. Vieve had known better than to think she could hide this incident from Harriet; yet she meant to guard the details with all her might. When Harriet held the glass toward her, she could see that her servant's hand trembled and her eyes held a deep concern. "Harriet, the less said right now, the better. I should like to bear this alone for at least one day."

The old woman looked closely into Vieve's eyes. "Are ye hurt, lass?"

Vieve smiled a light and reassuring smile. "There are no bruises, Harriet. Let me be."

"Will the hearty be called to..."

"I have asked only one thing of you," Vieve said sharply. "One day of silence on the matter. Then you may question and scold, if you feel the need."

Harriet hung her head and, gathering up the soiled clothes left by the tub, moved toward the door. She paused as her hand touched the latch. Then, turning back, she plucked out the chemise that bore the stains of Vieve's lost virginity. She tossed the garment into the flaming hearth and with a sharp nod of her head took up the bundle and left the room. An hour later she returned with a second brandy, though it had not been requested.

Vieve reclined against the propped-up pillows in the four-poster and watched the candles burn down and the hearth wane. The minutes dragged into hours as she thought of how far from her own desires she had fallen. The proud Vieve, stripped bare of dignity once and for all. After a year of fighting Andrew's advances, the Yankee had but to command her, and she was without resistance. She damned her golden hair, her clear blue eyes and shapely maiden's form, which men cursed as their own demise. Was she not just a woman, after all? How strangely men drew themselves that they could test the limits of her resistance, begging for her response, and yet when that acquiescence was found, make hers the sin, for she was pretty, or tempting...or in love.

What Andrew had begged for the sake of love, he had been willing to steal from her. And what Tyson had accused her of yielding, he had forced from her. It did not matter that Tyson's form of force was a sure finesse; he had seduced her with the intent to enjoy the pleasures of intimacy without commitment.

For a young noblewoman there was just cause to mourn a lost virtue, for it lessened her worth in marriage with any but the man who had claimed her. Oddly, though, it was not that sacrifice that caused her to cry late into the night. It was the other loss of knowing he would never learn the truth. His touch had caused all sense to flee, all will to crumble, all reason to disappear. She had not held him away for want of promises, for the only promise she sought was to be his, for a day, a month, a year. Could he not see that if she was moved by her father's want of money, she need not have yielded so much? And if marriage was her price, she'd not have given in for a farthing less? No other could draw from her what he could command. She loved him. She could not deny his simplest wish, because her heart dominated where her wits were mute.

She wept until she fell into exhausted sleep. Her last thought before night overtook her was his demand for her silence. By morning, she reasoned, he would be gone.

Tyson filled his pipe from his pouch, lit it from a candle in the foyer, and stepped out onto the veranda. He sought the evening breeze to cool his heated ire. In one short week he had been relieved of fifty thousand pounds of his family money, had warehouses to build, and would soon add a conniving young bride and her interfering father to his meager possessions. And all this, he realized, was his own fault.

The warehouse venture was not a disappointment, provided there had been no trickery in the contracts he had signed. He had not intended to leave the invested sum to go unchecked; even without the baron's request, his plans included staying through at least most of the building. But what had happened with Vieve still astounded him.

All of his adult life, Tyson had been cautious of women. He had not lived a celibate life, but his affairs had been few and generously spaced. Out of respect for his mother and the rest of his family, he had used discretion even with Lenore, denying himself on many occasions. But because Lenore was not prudent in her affairs, any man in her company was the object of speculation from the gossips.

From the time of his youth to the present, there had been few women who successfully charmed him. He had dealt with a mild stirring here and there, had become aroused by this one or that, but never in his life had he been at a woman's mercy. And those women before Vieve had not been wanting for good looks or sharp wits.

What simple idiocy, he asked himself, had this little vixen inspired? His mind had failed him, his good sense left unguarded. From the first moment he held her in his arms, he had wanted her. And when he kissed her and held her in the aftermath of Andrew's assault, he would not be denied. He had not thought, reasoned, questioned her, or even lightly considered restraint.

Her presence had rendered him mute, deaf, and out of control. Was she not only a woman, after all?

He banged his pipe on the veranda rail, sending a shower of embers down into the damp shrubs below. They had his money, his commitment and, indeed, his future in their hands. They had as much of him as he was willing to give. She may have successfully caused him to lose his head once, but she would not again.

Seven

When Vieve was dressed and ready to descend to the drawing room, where the family would gather before dinner, her father knocked on her door. When he entered and looked at her, she forced her hands to remain still and tried hard to appear poised.

"You look none the worse for wear, daughter."

She lowered her gaze to hide a blush, choosing to take his comment as a compliment. "Thank you, Papa."

"Captain Gervais came forward with a proposal for your hand," he said in a brusque, straightforward manner. There was no mistaking the finality in his eyes. "I accepted his terms. Should you like to know what he offered?"

"It's not necessary, Papa."

"You are willing?" Lord Ridgley asked.

Vieve bolstered herself to answer. "Until yesterday, I did not realize how important it is that a contract for marriage be settled. Nor did I see how impossible a choice Andrew Shelby would be."

Her father's frown bore down on her. "Your perceptions about Andrew Shelby could have used my counsel long ago, but by your actions I suspected you were not of a mind to listen to an old man's advice."

"I know, Papa," she said quietly.

Lord Ridgley cleared his throat. "It was enough that Shelby has lost his own inheritance through laziness. What his father left him was not grand, but a little good sense and hard work could have made more of it. Shelby showed no interest in our estate and always left our discussions from boredom. I may not be far wrong in guessing that he has nothing left. And if that is not dire enough, you couldn't have realized how he likes to drink and gamble." Lord Ridgley raised both bushy gray brows. "I don't think you would sit idly for that."

"No, Papa," she murmured.

"Good. Your marriage to Captain Gervais may be abrupt, but it will be done and you need not suffer through any more bidding."

"Papa? Did you insist on this contract?"

"I do not see encouraging him to take you in marriage as punishment for folly," he replied gruffly. "If it gives you any peace of mind, it was the captain himself who pointed out my advantage; I only agreed he was right."

"Is that a good way to have me married, Papa?"

He laughed suddenly. "Do you pity this poor beaten man, daughter? You discredit yourself. Let him play the angry groom and bemoan his poor disadvantage. He is a proud man, and his pride bites at him now. But he sees not the face of his own devil; the faces he sees are ours, which swim before him as the culprits who would abuse him. Still, he is a clever man, and in time he will name his devil and best him. For now it is enough that he behaves responsibly."

"But Father, if he is angry..."

Lord Ridgley's brows drew together. "You protect him in one breath and fear him in the next? Nay, child, this insult he feels will not leave a mark on your tender hide, for though he does not realize it yet, he is more angry with himself than any of us. I have tried to teach you to trust your feelings, girl. If you haven't already, you may begin now."

"What about Andrew?" she asked tremulously.

Her father touched her cheek, his rough fingers attempting a gentle caress. "I give you to the captain. Andrew will surely feel the rub for many years." She smiled into his eyes, for she appreciated the value he placed on her.

"I have used great restraint, Vieve." He tilted her chin to keep her gaze locked into his. "I have not demanded to know what events brought the captain to the fore. It is enough that his offer is acceptable and you are willing. I have no aversion to protecting what is mine, but I am an honest man. There is one answer I require of you. We do not cheat the captain? Andrew did not—"

"No, Papa," she insisted. "Tyson was..." she stumbled for the right words. "Tyson was in time."

"Good," Boris said. "Come to dinner. There is no need to say any more. Paul and Evelyn know only that you are to be wed, and as far as I'm concerned, the rest is no one's damn business. Not even mine." He held out his arm to escort her. "Let's do what we can to turn the rest of this evening into a happy one."

Vieve was still shaken by the abrupt change in course her life had taken. Paul and Evelyn handled their happiness for the couple with enthusiasm, as if all were proper, and asked no questions.

Tyson proved his ability to use charm when it suited him. If he was angry and suspicious, he carefully concealed such emotions. His eyes twinkled as if in amusement, his lips were turned upward in a confident smile. His clever use of innuendoes successfully hit their mark on her while seeming to provide romantic conjecture to the others. "I assured Lord Ridgley that you had already responded to my declaration very agreeably. I thought you would be pleased that your father is so willing to oblige us."

She bit her lip at the notion of any declaration, but looked up at him in what she hoped would be perceived as glowing adoration. Since the die was cast and her humiliation had already been great enough, she hoped to add nothing more to the imaginations of those around her. Tyson was playing the part of eager groom; she was smart enough to behave as a delighted bride. The others need not know her pinkened cheeks had any deeper meaning.

He had risen to the advantage very quickly, for she had been the one startled by this sudden marriage contract. But she remembered the details of the previous afternoon at least as well as he, and all she wished to see in those hard, diamond-bright eyes was an affirmation of love.

"Although Tyson did not put the question to me in a very straightforward manner, his actions were very firm in declaring what he wanted." She glanced at her betrothed, seeing his mouth tighten. "The captain would not be refused. He is most persistent."

"So long as we are bent on a single purpose, my love," he said. His voice was tender, his eyes burning. She thought she had learned to read those eyes, but she found herself wondering if she saw passion or fury.

"I never could have guessed you'd actually take my advice, Vieve," Paul said with a sudden laugh.

Vieve looked at her brother in confusion, while Tyson's cold stare curiously questioned him.

"Last spring," Paul went on, "on the very day of your arrival, I told my sister she would be better off setting her sights on you than wasting her time on Shelby." Vieve felt her cheeks grow hot. "Of course, I didn't even know you then, Tyson. And I was speaking more from anger with Andrew than true purpose. But as luck would have it, the two of you have fallen in love."

She slowly tilted her chin, looking up at Tyson. His lips were turned in a one-sided smile. How had Paul sabotaged her so innocently? She almost shook her head in denial, but caught herself in time. She swallowed hard, thinking that now there could be no doubt in Tyson's mind that she had deliberately planned what had happened.

"What an odd coincidence," Tyson said slowly, "that Vieve discovered her love for me at precisely the same time the baron discovered my abundant funds."

"Let's eat," Lord Ridgley commanded brusquely. "I am for putting business aside and finding the mood to celebrate." That said, he guided them all to the dining room, Paul and Evelyn in the lead.

As Tyson escorted her to the dining room, Vieve looked up into his eyes, showing fierce temper in her own. "You might have warned me," she whispered. "I had no idea you were going to make an offer of marriage."

"I thought we had decided to forgo warnings," he returned.

As they entered the dining room, Vieve resisted, her arm looped through Tyson's so that they lingered in the doorway. She looked up at him with what could be surmised as love and longing. She smiled, while her words bit out an icy remark. "I suppose you expect to find me grateful for your..."

Her words trailed off as she became conscious of the slow, rhythmical caressing of her bare arm. He smiled at her, but his eyes glittered with a menacing light. "Your father has ordered a more festive mood. I am for following his instructions, as I have already proven."

"Tyson," she began.

"Beware, my love, betrothals are toasted, not grieved. Unless you choose to shed more light on our sudden desire to be wed...."

"Come, come, there is enough time for all of that," Lord Ridgley said, standing before his place at the head of the table. He rang the bell for the meal to be served. Tyson dropped a rather husbandly peck on her brow and turned her toward the table, seating her between Paul and her father. Evelyn occupied the seat across from her husband, and Tyson sat beside her. Vieve breathed a sigh of relief that she was not next to him until she looked up from her plate to see his intense silver eyes directly across from her. She swallowed hard and hoped she would survive his anger.

Evelyn was delighted with the anticipation of planning a wedding, Paul was excited about the future profits of their combined families, and Lord Ridgley was lifting his glass with unusual gusto for a man who had issued a firm command for his daughter to be led to the altar.

"When can we begin making plans?" Evelyn asked.

"I can see no reason to delay," Tyson replied. "I think I have already revealed my greatest flaw," he said, checking eyes with Vieve. "I am a very impatient man."

"Then the wedding will be soon. Oh, it will be grand," Evelyn said.

"I'd rather it be small," Vieve said, trying not to look at anyone in particular.

"If Vieve wants an intimate wedding, all the better," Tyson said. "I will not be contributing a long guest list."

"Small weddings are sometimes prettier, more memorable," Evelyn agreed.

Vieve began to lament the lie into which her family had been innocently drawn. In a sudden pang of conscience she considered the meager benefits of blurting out the truth. An offer of marriage under these conditions was not what she had ever wanted.

But before she could confuse the situation with any sudden confession, she turned to see who had entered the dining room. Charles Latimer stood in the doorway. He was wearing his riding clothes, which in itself was rare, since he preferred taking coaches and was not much of a horseman. And his expression was especially fierce; even his smile was a little more wicked than usual. "Well, you're all gathered. It almost appears as if you were expecting me."

Lord Ridgley cleared his throat, a pained expression on his face. "Had we known you were coming, Charles, we'd have set another place. Come in," he said. "You're welcome to join us."

"I did not come to dine," he said flatly. "I did not come to spoil your dinner, either, but then I thought you would be finished by now. I'm here on some unpleasant business, and it involves all of you. I have spent the entire day listening to the woeful tales of Andrew Shelby. It seems he had nowhere else to turn."

Lord Ridgley retorted instantly. "I don't doubt that, Charles," he said. "Andrew has cooked his own goose. He has treated my daughter quite dishonorably."

Charles laughed as if the comment was a poor jest. "Oh, really? Is that what she told you? Why, the little vixen has been carrying on with Andrew for quite some time now, and he expects only what is fair. He wishes to become her husband now. He tells me that money is no longer a reason to delay."

"Money was never a reason," Lord Ridgley said. His face became more red as he spoke, and he refused to stand in his brother's presence. "I think Shelby ought to be glad no one calls him out. Aye, I've heard a tale or two, and if I had not heard so late, I would have taken care of Shelby myself. And you, Charles, will not speak about my daughter with less than the utmost respect in my house."

"Why, Boris, I only appeal to your honorable nature," Charles said. He betrayed his inner calm by the way he twitched the crop at his side. "The girl has been with Andrew for a long time. Their behavior together has been most... most... They must marry. In the name of decency."

Vieve looked uncertainly at Tyson. He braced his elbows on the table and leaned his chin on his hands. For a moment she saw a slight curve of his lips and a twinkle in his eye.

She became calmer as she watched him. It was an odd sensation to fear him one moment and the next find his quiet strength so sure and reliable. He could have intervened at any moment, but it was as if he held greater control by his silence. She relaxed slightly in her chair and decided to follow his silent instructions, remaining quiet and observant.

What amazed Vieve most was that Andrew had had the gall to go to yet another member of her family, especially her uncle. Charles Latimer had never cared one hoot for her.

"Worry about the decency of your own daughters, Charles," the baron grumbled. "If my daughter's behavior displeases you, it is my concern and not yours. Go home and tell the whining young whelp that he's lucky Tyson didn't do worse to him. Had I known the things he dared with my daughter, I'd have whipped him myself."

Charles stuttered and coughed. "Do you have any idea what's been going on because of your daughter? Well, clearly you don't, or you'd have done something. This man here," he said, pointing to Tyson with his crop. "This man you treat with such generous hospitality attacked Andrew for no reason at all. By his bruises I'd say the captain here meant to kill him. And when Andrew went to his closest friend to seek help, your son turned him out."

Paul stood up and faced his uncle. "It seems to me," he said slowly, "that Andrew should have been turned out a long time ago."

"Boris." Charles turned to his stepbrother. "I appeal to your decency."

Lord Ridgley's hands hit the table and he came to his feet. "I've had enough of your damned appeals. You've been a pain in the gullet for better than forty years, and by God I've tried, with respect to my dead mother, to treat you civilly, but you will not question my daughter's virtue in my own house. This is none of your bloody business; Vieve's marriage plans have nothing to do with you, despite your determination to get involved. Get those simpleminded scarecrows of your own married." He gave a flourish of his hand that had the appearance of dismissal. "Give one of 'em to Andrew, now that you have him sitting right in your house."

As Lord Ridgley bellowed, Charles's posture became more rigid. "You'll be sorry, Boris. Perhaps when you need me, I won't be here."

"Hell," the baron scoffed as if frustrated by Charles's assumption of importance. "I've never needed you. I've had my troubles, more because of you. You flaunt your money and tempt me, and when I won't take your charity, you sulk away. But then you come back, if only to make certain everyone can see how willing you are to be my benefactor. Once and for all, neither your money nor your relation to me is of any influence here. You're nothing but a braying, screeching braggart. Now get out."

Charles broke into a wide grin, but his eyes sparked with rage and his cheeks were flushed. The crop twitched at his side, hitting his boot. "You'll be sorry when you get the slut married and she's turned back to you as a dirty bride. Shelby's had his way with her, you know."

Tyson rose, the last of the men to stand, and when he came to his feet, he seemed to fill the room. Charles even seemed to cower slightly. But Tyson's voice was smooth and carefully controlled.

"You may leave the proof of virtue in my very capable hands," he said slowly. "The woman will be my wife, and you may tell Shelby that if he ever touches her again...I will kill him."

"Wife?" Charles croaked. He looked at his brother in stunned wonder. "You can't just let the wench change her mind now that she's become bored with her intended." Charles met with the hard, implacable eyes of three angry men. He laughed suddenly. "Good God, Boris. You'll marry your daughter to this colonial? What about your family name?"

"Good night, Charles," Lord Ridgley said, keeping his anger in check. "Do not return to this house without an invitation."

Charles stared at them one by one and then, with an angry snap of his riding crop, left the room. The three men slowly resumed their seats. Vieve's cheeks grew warm and she stared at her plate.

"If you were having such trouble with Andrew, why didn't you come to me long ago, Vieve?" she heard her father ask.

She looked up at him with tears in her eyes. "Papa, I was afraid you would blame me."

"Blame you?"

"It is what I am accustomed to," she said with a hurt shrug. "Whenever Andrew misbehaved, there was always someone close at hand to tell me why he could not help himself." She looked at Tyson and nearly laughed aloud, because the color in his own cheeks had ripened. Then her gaze was diverted by Paul reaching into her lap to squeeze her hand. She turned to look into his guilty eyes. "Even Andrew blamed me for the fact that he had little control over his own actions." She looked back at her father. "May I be excused, please? I have lost my appetite."

Her father nodded, and the look of sympathy in his eyes was obvious. She wished she could erase the last year of her life.

As Vieve left the room, Tyson pushed his chair back from the table. "My lord, is it your brother's custom to make even matters of your daughter's marriage his business? Is he a longtime friend of Andrew's?"

"Charles has always presumed upon even my most personal affairs. And I do not think his friendship with Andrew goes beyond acquaintance, but that has never stopped my brother before."

"I cannot make a contract of marriage with a woman and deny her desirability in the next breath, but I wonder if you have ever considered the strange partnership between Andrew's desperation to have Vieve and Charles Latimer's uncanny support. Until tonight, I faulted the young man's behavior, but I did not see anything suspect in his desire. Now I think you should consider your brother's motives." He tossed his napkin onto the table as he stood. "Excuse me. I think I should assure myself that she is all right."

"Perhaps I should go," Lord Ridgley said, making a motion to rise.

"Sooner or later you will have to entrust her welfare to me, my lord."

He did not wait for Lord Ridgley's permission, but he did listen for some verification that he was not followed from the dining room. He called out to her as she reached the bottom of the staircase. She slowly turned toward him.

"Somehow I did not expect this reaction from you," he said. "From your own lips, marriage was the price you put on your virtue. I have met your price. Yet you act as if you've been greatly wronged."

"It is not an act, Captain Gervais."

"Whatever it is, it is best stopped now." Although he kept his voice low, he was no less stern. "Unless you have a better solution for our predicament, I should appreciate a more graceful acceptance of our lot."

She shook her head, furious with his assumptions. "You have obviously accustomed yourself to making all the decisions alone, Tyson. Do you not even see the necessity of asking me if I will have you?"

He smiled roguishly and reached out a finger, gently lifting a curl off her shoulder. "My mistake, petite. As I recall, you staked your claim already."

"You made the claim, sir, I..."

"Vieve," he warned, his fingers dropping to caress her shoulder. She was stilled by the look in his eyes. "If it is your desire, we can go over the details again; we may argue endlessly whether I urged or forced you, or whether I met with seduction or resistance. You may already carry my child. The argument pales in the face of that single possibility."

Her eyes widened with astonishment. In all her confusion it was that single fact that had completely slipped her mind. She had thought a great deal about her lost virginity, but had not considered a more serious consequence.

He laughed lightly. "I knew it unwise to meddle with one so young. Your body beckons, but your mind is still chasing butterflies with the other children."

She fought the urge to slap his face. Instead she smiled wryly. "You are not so clever as I thought, Captain. You had but to insist that Andrew had violated me before you arrived at the old keep. My father would have believed you, and Andrew would have thanked you."

His eyes darkened, and a muscle in his cheek began to twitch. Without looking down, she could sense that his fists were clenched. "If there is a chance I misunderstood your preference, madam, speak quickly."

"I do not desire him, but do not place yourself so high above him. Andrew, too, was willing in marriage. You are no better than he; only more experienced."

Etched on his face was the effort he employed to raise his hands slowly to her upper arms. The anger in his eyes burned into her. He squeezed her arms. "Your memory fails you," he said hoarsely. "I am much more efficient than Andrew. Though I did not fully realize what I bought, the price I have paid for you is high and you are mine now. Be careful to remember that."

"You make it difficult to forget. You have my wedding planned, though I had nothing to say of it."

"If you corner a bull, my pet, do not be surprised to find he will charge."

"You think I planned what happened," she said, her eyes smarting with angry tears.

"It happened very easily," he said with an insolent shrug. "I reserve judgment on your plans, for now."

"Did you let my father believe that you should meet your due with marriage?"

His frown bore down on her. "Your father did not require any admission of guilt from me before using the threat of his great influence. The truth is irrelevant to him, but know this: you can do me much ill by this virgin's despair, but no more than you can do yourself. You expose me as a villain only at your own expense; you cannot escape public shame and humiliation if you name me as a rogue who used you against your will. For that your father could see me hanged, which I perceive as slightly more uncomfortable than being firmly led into wedlock." His finger lifted her chin roughly. "And it would be a lie, for I touched you and you answered me willingly."

"I did not trap you," she said in a strained whisper.

"Nonetheless, I am trapped."

She shook her head in denial and found that he could quiet any argument easily with his lips. Although the quick embrace and hard press of his mouth against hers came as a surprise, gradually her eyes closed, and she did not attempt to resist him. When he released her mouth, she opened her eyes to see that he regarded her with a mocking grin. "Still so eager, my vixen, but unless I was mistaken, you do not know the ecstasy of your reward. You are still a virgin in that sense."

"You are a wretch," she accused, seething at his mocking games.

He laughed at her rage and released her. "You need not expect satisfaction too soon, my love. I will find my diversions in London until our wedding day. I don't want Lord Ridgley to be tempted to do his worst."

"You leave?" she asked. She heard the panic in her own voice, and to think he might have heard it also almost sent her fleeing from his sight. She raised her chin proudly and took a different pose. "You will not return."

He regarded her with amusement. "You should hope I flee, petite. Marriage to me may not be all you have dreamed of." He turned away from the staircase to return to the dining room, as she climbed the stairs to her room. She reasoned that he must have announced her flustered mood, for she was not bothered by anyone, even Evelyn, through what remained of the evening.

He had made his point and left her to sleep on it. That she hungered for some word of love from him was her problem, for he'd made it quite clear he did not love her and marriage was not his desire. Yet there was no one to relieve her of this plight but him.

I hate him, she thought. And with that thought, her anger suddenly fled as her heart was plunged into sudden despair. He hates me. He may always hate me.

The tears that came that night were of another variety. No longer did she lament the absence of words of love and longing. What was the Yankee to think, with all that had transpired, but that she had deliberately tricked him to help her family? Even Paul had nearly confirmed that possibility. When he had touched her, she had yielded, helpless to deny him. If she had been stronger, she would have fought her own feelings.

And now she would wed a man who felt abused and would die before answering her love with his own. If she could not convince him that she had innocently acquiesced to his passion, without plot or contrivance, could she perhaps convince him that marriage with her would not be so horrible? Even if he could never believe that she had fallen in love with him, could she somehow prove that she meant to be a good and loving wife to him, despite the disastrous beginning?

It was shared passion that brought them together. Could love not grow enough to keep them so?

When she rose in the morning in a stronger state of control, it was in her mind to seek him out and apologize for her share of the angry words. She wished to tell him that she understood his ambivalent feelings toward her, but that she would strive to be a good wife, holding nothing back in the effort.

But she found he was already gone.

Tyson sat in the captain's chair of the Lady Lillian with a half-bottle of rum amidst a generous pile of paperwork. He leaned back in his chair, feet upon the desk, and a large padded parchment braced on his leg. He made smooth strokes with his brush, using watered ink to try to capture the slightly grayed light hair that he remembered showing on the temples of Michael Everly.

Tyson had begun sketching as a pastime early in his youth. He had started with a twig in the dirt, and when he was a little older, he sat on the fence of the corral with parchment and slivers of charcoal in hand, and had captured the graceful lines of a stallion's flanks. When he was alone with some worry he frequently drew as a means of relieving tension. During the traumatic days leading up to the duel, he had almost absently developed several facial likenesses of the despised man. He had brought them all to England with him. Looking at the various drawings, he sought to make a near perfect one.

When Tyson was sixteen and the long-brewing revolution had exploded into gunfire, the Gervais family had been forced to defend their land and possessions against British attack. His father had died two years later, leaving Tyson, the eldest son at eighteen, as the manager of a large plantation and having to care for a mother and four younger siblings. His entry into manhood, under such a weight of responsibility, had not been graceful. But no one had ever questioned his ability to take on the obligations his father had left behind. He had not resented the burdens and was proud of his ability to meet them.

It was just a year ago, when the youngest in their family had married, that his mother had spoken to him about all that he had accomplished and what he now must do. "You have put your own happiness aside for too long. They are all cared for now. Our family thrives. You must not wait any longer to find something of personal pleasure for yourself."

He had disregarded her fretting, arranged a footstool under her feet, and told her for the hundredth time that he did not delay in his own happiness. He loved his duty; he was as happy as he had ever expected to be.

"There is more to life than work," she had pressed.

"I want nothing more than I already have," he had replied.

"I cannot criticize you, Tyson. You are fully a man and no longer a child for me to command. You do well by your family, your town, and your country. However, I would ask one thing of you—do not commit yourself to a life of misery by knowingly marrying a woman of low virtue."

Tyson had frowned, accustomed to his family's criticism of Lenore. "I thought I had given my word that she would not become my wife."

"I know you think yourself very cautious with her, Tyson, but she has much of your affection. I would not want you compromised by it."

A mere two months later, his mother had passed away. An epidemic of cholera had claimed many lives that summer, and their family had lost only one. It was not until the quiet of the house became oppressive that he took stock of what she had said and examined his life.

His behavior over the following months had left his brothers and their wives shaking their heads in confusion. And when it was finally done, he had sailed to England despite their protests. He had thought to find information about Everly, but he had found a great deal more than that.

The ship rocked gently beneath him, and he poured himself another drink. He had done what he intended in the month away from Chappington. The Lady Lillian was still dockside, full of cargo from the English merchants, the agent bribed at high cost to release her, and ready to be towed out in one more day. She would make Virginia by Christmas. He, himself, would stay behind and accommodate the baron. He would return to Chappington, leaving the drawing for his hired man, Mr. Humphrey, to use in an extended search for information about Everly. Then, on the first day of October, he would be married.

He sighed and lifted his mug to take a drink.

"I don't suppose you have another cup?" came a familiar voice.

He looked up to see Doré Gastión standing inside the cabin door. They had met seventeen years before on a revolutionary battlefield when Doré was a young French militiaman and Tyson a boy defending his home and family. There was no man whom Tyson held as a closer friend. Tyson broke into a wide grin.

All his life, Tyson had learned to control his behavior before business associates, neighbors, and family, allowing only his strength to show and never betraying any vulnerability. But he and Doré had cried together in fear, both of them verging on manhood in the midst of war.

"How do you come to be here, Doré? This is not a good place for a Frenchman."

Doré smiled. "I am careful with my accent. Unless I drink too much, few people notice."

"But your name?"

"It is a good aristocratic name," he shrugged. "You, too, carry a bit of the French blood, and you are American, now in England. Perhaps we are both mad?"

"Undoubtedly," Tyson said. "I laugh over it every morning as I rise, and I look over my shoulder all through the day. We killed a few of these English, Doré. Do you hate them still?"

"What good is hatred? It gets in the way, does it not?"

"Indeed, it does," Tyson chuckled, rising to rummage through his shelf for another cup. He poured from the bottle of rum and passed the drink to Doré. Both cups were raised, but it was Doré who made the toast. "To your mother, may she rest in peace."

Tyson hesitated, but he drank. The effect Doré had on him was at once perfect and disconcerting. Doré was the one man from whom Tyson could not seem to conceal his feelings. When he looked again at his friend, his eyes were misted.

They were equal in size, but opposites in almost every other way. Tyson was dark, while Doré had lighter coloring, brown hair streaked by the sun, and penetrating, dancing blue eyes. The Frenchman's perennial wide, playful grin contrasted Tyson's more serious, impatient personality. The Parisian smile had charmed many a lady in a swinging skirt, while Tyson's hypnotic silver eyes had caused women to shiver in anticipation. Tyson had the hard good looks of a swarthy devil; Doré had the frivolous handsomeness of a young prince.

"You received my letter?" Tyson asked.

"Yes, and when it was possible for me to leave France, I traveled to your home to visit you. But you had already departed."

"I had not expected you to endure such extensive travel on my behalf, but I knew you would want to be informed of my mother's death."

"I thought to pay my respects on behalf of Madam Gervais, who did not approve of me." Doré laughed good-naturedly. "When we went abroad together, your mother worried and accused. She said I was a bad influence on you. It was much the other way, in my recollection."

"She liked you, Doré. More than that, she thought of you as another son."

"Another misguided son," he chuckled. His expression became serious. "Your brothers, Tyson. They are worried about you."

"They needn't be," he said gruffly, turning away from his friend's close scrutiny. How like his younger brothers. They seemed to have replaced his mother as nosy guardians. They had no doubt encouraged Doré to travel to England, suspecting they sent the one man Tyson could not ignore to inquire about his welfare.

"I am worried, Ty. I have heard this tale, that you left the woman, Lenore. Mon Dieu, such a wonderful whore. And where did you flee? The Gervais men tell me that you began to court many young virgin ladies. And I have seen you maul so many harlots. You were in a rush, I am told, to marry."

Tyson had drifted from Lenore on many occasions, but had confronted her with a formal departure after his mother's death. His pattern had been broken and he had taken a quick, close look at all the marriageable women of Richmond. Tyson turned back toward his friend, raising one dark brow with a broad smirk. "Is it said that I handled myself poorly? I thought it was time to rise above the likes of Lenore Fenton."

"Bah, it was too sudden a change, my friend. The woman did not take kindly to your abandonment. How is it she tricked you into this duel? As if you have not killed enough English."

Tyson sighed and rubbed the back of his neck. "I don't know how she tricked me. I did not want any part of a duel, and I knew all the while that the business of her embarrassed reputation was only an act. But I thought the pretense was for the benefit of the Englishman, Michael Everly. I refused to meet him until he began tormenting my family, making his insult a matter for public conjecture, and challenged me in front of spectators by calling me a coward. He would not cease until I gave him his chance to defend the honor of his fiancée." Tyson shook his head and took another drink. "Such a farce had never before been played for Richmond. The town quite enjoyed it. But I have never killed with pleasure."

"Mademoiselle Fenton did not pressure you before your mother's death. It is clear that the great Richmond matriarch, Madam Gervais, held even Lenore in check. But how much time after Madam's death did she wait before pressing her desires?"

"Three months," Tyson confirmed. "Maybe four."

Doré laughed in good humor. "Your little mama, she carried a big stick. A tiny, silver-haired widow who had but to blink her eyes and whisper to bring four large boys to do her bidding. I never understood how she could hold such dominion over people. Yet even I shook when she scolded me, as if I were some boy to be mothered."

"She appeared soft," Tyson said in fond memory. "But there was no mistaking her command." And then he added very softly, "She died too soon."

Doré walked over to the desk, looking down at the likeness of Michael Everly,. "And that is why you are here?" he said, pointing his cup toward the parchment.

"I would like to learn something of this Englishman who descended from such high, noble circles. No one seems to know anything about him."

"What will you gain, Tyson?"

"He had no connection in America, but his sudden engagement with Lenore still mystifies me. I should like to know how he came to Virginia, if nothing more. And there is the matter of restitution. I did kill him."

"It is regarded as self-defense in your country. But here?" Doré gave a low whistle. "And your brothers tell me that you have achieved some business agreement with an English lord. Tyson, I worry that you have gone mad."

"It was a prime opportunity. We are not friends with the British, but there is money to be made by both countries if we are clever and careful. We speak about the war only a little, and if we hold each other in any contempt, when there is money at stake our dislike is a great secret. I have never let my personal feelings keep me from making money."

"You have enough money."

"The family grows," Tyson said.

Doré sighed. "Very well, I will help you with this business. We will find this Everly family, settle your contracts, and go on to a country where we are welcome. Your brothers tell me you are bent on taking a long rest away from home, so you will come to France and be my guest." He took a drink and grimaced. "And we will drink decent wine."

"I don't need any help," Tyson said, not bothering to hide his irritation.

Doré laughed. "That tone works on the brothers, my friend, but we have been through too much for such a lie."

"I must stay here for a while, Doré. My business cannot be completed quickly."

"You do not make me welcome," Doré said suspiciously.

"The baron of Chappington, Lord Ridgley, has accepted an American guest. Do you think it wise to test his good mood by adding a Frenchman?"

Doré shrugged. "This marvelous world. So many possibilities."

"Not so many as you might think. He is a staunch Englishman."

Doré smiled lazily. "I am a rich Frenchman."

Tyson stiffened, bracing himself. "I am going to marry the baron's daughter."

Surprise showed on Doré's face for only an instant, melting into a wide grin. "I will make you a good witness then."

"Knowing you, I shouldn't let you within an ocean of her," Tyson grumbled.

"She is pretty, then? I should think so. You left the most magnificent whore in all the world."

"Of course, they know nothing of her," Tyson hastened to tell him.

"I should think not," Doré laughed. "These British are hard on such etiquette."

"I am not sure it would be wise for you to attend me."

"But no, Tyson. This poor family, they must think Americans so ill-tempered if they know only you. A little of the French charm, it will soothe your bride. Tell me, does the baron hold a pistol to your head for the vows?"

Tyson sighed heavily. "I have given the man fifty thousand pounds. If he wishes that I oblige him further by marrying his daughter, I cannot see the wisdom in refusing. I will trust you to behave yourself. She is quite young."

"Young? Yes?" Tyson mumbled a response and Doré leaned forward. "Speak up, Tyson. I do not hear you."

"She is seventeen," Tyson said more loudly.

Doré relaxed again, but his smile was teasing. "I find these English so dull, but I see they know the value of money. How is it the baron has convinced you that this marriage is what you want?" Tyson was silent, but the deepening color of his skin caused Doré to chuckle. "Well, my friend, I hope she was worth it."

"So do I," Tyson said with no small amount of irritation.

"You have a most interesting reaction to falling in love, Tyson. One would almost think you dislike the notion. But then, it is not at all what you are accustomed to, I suppose. In my country we fall in love more gracefully. And more frequently."

Tyson did not like the idea of having his friend witness his discomfort, but at the same time he could hardly deny the satisfaction of having someone close at hand whom he could trust. "But, monsieur, I shall expect you to exercise great restraint."

"Ah, restraint. Are you the man to teach me this virtue, Tyson?" he asked playfully.

"You don't know the half of it," Tyson grumbled.

"Not yet," Doré acknowledged. "But very soon I shall."

Tyson and Do refilled the night with rum and nostalgia, going over the details of their past together. There were stories enough to put them well past midnight with their tales. Neither had yet suggested sleep, for it had been almost two years since they'd been together.

The conversation had only just begun to lag slightly when a shout from outside caused Tyson to stiffen in his chair. There was another shout, and within seconds the bell on the quarterdeck began to ring frantically. The sound of yelling and running quickly followed, and Doré and Tyson made a dash from the cabin to the quarterdeck, greeting many half-dressed, sleepy ship hands bumping into each other and the thick, black smoke rising from the ship's hold.

"Fire."

Tyson stopped dead in his tracks. His cargo was burning. Without fast action, his ship would go down—his first and favorite vessel.

"Buckets," he shouted. "From dockside over the plank. Hop to, mates. We have a fire in the hold."

Tyson grabbed two buckets and was down the plank, on the docks, Doré fast behind him. Tyson called for hooks to lower the buckets from dockside and had to get to his knees to fill the first one. He nearly panicked at the time it took to secure one full bucket and surveyed in his mind the amount of flammable cargo he had purchased. He handed off to the nearest man, recognizing Bevis, his face darkened by smoke. Bevis was wheezing, but did not delay. He ran into the ship with his bucket while Tyson handed the next full pail to Doré. Within moments there was a line of men passing the water across the wide plank that had been used for loading cargo all day long. Tyson furiously filled buckets until he couldn't stand it any longer and then called for a replacement and began handing water into the hold.

The flames were not so dire as was the smoldering of wool and silk. The blackness of the smoke was suffocating, and the salt water from the Thames was not doing the job. He ran out to find Doré, and they had a quick conference to devise a better plan.

"Keep on those buckets, mates," he shouted. "Bevis, Tommy, Drexel, and Mack, come with me."

Six men on the deck strained their muscles to move the large barrels of the crew's drinking water, all ready for the next day's departure, to stand beside the deck hatch from which smoke strained to escape. When a dozen barrels stood in a line, Tyson rushed to the side. "Clear the hold and close her up. We're taking the fire from the deck."

He ran back to the hatch, where two men were positioned and ready to lift it. He braced his shoulder against the first barrel, Doré joining him on the opposite side. When he heard the closing of the cargo door, followed by a shout that all was clear, he gave a slow nod to Bevis and Tommy.

The men lifted the hatch, and smoke poured out into their faces. Tyson and Doré grunted with the effort to tip the barrel. Water poured atop the smoldering cargo. Two men behind him pushed a barrel forward and repeated the tipping, and so on, until all had been emptied into the hold. Then they stood back, over fifty men in all, and watched the black clouds wane and dissipate. The fire was beaten, and the men cheered.

Tyson stood and looked down into the hold. His cargo was very likely destroyed. His ship might have been also. He saw Bevis sitting on the deck, leaning against the rail.

"I think we got 'er early, Cap'n," the man said, the sound of wheezing still apparent in his voice.

"Do you know the cause, mate?"

"I'm thinkin' it were the lantern, Cap'n. I woke up the first whiff o' smoke and seen some glass broken by the crates."

Tyson scowled. "Did you see anyone?"

"I 'eard somethin', Cap'n, but I got to the fire first, sir. Didn't think of chasin' the scoundrel."

Tyson was silent for a moment. "You did right, Bevis. You may have saved the ship." He regarded his crew, most of them shirtless, some of them barefoot and wearing only hastily drawn up britches. "Well assess the damage at daybreak. Everyone who fought the fire will find a bonus."

His men began to drift away from the disastrous scene to get the few hours of sleep left before the sunrise rousted them again. Only a few remained on the deck when Doré put a firm hand on Tyson's shoulder.

"Deliberate, Tyson. There is no doubt."

"I know."

"Who?"

Tyson considered the possibilities. Would Lord Ridgley go so far as to damage property to keep Tyson's money? Surely the baron could press his advantage legally. And Shelby would certainly profit by Tyson's problems. Even Charles Latimer had shown his obvious displeasure with both the business partnership and marriage. In addition to these three, there was a city full of British citizens disgruntled by Americans in port.

"I could have lost my ship."

"You could have lost your life, Tyson," Doré pointed out. "I would choose the dark of night to set a fire, but with fifty hands and the captain sleeping aboard ship, it is as much an attempt to murder as damage goods. Did you see how it began?"

"Bevis was my watch, and he slept..."

Doré slowly shook his head. "You were too busy with the fire to notice that the hatch was unlocked. Whoever did this simply lifted the hatch and dropped in the lantern. It was not necessary to creep past your guard into the hold, but only to come quietly up the gangplank to the deck and drop the lantern onto your cargo. A child could have done it. Bevis might have missed the action even if he'd been awake."

Upon consideration, Tyson realized that Doré was right. A darkly clad youth could have tiptoed past any drowsing sailors and lifted the hatch enough to slide the offending lantern into the hold. Bevis's post was near the cargo door, in watch for thieves. No one could get past him to go in, or carry goods out.

"I suggest you leave your new business partner and take Lillian to Virginia," Doré said.

"And run?" Tyson laughed shortly. "You know that is not my way. I do not run from my enemies."

"Do you know who they are?"

"I would be even less likely to retreat if I knew them. Now finding them is the greater challenge."

Eight

Tyson assessed the damage to the ship and found the Lady Lillian to be seaworthy, but half of the cargo destroyed. While his men were put to the task of emptying out the charred cargo, Tyson knew it was time to pay a visit to his mother's cousin. He had known for some time that the earl of Lemington had a residence in London, but he had been uncomfortable about a meeting. He thought there might still be hard feelings, since his mother had abandoned her homeland for an American. Now he wished he had met the earl sooner. He hated to press a British noble, family or not, for support, but he obviously numbered more enemies than allies.

Tyson had sent a message to the earl upon his arrival months before, and the reply had indicated that Tyson would be received, but it was barely cordial and certainly not enthusiastic. His second missive, after the fire on his ship, stated frankly that he needed to see the earl, and the earl replied he would see him at once.

His lordship of Lemington, Farrell Moresay, was a small, reserved man of nearly sixty. He seemed to receive Tyson with some initial resistance, but their acquaintance began to warm as Tyson found out the reason. "Your mother was my favorite cousin, and when we were young I actually hoped to marry her. I was angry for a long time after she fell in love with that colonial." The earl smiled. "I should not complain, as I've had two good wives and seven living children. And by your acquaintance, I see that Lillian did well for herself."

"When we were children, Mother talked often of the English nobility," Tyson told him. "She told us stories of princes and princesses that kept us begging for more. Yet, I know she was happy with her life in Virginia, and my father was a good and prosperous man."

"You have followed in his footsteps, haven't you? A merchant captain, a plantation owner, looking for business in England." The earl chuckled. "The Gervais men are ambitious. Perhaps I would have been a world traveler, if not for my father's title. But I don't complain. I envied your father, having made his own way, and when he took Lillian to Virginia, I think I hated him. But I am too old for such hostility now. I wish I had made just one trip to America, though. I wish I had told your mother that I was no longer resentful that she did not accept my proposal of marriage."

"She spoke well of you, my lord. I'm quite sure she never worried that you were still angry. She extracted many promises from me that should I ever visit England, I must certainly find you."

"I'm glad you did, and I'm pleased that you've done so well for yourself."

"The first ship that I purchased with my own earnings I named for my mother. She is christened the Lady Lillian, and I have done well with her. But I'm afraid that since my first message to you, I have found myself in need of counsel from someone who knows the laws of this country. Would you take a ride with me, my lord, and let me show you my ship?"

The ride to the wharves from Lord Moresay's fashionable house consumed nearly an hour. During that time Tyson explained his investment, his impending marriage, and the fire, careful to keep accusation out of his narration. It was true that resentment of any American profiting in England might come from many sources. A sailor, down on his luck. A redcoat who had suffered losses or injury in the Revolution. The possibilities were endless.

Lord Moresay admitted that he had known Lord Ridgley for a long time and had the utmost respect for him. He was appalled by the damage to the ship, but cautioned Tyson. "I do not think you need question Lord Ridgley's honesty, if it has come to that. Perhaps this young man you mentioned...what was his name? The one who hoped to marry the baron's daughter?"

"Andrew Shelby. I have considered him."

"What will you do now?" the earl asked.

"I am sending the ship to Virginia without replacing the cargo that was lost. I'll lose money on the shipment, but I think it best that she be out of port. I will go to Chappington for my wedding, and if Lord Ridgley does not object, I will bring my wife here so that I'm close at hand to oversee the warehouse rebuilding. I will send you a note when I return."

"Can you think of a way that I can help?" the earl asked.

"At present I mean only to inform you that I may later seek your help. If you would put the contracts I have signed with Lord Ridgley in safekeeping, that would assist me. Beyond that, there is nothing, and I am afraid I will be late for my own wedding if I don't hurry."

The earl shook Tyson's hand. "I look forward to entertaining you and your wife. And, on behalf of Lillian, I will assist you, Captain. I only hope you don't find yourself in need of someone to help you fight Lord Ridgley. That would be difficult for me to do."

"If that is what I need, my lord, even you may not be able to help me," Tyson said boldly.

"I doubt the baron would wed his own daughter to a man he intends to harm."

"You know him better than I do."

"If you have these suspicions, why have you entered into both a business partnership and a marriage contract?"

Tyson took a deep breath. "Both, my lord, were irresistible."

Tyson could not easily dispel the suspicion that Lord Ridgley might have set fire to his ship, hoping that Tyson would take to the sea, leaving behind one slightly damaged young woman and a large sum of money. Even with Lord Moresay's endorsement of the baron, Tyson's curiosity was peaked. There had been no word from Chappington.

In spite of Tyson's desire to brush Vieve from his mind while he readied his ship for departure and finished other business, he found himself musing on whether her maidenhead had been worth his invested sum. He suspected her family of foul play, yet had never before had such disruptive, torrid dreams as had plagued him since that day in the old keep. And when he had sought to find some base pleasure with a prostitute, he had found that his virility would not serve him. He had commanded his mind to pretend that it was Vieve's velvet flesh he caressed, her thick golden hair that spread across the pillow, and her sweet fragrance that aroused him. But it was useless, and he left the whore in frustration.

Of all the things that Tyson could find to worry about, the worst was the fact that memories of Vieve haunted him, hindering his usual control. He had hoped that the month away from Chappington would help him to develop an indifference toward her, yet instead he felt drugged by her beauty and sensuality more from afar. He had not even been able to name the threats he faced, which might indeed come from her own household, yet he was forever in want of her body. He had thought the wedding a trap, but it paled in light of the larger snare of his desperate longing.

Such thoughts occupied him as he folded the clothing he placed in his trunk. In a few hours he would be under way with Doré. The conflict in his mind grew apace with his physical tension. He wanted her, but resented the desire she inspired. He longed to make love to her, yet despised the torment of such longing, feeling weakened by it. His thoughts were ever turned to her, seeing her face, her body, her lustrous hair so clearly in his mind that she might as well have been standing in front of him. He had never before been so consumed, nor had his concentration been so insistently drawn away from the more serious business that should occupy him. He thought he'd been cheated, tricked, trapped, and coerced into a state that made him more vulnerable than he had ever been before. He struggled to think of a way to get the better of such debilitating feelings.

"I'll pack 'er up for ye, Cap'n," Bevis said, pulling Tyson out of his daydream.

Tyson peered at his servant quizzically. "I hadn't expected the offer."

"Aye, it's a good gentleman's lackey I aim t'be," Bevis returned sarcastically.

"Oh? Shall I brace myself for a change in attitude?"

"Ye 'ave some complaint 'bout the service, Cap'n?"

"Oh, no," Tyson laughed, backing away from his trunk.

Bevis McCauley made a good mate, qualified by knowledge of the sea and ships to pilot any vessel. Although short, Bevis was as strong as an ox, determined by nature and accustomed to the rugged life aboard ship. When in port, he was more given to brawls than women. At nearly fifty, Bevis had served on many a ship, although since he had worked for Tyson for ten years he now called Virginia home. He preferred the company of men, but he had had three wives, two of them simultaneously. When Bevis saw a pretty smile, he married indiscriminately, and seeing his error, took his leave with due haste.

Tyson had found much to fault in Bevis's performance as a manservant, but he wished to keep Bevis close at hand because he was loyal, strong, and shrewd in his own simple way. Bevis had not argued overlong when Tyson required him to act the part of manservant and driver for three quick trips to the country, but when Tyson had told him that he must play that role for an extended length of time, the disgruntled mate protested so loudly that Tyson wondered if Bevis would find some other ship to employ him. In the end, Bevis grudgingly agreed to stay with Tyson while he finished business in England, but not without a daily complaint and a great deal of discontent.

"Ye're goin' through with it then?"

"I thought that was quite clear."

Bevis shook his head. "Ain't clear t'me atall, Cap'n. Ye never thought t'marry before, an' this little one, she got 'er a right powerful pa. If ye don't mind me sayin' so, Cap'n, it ain't goin' to sit well with that old Ridgley bloke if ye goes back t'yer old ways."

Tyson raised both brows in amusement. "My old ways?"

"Aye, sir. Loose women, sir. I understands it, I do. But if ye likes yer women cheap an' bawdy, what be ye doin', marryin' high and decent like this?"

"Is that how you see the baron's daughter? High and decent?"

"Blast it, Cap'n, I don't know nothing 'bout women—but I knows a thing'r two 'bout them what come from strict 'ouses, an' if ye marry an' bed this'un, ye'd better change yer ways."

"Why, Bevis," Tyson laughed. "Fatherly advice from you. That quite exceeds my expectations."

The man snorted and began folding clothes. "I said what I 'ad t'say. Ye go an' do what ye'll do, but if ye don't like this 'usband business, ye be right careful where ye plays. That little slip's pa'll put ye in the 'ole, 'e will. If 'e don't shoot ye straight out."

"So, you old goat, you think I'll make a poor husband? Is that it?"

"If I 'ad a daughter, I'd keep 'er locked up tight 'til ye was well out o' port."

Tyson laughed as he went to his desk and picked up a quill to sign the log. "It's a blessing, then, that Lord Ridgley did not ask for your advice. He happens to think he got a good bargain out of me."

"Aye, sure he does, since ye 'as enough money fer 'im. But mark me, Cap'n, if they don't like the way ye treats the girl, they'll keep yer coin an' take 'er back. An' what they'll do to ye, I'd dare not guess."

A slight frown creased Tyson's brow. "Rest easy, Bevis. I'm well aware of the impending dangers."

Bevis turned away from the bunk on which he was folding Tyson's clothes. "I ain't fer empty talk, Cap'n. Ye're young, ye're good, but ye ain't never been careful with women."

Which was why, Tyson admitted only to himself, he was on his way to his own wedding. He'd lost his head and bedded her. She filled him with a strong longing, and he'd moved quickly and carelessly to take her. But he did not intend to pay a dearer price in the end than wedding her. He hoped to still leave himself a way out.

"Everything is ready but my trunk," Tyson told his servant. "I'm going to see if Doré is ready to leave."

"Ye'll find 'im on the quarterdeck, Cap'n."

"Good. After you've loaded the trunk on the coach, we have a few errands to take care of in London before going to Chappington."

After the trouble on the Lady Lillian, Doré was not so unreasonably pleased to be going to his friend's wedding. He questioned Tyson liberally about his bride, her family, and the business venture, and he requested that Tyson go over each event again and again, no matter how much Tyson chafed at the prospect. Although Tyson resisted giving each intimate detail, he realized he was telling the story repeatedly, beginning with his initial arrival in London in early April.

Tyson gave Doré a brief tour of the furnished town house he had rented.

"But I thought the baron wished to keep his daughter close at hand."

"He made me agree not to take her out of England, and England is quite large.

"One more stop," Tyson announced. "The picture I made of Michael Everly is displayed in a shop window near Hyde Park. It seemed a good place to be viewed by passing gentry and peasant alike. Mr. Humphrey has a room nearby, keeping an eye on the people who stop to look at it, and making himself available to anyone who might know Everly's identity."

Doré looked at the picture displayed in the shop window. Written above the likeness were the words "Do you know this man?" Below, smaller, it said, "Inquire Within."

"I think that's the most foolish thing you've done so far, posting that portrait."

"I plan to leave here with at least some information about the man."

"I only hope, my friend, that these English do not find an excuse to hang you."

"No one is going to know there is any link to me. Mr. Humphrey is well paid."

"I think that should Lord Ridgley or this other man, Lord Moresay, discover that you have killed a man in a duel, your problems will only grow. Perhaps you should tell at least one of them."

Tyson banged on the coach, indicating they should proceed. Bevis called to the horses, but their passage through the busy London streets was agonizingly slow. Tyson gazed out the window at the tenders and peddlers, the richly garbed ladies, the gentlemen, and the commoners who jammed the streets.

"Tyson," Doré pressed. "Should you not confess this duel to the baron?"

"If he is looking for a way to disadvantage me, should I give him more fuel for his fire?"

"And if he finds out?"

"How?"

Doré sighed in frustration and held his tongue. He, too, gazed out the window as they passed through Hyde Park, slowly moving past the busiest shopping district in London near the Exchange. It seemed that they dragged through the crowded streets, and both men were quiet for a long time.

Doré's eyes were caught by one particular woman in the teeming masses. "Magnifique," Doré whispered, amazed. "She should bring her talents to France, where she can be appreciated. Tyson, look at that woman."

Tyson looked briefly and shrugged. "So?"

Doré laughed. "Could you have lain with her for so many years and not recognize her? It is she: the most wonderful whore in all the world."

Tyson regarded the profile of the tall, auburn-haired woman. She was fashionably dressed in a fox-trimmed cloak of pale green, carried a muff, and wore a plumed, wide-brimmed hat. Jewels sparkled at her ears and on the fingers of her uncovered hand. Could she have had any reason for coming to England except to find him?

He never for a second believed that the foppish Michael Everly had been anything to her but a pawn she had used in a deadly game.

"Lenore," Tyson said.

"Do you know the man with her?" Doré asked.

Tyson considered him carefully, though he could not see his face. "I don't think..." He stopped himself and waited as the couple turned to walk away. "Good God."

"Who is it?"

"His name is Charles Latimer," he said slowly. "He is the baron's half-brother."

"Mademoiselle has known many men, but an Englishman related to your bride's father? This is too much?"

"Doré, when you were in Virginia, did my brothers mention what Lenore was doing?"

"It was June and I kept my visit short. She was said to have been somewhat retired, with the gossip about her being most malicious. But I believe she was there."

"I arrived here in April, our voyage a good one at six weeks. If the baron had sent an agent to Richmond to investigate my worth last May when I originally suggested my offer, there would be time for Lenore to have been found and brought to London to be a witness against me. Five months would accommodate a round trip to America."

"Could it have been this brother the baron sent to America?"

"No," Tyson said. "No, I have seen him in England twice since last May."

"Perhaps Mademoiselle Fenton came of her own accord and simply met this man."

"It couldn't be such a neat coincidence. Lenore has never been to England, and Latimer didn't seem to know the first thing about the colonies. His trade has been confined to England as far as I know. He is quite wealthy, but not a world traveler. Lenore would not have known how to seek him out, for though I wrote to my brothers about my business venture, I did not name my partner. Charles Latimer knows that I am invested with the baron, but it is not common knowledge."

"Should we assume that your future father-in-law seeks the aid of his brother?"

"If Lord Ridgley is working to dig up my past with the help of Latimer, their plans for me are more grim than I feared. I have not been pleased with the baron's advantage, but my instincts warn me more against Latimer. And the baron's dislike for his brother seems obvious."

"So, we do not mention this rare sighting, eh? No one knows discretion better than a Frenchman," Doré said. "It is good; you can make use of my help after all."

Tyson looked at his friend. He felt some relief, but at the same time he had not wished to put anyone else in jeopardy.

"No friendship need go so far as this, Doré. I have no way of anticipating the possible risks, for this trouble grows more complex with each day. You may excuse yourself now, with no criticism from me."

"There is more safety in numbers. Now, let us go over the details again, starting with this duel. I'm sure there is something you missed."

"More, it appears, than even I perceived. Fortunately, the ride to Chappington is a long one." He raised a brow and smiled. "You have always envied my association with Mademoiselle Fenton. After we have accomplished this wedding, I suggest that you return to London and renew your acquaintance with her."

"Ah, it is my pleasure to be of help to you, Tyson."

Doré found the Chappington manor to be a most interesting place. It was large and filled with many beautiful and expensive objects. Having visited England many times, he was not surprised by the magnificence of the very old, refined collections that decorated the place. But it was the family to which Tyson would tie himself in marriage that fascinated him most.

The baron was more receptive to his meeting than expected. He seemed gruff by nature, but friendly nonetheless.

"If it is not enough that I allow my daughter to marry an American, his closest friend is French. My neighbors will declare me mad."

"Not if you are careful to remind them, my lord, that your new son and his friend are very, very rich."

There was laughter as all acknowledged that money made friends in an otherwise hostile world. Doré could not help but notice that the baron's temperament strongly resembled that of Tyson's father—a crusty edge covering a soft heart. Doré immediately began to doubt the baron's wickedness.

Paul and Evelyn were a reserved couple who seemed less than worldly, yet noble and amiable. They could endure even a Frenchman, if he was polite and a friend of Tyson's.

But Doré had not been prepared for Vieve, who met him with a charm, warmth, and grace that left him gaping in astonishment. Tyson had prepared his friend for a scheming wench whose calculated plotting had rendered Tyson a victim. He had described her as conscious of her good looks and bent on achieving wealth through her carefully designed seduction of an American guest.

She was beautiful. Although she seemed intelligent, he soon doubted her capacity to seek out and trap one such as Tyson.

In a very short time Doré suspected that this young vixen had caused Tyson to trap himself, for her father was a serious-minded man who kept a careful eye turned to her welfare. Perhaps Tyson was too close and too confused by emotion to draw a more objective conclusion. It is good I am here, Doré thought, to untangle the poor man's mind.

"Now that I've made your acquaintance, I understand my friend's mood much better," Doré told Vieve.

"How so, sir?"

"He has been so out of sorts, so reluctant to share his good fortune with me. It is said, mademoiselle, that you can trust a Parisian with anything but your woman."

The lovely young woman smiled, but her brow was knit in confusion. Doré looked into her eyes and saw that she was not prepared for such flirtation. She was indeed young and guileless. And Doré, with great amusement, reminded himself that Tyson had very little experience with innocence.

He tucked Vieve's hand into the crook of his arm and requested a tour of her beautiful home. As they walked through hallways, sitting rooms, parlors, and galleries, they spoke about the captain. "I suppose you were not prepared to meet someone like Tyson."

"He is not like any other man," Vieve returned.

"Forgive me for such honesty, little *cherie*, but I will warn you that these Americans know very little about being in love. Tyson will even admit he has never been much distracted by women."

"I would have thought there had been many beautiful women in Tyson's life," she said quietly.

"Is that what he told you?"

"No...but... actually, he hasn't told me much about his life before he came here. It's just that... I assumed there must have been many."

"Oh, there have been women, damoiselle, but none like you, I assure you."

"I am not very different from others."

"Mon Dieu, but you're very different from the women Tyson has known." He could not suppress his laughter. "I'm only surprised that you accepted his proposal. You are so young and sweet, and he often behaves like a mean-tempered scoundrel."

Vieve smiled brightly and Doré nearly sighed with envy. "He does have a rough exterior, but monsieur, you've met my father. I am accustomed to such a disposition."

"Had you known Tyson's father," Doré added, "you would be even further astonished. He was very much like Lord Ridgley: gruff, stern, and his outbursts frequent. It is plain that Tyson is destined to be exactly like him."

"He is easily angered," she admitted quietly.

"Ah, *cherie*, you must be patient with him," Doré said soothingly. "Those very traits that make his faults are the same qualities that have made him a rich and powerful man. He is very important in his country; when you join him there as his wife you will be surprised by the deference with which he is treated. He is stubborn and impatient, true, but he is a kind-hearted soul. He behaved as a doting father to the women in his family."

"It is hard to think of Tyson as doting."

"Ah, he is a good merchant trader. He is afraid that if anyone finds out how deeply he cares, he will suffer some expensive disadvantage in the bargaining. He has learned how to cover his soft heart very well."

"You could be describing my father," she said. "I admit, I had some doubts. You make me feel better about him. Thank you."

"Doubts?" Doré questioned. "It is not too late, little petite. Did you ever consider rejecting his proposal?"

She shook her head, and her smile took on a wistful quality. Her eyes were positively aglow. "Not for one moment."

"If he disappoints you, mademoiselle, you must tell me. I am a good friend. I will help you in any way."

Vieve laughed at him. "You flirt like an able courtier, monsieur. I will manage, but I thank you just the same."

Doré shook his head in bemusement. Tyson's family would share his surprise when this little Tory flower joined them in Virginia. Much to his mother's consternation, the only women who had previously interested Tyson had been ones like Lenore Fenton. But Vieve bore no resemblance to Tyson's past preferences.

This little Vieve could trap even a man of Doré's frivolous nature. If it was not enough that she was everything a man could want, she adored Tyson. "I doubt that Tyson is quick to see his fabulous good fortune," Doré said. "But you will give him time."

"I hope, monsieur, to give him many, many years."

Still trembling inside with silent laughter, Doré returned from his tour of Chappington Hall to the drawing room, where all the others were gathered. He was involved in light conversation with Vieve as they entered, and met, as he had expected, Tyson's suspicious frown. It was good to know that he could still read his friend so well. Tyson was actually possessive of this woman, a rare thing indeed. Doré passed Vieve to her intended very quickly and graciously.

"Your friend is a welcome addition, Tyson. He speaks very highly of you."

"I can imagine," Tyson said somewhat testily.

Vieve smiled brightly. "He assures me that you are quite charming, when you have left me to fear your temper."

"And you believed him, I suppose?"

Doré smiled in good humor. "He is afraid, madam, that I will take you away from him. These Americans have always been jealous of the French. We are so much better with the ladies."

Tyson made a mocking bow. "My thanks for the warning. It would please me if you would leave the rest of the revelations for me to share."

"With pleasure, Tyson," Doré returned.

Late in the evening, when Evelyn and Paul and Vieve had all retired and a long discussion with Boris had come to an end, Doré took the liberty of pouring a brandy for himself in the downstairs drawing room. He took the drink with him upstairs to enjoy in the solitude of his room. At the top of the stairs he could see the figure of a man who stood motionless in the hall. As he approached, Tyson turned.

"Are you lost, Tyson?" he asked teasingly, quite certain that he lingered outside the door of his bride's bedroom.

"I'm on my way to bed," Tyson said shortly.

"I thought it was the custom to wait until after the vows. Isn't your room further down the hall?"

"I assure you, monsieur, I can find my room without any help from you."

"You do not seem well, Tyson. Is something wrong?"

"I'm fine," Tyson gritted out.

"Good," Doré said. "Don't despair, my friend. Even the most worldly of men enters marriage with caution. I doubt you will be misunderstood. This confusion and fear, it is normal, I promise you."

"Thank you, Sir Prophet, but I assure you, I am not confused about what I am doing. I have given a dozen explanations to you, and you know quite well what problems have emerged."

"Yes," Doré confirmed. "You do have problems, but I fear you mistake them. You have been so concerned that the woman betrays and uses you, and I think you are wrong. Her father may seek some advantage for her in both business and marriage, but it is a father's quest. And the little one loves you. Make it right with her, if you can."

"You are free with advice for a man who is older than I by one year and has yet to marry."

"I have not married, but I am a connoisseur of women; I pride myself in my ability to judge their worth. I warned you long ago that Mademoiselle Fenton would one day poison your wine and you must see her for what she is; and I warn you now that this little Vieve, this golden flower, has not done what you think she has."

"You have only spent one afternoon in their company, while I have known this family for months."

"Ah, but Tyson, you granted Lenore far too much rope for which to hang you...and you will tie your hands with this woman who deserves your affection. Upon ships and battlefields, you were always the expert, but when it comes to women, I am a quicker judge." Doré shrugged meaningfully. "I know it is difficult for you to trust women, my friend, but do not go too far to abuse yourself."

"Vieve is my problem," Tyson said tersely. "You may acquit yourself of responsibility where she is concerned. I accept your assistance on the other matters."

"Very well," Doré said with a smile. He passed Tyson and went on to his room, turning back toward Tyson when he was well down the hall, finding him still lurking in the shadows in some kind of panicked indecision. "Poor bastard," he said to himself. "This passion does not sit well with him. He is too light of French blood."

Vieve had chosen a pale blue, almost white satin gown to wear for her wedding day. She asked Harriet to arrange her hair in a curled, upswept coiffure that would lend her height and a mature appearance. The satin décolletage was lined with sparkling stones, and a sheer batiste of the same color rose to her throat. The sleeves of the dress were tightly fitted and the waist pinched, which left a long train of ice blue satin to trail behind her. The color gave depth to her eyes, and the style made her appear trim, but generously endowed. As she viewed herself in the mirror, her reflection pleased her.

Vieve was serious, but not in the least grim. Her thoughts had raced well ahead of the afternoon to the future. Tyson had been wise to leave her alone in her father's house for a month. It had taken every moment of that time for her to steady herself for the wedding. She meant to show him, rather than tell him, that she could do him honor as his wife. Her temper was in check and her manners were impeccable. He might be suspicious, angry, short-tempered, and intractable. But he would be hers.

Vieve was fortunate, because in addition to her tenacity and spirit she was also intelligent. She reasoned that a man of Tyson's age, temperament, and experience would have little patience with an adolescent bride. She conceded that such a pose might have made him wary of a life with her.

The wedding took place in the parlor, for only the immediate family and a few special servants attended them. When Lord Ridgley arrived to take her down the stairs, she took a deep breath and reminded herself of her decision to soften Tyson's suspicion with understanding, his temper with docile obedience, his irascible nature with sweet compliance. And soon she hoped to answer his kisses with her own. No matter how long it took, she was determined that one day he would love her as deeply as she loved him.

Her voice was firm as she spoke the vows, and his wedding kiss gave her cause to tremble. During the celebration that followed, wineglasses were kept filled, and the dinner was a delectable repast of roast beef with many side dishes of sweet cakes and pastries. When she could not imbibe another drop of champagne, she let Evelyn urge her away from the table. She paused to briefly kiss Tyson's cheek, hoping that he would perceive this as a gesture of affection and decide, as she had, that they should move ahead in this marriage with some tender feelings for each other. By his frown, she worried that it was going to take a great deal more than a little kiss to soften him into marriage.

Again, she approved her reflection as she posed before the mirror in her bedding gown. The sheer cloth was identical in color to that of her wedding dress and left little to the imagination. When Evelyn unbound her hair and brushed it to a high golden sheen, she stood back to survey her work. "You are even more beautiful now," she sighed. "Are you frightened?"

"No," Vieve said honestly. She had already had the briefest glimmer of the pleasure that could be found in the arms of a lover. In the month that Tyson had been away, he had grown even more desirable in her imagination. While wary of his moods, she was not frightened of his lovemaking. She had considered such intimacy to be one of the benefits of being his wife.

"You will be happy," Evelyn said confidently. "I'll leave you so that he can come."

Vieve bit her lip in sudden apprehension, but smiled for Evelyn. The quilt was drawn back and folded at the foot of the large four-poster, the pillows fluffed at the head of the bed, but Vieve had chosen the stool before her dressing table to wait. When Tyson entered, she rose, and her legs trembled beneath her.

He leisurely viewed her. The nightgown was so transparent that it did no service in concealing her nakedness. He wore an odd look on his face, and his eyes warmed her from her toes to her brow. She was amazed at how the flush crept over her cheeks. She thought she was ready for this.

He smiled as he looked at her. "You are lovely," he said softly. She lowered her gaze, pleased by his appraisal. "We have not shared a private word since I left you. Have you anything to tell me?"

She tilted her head slightly as she looked at him. He began to shrug out of his jacket, tossing it aside to a nearby chair. She said nothing. There were many phrases burning in her mind, but she was afraid to voice any of them. He chuckled at her silence. "Are you with child, my dear?"

"No," she said softly. "Have you been concerned?"

He laughed and began untying his stock as he approached her. He loosened his shirt, and her eyes were drawn to the thick mat of black hair on his chest. "Once I realized my mistake, I denied myself no share of pleasure. I gave you my best."

She felt her cheeks burn with embarrassment. In the face of his candor and experience she felt at a terrible disadvantage. Intimacies shared were enough of a new experience; actually talking about them was too disconcerting.

"I was right. You did not realize it. There are certain techniques I could have employed to forestall pregnancy. I could have withdrawn upon noticing you were intact... but I did not."

Although her face felt on fire, she tried to respond in a way that would give him some reassurance. "I doubt that once is a good test, Tyson. Surely there will be children."

He came to stand close to her. His hand rose as he held her gaze with his. He gently teased her erect nipple with his thumb. "Not too soon, I hope. I have no intention of being the father."

Her eyes widened in surprise. For a moment she thought she had misunderstood. "Is...is there something wrong?"

"Oh-ho," he laughed, not ceasing his casual caress. "I think I have committed enough of myself to this family. Has your father told you the sum? 'Twas fifty thousand, at our last accounting. You have a married name; I made right my act. You will no longer face shame for your sins, and mine have had a weighty cost. Tell me," he said softly, as he continued to stroke her breast. "Did Andrew do this for you?"

Her eyes flared suddenly and she brushed away his hand. She tried to push him away, but he pulled her back, and his commanding tone hushed those curses she would have hurled at him. "Be still," he said. "I do not intend to deny myself all the pleasures I bought."

His touch no longer titillated her desire. She could not have seen how deep his anger had penetrated. She had meant to be a willing bride, but not his willing victim. He held her close against him, and as she looked into his eyes, she saw that he was very pleased with himself. "And what is it you think you bought, Captain?" she taunted.

"A wife," he said with a shrug. "So you will play the wife. But you must go without your pleasures, for though I have no intention of bedding you again, I will not condone adultery in you."

She pulled out of his embrace and retreated. "You are an arrogant fool," she said angrily. "Whatever do you hope to gain with this idiocy?"

"I save my neck and watch my money," he said with a sly smile. His eyes roved over her again. "And I shall enjoy some of the benefits. You have a most alluring body, my sweet."

"Why the devil did you bother to marry me?"

"It was required. I took the prize without payment, but now I have cleared the debt. I refuse to incur any more debt to my name. Tell me, my pet, does marriage still hold the promise you expected?"

"You have some notion to make me pay for your mistake."

"You craved passion," he told her easily. "But more than that, money. Well, your family has my money, but I'm afraid the rapture you hunger for will have to wait. I know that you are hurt and wanting, my little temptress, but I am determined that you shall be denied."

As he spoke, her eyes glittered with white-hot rage. Her hand found a porcelain figure on her dressing table, and she hefted it as though it were a rock. "You think to make me suffer?" she asked loudly. "You know more of this promised passion than I. I have felt no such thing from any man—least of all you."

He threw back his head as if genuinely amused by her denial. "That's hard to imagine, petite, since you appear so willing."

With an insulted cry she fired the porcelain decoration with clear intent to split his skull, but he ducked the piece easily and it crashed against the door.

"You despicable coward," she cried. "You were afraid to test my father's force and now you turn on me. How long before you flee?"

"My investment is large," he said good-naturedly. "I'm certain we shall enjoy many more of these tender moments together."

Her hand found another figure, and with a shriek of outrage, she fired at him again. Again he ducked, his laughter loud.

"My father will..."

"Will find you a most fetching sight, but I fear he will weary of your complaints." She stopped her tirade instantly. "Come, my love, you can find more here to throw, and hearty screams to bring everyone running. Then you may stand in all your naked glory to tell our wedding guests how I punish you by refusing the conjugal bed. I, for one, will watch the scene with amusement."

The shock settled over her as she realized how foolish he meant to make her appear. She whirled around, presenting her back. Her breath came in short, furious huffs, but her throat ached with unshed tears.

"Your father could see me imprisoned or worse for stealing your virtue, but I doubt he can punish me for my poor performance as your stud."

The tears spilled over her lids and ran down her cheeks. She shook her head in wonder. Would she suffer through years of such cruelty?

"I know you had your heart set on passion, *cherie*, but I shall have to disappoint you. Andrew Shelby may have warmed you, but there is no one here to fan the flame."

She stood silent, refusing to add any words as fuel to his hostility. She felt his hands on her upper arms. "What is it, love? Do you feel humiliation?"

She nodded weakly, a sob escaping her. "If that was your intention, Tyson, you have success."

He slowly turned her back to face him. He gently brushed a tear from her cheek, and the look in his eyes was no longer amused. She could read the inner conflict in his eyes. "Do you think your humiliation is nearly equal to mine?" And in a very soft voice, he added, "Do you think you can match me in feelings of embarrassment, fear, and loss? Perhaps you can lend yourself trustingly to marriage, since your father sits below in wait for any cry from your lips...but I? You must consider what has been done to me, love."

"And so you think the only solution is this retaliation?" She raised her chin as proudly as possible when she stood naked, physically and emotionally. "You were wronged, but you add to your mistakes, Tyson. Even now, after you have felt the proof of my virginity, you speak to me as if I am a common whore. And I, your wife." She shook her head sadly. "It is too bad for you."

He lost the anger in his eyes. "Perhaps you will thank me one day, Vieve. My performance with a woman is so much better when there is no noose around my neck."

"You act as if you expect me to argue, m'lord," she said softly. "I assure you, my designs on you are not so well thought out as you accuse. I meant only to be willing and pleasing, but if you prefer your celibate ways, I think you hurt yourself more than me."

He frowned slightly as he looked at her. He gently caressed her neck with his hand. "Go to bed, Vieve," he whispered. "I will join you after I have a drink."

She sought the bed willingly, pulling the quilt over her and turning her back on her husband. He dimmed the room by extinguishing a few candles and helped himself to the liquor kept there for his convenience. Although she lay still and pretended to be sleeping, she was fully aware of the great length of time and the number of drinks he required before he took his place beside her in bed . . . still wearing his trousers.

When the bride and groom had retired, Lord Ridgley moved the wedding guests into the drawing room to continue the party, though on a quieter scale. He served his favorite Madeira to Paul, Evelyn, and Doré. Bevis McCauley had to be encouraged to stay on, for it was the servant's desire to disappear when his master had. But the baron found the manservant amusing, chafing as he did under the weight of formal clothing. And Harriet smothered a yawn, for which the baron teased, "Good Lord, Mrs. Harriet, it's early yet and you've barely gotten a good day's wear out of your best dress. Have a cup of tea at least."

All had been served their requested libations when the sound of a crash was heard from the bridal chamber above them. Bevis slid down into his chair weakly. Harriet's eyes gleamed with the feral intent of a lioness whose cub was threatened, and Paul shot to his feet. Evelyn looked a bit frightened. But Doré smiled knowingly, and it was to Doré that the baron addressed himself.

"You have known the captain for a long while, monsieur. Can you tell my son why he should sit down and relax rather than rush to his sister's aid?"

Doré gave a nod. "You may rest assured that the captain has a high regard for the property of others and will not damage any of the baron's household goods."

"But..."

"I see no need for concern," Lord Ridgley said. He motioned to Paul. "Sit down." He turned again to Doré. "Do you have an interest in trade as well? Perhaps before you leave, the captain and I can..."

The baron was cut off by a shriek and another crash. Again Paul was on his feet, almost indignant now. "Father, I demand that—"

"Sit down, dammit," Lord Ridgley snapped. "Have you seen the size of the man who married my daughter? Surely he has not been reduced to throwing glass objects around the room in a fit of temper. After all these years you ought to know the sounds of Vieve's outrage."

"But what if he is hurting her?"

"He would not dare," Boris told him with assurance.

"Well. .. then...if Vieve is having some tantrum—"

"She has a husband now," Lord Ridgley said with finality. "It is their wedding night. Not everyone is as mild-mannered as you... and least of all, those two upstairs. Now, if the lot of you cannot turn a deaf ear to those sounds, go out for a walk. But no one puts a foot toward the stair."

Paul sat down, although his expression and others around the room were unchanged. Boris considered them only briefly. Harriet, for her many complaints about Vieve, was hell-bent to tear asunder anyone who would lay one finger to the lass's head. Bevis McCauley, although clearly loyal to Tyson from his toes to the top of his shining pate, shrunk into a small figure in his chair, concerned about his master's wisdom in allowing this tirade to proceed in the baron's own house. Paul, who was gentle by nature, could not take the wild sounds, and since Evelyn had never doubted Vieve's spirited nature, her eyes widened with her imagination. But Monsieur Gastión smiled as if he knew what Lord Ridgley knew.

"So, monsieur, before you make a hasty departure, perhaps we can discuss the warehouses and the ships...and entice you into some deal."

"Something tells me, my lord, that you are more clever at making these deals than either Tyson or myself."

Lord Ridgley threw back his head and laughed. "Perhaps I am, at that."

Nine

Tyson rose early and, after a last look at his wife's sleeping form, went down to the dining room. Although the night had been far from restful, he at least felt he was in control again. He frowned at the thought. Such control; an ache in his loins, sultry dreams, and the torment of lying discontented at her side.

But he was decided. It was essential to protect himself from any further designs this family had on using him. With a little luck he could recoup his investment, and, if necessary, even forfeit the money and leave England hastily. He had retreated with due speed on other occasions; he knew the path of escape quite well.

Of course she would come with him, he secretly mused. And in his own time, in his own home, he would make love to her again, but the next time would be right. It would not happen on the ground of an abandoned building, and there would be no mistaking the reasons. He would not be moved by a jealous fit, and he would be assured that her motives had nothing to do with her father's need for money.

He sat at the dining room table and after an astonished look from a breakfast maid, managed to get a cup of coffee. The servants were surprised to see the groom about so early. Disappointed, perhaps...but no one moreso than himself. He resented the fact that his past made him wary of the devices of women, so that he felt it necessary to deny himself one of the greatest pleasures he craved from marriage. *I have earned my suspicions at a high price*, he told himself once more. And his wife's reaction to his cruel taunting had him nearly convinced that she was innocent of schemes, even if her father was not.

"You are about early on the morning after your wedding," Lord Ridgley said when he entered.

Tyson gave a curt nod. "Your daughter fared the night well and is still abed."

Soon Doré pushed open the dining room door and looked at the two. "So many of these foreign customs confuse me," he said with a chuckle. "In France, we do not expect to see the bride or groom for days following the ceremony." He checked eyes with the baron. "But the two of you are both men bent on hard work; I should have expected that you would give no time for pleasure...even on the day after a most beautiful wedding."

Tyson glowered at his friend, but Doré seemed not to notice. Instead he looked at the baron. "You seem a possessive father, my lord. Will you press the company of your daughter and her husband for a generous length of time?"

Boris cleared his throat. "I thought to entice even you to stay, monsieur."

"Ah, you are kind. But there is business in the city that I wish to engage...unless you are hiding some beautiful woman in this hall who has not yet been introduced."

"There is a woman in London who interests you?" Lord Ridgley asked forthrightly.

"Indeed, there is," Doré confirmed. "Tyson, would you lend your coach for my return to the city? I will send your man back to you with due haste."

Tyson peered at his friend. "Immediately?"

"I think it is best not to wait. I can be of more use in London, and you do not need me here. My lord," he said, turning again to the baron. "I do not refuse your offer of business, but perhaps I can postpone my involvement for the time being. I trust we will have another chance to speak of terms."

Boris nodded and rang his bell to hurry the service of breakfast. "I will extend my hospitality to my son-in-law for a while longer," Lord Ridgley said. "If that meets with no objection."

Tyson smiled cynically. "I admit, I have expected your generous invitation, my lord."

Doré did not waste time making his departure. The coach was called, and Bevis, though a bit ragged around the edges from a late and worrisome evening, was soon atop and holding the reins. Doré shook the baron's hand, thanked him for his hospitality, and then turned to Tyson. "I shall make use of a house a friend of mine has acquired in the city. I shouldn't be too difficult to find if you have need of me."

Tyson nodded, knowing that his friend intended to live in his own house and seek out Lenore Fenton. He stood in the circular drive until the coach was out of sight and then turned back toward the manse. The baron waited on the step outside the front door. "So, my lord, how long will you insist upon my residence here?"

Lord Ridgley frowned. "You wear your anger on your breast like a shield, son. For what purpose?"

"My shield, whether of anger or simple prudence, may protect me from yet another thrust of your powerful dagger. You have damaged me twice, through both money and marriage. A third time might be more than I can take."

"You do not give yourself much credit, Tyson. You are stronger than you would have me believe. But, come along with me. You have managed a family home and farmlands for many years. I will show you the ledgers for this estate. Perhaps you will have a few suggestions before you bequeath it to Paul."

Tyson joined the baron on the step. "It is not necessary, my lord. I am content to have the warehouse venture transferred to me."

Lord Ridgley's hand rose to Tyson's shoulder, and his blue eyes hardened. "I should like you to review this holding. Unless you fear you will not understand the simple ledgers."

"How long do you imagine it will take?" Tyson asked impatiently.

"That depends entirely on what you are willing to give to the study of this property. Come now, you are too resistant. I do this as a favor to you."

Once in the baron's study, Tyson was shown the ledgers and left alone with several bound books of figures, maps, contracts, and lists. He became instantly enmeshed in the study of the accounts, for the baron's ciphering and record keeping was even more impeccable than his own. He asked to be served lunch in the baron's study, and later, when Vieve and her father were already in the dining room awaiting him, he found it difficult to leave the work.

"You have kept careful records of your own possessions and, in addition, some of the acquisitions of others in your dominion."

"I have," Lord Ridgley confirmed.

"Your father has invited me to survey the records of this property that was to be yours," he told Vieve.

"Was?" she questioned.

Tyson looked at Lord Ridgley. "We have made an agreement whereby this British soil should more appropriately be joined with Paul's Dumere demesne, since I have land in America."

Vieve looked at her father. "If Chappington is to be Paul's, why do you make Tyson study the property?"

"It is a family business, Vieve. Tyson is of our family now."

She looked between the two men, and her brow wrinkled in some confusion as if she doubted the simplicity of family ties. She finally shrugged and returned her attention to her dinner. Tyson found it odd that she had not been told of this arrangement.

"I am beginning to see why it is preferable that I focus my attention on warehousing and shipping. There is little that can be done in the country."

"In only one day you have seen so much?" Lord Ridgley asked. "You are very apt, Captain, but please, do not make any hasty assumptions. My stable has a few good riding steeds; survey the towns and tenant lands for yourself. The records that you are studying have taken over forty years to compile. Give them a chance to show you the lay of the land with equal opportunity to see it for yourself."

"There is a strong resemblance among your records of estate to those records of trade that I examined a few months ago."

"Yes," the baron said. "It is interesting, is it not?"

"Papa," Vieve questioned, "why do you make Tyson work while he's here? Surely he deserves a rest."

Lord Ridgley smiled at his daughter, but peered askance at Tyson. "Your husband has a strong attraction to hard work, and one day you will appreciate his dedication."

The baron left the study of holdings to Tyson's private perusal, and it was not necessary to question Lord Ridgley, since his work was so meticulously laid out. Tyson took the offer of a good mount and rode the property lines of the Ridgley domain and the Dumere estate. He went so far as to talk to the citizens of the Chappington town, introducing himself as the husband of the baron's daughter. He made the acquaintance of one knight of the realm who paid revenues to the baron and two country squires who likewise had acquired property in Lord Ridgley's titled land. In addition, he rode the perimeters of the property of the baron's half-brother.

Tyson rose early and retired late, but still he was distracted by sharing a bedroom with Vieve. Although she began wearing concealing nightgowns and was most often in bed when he retired and still asleep when he rose, the softness of her beside him at night and the sweet scent of her bath soaps caused him sleeplessness. Many nights he considered taking her in his arms, giving her both comfort and love, but it was the disconcerting information he was finding in the baron's records that was holding him at bay. His shield had not been tough enough, for the baron had found a third way to bind him.

Vieve took quick control of certain wifely tasks, and this did not escape Tyson's notice, though he made no mention of it. When she discovered that he rose early, she began to lay out freshly laundered clothing for him before she went to bed. When she observed that he preferred his bath just after luncheon, he would find his tub steaming and the bedchamber empty at that time. Although Bevis had returned, Vieve took it upon herself to excuse the servant and began to examine his clothing for mending needs herself. She assumed the task of laying out his towels and soap, even going so far as to deliver his boots to the manservant's room over the stable for polishing. When Tyson complimented Bevis on his improved stitchery, he was corrected. "Ain't me, Cap'n. The mum done it."

Though he gave close attention to the baron's accounts, he did see Vieve's comings and goings, but when new and costly stockings replaced well-worn ones, he realized that she had gone to the town to make purchases for him. His initials appeared on new handkerchiefs and on the cuffs of his shirts. His waistcoat was brushed free of lint and hair, his frayed sleeve was darned, his torn pocket repaired.

After ten days of study, he went to his bedroom earlier than usual. She turned from her place at the dressing table, surprised to see him, and, murmuring a quiet good evening, went directly to her coffer to gather a robe to wear over her nightgown. He poured himself a drink and sat down on the settee to watch her brush her hair. His fingers lazily dropped to a white linen in a hoop; her sewing still lay where she had left it. He smiled to himself as he discovered that it was one of his shirts.

"Have I said that I appreciate your wifely talents, madam?"

"No thanks is necessary, Tyson."

"You make poor Bevis look bad."

She turned to face him. "He is not such a good lackey, Tyson. He told me that he much prefers work on shipboard to acting as a manservant."

"You have been in conversation with him?" Tyson asked. "I hope he has not divulged any family secrets."

She smiled at his discomfort. "I think he guards your past at least as well as you do yourself."

"Vieve," he said as she turned away. "Tell me why your father and your uncle do not have much mutual regard. They behave politely, but their hostility is obvious."

"There is not much family love between them, and Father says it has always been thus. They come of different fathers, and Charles's sire was a common tradesman who abandoned them both when Lady Dyana died shortly after Uncle Charles was born. I do not know why my uncle resents my father so, especially since Lord Ridgley was left to parent Charles and see to his rearing."

"Your father's accounting shows a relatively large sum spent over the years to help Charles Latimer establish himself. Does your uncle show any gratitude for this?"

"It is worse than a lack of gratitude," she assured him. "Although Uncle Charles has managed to do quite well for himself, better in fact than my father so far as money goes, he acts as if he has been greatly wronged." Her brow furrowed as she considered this. "I have never understood how my father can continue to welcome him in our home when it is so obvious that Charles is happiest when he can belittle my father and paint him a failure."

"Do you have any idea what your uncle owns?"

"No, but I am told he prospers." She looked at him over her shoulder. "When you appeared with money to invest in Father's warehouses, my uncle nearly collapsed in disappointment. It offends him whenever my father makes a modest gain."

"Yes," Tyson said with a frown, "I have noticed."

There was silence in the room as Vieve finished her grooming and Tyson watched. When she was done, she approached him. "Is there anything you would like me to get for you, Tyson?"

He considered her for a long moment. His brows drew together as he observed the high-collared nightdress, her demure wrapper, and the way she tied her hair back rather than letting it flow freely down her back. It was almost as if she tried to conceal herself from him, and he knew it was the result of the way he had shamed her on their wedding night. He met her eyes and tried to smile. He pulled her hand into his and gently kissed it. "No thank you, my love. Go ahead to bed."

She put out his morning clothes and chose a dimly lit corner to shed her robe. He sat before the hearth in the bedchamber for a long time.

He had told himself she was only a woman, and women need not linger long in his thoughts. He knew full well that her alluring body had wrapped chains around his desires, but he had not anticipated the other ties that would gently bind him. He enjoyed the sight of her graceful footsteps about their common room. He admired her ability to discover his needs even before he had himself. Her manners and actions showed him a glimmer of the loyalty she was capable of, and her gentle compliance promised many years of giving and devotion.

He had thought to satisfy himself with her body, but was stunned to realize that he wished more from her. The musical lilt of her laughter, which came less frequently now, teased his memory. The soft sound of her voice as she answered his questions without hesitation, the pride that would not allow her to cower when facing his anger, the dignity with which she bore the insult of a forced marriage wrought of a shabby beginning of their romance, and the way she yielded to his power like finely tempered steel, even when he had never been more cruel—all these things were Vieve. Here was a woman, despite the many problems that had assailed them, who could stand strong and faithful at his side, serving him as wife, lover... and even friend.

He suddenly wished that he had not cruelly rejected all those possibilities on their wedding night when she had been eager for his touch. He had lashed out at her when it was the baron who deserved his anger. But there was time ahead when he could be alone with Vieve. With that thought, he joined her in the bed and again rose before her in the morning to breakfast in the dining room.

Lord Ridgley was up, as was his custom, and as Tyson joined him, he called for the captain's breakfast.

"I need not spend any more time with your accounts, my lord."

"Good," Lord Ridgley said. "Were you impressed with my record keeping?"

"Oh, yes, my lord. As well you knew I would be. I must say, my worst fears did not prepare me for what you have obviously intended from the first. I thought I was being rooked, but I did not see the full load you wished to have me carry on your behalf. Tell me, what will you do to me if I refuse?"

Lord Ridgley frowned. "I don't know how households are managed in your country, Captain, but in mine we are careful to keep our accounting private. It is dangerous to tempt a servant with any exciting information." Their eyes met, and they stared at each other for a moment. "Finish your breakfast and we will go for a ride."

Tyson let the baron lead the way, riding with him over the rolling hills, past the ancient trees, across the countryside that composed Chappington. Although Tyson had surveyed the land, he had not ridden to the top of the hill that the baron chose to ride toward. The sky was a deep blue, and the sun shone brightly on the fall day. The fields were either brown or barren, the trees dulled to their winter hues of brown, orange, yellow, and red, and the air brisk and revitalizing. As the baron reached the top of the hill, he dismounted.

Lord Ridgley turned full circle in his appraisal of his land. The neat little town with one road running through it and fields behind it stood to the north. Chappington Hall was to the east, the old keep to the west, and to the south was the coast. The rocky coast was out of sight, but far into the distance where the sky seemed to reach the ground there was a slight haze that was the ocean. "Can you look at all this and deny the beauty of it?" the baron asked.

Tyson's jaw felt tight. "I concede its beauty, my lord, but I am hard set to know why you chose me as the man to trap."

Lord Ridgley sighed. "Tyson, I am not so clever as you think. I did not seek you out for this, but had you known what your generous investment would mean, you might have declined. I am an old man; I will not live much longer. My brother had almost ruined me and I was close to defeat. Your money made the difference."

Tyson laughed bitterly. "Oh, what a difference. Your records are good, my lord. Your brother has run off and bought out most of your neighbors, including the land surrounding your own son's newly acquired estate. He has profited from every accident that occurred; I think you believe he had the warehouses burned. He was damn close to wiping you out completely. Why haven't you had him arrested?"

"I have no proof. He may keep some record of payments to scoundrels for illegal acts, but you may rest assured, he does not let me survey his accounts. It is not illegal to have money and to buy property."

"But your own brother must pay the majority of your revenues."

"Two squires and a knight pay me on behalf of tenants. Charles thinks he is clever to have these agents and that I don't know who the real owner is. But the countryside is poor. The tenants have their own problems with fires, death among the people and livestock, meager harvests. And I can only go to the tenants themselves for rents and revenues; the law protects the owner of the farmlands from paying revenues from his other businesses. In addition, a ship and two warehouses have been lost. Thus, my misfortune has been crafted by my own brother."

"Why do you stand for it?"

"How do I stop him?"

Tyson smiled cynically. "Do not play me for a fool. I know you have a plan. What does he want?"

"My title," Boris sighed. "My lands, my life, my comeuppance."

"Why?"

"He sees himself as greatly abused; our mother died, his father absconded with whatever movable wealth he could carry, and Charles was dependent on me for everything. He has always hated me for that."

"Jealousy? It can't be as simple as that."

"Perhaps it is my fault. I was sixteen when our mother died, and though I thought I was doing my best, I did harbor great anger at what had befallen me. My entrance into noble circles was marred by the gossip of my noble mother who, once widowed, began an alliance with a carpenter, drawing him into her home and giving him a son. My mother was forty years old, Charles's father was twenty. The man did not even stay long enough to see my mother buried. I suppose I let my resentment show to the boy, for he was alone to bear the insult and the pain it brought me.

"But I spared nothing to see him do well. True, I have denied him the one thing which he felt was his due. He wished to be my heir, to become the baron of Chappington, but I reserved that for Paul."

"How long have these thefts and accidents been taking place?"

"I have suspected him for fifteen years. As I grew older and nearer death, Charles became bolder in his assaults. I am quite sure that he has done me harm during the past two years."

"Does Paul know the extent of this?" Tyson asked.

"He only knows that his uncle prospers as our own wealth declines. I had planned to tell Paul that I thought Charles responsible for many of our miseries, but then you arrived with money to invest."

Tyson laughed at the irony of it all. "Yes, and my arrival and my money did its part to throw Charles Latimer's great design into the gutter. I arrived when your brother was nearly in control of you."

"And now," the baron said, "he will either cease in his plan to destroy me, or he will forge ahead."

Tyson looked at the baron with cold eyes. "He moves ahead, my lord. Your brother has already been hard at work looking for my weaknesses. I saw no need to mention it earlier, but there was even a fire deliberately set on my ship."

Boris raised his brows, but chuckled ruefully. "Somehow, that is more what I expected."

"You are amused? Had I invested with anyone else I would not be required to end a long family feud to save the sum. You did nothing to warn me, you did nothing to caution me, but pulled me into your crisis with much malice. Just what is it you expect me to do?"

"Beat him for me," Lord Ridgley replied easily. "I know you are clever enough. Charles must have records, and now that someone has come from America to save my family, he will become careless and desperate. Spy. Cheat. Set him up for the fall."

"Why have you not used the talents of your own son to help you with this problem?"

"Paul may have the heart for such a battle, but he has neither the money nor the diligence."

"And so it must be me?"

"I took a careful look at you, Captain. You are capable of dealing with Latimer. You have enough devious enterprise of your own, and you have the money to push him over the edge."

"You tricked me. You purposely put me between you and your brother; you laid your demise on my head and had me buy into both a family and a business proposition where I had no chance for profit or even survival unless I won a battle that has plagued you for over forty years."

"There is trouble," the baron agreed, "but there is also reward. Once Charles is stopped, there is plenty to enjoy."

"By God, you have no damned conscience about it. The minute you had my money, you used all the available force at hand to lock me into your bitter war. You could have exercised some honor and told me beforehand."

"I am an old man," the baron said. "I could not take the chance that you would refuse."

"And so adding to my disadvantage, you forced me into marriage with your daughter."

"Vieve knows nothing about this," Lord Ridgley said hotly. "I backed you into my family troubles through the warehouse investment. Your marriage to my daughter is another issue."

"Does it matter to you that I have my own family to be concerned about? What the devil made you think you could use me to this degree?"

"The way you looked at my daughter made me think so," the baron shouted. "I was not too old to see the naked lust in your eyes. Nor am I a fool to give her to any man. Prove yourself worthy of her and you will have many good years." Lord Ridgley smiled into Tyson's glowering eyes. "You are put out by this arrangement, eh? With whom did you think you were dealing?

Some dribbling old man who couldn't wait to gift you with four ships and two large warehouses and a beautiful woman to boot? You want it all? Then get it. You will find a way." The baron rocked on his heels as he looked out over his threatened demesne. "You know the price. You know the villain you fight, and if you don't know the reward, you have not opened your damn fool eyes."

Tyson's fists were clenched at his sides, his fury was so great. He seethed with the knowledge that Latimer was already busily plotting against him and had gone as far as America to find his vulnerability. The careful records had shown Charles's intention to destroy Lord Ridgley; now he would have to remove Tyson to have a clear path to the baron. To fail to help the baron would cost him everything, including Vieve.

"It would have been wise to resist the warehouse temptation," Tyson said. "Then your daughter's wily seductions would not have cost me so much."

Boris whirled in sudden anger, his fists tensed. Tyson laughed at the old man's distress. "Oh, your price on the rebuilding of storage space was good, and your commission on four ships was enticing, but it was your daughter's beckoning lips and rosy breasts that sealed the deal." He laughed again at the stormy look on the baron's face. "I might have fled after my first taste if not for the grand sum I..."

Tyson's head exploded in sudden pain as the baron's fist met his cheek. The strength of the blow sent him reeling hack into a heap in the tall grass.

"Get up and fight, you worthless son of a bitch," Lord Ridgley growled.

Tyson touched his eye, feeling the rising welt of a bruise, and finding blood on his fingers. "My lord, I..."

"That is my daughter you speak of. I have stood for much from you, but to malign her goodness is too much. Had I known you were a complete fool, I'd have had you killed for touching her. Now get up or name yourself a coward, you miserable jackass."

Even through the baron's waistcoat Tyson could see the rippling of muscles in the old man's arms. The fist that had struck him was already swollen with a bruise, and by the look in the baron's eyes, there was more from where that had come. Tyson did not move. He was not about to fight a tired and desperate old man. He had pushed the baron past the point of pride, and this he regretted.

"I don't give a bloody damn what you think of me, Captain," Lord Ridgley growled. "Refuse this nasty business if you like; I don't need you. I may be old, but I have a little time. Just know this," he said, gesturing to the vastness of his holdings. "I treasure what my parents passed on to me, but I value my children more. If you ever hurt my daughter, I will hunt you down and kill you."

That said, the baron mounted his horse and gave a quick heel to the beast. By the time Tyson rose and held the reins of his own mount, he could see the baron's dust on the road toward the hall. Tyson winced as he touched his cheekbone below his eye. "By damn," he cursed. "He must have been hell to tangle with in his younger days."

Vieve found it hard to relax with her sewing. She had been sitting mending her husband's shirt in the parlor when her father had stormed into the hall in mid-morning. He wore a furious glower on his face and was muttering curses that bore her husband's name.

"Papa, what is it?" she had asked in surprise.

"Leave me be, girl," he snapped, going immediately to his study and slamming the door. When Vieve inquired of servants and stable hands, she learned that her father and husband had ridden out together, but had not returned with one another. She found herself pacing between parlor, foyer, and back hall, waiting for Tyson to appear.

By afternoon, he was still absent. His bath stood cooled and unused, and he was not present for either the midday meal or dinner. As Vieve picked at her food that evening, she noticed that her father's knuckles were bruised and swollen. "Father," she asked suspiciously, "what happened to your hand?"

He glanced at it abstractly, then back to his plate. "An accident in the stable," he grumbled.

Vieve put down her knife. "Father, did you have a disagreement with Tyson?"

"Minor. Nothing to worry about."

"Did you fight with him?" she pressed.

"Why would I be fool enough to fight with a young man of his obvious strength?"

Vieve frowned her displeasure, knowing better than anyone her father's temperament. "Will he return?"

"You will be better off if he doesn't," he snapped.

"Papa, if you've..."

"Leave me be," Lord Ridgley demanded. "I am finished with the self-centered whims of that young man," he ranted. "Always thinking of his personal wants. If he is the simpleminded whelp to flee because responsibility is too much for him, let him go. No one gives a damn—least of all me."

"Father," she said sharply. "If you have insulted my husband and driven him away, I doubt I can easily forgive you."

Lord Ridgley glared at her for a moment before he rose and left the dining room. She heard the door to his study slam shut, and with a sigh she finished her dinner alone.

When she heard the foyer clock strike eight, she retired to her room. She sent for Bevis to stoke her fire. She pulled her shawl tightly around her and stood quietly aside as the manservant entered with fresh firewood.

"My husband has not returned from his ride," she said softly.

Bevis shrugged. "Ain't unusual fer the cap'n to take a spell away, mum. He does that sometimes when he aims t' think 'bout some problem."

"I have been afraid that he has gone for good and all," she whispered.

Bevis shook his head. "I wouldn't worry, mum. The cap'n's a little foolish sometimes, but he ain't a fool. 'E'll come 'round."

She nodded and gave him a little smile of thanks, and when the servant had gone, she donned her nightgown and wrapper. She sat before the flaming hearth with her sewing, but the needle and thread never touched the worn shirt. At times she held the linen to her face to breathe in his lingering scent. Two hours passed before she heard footsteps on the stair and looked toward the bedroom door in apprehension.

The grime of a long day's ride showed on his clothes. His growth of dark beard cast a shadow on his face, and his hair was tousled. She smiled as he entered, but the smile gave way to a worried frown when she noticed the purple bruise around his eye. She rose to approach him. "Tyson? What happened?"

He ducked away from her close scrutiny with a mumbled curse. "A loosened board in the stable," he grumbled.

"I was worried about you," she told him.

"You needn't be worried, madam. I am not likely to report my whereabouts to you; I have been my own steward long enough."

"I didn't mean to imply that I expected..."

"I missed my bath and roused Bevis to fill the tub. You needn't let my altered schedule disturb your routine; after he has gone, you may retire if you like."

He stalked past her toward his trunk and began to remove his waistcoat. She sighed and went to stand behind him, taking the shoulders of the coat to help him out of it. "My routine is not so important as your injury. Does it pain you?"

"Not so much as it pains my mood," he threw over his shoulder.

"Let me see," she gently urged, turning him around to face her. She looked up at the split skin under his eye. She gently touched the bruised area with a delicate finger, but even her light touch caused him to wince. "Well," she sighed, "I see he has not lost his touch." The door creaked slowly open as Bevis cautiously entered with two buckets from the cookery fires. "I will get you something to put on the wound," she said, extracting herself from the bedroom.

Vieve went to the kitchen in search of the salve and cloths that the cook used for her own cuts and burns, but she lingered long downstairs, giving Tyson the privacy he needed for his bath. She filled a tray with meats and breads left from the evening meal and wisely included a large snifter of brandy to assuage his aching disposition. She carried the heavy load to her bedroom.

He was leaning back in the tub, easing his tensions from the long day when she entered. As she came closer she was relieved to see that the water was clouded from soap and the grime of his day astride, so as not to injure her delicate sensibilities. Albeit no longer a virgin, Vieve had yet to see a totally naked man.

She put the tray on a nearby table and approached the tub, folding back the sleeves of her wrapper. He raised his brows in question, but made no protest as she leaned toward him. "My father is stubborn, Tyson," she said without looking at him. She picked up a cloth from her tray and, dipping it in his bath, bent to the chore of cleaning the dirt from around the cut. He winced away, but she used a soft and commanding tone. "Let me," she said sternly. "It will only get worse if you don't have it tended."

She turned away and returned with a bit of the salve on her fingers. "Try not to be too hard on my father, Tyson. He means well, truly, but he is proud and he ruffles easily when his plans go awry."

"He told you that he struck me?"

"Of course not. In fact, he met with the same loose board in the stable that injured you. But when my father comes growling into the house with an injured fist, and my husband, in an equally poor mood, sports a nasty black eye, it does not require a great mind to see what has transpired." She leaned away from him after the salve was spread. "I doubt you deserved it, Tyson, and I make no excuse for my father, but he is worried about many things and is not very patient."

"Do you know what worries him, madam?" Tyson asked tersely.

She shrugged. "I know that he wishes to do well by your investment. And when Lord Dumere passed away, Father began to fret about his own time that is left. I don't like to think of ever losing him...but he is right." And very softly she added, "I suppose I can't expect him to live forever."

Tyson turned away from the sad look in her eyes and raised the sponge to scrub the dirt from his shoulders and arms. Then he moved in the tub to wet his hair and began to lather his head with a bar of soap. When he sat upright again, Vieve was ready to pour more hot water from a hearth kettle into his tub. He watched her with interest, sighing in appreciation as the hot water soothed his aching body. Then her hand stretched toward him with the brandy snifter. He raised a brow in question, but accepted the libation, taking a hearty gulp. She withdrew again to fetch a linen towel and placed it near his tub.

"Your ministrations are welcome, Vieve. You act the wife as if you've been well trained."

"Despite the many accusations to the contrary, Tyson, I have wished to be a wife, and not the many other possibilities to which you've alluded."

He laughed good-naturedly, for his injury, his exhaustion, and his mood had begun to ease. "Touché."

"There is food when you are finished washing."

"I admit, my appetite has returned. You may seek your bed, if you desire, for tomorrow will be a full day. We journey to London."

"We?" she asked in surprise.

"You and I. As soon as you can be ready, we will leave."

"Does Father..." She stopped her question before she asked it.

"I have not asked him for permission, nor will he accompany us. I think, however, he will allow this." He smiled at her. "That is, if you can find it in your heart to tell the baron that you do not fear to live outside of his protection."

She considered what terrible strife existed between her husband and father, but decided that it was not hers to work out. She would refuse either side. Somehow she intended to be sure these men knew she loved them both. However, they were equally stubborn. She braced herself to exercise patience.

She bent to place a wifely kiss on Tyson's brow. "Thank you for not hurting him, Tyson," she said softly. And then she withdrew to the dark side of the four-poster so that when he rose from the tub she would not be close at hand to view his nakedness.

It was a very long time before Tyson joined her in the bed. She had begun to drift into sleep but roused slightly as she felt the bed dip with his added weight. She huddled deeper under the folds of the quilt, sighing sleepily, feeling his presence close by. A strange motion caught her attention, and she became aware that he gently stroked her hair. She was still, as if asleep, while his hand gently caressed her freed tresses.

"Oh, Vieve," he sighed. "Did you fool me, or am I just a fool?"

Boris Ridgley stood on the landing in front of Chappington Hall and watched the loading of both the coach and an extra cart. His hands were plunged into his pockets as he regarded this hastily arranged retinue. The maid, Harriet, emerged from the house garbed in a heavy wool coat, a small black hat over her graying locks, and carrying two hatboxes and a small bag. "Here, missus," he said. "Let me get that for you."

"Never mind, m'lord. I'll manage. London," she snorted. "Wet. Cold. Stinking gutters." She hobbled down the steps toward the coach, allowing Bevis to take her parcels. She lumbered up on the stool to throw herself into the coach. Boris's shoulders shook with laughter.

A final trunk was added to the cart, making it ten large parcels that had been packed for the journey. He doubted that one simple shawl remained in his daughter's room. He mused on the loneliness of the winter.

Vieve came onto the landing and paused before her father. She wore a tailored coat of deep blue wool edged with mink around the collar and sleeves. Her golden hair was neatly tucked under a hat of the same fur, and her eyes were a deeper sapphire than a summer sky. She rose on her toes to kiss his cheek.

"You are certain you wish to go with him?" he asked gruffly.

She nodded and her eyes misted slightly. "It is not so far. You will visit."

"Not very soon. I have pushed him far enough. You need some time alone with your husband."

"I could as well abide two angry old mules," she assured him.

"Go ahead, child," he said, feeling his voice catch slightly. He was amazed at how his own eyes watered at her departure.

"Take very special care, Papa," she whispered.

The door from the manse opened as the very last traveler emerged. Vieve moved quickly toward the coach. She inspected the stacked trunks herself and stood quietly talking to Bevis.

Lord Ridgley looked at his son-in-law. Tyson stood a head taller than the baron, but appeared somewhat humbled. "One demand made of me during my upbringing was respect for my elders, my lord. I would withdraw the words uttered in anger."

"Someone likely told you to treat an old coot gently," Lord Ridgley replied good-naturedly.

Tyson laughed. He winced and touched his delicate cheek. "Aye, my lord. I can see I was given." He held out his hand to shake the baron's. "I will send word on my progress."

"Take care of her, Tyson. That is the most important thing."

"All will be well."

The baron grasped Tyson's hands in a solid grip. "I, too, would withdraw the insults. Do not judge me too harshly, son. Old men are oft in a hurry to settle their accounts."

Tyson looked toward his wife. "I cede you are right, my lord. I will reserve judgment until I have seen myself do better than you in as many years." He grew serious. "Have you considered sending Paul and his wife abroad until this is past?"

Lord Ridgley shook his head. "I will tell him of the problems that exist and urge him toward caution, but he is a man with a family now. I don't have much time, Tyson. I cannot continue to coddle my children as if they are babies. I think, sometimes, that those of us who were abandoned through our parents' death and other hardship are better off in the end. We all have to come through the rough to our adulthood." He sighed. "It is not easy, but it is essential."

"Watch carefully," Tyson said. He stepped away from the baron and moved toward his wife. He stopped short as he noticed the heavily laden cart. "Madam, have you packed everything you own?"

She flashed him a smile that would melt the ice around any heart. Lord Ridgley watched her in appreciation. "Yes, Tyson," she said sweetly. And then, blowing her father a kiss, she let Tyson help her into the coach. As Bevis took the reins and gave his horses their start, Tyson leaned out the window and raised a hand in farewell.

Lord Ridgley stood as the solitary watch until the coach was out of sight. When he returned to the house, it seemed suddenly silent and empty. He listened for the familiar sounds of laughter, shouting, arguing—the sounds of living. His children were married and gone.

He went to his study, and he smiled. He was confident of the future for the first time in many years. He complimented himself on his cleverness.

Ten

Lenore Fenton had been three weeks in London. She had quite enjoyed the time since Mr. Charles Latimer became her benefactor and she resided on his account. Additionally, there was a stipend provided so that she would not suffer boredom. She had one hired woman, Clarissa, retained a large and comfortable upstairs apartment of rooms, and frequented supper taverns in the evenings and the Exchange, coffeehouses, and the theatre in the afternoons. She had made a few acquaintances, had male escorts on occasion, and found the diversions in this old city to be very pleasurable. All this was provided because Lenore had convinced Mr. Latimer's representative that she had information about Tyson Gervais that would be useful in putting him at a disadvantage.

The agent had arrived in Virginia in July. He had come on the false pretense of buying a surplus of harvested goods for shipment to foreign ports and was immediately directed to the richest plantations surrounding Richmond. In investigating their solvency, he discovered that the gossip about the Gervais family was still hot. Lenore was easy to find.

The late spring and early summer had been dreary for Lenore, for since the duel even the most tenacious of her male friends were reluctant to continue the acquaintance. She had suffered a great deal. Being cut off by the women was never much of a problem for her, but abandonment by the men was more than she could bear. Had she been totally ignored by all men it might have been even better, for her reputation had worsened and the low-class mongrels from Richmond began to presume upon her for favors. Never had she been so humiliated as to judge the poor quality of men who bothered to knock at her door. Whereas she had once been courted by plantation owners, bankers, business-men, and the like, she began to have visits from overseers, common hands, and apprentices, and even the scurvy likes of shiphands and dock workers.

When she realized the agent from England was looking for a way to best Tyson Gervais in a business venture, she used coy negotiations to get a good return on her information about him. And when he offered the trip to London, where she would not only be a pampered guest, but would see Tyson once again, she jumped at the chance. Lenore was careful to assure Mr. Latimer's representative that Tyson had used his obvious advantage with firearms in a duel in which an Englishman was killed, and which she had witnessed.

Lenore was a social creature and did not spend much time alone in her apartments. If there was no new acquaintance calling on her, she took Clarissa with her to the shops and coffeehouses. In London, unlike Richmond, women of quality did not venture out alone... and Lenore meant to be regarded as a dame of gentry in this city, at least by daylight.

On this particular October afternoon, the sun was bright and the air was cool, and Lenore was examining imported laces displayed by an outdoor vendor.

"Ah, Mademoiselle Fenton."

She turned, and to her complete astonishment a very handsome man was standing behind her. She smiled flirtatiously, but her eyes held some confusion.

"I am hurt that you do not remember me, mademoiselle. I am Monsieur Doré Gastión...we have met on two occasions in Virginia. My friend is Tyson Gervais."

"Of course, monsieur. Yes, I remember you now."

"It is such a pleasure to see you again, *cherie*. Certainly you are here because of Tyson."

"Because of..."

"He sent you letters, of course. But does he know you have come? Ah, he will be so relieved. It will mean the world to him."

Lenore frowned in genuine confusion. She had no idea what the man was talking about. "I have not heard from Tyson," she said carefully. "I have no idea where he is."

"Mon Dieu, that cannot be so. He is here, but he told me that he wrote to you. Several long letters went to Virginia; he was sending them on every packet bound for America. But you received none?"

"When did he say he wrote them?"

"He was not specific, mademoiselle, but he did admit that he was feeling a ruinous anger when he left Virginia, and it took him a bit of sea travel and time to think to realize his dreadful mistake. You know Tyson so well, *cherie*. You understand much of his temper and jealousy."

"Jealousy?"

Doré laughed and shook his head. "Ah, he was enraged that you had found another to replace him...and then there was a duel? Poor Tyson. He is so bullheaded. His anger often seeks those he loves the best."

Lenore stiffened slightly, and her mouth was firmly set. "Monsieur, surely you have misunderstood Tyson. There would have been no duel had he made right his affections, and he was most determined to cast me aside when he left the country."

"Who is to say when the man finally came to his senses? What he told me not a fortnight past is that he realized he had made a terrible mistake in not marrying you when he had the chance and wrote his explanation and apology in many missives to you. Clearly he loves you, *cherie*. When I saw you, I assumed you had returned to him."

Lenore raised her eyebrows, wondering if there were several long, loving letters awaiting her in Richmond. It was difficult to comprehend. He had been cruel in his rejection, and she had come all this way to enjoy the spectacle of his downfall. "If he realized his mistake, why did he not return?"

"He is in terrible trouble, *cherie*. He is virtually a prisoner in this city, trapped by a crafty old baron."

Lenore crossed her arms over her chest. "It is hard to picture Tyson as trapped," she said almost angrily. "I cannot imagine him standing for any maltreatment. If he chose, he would hop a ship bound to any port and get passage behind him."

"Yes, this he could do. But the complications would be many and so long enduring. He would lose all the money in the world and would have nothing to spend upon his return to Virginia...and, in addition to that, he has been forced into a marriage he does not desire. Tyson does not flee because he has a plan both to free himself from the marriage and have his money returned. You know that Tyson is too proud to go home to Virginia a poor man and unable to marry you."

"Marriage to whom?"

"It is a long story, *cherie*, but if you wish, I will explain. Shall we go someplace where we can talk?"

"Indeed we must talk, monsieur. I must hear all these details at once."

Doré smiled and tucked her hand into the crook of his arm. "Come, *cherie*. I will explain for my friend and later I can tell him that I've seen you. He must not know you are here, but he will be so happy to learn this. I am certain that we can be of help to him."

Mr. Humphrey occupied a modest two rooms above a tailor shop. Part of his rent paid for one meal a day with the tailor's family, free cleaning of his room, and a window that overlooked the street. He had seen many people pass by the picture the American captain had told him to post. He had had many inquiries, since great curiosity was stirred by the idea of such a search. Mr. Humphrey had learned to trust his instincts to discern the motives of those who asked. Sometimes he replied that the man was due a reward, and sometimes that the man owed a debt. But since he had very little information about the purpose of the search, he could not reveal much.

The likeness had been posted for almost a month, and Mr. Humphrey had not yet talked to anyone who he thought had legitimate information. Captain Gervais had told him that the man had been a visitor in America. Then he had disclosed, "I fear he will not come forward himself, but I would like to find some family member or acquaintance of his. Find out what you can whenever anyone inquires, but take great care never to reveal that it is I who wishes to know." Humphrey began to suspect a crime, a debt, an adultery, or other such intrigue.

One afternoon when he heard a light, hesitant knocking at his door, he found a nervous young woman standing there. She was poorly garbed in peasant wool of dull gray and brown, and the shawl that covered her head had been chewed by vermin and was badly frayed. His first reaction was to pity her and wonder if she was cold. He urged her within to warm herself by the hearth.

"I am curious about the picture you have displayed." She twisted her hands uneasily. "Is the man...in some kind of... trouble?"

Mr. Humphrey smiled kindly. "Indeed no, madam. But his family is being sought. Do you know him?"

"The face is very familiar to me," she said quietly.

"Can you place a name to the face?"

"Do you have a name, sir?" she asked in return, as if unwilling to venture any further with her information.

Mr. Humphrey thought very carefully. He was not about to let a legitimate possibility get away from him. He had been at this job for the captain for a long time already, knocking on many London doors before the picture was drawn. "I'm afraid I have only a first name. Michael. Does that help you?"

Recognition darkened her eyes, and she flinched slightly. Then, realizing her reaction, she collected herself. "I can say nothing more until I know why you are looking for him."

"Sit down, madam," Mr. Humphrey urged, hopeful that his reward was finally close at hand. This woman was the first to actually react to the likeness. Surely there was something to it. "Let me get you a warm drink from the proprietress and talk with you awhile. I assure you, the man's family and friends need not fear any trouble. My employer only wishes to know a few things about him."

It took a great deal of patient coaxing and two warmed cups of goat's milk to relax the young woman enough to reveal that the man called Michael was her husband. He was an actor, she hesitantly explained. He had secured two seasons at the royal theatre. Then his troupe had gone abroad to America, where it was rumored there was a great need and rich pay.

"As I was carrying our firstborn, I could not travel with him. But he has been away now nearly two years, and there has been no word."

"And you have no income, madam, for you and your child?"

"I was once a player on the stage," she said, a certain brightness glowing behind her tired eyes. "I am a charwoman now, since I must care for my daughter."

"You must have been a very good actress," Mr. Humphrey assured her. "Your speech is sharp and refined."

"I cannot play in the theatre and support my child."

"Why did you fear that the man might be in some trouble?"

The woman hung her head. "Although I loved my husband deeply when I married him, sir, it was not long before I realized that he was more than an actor on the stage. He chose to act his way through life. He seldom told the truth; in everything he saw a good chance to perform.

"That I was with child was not the reason that I could not go with him," she said. A moment passed before she raised her eyes, and they were moist with emotion. "My husband had chosen another woman to play against his lead. I suppose I must accept that he abandoned his child and myself."

"Surely you are mistaken, madam. How could he leave someone so lovely and sweet?"

She laughed, but it had a hollow sound. "Actors are a very strange sort, sir. I think my husband was the most talented man I ever met. Even though I believed him in everything, now I see that it is possible he never told me the truth."

"His name, madam? Will you tell me?"

"I'm sorry. I have been so afraid that someone would come to me to demand restitution for something he did. His name is Michael Earwhick, though he carried several names for use on the stage: Waverly, Erling, Everly, and Warwick. Is he...in serious trouble?"

"No, madam, he is in no trouble of which I am aware. How can I find you if I am in need of further conversation?"

"I occupy a small room in the residence of the Duchess Dunkirk on Larks Square. 'Tis large, and I earn four hours a week of my own time. You may seek me by asking in the cookery, but I beg, you, do not anger the lady of the hall. Leave word for me in the kitchen to meet with you on only Wednesday afternoon."

"Your name, madam?"

"Mary Earwhick. Late of the theatre," she said with a spark of reminiscence.

"You have already helped me a great deal. And I have been instructed to pay four shillings to the person who has information," he lied.

"Oh, you are so generous. Four shillings is as much as I earn in a month."

"Then I know you will find good use for it," he said, thinking that he should like to see her in a warmer shawl, at the very least. "Perhaps your little daughter has some need."

"She is such a pretty child," the woman said wistfully. "And in spite of what I would have for her, she already shows that she prefers to perform for anyone who will watch."

Mr. Humphrey was taken with the young woman, who he thought would be lovely if her eyes were brightened by hope and her despair wiped away.

At the door she turned to him, and curiosity burned brightly in her eyes. "How does a man retain employment like this? Sitting in a room, waiting for a reply to a picture?"

Mr. Humphrey smiled. "I am a barrister, madam. A clerk in the law often finds that there is an acquired skill for gathering information, and a young barrister needs help in getting a start. I am not too proud to work for honest pay."

"You are wise," she said. "I defied my parents, defied custom, and I have been rewarded for my foolishness."

The ride to London was a two-day affair and included a brief stop at a modest country inn. By the time Vieve reached the city and put her feet on solid ground again, she felt as if her bones still rattled from the jostling of the coach.

The house that Tyson had leased was a beautiful three-story, brown brick, with a handsome carriage house attached to the west wall. A waist-high wrought-iron fence with a gate fronted it, and a stone walk led up to a massive oak front door. From her first sight of it, Vieve thought the house exquisite, and her delight showed on her face.

A large foyer with a marble-laid floor made a rich entry. To the right was a set of double doors, which Tyson opened to display an expensively furnished front parlor; the left a wide and open staircase led up to the second floor. They had only been in the foyer for a moment when Doré appeared at the opposite end, having come from another room on the first floor. He greeted them happily, first shaking Tyson's hand and then bowing elaborately over Vieve's.

"I should have expected to see you here, Monsieur Gastión," Vieve said.

"He did not warn you that I would be here?" Doré asked, looking between the two. "I hope it is no imposition, madam."

"To the contrary, your company is welcome."

Tyson dropped a possessive arm about her shoulder, and she smiled at Doré. While Tyson seemed to trust his friend a great deal, he was always a little more affectionate in front of Doré, as if the Frenchman's flirtations threatened him. "I must speak with Doré, Vieve. May I leave you to investigate the house on your own?"

"Of course," she said. "I will keep busy. I see that it is at least partially furnished, but what about staff? Shall I be looking for servants?"

"The owner left all the furniture, a cook, and one scullery, but I have done nothing more. You have my encouragement to set the place to your usual standards."

Her face brightened with enthusiasm. "I'll see to it," she said. Managing for her father had been simple enough; she had been overseeing the same servants for the past two years. Some of them had been there since her birth. But putting a house to rights for her husband was as exciting a venture for her as she could imagine. If she was able to please him with modest stitchery and a few simple chores, this challenge would surely help her to prove herself.

She did not take the time to look through the rooms on the lower level, for she knew that Bevis would wish to get the trunks and bags unloaded. She asked Harriet to go around to the cookery and find those two aforementioned servants. She herself went to the bedrooms.

At the top of the stairs Vieve stood to look down the long hall. All the doors to various rooms were closed, and she could make no sense of the plan. She began opening doors, finding covered furniture and closed curtains in each room. She pulled draperies back to let the light in and then went back into the hall.

Before her were four large bedchambers; the one farthest from the stair had obviously been claimed by Monsieur Gastión. There were two moderate-sized sitting rooms, one of which was joined to the largest bedroom and had a small veranda that looked out over the top of the carriage-house roof.

The master room had a writing desk, a wide hearth, and a generous wardrobe. The bed was modern and large with a canopy from which hung many yards of deep purple velvet. A bit farther down the hall was a room of humbler size. There was a bed canopied with a sheer white cloth, a dressing table, breakfast table, and one commode. A man and his wife could comfortably occupy the master bedroom, and the other seemed to be just right for an older daughter.

Vieve looked longingly into the largest bedchamber. Two small stools on each side of the four-poster could be used for entry by a man and woman. Twin stuffed chairs with matching hassocks stood before the hearth. It was generous of space, which could even accommodate a dressing table. Though it already appeared furnished for a pair, she was certain she would not be welcomed there.

He seemed pleased with her efforts at wifely servitude, but he'd lain beside her night after night with his trousers on, as if she might assault him in his sleep. She felt a little nearer to his affection than she had on her wedding night, for he was at least kind to her. But after the cruel things he had said about her when she had been willing, she did not dare go even so far as to try to show him her acquiescence. She definitely lacked the courage to have her things placed in the same room with his.

She heard the door open from below and the grunting, shuffling sounds of Bevis laboring up with the first of many trunks and knew she must make the right decision at once. She knew that Tyson had made very few decisions of his own accord. He still felt the rub of her father's insistence, and it was reasonable, she sadly relented, that he wished to protect himself from her family. With a heavy sigh, she decided it was essential that he choose her for his own reasons.

"The master will take this room, Bevis, and I shall use the room with the white lace canopy," she said with a sigh. *Perhaps one day,* she thought, *I will find myself in that wonderful, large bed.* "If you can get the trunks into the right rooms, I'll go to the next flight up and see what there is for you and Harriet."

She found four rooms on the third level that would house the servants, and by the time she returned to the second floor all the trunks were in place. Bevis declined the housing offered and made his preference for the carriage house felt, for it seemed the shiphand-turned-lackey disliked the comforts of a gentleman's home. As for Harriet, she accepted the servants' abode on the third floor, but Vieve reconsidered when judging her woman's age and size and put her on the second floor, next to Monsieur Gastión.

There was much unpacking to do, finding fresh linens for the beds, shaking the dust out of quilts, airing the rooms and then, as quickly, laying a fresh fire in the hearths to warm the chilled rooms. And all this was done with minimal staff, for the scullery could not be found and the cook was struggling to increase the nightly fare from a size that would serve the Frenchman and herself to a meal that would serve six. Tyson would be of no help, for after he had passed only an hour or two with Doré, the two of them excused themselves. They made a quick, parting request for something to be saved for them to eat if they were late.

Vieve took pride in her ability to lay out the rooms and put away her husband's clothing with loving hands. She arranged his soap, brush, shaving strop, polishing cloths, and other grooming tools with care on the floor of his wardrobe and even had Bevis place the brass tub before the hearth, so that Tyson might enjoy a steaming bath before a glowing fire. She was not disappointed when Tyson did not return by the dinner hour and, in fact, was greatly relieved, for she had put all her energy into settling his room. Now she and Harriet together could arrange her belongings. When she had finished and bathed to remove the clinging odor of traveling dust and perspiration, she donned her high-collared wrapper and asked Bevis to lay fresh firewood by the hearths in both Tyson's room and Doré's. She then prepared trays of stew, bread, and wine to place near their hearth fires to welcome them to well-settled bedchambers. She lit tall taper candles to brighten their abodes and surveyed her finished work with pleased exhaustion. She left Tyson's door ajar so that he would have no trouble recognizing his chamber.

Finally, her own room welcomed her. No more did she grieve that he set her apart, for she had done a good day's work toward gaining any small amount of his praise. She rubbed oil of roses on her swollen feet and chafed hands and brushed out her hair. Her legs were sore from hurrying up and down steps, and her eyes were scratchy with sleepiness. She lounged on the daybed before her own hearth and watched the flickering of the flames, though she was more than ready to find her bed. Finally, when the clock below had struck eleven chimes, she heard the door open and men's voices below. She smiled to herself, for there was no possible way he could be displeased with her now.

It was only moments before the door to her room opened and he looked in. Feeling very pleased with herself, she smiled brightly. This was the moment she had waited for all day long. He was surely impressed with her talents and would value her more highly now.

"I see that you are all settled," he said somewhat testily. "You are pleased with this room?"

"Yes, Tyson. Have you been to your room?"

A rueful movement shook his shoulders, and he wore an odd smirk. He entered her room and closed the door, moving to her dressing table, where he toyed with her articles of grooming. "I found my room."

Her eager smile faded as she detected anger in his eyes. "I... I hope it is . . . adequate, Tyson. Is everything all right?"

"What do you think, madam?" he asked with a note of sarcasm.

"I was very careful," she said in confusion, sitting up from her reclined position. "I even brought your dinner to your room when I realized the lateness of the hour."

"The dinner is there, as are my clothes. Are you quite proud of your accomplishment?"

She looked around her room in confusion. She had no idea what she had done wrong. "You are displeased?" she asked, incredulous. Her mistake completely eluded her, and she was a bit too tired to think.

"You have taken a lesser room. Do you have an aversion to sharing one with me?" he asked bluntly.

"No," she said evenly. "I thought the aversion was yours."

"We did well enough at Chappington. How were you disadvantaged in that, madam? Were you accosted, in danger? Is it that you'll take fewer chances now that the baron is not just down the hall to save you?"

"You were very clear, Tyson, that we would not be living as man and wife. I thought you made do with my room at Chappington only because you were not accorded one of your own. I thought you would be pleased."

"You've made your point," he said with irritation. "You were willing enough when the act would buy your marriage and when your father would support my conjugal rights, but now that we are alone in London, you place yourself down the hall and out of my reach."

"But you said that you had no intention..."

"Did it ever occur to you to ask me if I had changed my mind?"

"It certainly did not. I do have some pride."

He threw back his head and laughed loudly. "Pride, is it? You were not too proud before we were wed, nor were you shy on our wedding night... but now it is a matter of pride."

"What is the matter with you?" she asked as she rose from her couch. "You hear the sounds of resistance and forge ahead unchecked. Then it is willing and proper I am and you reject me. Now it appears I have erred again, for you expected me to grovel to you and kindly ask if you have changed your mind. Humph," she finished, crossing her arms over her chest. "You are impossible to please. One would be foolish to try."

"It appears that I am the foolish one, my dear. Over and over again I meet yet more new requirements...raising the price again and again, and yet finding that my payment is never complete. Why don't you just move your prissy butt into my room. Now."

Her mouth tightened in rage. "While 'tis difficult to refuse such loving seduction, Captain," she sneered, "I shall do so when it snows in July."

His face reddened. "Your little games make the chase all good fun, madam, but you will see that I am tired and short-tempered, and in no mood for argument."

"And you think that I have been lying abed the day long, awaiting your pleasure? Go to hell."

"Madam, I am warning you..."

Deeply stung and angry, her hand waved in a gesture of impatience. "Your warnings are all double-edged lies," she ranted loudly. "You must think I'm an addlepated fool. Your whimsy bears much consequence with your changeable moods. You will it this way, then that, then this, then that.... You may change the hands on a clock so easily, Tyson, but my God, I am a person."

He frowned darkly. "Past problems are regrettable, but..."

"Regrettable? Indeed," she nearly shouted. Her anger built up until she thought her hair might catch on fire from the sheer heat of her rage.

"Lower your voice, madam," he urged.

"Why? It pleased you once to hear me rant and shriek. Are you afraid that if everyone comes running tonight, you will look the fool?"

"Vieve..."

"You arrogant moron, it met your mood to take me before there were exchanged words of love or promises, and when wedding vows were made, and I would willingly yield to you, you accused me of tricking you into marriage. When I humbled myself to play the pleasing bride, you called me wanton and would not touch me. And now..." She laughed at him, shaking her head, though tears traveled down her cheeks. "Now I am to know you have changed your mind. Well, so have I."

"Vieve, I..."

"Take your whimsical ways to your celibate chamber, you useless jackanape," she yelled. "A woman is more than the flesh that serves your base needs. You must do more than snap your fingers to have me satisfy your desires."

"You surely test my temper, Vieve. It is not as if I have paid less than my due for what I desire. To the contrary, the gun is forever at my head, and the benefits of this marriage are yet to be seen."

"Perhaps you should not have stolen the benefits first, Captain."

"I have paid for that crime. You are my wife."

"And if I walk down yon hall and yet again seek to please your whimsy, will you once more hold me at arm's length and call me schemer, thief, whore, and tease? Ha. In anger you take me, then cast me aside and mock me, and then seek to take me again. Have you no consideration for a woman's plight?"

"You are mine," he stormed.

"I am your scullery and laundress and seamstress and slave. By what action am I your wife?"

"You have lain with no one but me."

"And you scorned that fact and thrust me away for a route of escape from those very bonds."

"You will be mine again, like it or not."

"I will be no man's without a word of love or a simple promise."

"We shall see," he said, striding toward her.

"Don't you touch me," she screamed.

But he advanced, an ugly scowl on his face. "No, Tyson, no," she said in panic, backing away. He grasped her by the upper arms, and she thought surely she had pushed him too far. But the door to her bedroom slowly opened, and in its frame stood Doré, a serious frown on his face as he watched the scene before him.

"The angry words, my friends, will kindly be held with tight lips, for those of us who hear this terrible fight hold you both dear." The intensity of Doré's blue gaze burned into them both. "Do not make us witnesses to a more brutal event," he said very softly.

Tyson let his breath out slowly and released his wife. He walked past Doré out of the room. In the hall stood Harriet, glowering at him from under her ruffled nightcap. He escaped quickly to the chamber that Vieve had prepared for him and slammed the door.

Without causing Vieve any further embarrassment, Doré softly pulled her door closed. In the hall he stood for a moment, considering what he had heard and seen. Harriet looked at him, her anger still vibrating. "The poor lass worked 'til she near dropped, an' he hasn't a word t'say in the way of thanks. He cares naught fer her, but wants his booty. His lordship did her ill, givin' her to him."

Doré shook his head sadly. He had seen the improvements in his own chamber as a result of Vieve's hard work, and knew that Tyson had made yet another terrible mistake in dealing with his wife. Doré had never before interfered between a wedded man and woman, but this once he knew it was essential.

Tyson was finishing breakfast the next morning when Doré entered the dining room. They eyed each other warily before Doré sighed and pulled out a chair to sit. Tyson leaned back from the table to await the lecture he knew was coming.

"You amaze me, Tyson. I have known you for so many years, and I have seen you behave in a gentle and generous manner to even the lowest lady of the evening. In matters of business you display brilliance which sets you instantly apart from all others. Yet, in the simplest venture of wooing your own wife, you become the rogue bull. Do you not see that if you play a sweet tune for her, she will dance for you?"

Tyson sat mute, looking coldly at his friend. He knew well enough how miserably he had failed with her.

"Have you nothing to say?" Doré asked impatiently.

"Nothing," Tyson said evenly. "Are you finished?"

"It seems you will not listen to reason. You are determined to destroy the one good thing that has come to you."

"You are finished now?" Tyson asked.

"I will say no more," Doré replied with a heavy sigh.

"Good. Excuse me."

He went to his wife's room directly, leaving Doré alone to have his own breakfast. The household had worked so hard on the previous day that the breakfast hour was fairly late, and he assumed his wife's absence from his table meant that she intended to hide herself in her room. He knocked on the door and entered upon her quiet permission.

Vieve sat at a small breakfast table with a cup of tea while Harriet stood within the room folding towels to place in a bedside commode. "Will you excuse us for a moment, missus?" he asked. Still, the woman stood tall and firm until Vieve gestured with a wave of her hand for her to comply. He stood just inside her bedroom door until the woman was gone and the door was shut.

"I apologize for my actions."

She looked at him with red-rimmed eyes.

"I was brutish."

"You were," she confirmed.

"I would not have taken you by force. I was angry, but I have wooed you before, and you know force is not my way."

"Indeed, I know many of your ways...and few of them are within my understanding."

He sighed heavily. "Much has transpired that you do not understand."

"Oh? Are you quite certain of that?"

"Vieve, do you wish to see me beg forgiveness?" he asked tiredly.

"What I wish, Tyson, is the smallest bit of respect. You have had your troubles, and perhaps my father has been too forceful with you, but this is little of my doing and I have tried hard to please you. I cannot help that I never know what to expect."

"You need not fear me, madam. I assure you."

She looked down into her teacup. "That will take time, Tyson. What has passed between us these many weeks since the old keep does not fill me with trust."

Tyson sighed heavily. "You are within your rights to deny me. I admit it is a thorny bed of my own design. You may accomplish your vengeance thusly, if it serves you."

"Vengeance?" she questioned. "Oh, Tyson. How little you know of it. It is hard for me to believe you are so ignorant of women."

"I am a man of business, madam, and coddling the whims of ladies has not been much a fancy of mine. If you find me less than skilled in these courtier's games, it is because I have been more concerned with my work than chasing virgins."

She almost smiled at him, but seeing that he was serious in his explanation, she held her tongue and simply nodded. "I see. I wouldn't have guessed."

"My apology is accepted?"

"I cannot see the wisdom of extending the hostilities."

"Very good. You needn't hide yourself away in your room in fear of my temper. I will see you at dinner."

Vieve nodded, though the corners of her mouth twitched in the temptation to smile. When Tyson left the room there was no need to conceal her amusement.

He was a dichotomy that amazed her. She had seen him forge past her meager protests, or refuse her entirely. She had feared both his rape and his total indifference. She shook her head in wonder at his radical moods. If indeed he wished to have a wife, tender in giving and loving, to share his bed, why did he not simply embrace her with his arms and voice his desires gently?

For the week following their bitter fight, he was cordial at their common table. In the next week he spent time in her room, sharing an evening or mid-morning libation and discussing his home or his business in Virginia. A third week came and he drew closer, displaying little gestures of affection such as an arm casually draped over her shoulders, a light caress of her waist, or a soft hand on her back. In the fourth week she knew for certain that she was being courted, for he had added light, delicate kisses of greeting or good night. But he was cautious. And she was not about to make it any easier for him. There were some mistakes she was not willing to make twice. The next time she was edged toward intimacy with Tyson, she would be certain that the path she traveled was a safe and secure one.

Vieve was delighted by the earnestness with which he moved toward her. She had never had any courtship with this man. He had entered her life so boldly and been pushed to marry her so quickly that there was much missing. She did not know him at all and had only faced either his lust or his anger. There was a great deal more to learn of him. And in these weeks of his amiable courtship, she savored each little part of him that she came to understand.

During the fifth week of his effort, she went with him to some business appointments, dinners, and afternoon soirees. She was impressed to meet the earl of Lemington, a distant cousin of Tyson's. She was able to view the building that was being done on her father's burned warehouses and listened attentively while Tyson spoke to the builders and workers. It was like falling in love with him all over again, for she was finally getting to know all of him.

We came through our knowledge of each other backward, she reasoned. The physical desire they had shared was mutual, spontaneous, and immediate, but they had known nothing of each other. No wonder there had been so many sparks flying.

She saw him perform stubbornly in business, or generously offer an underpaid worker a chance to earn more with additional labor. He was shrewd, but honest in his dealings. He was polite in the company of the English he had met, charming enough to soften the hardened hearts of old dowagers, yet he was no fop, and the men listened respectfully when he spoke. He lost his temper once when a careless carpenter left a loosened board that could cause injury to others, yet patiently explained an error to another worker. When she questioned this action, he explained that the first man had a reputation for being too lazy for the work, while the second was conscientious and rarely made a mistake.

"But how do you know, Tyson?" she had asked.

"It is an employer's business to ask the right questions and get the correct answers. It is simply my obligation to know."

His wisdom, kindness, and dedication warmed her, and she knew that in him was a man she could trust and love for the rest of her life. She could give him the same, but she allowed him to earn that from her, for the one thing he possessed in abundance was a fierce pride. She followed his lead devotedly...and patiently.

Tyson had seen Lenore Fenton several times, and though the meetings were distasteful to him, the bawdy woman was convinced that Tyson needed her help and would reward her in the end with his everlasting love.

Although she betrayed no knowledge of Charles Latimer, she displayed discomfort when questioned about how she came to be in London. Finally, she fell headlong into her own trap. "All right, you tease," she laughed. "It was because of your letters."

Tyson had raised a brow in amusement. "You did receive them?"

"I didn't want to let on. You treated me so shabbily."

Avoiding her bed was delicate, for Lenore expected a great deal more clarification of feelings, but invariably she settled for what Tyson was willing, or not willing, to give.

The day was the tenth of December, and the weather was cold. The warehouse building was going well since the snowfall had been light, and the Latimer family had been settled in their rich London house even before Tyson and Vieve had arrived. Doré used his time equally watching either the Latimer household or Lenore's apartments. They slowly collected information whenever they could, building what they knew about Latimer, his dealings, and his associates.

Tyson was a methodical man. He was well-organized and obsessive about the nature of his work; things were done perfectly according to a well-thought-out plan. He was only just discovering that he was the same in his personal life, for he had cautiously courted his wife for many weeks, each day moving closer to her. Soon he would voice his desires and invite her to share his bed. But he had set much awry with his impatience, at times pursuing her with such clumsiness or anger that he had hurt and frightened her. These actions, he knew, would be wise to correct. Where she struck good sense from his skull, he sought to restore it. He had rushed into her life with the force of a fire-breathing dragon, ultimately punishing her for his own mistakes. She was young and gentle, and he meant to win her not for a night, but forever. His courtship was patient, but inflexible, for he had his eye turned to many years with this woman close at his side.

On this day he had made a special purchase, and he looked at the sky as he approached his house. It was approximately four o'clock in the afternoon. Vieve had developed a pattern of bathing in the late afternoon, before dinner. He smiled as he opened the front door of his house. He grinned broadly as he saw she was not in her usual afternoon seat in the parlor. He mounted the stairs to her bedroom and opened the door without knocking.

So startled was Harriet at this interruption that she gasped in surprise and dropped the dress she was holding. In her tub, Vieve looked over her shoulder and frowned at him. But Tyson did not notice. He stared at Harriet for so long and with such intensity, that she retrieved the dress, spread it on the bed, and fled. He stepped aside as the hefty woman beat a hasty retreat and chuckled as the door was swiftly closed.

He leisurely walked toward the fore end of his wife's tub and smiled down at her. "You shouldn't do such wicked things," she said in a scolding tone. "Since you came into my life you have cost poor Harriet ten years of hers. She has no idea what goes on with us, and I know she worries constantly that you are cruel to me."

He raised a brow and smiled. "That again? Come, my dear, I have been on my very best behavior... for a damn long time."

"I think you send my woman off in a flutter purposely, so that she will think the worst."

He threw back his head and laughed in delighted glee. "Or the best, madam? Come, where is your spirit?"

"I am at my bath, Tyson, and I know you think you should be allowed great liberties, but this is too much. Excuse yourself."

"You are such a spiteful wench when denied your pleasures," he said teasingly. "Be easier on me. I've brought you a present."

"A present?"

"Do you forget your own birthday? Today you mark eight and ten. A woman, some would say."

"That's ridiculous. My birthday is..." She thought for a moment. "It is my birthday. How did you know?"

"I did sign marriage contracts, madam, even though much about our marriage has not been customary. And look, you are wearing the same thing in which you were born."

She ruffled the water with her fingertips, attempting to splash him. "Can we not discuss my birthday another time, m'lord?"

He pulled a chair from near the hearth to take his leisure, sitting down and propping his feet on the end of her tub. "Tell me, my sweet, if you could have anything you wished, what would you claim for your birthday present?"

"Do you pretend that you will bequeath your affection as a birthday present? That is rather arrogant, is it not?"

His eyes gleamed with mischief. "Tell the truth, woman. Is that what you want most?"

She groaned and slid down into the water. "You are the most insufferable man in the world. Did no woman leave your bed disappointed in your talents?"

"Never," he insisted. "But think of something less wonderful for your present." He pulled a long, slender box from inside his jacket and watched with amusement as her eyes took light. He opened it and looked inside.

"Diamonds," she said, the corners of her mouth turning upward.

"Diamonds?" he laughed. "But I have given all my money to your father. You remind me on purpose. You are a vindictive wench."

"Ha. I do not interfere with your bath. Rubies and emeralds then," she said, rather enjoying the game.

Out of the box he drew upward a long string of pearls, gleaming in satiny brilliance, and dangled them before her eyes. "Oh, Tyson," she said breathlessly. "You really did bring me a present. I thought you had come only to taunt me."

"Madam," he said sincerely, rising to lean over and fasten them around her neck. "I assure you, the torment is more mine. I am not naked."

"Tyson, please, let me dry off," she protested.

"The water is their natural habitat. They will be at home. Let me...I have thought of this sight all day long."

He closed the clasp and pulled away. His eyes were drawn to the sight of the pearls, dropping to the top of her milky breasts. He smiled roguishly. "I am too selfish and cannot deny myself the sight of the woman I wed." He stood back, looking down at her. She reached out of her tub to gather her towel. "Please, madam, do not rise. My control is strained enough, and I forget my promises. If you stand now in all your naked glory, I shall be forced to do my part as a husband and end your miserable wanting."

She laughed at his misery. "Oh, please, Captain," she said, lifting the pearls with a finger. "You have been generous enough." She grabbed the towel without exposing any more of herself. "Turn your back then, Tyson."

He turned away as she stepped out of the tub, wrapping the towel about her. "Dress," he instructed, moving toward the door. "Monsieur Gastión and I will take you out. Wear something that will draw attention to the pearls."

"Doré goes with us?" she asked brightly.

He turned back to notice the towel wrapped about her, making her resemble a Greek goddess. "Does that please you, my dear?"

"Greatly," she said. "Should you become brutish, I can trust him to protect me."

He raised both brows in question. "And if I am mannerly?"

"Why, then, Doré will excuse himself. No one knows discretion better than a Parisian."

"Madam, if I did not know better, I would swear you've schemed all this from the very beginning and have the rest of my life laid out in some neat little plan."

"Don't be silly," she laughed.

With a nod of his head, he left her to dress. The moment the door was closed, her lips turned up in a sly smile. "I cannot see my plan for longer than the next ten or twenty years."

Elizabeth Latimer took her morning tea in the breakfast parlor of the London house that was once her father's. She was alone and relished the solitude. Her son, Robert, had already left the house, and her daughters were still abed. Charles, she suspected, was in his study. The only sounds on this morning were those of the servants, quietly performing their duties. The sky was a murky gray, the air was wet and cold, and Elizabeth's mood was equally dour. Ten days would bring Christmas.

Because Elizabeth was quiet by nature and strictly obedient to her husband, everyone tended to believe that she was unaware of what was going on around her. If any unscrupulous dealings existed in her house, she concealed her knowledge behind the mien of a dutiful wife. When she was upset, frightened, or angry, she simply withdrew until the disruptive feelings passed and she felt her quiet control again. This demure and shy posture not only caused people to think she was innocent of any conspiracy, but allowed her a much closer look at the same. Charles, most especially, doubted her capable of passionate feelings, opinions, or actions of any kind.

Elizabeth was thirty-seven years old. For twenty years she had known of her husband's single obsession to best his brother. She was amazed at Lord Ridgley's uncommon longevity and had been convinced that by now the baron would be dead and Charles would be in control of the baron's heirs. She had not foreseen that it would last so long and that her own existence and that of her children would be compromised.

When she had met Charles Latimer, she had been very taken with him. Her father, Silas Markham, had been a wealthy master printer who owned both a rich London home and a country manor northeast of the city. Charles, at twenty-five, had owned his own iron forge and was part owner in a second shop. He was tall, lean, and handsome. Elizabeth, who was demure, plain, and small, adored him.

She was an only child with a rich dowry, and when Charles asked for permission to marry her, Markham refused. He had worked hard and hoped to have had acquired enough to buy his daughter a titled marriage to a nobleman. Six months later, Elizabeth found herself pregnant by Charles Latimer, and the request for her hand was supported by Lord Ridgley. Markham changed his mind, but died before his first grandchild was born. And the passion that had consumed Charles before the wedding began to wane immediately.

With the marriage Charles acquired Markham's lucrative printing business and the deeds on two large houses left to Elizabeth, and this multiplied his wealth very quickly. By the time Charles was thirty years old he held half-interests in a dozen merchant operations. He used his profits to make loans, and when they were not repaid, he added to his acquisitions.

Elizabeth loved him desperately in the early years, but as her devotion yielded to acceptance of a less than perfect marriage, she strived only to keep her family life somewhat stable. She knew about one or two mistresses Charles had kept, and his occasional dalliance with a housemaid, which seemed the route for successful marriage. So long as she and the children were well kept, she could look the other way. Charles was not patient and seldom kind, but he was rich and Elizabeth had almost everything she needed. She had learned to make do without devotion, but she would not live on a farthing less. Most of all, she was determined that her children would have a sound future.

She felt there was little she could do to save Charles, but she would not allow her innocent children to be harmed in the course of their father's obsession.

Robert Latimer was already much aware of his father's unscrupulous plans and chafed at the maltreatment of his mother. Elizabeth had long ago identified the sneer on her firstborn's face when he looked askance at his father, and no amount of reassurance that she was as happy as she wished to be would dissuade Robert's growing hatred. And Faye, at only fifteen, was suffering from a terrible melancholia because she thought herself deeply in love with Andrew Shelby. The happiness and future of two of her three children was already hanging in the balance of Charles's schemes. She desperately wished to see this finally done.

She meant to save herself and her children.

She shook the small crystal bell beside her plate and asked for more tea. She thought her plans through once again in her mind before she asked a maid to see if her husband was at work in the study, and then, bolstering herself, she entered.

"What is it?" he asked impatiently, not looking up from his work.

"If you have time, I should like to speak to you about our daughter."

"Which daughter?"

"Faye."

Charles sighed heavily. "Will it take long?"

"It is important, my dear, but I doubt it is very complex." Elizabeth stood calmly, determined in this request. He had only struck her a few times, and she was no longer afraid of him.

"Very well," he said. "You may sit down, but please be brief. I have a great deal to do."

Elizabeth took the chair he indicated. "When Andrew was visiting our house frequently," she began, "Faye developed a very strong attraction to him. She fancies herself in love with him, and she is inconsolable now that he is gone. She is mature and it is time to secure a husband for her."

"Mature? I had not thought so."

"She has come sick every month for two years, Charles. Soon her body will move her if her heart does not. Have you anyone in mind?"

"Perhaps I will let Shelby have her," Charles said distractedly. "It would save me money. I could give him back his property as Faye's dowry. Do you think that would please her?"

"Yes, Charles. How soon do you think it can be done?"

"A couple of months, as there are other, more pressing matters to which I must attend."

"Is it the American captain? I've heard you say he worries you."

"He is less of a worry every day," he said abruptly. "I have managed to learn a few things about the captain. It seems that before he came here, he killed an Englishman."

"Murder?" she asked.

Charles cleared his throat. "I have made the acquaintance of a very good witness who says that the captain used every advantage. Perhaps in America it would not be conceived as murder, but here?"

Elizabeth's eyes widened in sudden worry. "Does Lord Ridgley know?"

"Even you are smart enough to understand, my dear, that the captain has obviously not told my brother. I will tell Boris when it suits me."

"Does Andrew know?" she asked.

"Andrew does not seem inclined to pay much attention... but perhaps he knows. It is unimportant."

"But if Andrew is truly interested in marrying Vieve, would he await the possibility that Vieve would be available for...?"

"By the time Captain Gervais has paid for his crime, it will be too late for Boris to save his fortune through his daughter's hand. And I do not require Andrew's poverty to further disable him."

Elizabeth swallowed hard. She was unconcerned about the baron's estate. It was Faye's happiness she wished to secure. Charles's threat carried the implication, of some drastic and costly move against the captain. "Whom...did he kill?"

"A British visitor to the Virginia colony. By summer I shall have obtained the captain's warehouse shares and he will be facing punishment for the killing."

"And Andrew?" she asked weakly.

"Andrew cannot serve me any further. I will let him take Faye to get his property back."

"Charles, Vieve has wed this American. Why do you ignore the heir? What of Paul?"

"I long ago took control of the country farmlands surrounding the estates of Dumere and Ridgley. The properties are poor. The money the captain has brought is the only thing that delays me from going to my brother to show him that without my help he will lose everything. When I relieve the captain of his share in the warehouses and the commission on my brother's ships, Boris will have no choice but to meet my terms."

"But how, Charles?"

"I have a plan. It needn't concern you."

"I only want my children settled, my dear," she said confidently. "I do not want Faye's marriage interrupted or Robert's inheritance diminished."

"I have told you, when I have finally finished with my brother, our children will all be better off."

Elizabeth sighed. "Charles, can we secure the betrothal between Andrew and Faye with due haste? The girl is so upset."

"I'll see to it as soon as I can. Is that all?"

"May I tell Faye that you approve?"

"I don't care, madam. Just so long as you leave me to my work."

"Thank you, Charles. She will be happy, I know."

Elizabeth quickly left her husband's study and went to Faye's room. Although it was nearly noon, Faye was just rising. She had not felt well these past few days. When she found her sad, sorry daughter, she embraced her fondly. "Darling," Elizabeth cooed. "I've spoken to your father, and he plans to bring Andrew Shelby to an offer for your hand."

"And if he is not interested, Mother?" Faye asked lethargically.

"Oh, sweetheart, your father is rich and powerful. How can Andrew refuse?"

Faye's eyes grew brighter. "Then Father will make it worth his while?"

"He promises, darling. Are you happy?"

"Andrew is all I want. How long must I wait?"

"It will be arranged within two months. Will that do?"

Faye frowned as she considered the length of time, and then she slowly smiled. "Yes, that should do nicely. Thank you, Mama."

Tyson had his coat over his arm and was ready to leave the house when Doré entered. They spoke quietly in the front hall. "How did it go?" he asked.

"I found the man's favorite servant. I must tell you, Tyson, it is possible that this Latimer has good taste in women. Perhaps he has some Parisian..."

"Did she agree to leave the Latimer house?" Tyson asked, cutting him off.

"Yes, she was eager to leave him. He has bothered her for intimate favors, and she does not like the affectionate merchant. He is not a generous man. So, the household is short by one servant." He shrugged and smiled. "I do not think the remaining staff will have trouble doing her work, but the master will be disappointed."

"I have in mind a young woman to replace the maid, and I don't want to endanger her. What do you think?"

"I am told that Mrs. Latimer keeps herself much in evidence and foils many of Charles's flirtations. I think the woman would be safe for a few weeks, at least. But you must be fair with her. She deserves warning."

"Mr. Humphrey is bringing her to meet me this afternoon. You're welcome to come along..."

"Tyson?"

Both men turned to see Vieve coming down the stairs. Doré's eyes glowed. He enjoyed looking at her on every occasion, but he took even more pleasure in watching the two of them play against each other. The little goddess teased her husband well, and Tyson seemed to have trouble with the game.

Vieve was dressed in a gown of pale green velvet and was bedecked in hat, gloves, and her matching cloak slung over her shoulders. Behind her stood Harriet, also ready for an outing.

"Are you taking the coach, Tyson?" she asked.

"I had planned to. I have an appointment."

"Oh," she said, disappointed. "Perhaps while you're out you could find a coach for hire and send it back for me?"

"Where are you bound? It can't wait?"

Her mouth curved in a coquettish smile. "It is nearly Christmas, Tyson. I wanted to shop for some gifts."

"Perhaps I could take you abroad tomorrow."

"You do not require so much time for your meeting," Doré intervened. "We could all go out together, and while you are at business, I will happily take Madam to do her chores. And then perhaps dinner in an inn?"

"That would be wonderful," Vieve accepted quickly.

"I don't know how long I will be engaged," Tyson broke in.

"It is of no matter," Doré said. "I am always pleased in the company of your beautiful wife. And I believe she is happy with me as an escort."

"I had planned to take Harriet with me...."

Doré stepped up one step and reached out a hand to Vieve. "But it is not necessary, petite. I will guard you better. Come, we will have a good outing."

Tyson glowered at the two of them, but neither noticed. Doré took possession of Vieve's hand, escorted her out the door, and helped her into the coach. Tyson hesitated too long to even get the space beside her for his seat. He was quiet as the coach rattled toward the coffeehouse where his meeting was scheduled to take place. While his every thought was turned to being alone with Vieve, her happy disposition and innocent flirtation with Doré was enough to ruin his day.

Tyson had heard his friend's liberal jests about his great talent for stealing ladies from other men. Doré had never trespassed before, but as this duration without intimacy with Vieve increased, Tyson grew more concerned about the depth of Doré's loyalty. Doré not only doted on Vieve, but had actually come between them once. When the coach stopped, Tyson got out and gave a stern message to the Frenchman. "I will meet you here in two hours—not a moment more or less. Behave yourself with my wife."

"How could you think otherwise, Tyson? I guard your prize as if she were my own."

"That is not what I asked you to do."

As he stood outside the common room watching the coach rattle away from him, Doré's advantage stung him. He regretted his rash decision on his wedding night, for he had established this celibate marriage, and now she held him to it. He was tired of playing the gentle suitor and wanted to win his place beside her in bed. Waiting patiently had not lent him a sweet and docile temperament.

The wait inside the common room was not long. Mr. Humphrey brought the young woman in and introduced her as Mrs. Mary Earwhick. Tyson observed her while they waited for their drinks to be served. She was pretty, though simply dressed, and quiet, she looked a bit tired, but Tyson had been informed that she worked hard and had only one afternoon a week to call her own. After a few moments of conversation, it was easy to see that Mr. Humphrey had been right about the woman's articulate speech and intelligence. If she was also a talented actress, much could be achieved. Only one thing gave him caution: as she lifted her glass of wine, her hand trembled.

"Has Mr. Humphrey told you why I wished to meet you?" Tyson asked.

"Yes, briefly. He says that you are in search of the family to the man in the drawing. It is possible that he is my husband."

"Your husband's name was Michael Everly?"

Her eyes flared slightly. "Was?"

"The man in the drawing is dead. I am sorry."

Her eyes closed as she attempted to steady herself. When she opened them again there was a look of serenity. "How?"

"You'll forgive me, madam, but before I disclose any further information, I should like to be certain that I am speaking with his kin. You understand."

"I am certain that we speak of my husband. Everly was one of the many names he used for the stage. He was a brilliant actor, but not much of a husband. He left me to go with a troupe of traveling actors to America, where the opportunity was better. I'm certain he did not intend to return to me."

"You appeared frightened until hearing of his death."

"Yes, Captain. Michael had done a few things in the past that were dishonest. If he could earn a few pounds by taking on a false identity for the purpose of a theft or conspiracy, he would do so."

"That is exactly what he did, but you will not suffer because of it. In fact, your honesty brings much relief to me, for I killed him in a duel."

Even Mr. Humphrey's eyes rounded at this information.

Tyson went on. "For several years I played casual escort to a woman who lived a short distance from my home. During this time I had no desire to marry, and the woman was liberal in her affections. I do not fault her for this, and perhaps I carry an equal weight in the wrong that was done. But I reached a time in my life when I saw marriage in a different light and broke away from her to engage in various courtships with young, virtuous women. She told me then that she desired marriage with me, but I declined. I encouraged her to find a suitable husband and even offered to bolster her dower purse. She was not without means, but the estate her parents had left her had dwindled considerably. She was a frivolous manager.

"A British aristocrat appeared as a visitor in our city, and the courtship between them began. Then the woman called me to her house on the pretense of business. I assumed she had need of money, but she surprised me with an entirely different request. I crawled into her bed again, and Michael Everly found us thus.

"In the course of the following days he made a public display of his anger. As he recounted the story, I began to sound like a jealous lover, while he stood up as the wronged aristocrat hungering for justice. He challenged me so that he could marry the woman. I tell you frankly that I intended only to injure him, but my aim was off and I hit his heart."

Tyson took a long pull on his ale, and looked curiously at the woman's faint smile.

"I assume the woman staged the event," Tyson continued. "But I don't understand how she convinced him to take a lead ball and end his life."

Mary Earwhick shook her head. "Pardon, Captain, but you said your aim was misplaced. Is that usual for you?"

"I will admit that I was agitated. I missed my mark by the whole breadth of a man's hand. That distance amazes me still."

"You did not wish to kill him?"

"I offered him every alternative to a duel. I have a reputation as a good marksman. I went so far as to take a disadvantage, offering swords, which I handle poorly."

The woman's eyes were alive with mirth. "My dear, I am certain that he declined the swords. Oh, Captain, surely you did not kill him."

"I looked for myself, madam. You may rest assured I killed him."

"There was a good deal of blood then?"

"A great plenty."

"Yes, I suppose there would be. Captain, my husband has played this role before. He does it well. He first attempted this on the stage, learning as he refined it. When the idea came to him, he thought it would make him the greatest actor in the world to be killed on stage. It was difficult for him to find someone to make the right props, for he needed a special, fragile glass. It is much like two plates, stuck together, but clay plates would be too strong and would not break easily. The glass had a small opening through which he could pour animal blood or thickened red dye. Real blood worked best. For the stage he tied the glass disk to his chest, and when a sword was thrust at him, he clutched his chest, breaking the thin glass, letting the red stain spread across his linen shirt." She laughed aloud. "The first time, he cut his chest so badly with the glass that he learned to protect his own flesh better, and of course he chose to use blood rather than dye, for the dye stain on his body was impossible to remove."

Tyson frowned. The duel was burned into his memory, and not a detail was forgotten. Everly had dropped his pistol and grasped his chest. "It is possible that he intended a hoax, but there was a dark smudge on his shirt where the shot had entered."

"A little powder on the fist that struck his chest would accomplish that effect," Mary assured him. "I'm sure if you were reluctant to duel, you told him in a great many ways that you would not kill him. He probably anticipated a wound, but if the woman paid well, he would do it. He was very proud of his skill as an actor. He could lie still and cold, even if he felt great pain. You see, if you were a bad shot and had hit his leg, he could not act his way through a chest injury. It is more likely you missed him entirely."

"If I missed him entirely, he could have killed me," Tyson said.

"If he had to be shot to be paid, Captain, he meant you no bodily harm."

"Do you think there is a chance he is still alive?" he asked.

"Oh, alive and far away from the site. Was the funeral grand?"

"Very quiet," Tyson mumbled.

"Then there was no challenge for him at all. He once played a dead man for two full afternoons and had to escape from a false bottom in a casket before he was buried. He earned a great deal for that, since an inheritance was at stake." Her expression sobered slightly, but her eyes still twinkled. "I'm sorry he put you through so much. I would have come forward with the truth sooner, had I known. Did the woman who hired him get her wish?"

"She wished to have me marry her, especially after the ruinous gossip about us. I have made many other mistakes, but I chose not to make that one."

"Then all is well," Mary said with a smile.

"A hoax," Tyson mumbled. "I never would have believed it."

The woman raised both brows. "Of course not. That is why this demonstration usually comes at a high price. It is not only dangerous, it takes a very talented actor to accomplish it."

"Well," Tyson finally said, "I had intended to offer you restitution. Perhaps I am premature."

"I'm certain that you are. And I would not have been able to take anything from you. Though my need may be great, Michael's deception has caused trouble for too many people. He will make a fatal mistake one day. I wish I could feel sorry for him."

"I commend you for your honesty, madam. You could have taken payment from me."

"Have we not learned, through Michael, how bad money will haunt us? No thank you, Captain."

Tyson was quiet for a long moment, thinking. He stared away from his guests, looking at nothing in particular, and a smile slowly grew on his lips.

"I'm certain you are outraged, Captain..."

He gave a short laugh. "To the contrary, I was not prepared for this relief. Although I felt I could defend my actions, I must admit that knowing no one was killed brings tremendous satisfaction. I had no pity or fondness for Everly, and that damned woman who plotted this did not have the least of my loyalty. But to think I was backed into a duel for her honor stung me deeply. She had no honor to defend."

"Even in this short time, I see you as a man who dislikes killing, Captain."

"Indeed, but don't misunderstand. I am married now, madam, and I value the woman highly. Were she to be compromised, I would meet the culprit and..."

His voice trailed off as he realized what he was saying. He could no longer make excuses for his feelings. Vieve's strong allure was the least of what bound him. He loved everything about her; he depended on her presence, her quiet trust, her proud and loyal bearing. The mere thought of returning to his lonely, unattached life-style seemed impossible.

He looked into Mary's eyes. "My wife's smallest comfort is worth the lives of ten men. To kill for her honor would bear no insult."

Mary's voice was soft. "She must be very proud to know how you adore her."

Tyson quickly considered that there must be no further delay in telling her how greatly he prized her. He did not share this with Mary, but instead cleared his throat to proceed to another subject. "Mr. Humphrey tells me that you act as well."

"Not for some time, Captain. But I think I was a marginal talent once."

"Did you ever participate in your husband's schemes?"

"Acting is for the pleasure of the audience, Captain. How could I bring pain to people?"

"Perhaps you would like to earn some money. Acting, so to speak."

She frowned suspiciously. "I cannot oblige you in any way meant to bring people confusion or hardship, sir. That is no way to use a talent."

"What I need is of that bend, but only to right a wrong and save lives. There is a man in London who has been plotting a course to ruin a local baron and myself. I had thought that he would be satisfied to rob us blind, but now I worry that he has more violence on his mind. All I wish is to place a servant in his household. If you were to take the position, I'm sure he would favor your presence. If you discover that the man is dangerous, you could possibly give me warning." Tyson smiled. "The greatest danger to you is that he will undoubtedly pester you with his passionate advances. But he has a wife and children, and surely you could get close to him and still safely avoid his amorous attentions. He happens to have need of a maid at present. His favored one has left his employ without notice."

Mary looked at Mr. Humphrey, then back to Tyson. She frowned as if the idea did not appeal.

"There is a great deal of money to be made, and the danger is minimal; if you find you cannot discourage his pursuit, quit his house hastily. I will pay you enough to keep you and your child for a long time."

"And that is all? I must take a position in his household?"

"And pay attention to the people who visit him and, on occasion, listen carefully to what is said. I am prepared to offer you a bonus sum if you can find an accounting ledger that will incriminate him and show a record that he has paid to have crimes committed against the baron and myself. If you are clever enough to retrieve that, I will double your pay."

"You wish to have me steal something from his household?"

"This theft would put him away as a criminal. My offer is this: one thousand pounds today for taking the job, another one thousand pounds for listening and watching in his household...and five thousand pounds total if you leave his house with any evidence that can be used to either convict or stop him from doing any further damage."

"Will you tell me what to look for?" she asked, her interest peaked.

Tyson grinned broadly. "It will be my pleasure, madam. Can you find a place to leave your child until this is over?"

"It is done, sir. The Duchess Dunkirk does not allow me to keep her at the house on Larks Square. I have been paying for her boarding with another family, but if this goes well, we will never be separated again."

"Very good. I rest easier knowing we do each other a valuable service."

"But if he does not give me a position?"

"Madam, you are an actress."

When Tyson emerged from the coffeehouse, he felt as if his whole life had changed. He had not been prepared for the effect of learning he had not killed a man. It was the overriding threat of what the incident could mean in this country that had plagued some dark corner of his mind since he had first sighted Lenore.

Had he come to love and trust Vieve before he had claimed her virginity, he would have taken on any of Lord Ridgley's problems to have her. So, he was late in knowing what he wanted, but he was not a fool. The love he felt for his wife went beyond anything he had ever felt in his life. Within that emotion was the energy to set her family troubles aright.

He faced only Charles Latimer. And he felt confident about that confrontation.

When his coach arrived, he opened the door and found his wife seated close beside her escort.

"Thank you, monsieur, for assisting my wife. Excuse me, I think you have my seat." Doré moved reluctantly, but smiled knowingly. Tyson sat beside Vieve and took her hand in his. "I think we should celebrate. A trip to the theatre and dinner."

Tyson was in high spirits, liberal with his coin, and seemed inclined to spend the rest of the day enchanting Vieve.

First he stopped at a flower cart en route to the theatre and purchased a small nosegay. They laughed through a farce at the theatre, dined at an expensive tavern popular among the noble class, and took a late drive through Hyde Park. His banter was never more mirthful; his affection toward her, whether in a brief caress or compliment, was delightful. While she had appreciated his attempts at courting her, tonight he behaved as though it was natural for him, and she felt adored.

The evening grew late, and she leaned her head against her husband's shoulder and sighed. He lifted his arm, putting it around her to make her more comfortable. "Thank you, Tyson," she said sweetly. "Today was even better than my birthday." She yawned sleepily and he kissed her brow.

"Tyson," Doré said softly. "The night is young for me. Will you drop me?"

Vieve roused herself briefly to bid Doré good night, and when he had departed their coach she turned eyes up to Tyson. "You have changed somehow. What is different?"

He gently squeezed her shoulders. "I had a problem that I had been wrestling with. Today, by some miracle, it was removed."

"My uncle?" she asked. He looked at her with a question in his eyes. "I have known since the day we left Chappington, Tyson. My father took me aside early that morning and told me what burdens he had thrust upon you. I don't know many of the details, but I know that Uncle Charles has been trying to ruin my father, and you have been assigned to the task of stopping him."

"You have known all this time?"

She nodded. "My father suggested that I leave the matter to you."

"Why did he tell you at all?"

"He wanted me to know what grudge you felt against our family. And if I wished to remain with him in Chappington Hall, he would support that decision."

The coach stopped in front of the London brownstone. "But you came with me."

"It is my place," she said very softly. "With you."

She saw the change in his eyes as the gray darkened to a deep and smoldering charcoal. His arm tightened around her shoulder, and he lifted her chin with a finger, gently touching her lips and then tracing them with the point of his tongue. Then his mouth was on hers, searing in its heat, searching, demanding. She felt the beat of his heart against her breast and heard his rapid breathing. When he released her mouth, she was breathless. "Tyson," she beckoned. "The coach has stopped."

He sighed heavily, released her, and opened the coach door. He lifted her down and took her through the open door and up the stairs. Halfway up she paused, stopping him. "Tyson, please wait a moment. There is something I must tell you."

"It can wait, Vieve. Come."

"No, Tyson, this cannot wait a moment longer. I am sorry that my father used his advantage against you, and I did not enter into his plan with him, but please understand that I love him the same. He is not dishonest, only desperate."

He nodded, and the soft glow in his eyes was warm and understanding. He continued up the stairs and stopped at the top.

He held open the door to his bedchamber. The room was dimly lit, the fire burned low. He looked back into her eyes. "I love you," he said softly. "I have not touched another woman since that day in the old keep. It is only you I want."

Tears came to her eyes, but she smiled. She touched a finger to his lips. "Will you stoke the fire, my love?"

Without waiting for an answer, she walked past him into the room. This was the moment she had waited for, and though a shiver of apprehension ran up her spine, her body quivered with passion's promise. She stood to the side of the hearth while he removed his coat and lay fresh logs on the fire.

She felt as though she had waited her whole life to feel his hands on her again. Though she knew little about lovemaking, she thought she knew her husband now. And she was determined that he would not be disappointed.

He rose and came toward her, but she put a hand against his chest to stop him. She smiled sweetly, and before his questioning gaze she began to slowly unfasten the tiny buttons that ran from her throat to her waist. She spread the gown over her shoulders and let it fall to the floor at her feet. Wearing only her sheer shift, she carefully unfastened her hair, tossing the pins and ribbons into the hearth fire, letting her tresses fall freely down her back. She kicked off her shoes, unfastened her garters, and drew off her stockings, still holding his burning gaze with hers.

She approached him, rising on her toes to plant loving kisses on his lips as her fingers worked the buttons of his shirt. His arms encircled her, and she felt his action to remove his cuff links, which quickly joined the other discarded articles on the floor. She pushed his shirt over his shoulders and caressed his muscled chest with eager fingers.

"Vieve," he whispered. "I have wanted you so, I have hungered for you."

"You shall wait no longer, my love. I, too, have been pained with this wanting."

His lips found her shoulder, and her shift shortly joined the heap of cumbersome garments. Her naked breasts against his warm chest stirred her passions, and she gave herself to his deep kiss. She opened her lips to his searching tongue, straining against him, her fingertips moving boldly over his body. "Let there be no doubt, my darling... I love you," she whispered. "I love you with my whole being."

He held her away from himself so that he could look at her shimmering nakedness against the firelight. His eyes gleamed as he filled himself with the vision of her beauty. "You concealed yourself from me for too long, my love. Now I shall finally see all of you." With a slow sweep his hand moved from her shoulder, over her breast, down her slim waist, over her firm thigh. "My God, you are beautiful."

She bit her lower lip, trembling inside from the pleasure of his hands on her bare flesh. Her fingertips found the buttons on his trousers. "Do you still find me wanton, m'lord?"

"I pray for it," he returned as her fingers worked the fastenings loose. "Give me all. Hold nothing from me. I must have all of you. Nothing less will satisfy."

His trousers and shoes disappeared, and he felt her small, quivering hands on his narrow hips. "I am yours, Tyson, as I have always been. There is not a corner of my body, my mind, or my heart that I would withhold from you."

With a gasp of longing, he pulled her hard against him. They stood before the brightly burning hearth, their lips desperately locked together, while with curious fingers they discovered every detail of each other's naked flesh. His muscled body grew taut and hardened under her gentle touch, and her soft skin shivered with delight. He bent his head to trace a line with his lips from her neck to her breast, teasing an erect nipple with his tongue. Vieve brazenly closed her hand around the bold and ready manhood that had robbed her of her virginity and sighed in awe at the heat and power she felt.

Tyson's mind whirled in ecstasy with her touch, and he lifted her into his arms, so eager for her that he only took one step backward to the chair, bringing her soft bottom to rest on his thighs. His lips at her breast, his arm holding her firmly on his lap, his experienced fingers made a feast of her, and he dined on her slowly, until her sighs of pleasure turned to gasps of desire.

Though Vieve might have expected to be invited to the nearest bed, Tyson's creative move seemed almost natural to her. It was easy to place herself within his power and allow him to instruct her. His lips and fingers quickly lay to rest any fear, modesty, or resistance. Her arms embraced him, her fingers locked into the thick hair at the base of his neck, feeling the hardness beneath her as he urged his way into her. Her thighs opened easily to his hand, and he lifted her but a little, filling her with all his power and heat.

Vieve gasped at the sensation. An ember of ecstasy was touched deep inside of her, and it grew until small sparks of delight traveled through her body, promising an explosion of rapture. Through widened eyes she saw the tightened features of her husband's face, eyes tightly closed, small beads of perspiration standing out on his brow. With a sigh of longing, she embraced him tightly, holding his head against her breast. Her hips moved naturally to the rhythm he paced with a firm hand on her hip.

Tyson buried his face in her full bosom, feeling every muscle in his body ache with the control he employed to bring her the full score of pleasure before claiming his own. He commanded his body to please hers, his movements subject to her needs, so that he quickened his thrusts with her writhing demands until he heard his name on her lips in a startled cry that declared her pinnacle of pleasure was met.

"Tyson."

With a deep moan of penetrating joy, he released himself from his own torment to match her rapture. And he had never before in his life felt anything to compare to it.

Their bliss melted around them, leaving their bodies glazed in a damp mist. Vieve's head lay contentedly on his shoulder, her hair falling down his arm like a shawl. She was limp in the aftermath of pleasure's peak, and his hand gently caressed her back as she slowly roused.

Her lips gently nibbled his ear. "Have I told you how much I love you?"

A light, low chuckle escaped him. "What I just felt from you, my sweet, bears more credence than words could." He softly kissed her lips. "Willingness and acquiescence I prayed for, but had I known how completely you would give yourself to me, I could not have waited as I have."

"And had I known the full reward that you denied me, you would not have escaped your obligations so easily."

He held her face in his hands and looked deeply into her eyes. "I cannot remove those days when I mistreated you, much to my regret. I see now that I have loved you from the beginning. You are my heart and my life, Vieve. That will never change. I love only you, and I need your love in return...for all time."

"All of me," she whispered. "Forever."

With a sigh of reluctance, he lifted her in his arms and carried her gently to the bed. He braced a knee on the bed, looking down at her, and smiled roguishly. "We have yet to make love in a bed," he said with a shrug. "Does it sit ill with you that my hunger for you comes before all other considerations?"

She locked her arms around his neck and drew him down to her. "It may prove inconvenient for the servants, my darling, but I shall try my very best to endure your whims."

Eleven

Vieve soon understood all the elaborate scheming required to trick Charles Latimer. Tyson was quick and detailed in his explanation of that situation. Tyson worked from a variety of angles to subdue the crafty merchant, and by the time he was finished, Charles would be both financially wounded and facing harsh evidence against him. From such a position, even Charles would find a further fight impossible.

They hoped that through Tyson's plan Charles would be forced to admit his guilt, return certain properties acquired dishonestly, provide restitution for damages, and swear in a written confession to desist in meddling with the baron's estate. But there was another possibility. Charles could be pushed into some desperate criminal action—and would be caught. While Tyson preferred the first outcome, he was prepared for the second.

When Tyson told Vieve about Lenore and the duel in which he had thought Michael Everly was killed, she finally understood the initial anger she had met in him.

"Oh, Tyson, when you discovered my father's need for money and my virginity, you must have been wild with suspicion. If only I had known..."

"The knowledge of your family's need and your submission to my desires was not nearly so disruptive as the violence I felt at the very thought of anyone but me touching you. It was my own deep need for you that most confused me. I wanted you for my own so desperately that I was outraged by that crippling emotion. I saw only my choices gone and failed to see the determination with which I chose you. Had you not yielded, married me, and by your special methods, tied me, I might still be sitting on shipboard alone, my head spinning in fear and confusion."

"You mock me. I cannot imagine you being afraid of anything."

"Oh, madam," he sighed. "What I feel for you is so strong and deep it can terrify the bravest man. When you took my heart, held it within your tender nurturing, you made it impossible for me to take it back. Now...I cannot live without you. Such is the plight," he tenderly explained, "of a man who has taken so long to know real love."

With the dialogue finally open between them, she could send Tyson off to his duties with a good feeling in her heart and welcome him home again, eager for his presence.

Tyson damned the presence of such conspiracies, for he swore he would be content to live somewhat retired now that his amorous wife made her demands. Yet, business of the most delicate nature kept him active outside of their London house, and when nightfall came and he had returned, Vieve used all her energy and imagination to show him how determined she was that they would always share a common bed.

Vieve's knowledge of Tyson's plans was still relatively new when her Aunt Elizabeth surprised her by calling on her. It was only a week before Christmas, and for once Elizabeth was not accompanied by her daughters.

"I realize that my husband and your father have had a falling out, but my dear Vieve, you have always been a favorite of mine and I did so wish to visit you."

"Does Uncle Charles know you have come?"

"Oh, my, no. He is still quite angry about their argument at Chappington. Please understand, I do not defy him; he did not say I could not visit you. But I saw fit to leave my visit unmentioned."

"Of course," Vieve said, inviting her aunt to the drawing room and asking a maid to bring tea. She was a bit confused. She had never felt like a favorite of Elizabeth's. Her aunt was always polite, but nothing more.

Elizabeth moved around the drawing room, taking her usual small steps, touching various objects with light fingers and remarking on Vieve's lovely home. Vieve stood in uncomfortable silence, watching her aunt's movements, listening to the compliments with a suspicious ear. Finally, Elizabeth found a comfortable seat, and the tea was served.

"You seem to be so contented, dear. Are you terribly happy with your Yankee husband?"

"He is a good man, Aunt. Yes, I am quite content."

"How good for you. You deserve happiness. And I have always thought the captain a fine figure; most handsome."

"Thank you," Vieve said quietly.

"I am only sorry that we have such limited social ties. I'm afraid Charles is too piqued to be friendly."

"It is understood. You needn't worry."

"My daughters would like to see you again, I'm sure."

"We have never been very close, Aunt. I understand that they are busy with other things."

"But family is so important. It would be good if Charles could settle his differences with your father."

"Perhaps they will..."

"Not, I daresay, until your handsome husband stops coming between them."

"Tyson? How does Tyson come between them?"

Elizabeth laughed softly and lifted her teacup to take a dainty sip. "Why, my sweet, Charles longs to be a part of this wonderful business they have together. The captain's brothers have become involved; why not Charles? He is good in trade; he has money to invest."

"That would be my father's choice, I suppose," Vieve replied. She looked at Elizabeth from under lowered lids as she sipped her own tea. Her aunt's sweet and soft expression caused Vieve to wonder how she could be so naive about Charles's desire for good business. But Elizabeth had always been removed, it seemed, from the seedier aspects of life. She was so preoccupied with manners, social graces, and conservative traditions, she would not pay much attention to her husband's business.

"Well, perhaps Charles and Lord Ridgley will one day repair their family bonds. They have had such ups and downs for many years, bless them."

"Many."

"Do you plan to travel to your husband's home soon, my dear, or will you be staying here for a while longer?"

"A long while, it would seem."

"Oh? The captain is not eager to go home? How can he be so comfortable in this country?"

"He means to give careful attention to my father's ailing business, Aunt Elizabeth. We may remain here for a very long time."

"Are you quite serious?"

"Certainly."

"But, Vieve, dear, an American working here would be subject to so many...ah...suspicions. It would be safer for him to be in his own land. There is no telling the number of angry British who might wish to disadvantage him."

Vieve looked at her aunt squarely. "Can you name any, Aunt?"

"Of course I would not personally know of any, but I was told just a few weeks ago of a man from New York who came here as an emissary and met with much abuse. He was accused of some petty offense and was quite harshly punished. Do you not fear such could befall your own husband, because he is a foreigner?"

"My father would support him. Lord Ridgley is not without influence."

"Certainly he has great influence, but enough? Surely you love your husband a great deal, Vieve. You should convince him to return to his homeland soon."

"Tyson is very heavily invested here. He would not lightly leave his obligations."

"If it is a matter of money, surely something could be arranged. Why, Charles himself hungers for a share of the shipping venture. Even he would extend a sum to make it possible for you to get your husband out of his weakened position."

"I doubt that would interest Tyson, Aunt Elizabeth. But if you like, I will tell him you mentioned it."

"I know very little about my husband's accounts. He has always managed the business affairs for our household. But I have heard him say that he was deeply hurt that Lord Ridgley would not accept an investment from him."

"My father must have had good reason," Vieve cautiously murmured.

"Who is to say, dear. We are women, and therefore bent to the whim of our men. But I assure you, if I were married to a Yankee, I would not encourage his extended stay in England."

"Would you use your wiles to hurry his departure?" Vieve asked with a sly smile.

Elizabeth laughed lightly, her cheeks even growing a little rosy. "I suppose I would at that. For your own good, I think you should."

Vieve slowly lifted her cup and took a leisurely sip. "You seem almost anxious for us to leave, Aunt. And just after telling me how favored I am in your eyes."

Elizabeth's expression became strained. "I meant no offense," she said.

"I only wonder why."

Elizabeth's mouth straightened to a stern line. Her small eyes twinkled. "I think I speak the truth when I mention the captain's disadvantage here. Many would be suspicious of him because of his citizenship."

"I suppose so, but Tyson is not worried. He also has strong allies. I'm afraid I must disappoint you, Aunt. We will remain."

Elizabeth placed her cup and saucer on the table before her. "I had not intended to be so blunt as this, my dear, but I'm afraid it is your presence in London that has become a problem. My daughter is soon to be betrothed to Andrew Shelby."

"Faye?' Vieve questioned, amazed.

"Yes, Faye. I think their marriage would begin on more solid ground if you would simply move on to your new home with your new husband. And there is no question but that the captain would be better off."

"Aunt, I assure you, I have no interest whatsoever in Andrew Shelby. I wish Faye well."

"Nonetheless, there was a good deal of talk about your passionate romance with the young man. Such gossip does not do well on a young bride...and Faye is young."

Vieve sighed heavily. "It is all useless gossip, Aunt Elizabeth, and surely Faye can rise above it if she loves Andrew. But I think you should reconsider, for her sake. Andrew is not always the most chivalrous."

"Faye must be the judge of that. However, it is most difficult for her to find happiness under the weight of your lingering presence and Andrew's fascination with you."

"Andrew. But..." Vieve stopped suddenly. She frowned. "Aunt Elizabeth, does Andrew resist a betrothal with Faye because of me?"

Elizabeth looked away briefly. "Your romance with him was far too obvious, it has not been long past, and it is understandable that it is his pride, not his true feelings, that distract him from making an honest proposal for my daughter. And my daughter should be granted the decency of a completely new start with her betrothed."

"How does my residence in London hinder that?"

"It is possible, my dear, that Andrew still holds some hope on your situation...changing."

"It cannot change."

"Not if you go to Virginia...but if you stay here? Who knows what misfortune may befall your husband. He is unwelcome here. The smallest problem could send him the route of that American emissary."

"Do you threaten, Aunt? Is there something you should tell me?"

Elizabeth rose, her lips pinched and her eyes narrow. "I have said what I came to say. You have tossed Andrew aside and wed the Yankee. Do this for Faye. Leave England with him as soon as possible so that she can be wed. I have never asked a thing of you or your family but this. Please."

Vieve stood to face her aunt, her insides trembling nervously. "Aunt, hear me, please. If Andrew resists marriage with Faye because of me, he is a fool, for I hold no feeling for him. And I think it would be unwise to tie your daughter to him in marriage. Here or gone, I cannot come between them if they care for each other, and if Andrew does not love Faye, please do not hurt her further by forcing him to wed her."

"You could rectify the problem," Elizabeth said impatiently. "You have your rich husband. Leave with him, that the rest of us might get on with our lives."

"I will go or stay, as Tyson wills it, Aunt."

Elizabeth's mouth twisted in a sarcastic sneer. "'Tis a pity, Vieve, that you are so spoiled. One day you will regret your lack of compassion."

Elizabeth moved away from Vieve and, without saying good-bye, quickly left the room. Vieve sank again to the settee, completely confused by what had just happened.

Only a moment had passed when Tyson entered the drawing room, still wearing his cloak. "What was she doing here?" he asked.

Vieve looked up at him, her brow wrinkled in bewilderment. "She came here to urge me to leave England with you as soon as possible. She said that Faye is to wed Andrew and my presence is an interference. I think, Tyson, that Andrew resists a betrothal with Faye...because of me."

"Have you seen Andrew?"

"Not once. Nor have I seen any member of the Latimer family before today. She said that you must surely be in danger in England and for safety's sake should consider returning to America. It was almost a threat."

"Or a warning."

"Could Elizabeth possibly know what her husband is doing? Or what he plans to do?"

"Perhaps, but more important, did she say anything to indicate that Charles knows I am onto him?"

Vieve thought for a moment. "No, but she did say that if it is a matter of money that delays our departure, Charles hungers for an investment in my father's shipping trade and probably would come forth with money. Does that mean what I think it does? That he would take your shares and finally own my father?"

"Certainly. He already controls most of the country property. Lord Ridgley's only advantage has lately come with my investment... which has foiled Charles."

"What will you do?"

"Ah," Tyson said, smiling shrewdly. "Well, we wouldn't want Charles to be disappointed. Perhaps something can be worked out after all."

As a part of the Christmas celebration in London, King George had extended invitations for many formal events at Windsor. The English noble, visiting aristocrat, gentry, and squire were given royal requests to attend various events. The earl of Lemington made a personal invitation to Captain and Madam

Gervais to accompany him to an evening ball held three days before Christmas.

Vieve had never answered a royal summons. Her father had attended a few, and she might have been presented formally had her mother lived. This was the first such event for her, and she was giddy with excitement. Although she knew the limitations of a party with so many guests, she hoped to view the royal couple from afar, or see the faces of some well-known members of Parliament.

She troubled over the selection of a gown, cautiously examined the minor jewels that her mother had left her, and forced poor Harriet to rearrange her coiffure three times. Her maid, sighing tiredly at this high pitch of excitement, tried to comply, unaware that Vieve's determination to look exactly right had little to do with how she might appear to those attending nobles.

It was Tyson's gaze she meant to satisfy.

When he told her about the invitation, he had imparted that they should be quiet guests at Windsor. The earl had subtly instructed it would be best to downplay his American roots.

"There are those who would happily see me hang for being so presumptuous as to marry an Englishwoman of blooded name," he said. "In fact, it strikes me that a rich American is in more jeopardy than a poor one."

"But I think you need not fear all the English alike," she said.

"I'd like to think that it is wisdom in those I trust, rather than fear of any of them."

"Will I face the same in Virginia? Must I ever worry that I will be judged for my ancestry rather than myself?"

"If you arrived without the close guard of your jealous and possessive husband, you would ruin the very existence of every unmarried women in Virginia...rest assured."

Vieve doubted her fairness was so great, but she was wholly satisfied that Tyson felt that way. She found him to be the most handsome man in the world and frequently wondered how he had avoided marriage for so long. "I don't know how you escaped the women who came before me, but thank heaven you did."

The gown she chose for the ball was a rare lavender color, a shining satin that glistened in the candlelight. A diamond pendant that had been her mother's sparkled above her low décolletage, and small diamond earbobs twinkled on her ears. A few feathers that matched her gown were woven into her hair. Her cape, lined with ermine, was sewn of the same lavender cloth.

She approved her appearance and then waited anxiously for Tyson's appraisal. When he came to her room, he stood for a long moment in the doorway, looking at her. When his eyes met hers and lingered there, burning in their intensity, Harriet slowly withdrew from the room and gently closed the door.

It would always be as it had been that day at Chappington, when he had returned to her father with his money to invest. The way he had looked at her then had branded her as his forever. She felt her pulse race and her breath quicken.

"I have half a mind not to share you with all the other men in attendance, but you have never been to a royal affair and neither have I."

"I have never wanted for royal parties. I would be a willing prisoner of your selfish whims."

He laughed softly. "It is a tempting thought, but then I would have to make an excuse to this noble cousin. He is stuffy and staunch. He would not understand."

"You could complain that you'd fallen ill," she attempted.

He frowned as if considering that option. Finally, he sighed and took her arm. "Come, petite, we go as much on your father's business as our own."

As he moved away from her to pick up her cape, it took great willpower not to dispense with the ball and enjoy a fire in their bedchamber...alone. When he placed her wrap about her shoulders, she was possessed of another feeling, and she turned abruptly, placing a hand on his chest. "Tyson, perhaps we should not go. All the English and you..."

"What is it?"

"I don't know...a feeling..." She shuddered. "If anything happened to you..."

"Your aunt has frightened you unnecessarily, Vieve. I have no one to worry about but Charles Latimer. And I'm certain I can handle him."

"But Tyson, what if he tries to hurt you?"

"You needn't be afraid. I have no intention of leaving you a widow."

She went with him to the coach, quieting her further arguments. Bevis stood at the coach door, wiggling with discomfort in his formal clothes. He smiled when he saw her, the wide, dark gap from a missing tooth appearing as a tunnel into his mouth. "Aye, mum, it's fine ye're lookin'. Mighty fine indeed," he said with a bobbing motion.

"You look very fine yourself, Bevis," she said. But he only hung his head as if disgruntled by the necessity to dress so.

As she stepped into her coach she heard him mumbling behind her. "Blasted peacock feathers... look like a whore, I do."

The ride was a long one, and Vieve remained uncomfortable. She couldn't name the fear that gnawed at her, but some danger seemed to loom. She hoped it would be a short evening.

Once they arrived there was such commotion that the feeling of dread passed and her excitement was renewed. She had never seen so many people pressed into the ballroom, moving in and out of hallways and alcoves. She waited with Tyson in the gallery for nearly an hour to get inside. All around them stood gentry and aristocrats wearing their finest, exuberant with the prospect of their own invitations, feeling their personal importance with high spirits.

She could not have seen how they were regarded, for she was too awed by the glamour all around her. Since they spied no acquaintances, Tyson took her to dance, and while that event was shared by many, there were whispers among the spectators as they moved together and apart, bowing, bending, and swaying.

Vieve's pale beauty against Tyson's wicked darkness perked romantic conjecture as they danced. His eyes held hers firmly, his steps graceful though he was a large, muscular man. "Who are they?" people speculated. Was the woman a visiting princess? The man a little-known aristocrat, exiled from his homeland? They appeared deeply in love, for they were so lost in each other that even the murmuring around them did not distract them. Their rich clothing, jewels, manners, and attraction to each other sparked a few fantasies. Matrons sighed with hope that their daughters would do as well; widows hoped for a similarly rich beauty for their sons. They appeared handsome, wealthy, and in love. There was nothing more to which one could aspire.

When the dance ended, Lord Moresay approached. "I didn't see you come in, but then among so many, how could I? I noticed you at the dance. I'm glad you've come. You've given everyone much to talk about."

Lord Moresay took them the round of a few introductions. Vieve watched her husband bow, kiss ladies' hands, and engage in passing conversation. He did as well as any noble, gently reared. She had known so little of colonials when they had first met, having heard that all were rugged frontiersmen, clods, bereft of any social graces. Why else would they rebuke control of their sovereign in rebellion? Even now, these Americans had formed a strong alliance with France. But their land was rich with crops that England could not provide for herself, and their treatment of them was cautious, if nebulous. The British in high places were learning to be polite to these despised revolutionaries.

"I suspect you will see many familiar faces tonight," Tyson quietly warned her. "Andrew among them."

"Do you worry that I have some soft place in my heart for Andrew Shelby?" she asked.

"No, my love. But be wary. Do not be fooled by his inconsolable smile or his broken heart."

It was shortly thereafter that she clutched Tyson's arm as she spied Andrew across the room. Her breath caught in her throat. Her past suitor looked haggard, tired. Although the night was young, he had had too much to drink and his courtly swagger was more of a drunken limp. He seemed to have fallen yet farther from his aristocratic pedestal. She felt as though she had never known him. She was torn with both relief that she had somehow escaped marriage to such a man and pity for his deterioration.

"Tyson," she whispered. "Andrew is over there. Look at him."

"I have already placed him," Tyson said irritably. "And the Latimer family is here in full regiment."

"Where?"

Vieve followed her husband's gaze and saw that Charles and Elizabeth stood in conversation with another couple. Nearby, Beth waited impatiently for any young man to approach, and Faye's eyes were lingering forlornly on Andrew. Robert leaned against a pillar not far from the rest of the family, caught in conversation with a young woman.

"Is Robert so much like his father?" Tyson inquired. "They share those strong Latimer looks, but Robert appears bored by his father's ambition. He pays little attention."

"I'm ashamed to say that I hardly know them. The fact is that when they were visiting, my mother begged me to be gracious and polite." She shrugged off the memory. "It always seemed as though we shared a mutual dislike, and so we were only together at our parents' insistence." As to the strong Latimer looks, all three children were big, like Charles, and while it might be an asset for Robert, the girls had suffered, for they were large, gawky, and homely. The features that made a man handsome were not always well placed on a young woman. "Tyson, look at Faye. I think that Andrew has hurt her."

"And how would that happen, Vieve?" Tyson asked, frowning. "Andrew spent the majority of his time prancing after you."

"She has always been jealous of me," Vieve said.

"How much time did Andrew spend with the Latimer family?"

"I have no idea. Until the night that Uncle Charles came to Chappington on Andrew's behalf, I thought they were only slightly acquainted."

"And that was only four months ago. It is possible that Andrew and Charles have been more closely associated than we realized. How else would Faye become so involved with him?"

Tyson stared at Charles Latimer for a long spell, and then, with a sigh, he pulled his wife with him toward Lord and Lady Moresay. Tyson and the earl of Lemington both looked in the direction of the Latimers and wordlessly nodded in agreement over some conspiratorial plan. Then they moved as a foursome toward Charles and Elizabeth. Not wishing to be obvious, they paused to speak briefly to acquaintances of the earl's, but finally stood before Charles Latimer.

"Good evening, Mr. Latimer," Tyson said amiably. "I thought to take this opportunity to introduce you to relatives of mine. Lord and Lady Moresay, the earl and countess of Lemington, these are my wife's uncle and aunt, Charles and Elizabeth Latimer."

Charles's eyes rounded slightly, but he heeled and bowed as expected. Elizabeth sank into the required curtsy and extended her hand to the earl. "Good to make your acquaintance, my lord," Charles said. "I was not aware that the captain had noble influence here."

"Had I failed to mention that?" Tyson asked.

"I am not of much influence," the earl scoffed. "I'm afraid that my importance is very slight. Lemington is not such a large state, and I serve only a humble position for the crown."

"I doubt that, my lord," Charles said, his smile gleaming. "I have heard nothing but good about Lemington."

"It is good enough for my family," the earl replied with humility. "But we spend little enough time there, since my position in London requires me most often. I work in His Majesty's courts."

Vieve did not miss the flaring of her uncle's eyes in surprise. "The courts?" Elizabeth asked. "That must be very interesting."

"I assure you, it is quite dull. I am forever trying to untangle disputes over property or theft or other such confusion."

"It mustn't be too difficult to establish whether a man has stolen, my lord," Charles said like a man of experience. "I've had many of my own people steal from me, and if they have the article that was missing, it..."

"I'm afraid I don't have the luxury of dealing with the common criminal, for I am not a magistrate, but appointed to the Court of High Commission. I must determine due course for the crown, so my work is limited to property, marriage, inheritance, and title. It is extremely dull. There has never been a second son that didn't think he was slighted somehow."

"My goodness, such an important role," Elizabeth said with a sudden surge of energy. "And how fortunate for our niece."

"Fortunate?"

"Oh, yes, my lord. I have been so concerned. While it is clear their marriage was ordained by the angels, I was terribly worried that Captain Gervais's long presence in this country might hinder him in some way. Though we would put such hostile notions aside, there are still those who dislike Americans. I am most relieved that someone of power is close at hand for support."

Elizabeth pulled Vieve's hand into both of hers. Vieve was stunned by the sweet smile, yet the hard set of her aunt's eyes. "How very nice for you, my dear Vieve."

Vieve was speechless, and a long moment of silence passed. The earl cleared his throat. "It's a pleasure to make your acquaintance, sir and madam. If you will excuse me, I should like to entice the captain's lovely young bride to dance."

"Certainly. I... ah, enjoyed meeting you as well, my lord," Charles said uncomfortably. As Vieve was whisked onto the dance floor by the earl, she glanced over her shoulder to look at her aunt again. Elizabeth stood with hands demurely clasped before her, a smile on her lips, and her small eyes twinkling in what appeared to be hot emotion. Vieve actually shook her head in dismay. Something about Elizabeth had changed.

The earl's step was not nearly as elegant as Tyson's, but his conversation was intriguing.

"I had never met your uncle before tonight, madam," Lord Moresay said. "But I have been acquainted with your father. When my cousin's son introduced himself, he was very quiet about his connection to your family." The earl chuckled. "Testing the water, no doubt."

"How long have you known my father?"

"Oh, some twenty-five years, I suppose. Good man, Lord Ridgley."

"And have you been involved with the matters of law and property and titles for a very long time?"

The earl laughed lightly. "I have only been involved in these legal events since...oh, I suppose three or four days now. I suppose the news would quite surprise His Majesty."

Vieve laughed aloud as she looked into Lord Moresay's twinkling eyes. How wonderfully devious Tyson had been. "My uncle must be quite undone by the news." And then more softly she added, "Thank you."

The earl gave her hand a reassuring squeeze. "Enjoy yourself, my dear. Our work is done for tonight."

Once the earl of Lemington had concluded his dance, he passed Vieve to the next ancient partner, and a long train of partners followed. She had danced with ten men when Andrew approached her. She looked frantically for Tyson, but could not find him among the guests. Rather than create a scene, she accepted warily.

"Do be careful with your manners, Andrew," she warned him. "My husband has good reason to hate you."

"I frankly don't know why he should. He won you, after all. Do you still hate me?"

"I do not trust you, and I would not be so foolish as to accept your friendship again."

He laughed bitterly. His eyes were glassy from drink, his steps as they danced less than graceful. "I am the one person you should wish to befriend."

"What do you mean, Andrew?"

"Beware, pretty Vieve, there is much about your husband you do not know. He will leave you...and when he does, I will be here for you."

"Oh, Andrew, you must forget about me. I belong to another man now, and that will never change."

"You actually care for the pompous bastard, don't you?"

"Andrew, I love him. I know you've been hurt, but..."

"I had heard that he was forced to wed you. That your father trapped him to get his money."

"You heard..." She stopped suddenly. This conspiracy was new to her, but she had been informed. Tyson had worked hard to convince Lenore that he was unhappily bound to England and wished for a way out. Lenore was here by route of Charles Latimer. And now the chain linked around Andrew, for Lenore was the only one to be told such a tale. So, he was a part of Charles's whole scheme.

Although she struggled with fierce anger, she lifted her chin and tried to sound convincing. "Tyson might resist me, but I hope to change his opinion."

"And who better than you," he sneered contemptuously. "I will be waiting, my pretty, and perhaps I will take mercy on you when he's gone."

"You should not hold your hopes on that, Andrew. For your own sake I tell you that no matter what becomes of me, I will never accept marriage with you. Never."

His finger touched her chin, and he smiled confidently. "If I want you to, you will."

Vieve stopped in the middle of a dance step and looked in awe at Andrew. His eyes shone with bitterness, his mouth twisted in a hateful grimace. "Save yourself if you can, Andrew. I fear you work too hard to destroy yourself."

She pulled away from him and walked briskly toward where she had last seen her husband. As she approached the crowd that had gathered on the fringes of the dance floor, she was stopped suddenly when she spied him in conversation with a beautiful, statuesque woman. Vieve's coat was draped over his arm, as if he was ready to leave. She approached them slowly, a nervous flutter beginning anew in her stomach.

The woman was some years older than Vieve and wore a stylish gown that glistened with twinkling jets, her auburn hair done in a modern, upswept coiffure. Vieve felt small and young in comparison, and, reasoning that this must be the ill-famed Lenore Fenton, she was frightened as well.

It was Lenore who noticed her. Tyson turned. "My dear, I've been surprised by an acquaintance of mine from America. Miss Lenore Fenton, I should like you to meet my wife, Madam Vivian Gervais."

The woman looked down her long slim nose at Vieve. "A pleasure, madam," she said smoothly, looking directly back at Tyson. "Although you said she was young, I was not quite prepared for her. Now I understand the problem."

Vieve tried to stand her ground proudly, but it was difficult. The woman was brazen. She was afraid for Tyson.

"If you will excuse us, madam," Tyson said with a smile. He kissed Lenore's hand, and the woman made the requisite curtsies, after which Tyson pulled Vieve away from her.

"She has chosen this very evening to test my clever lie, Vieve," Tyson explained as he led her through the gallery. He paused only long enough to send a page for his coach. Then he turned Vieve to look at him. "She says she has secured an offer for my warehouse shares and that if I won't speak with her tonight, she will be forced to believe I am disinterested. I suggested a daytime conference, but she is clever. She means to assure herself that I am not interested in our marriage. I am going to send you home and go with her."

"Tyson, she frightens me. Can't you make some excuse?"

"I have worked hard to build this lie with her. She believes that I seek escape from my marriage and England."

"You must beware. Even Andrew is a part of this."

He frowned slightly. "I know that."

"You know? But..."

"I have suspected for a long time that Charles Latimer was trying to arrange your marriage with Shelby. Paul's marriage, though not by your uncle's doing, caused further debt to your father's estate. Had you likewise married poorly, Charles would have finally had the upper hand."

"And he would have approached my father?"

"Yes. Charles wants to be named as your father's heir, setting him up to become the baron of Chappington upon your father's death. Charles would have offered to save the family estate from certain ruin. He has been working for this for many years."

"Does he control them all? Lenore, Andrew, Elizabeth?"

"Lenore is rather difficult to control, and I'm counting on that. I think it is obvious that your aunt knows what her husband is doing. As for Andrew, how else could Faye have become so infatuated, unless Andrew has been much around their household? Andrew's desperation for you was surely encouraged by your uncle's money."

She gave a short and bitter laugh. "And all this time I thought he was half crazed with wild love for me. What a fool I've been."

Tyson smiled into her eyes. "I don't doubt that he wants you for yourself, Vieve. Perhaps, without your uncle's interference, he would have used some sense in courting you."

Bevis drove up to them, and Tyson gave her a quick kiss before handing her in. "Please be careful, Tyson. I'm afraid she has set a trap for you."

"Then she will find her plans changed, for I will not allow her to trick me again."

"I will wait for you."

"Please understand, she will detain me for as long as possible. Can you trust me?"

She brushed his cheek with her hand. "Of course I trust you," she whispered. "But hurry home."

The fire had burned to glowing embers when Vieve was roused by a sound. She had dozed in the chair before the fire, waiting for Tyson. She listened alertly. A door opened down the hall, and she sighed with disappointment. She attributed the sound to Doré's return.

She heard another door open, and she listened again. Why was he opening doors? Could it be Harriet? She moved to light a candle beside the bed and then crept closer to the closed bedroom door. She could hear someone in the hall outside her door. And then the latch moved.

Vieve withdrew from the door and stood with her back flush against the wall. The door slowly creaked open. She held her breath in sudden terror. Where was Doré? Bevis? Harriet? Tyson? Was she completely alone? She thought briefly to scream, but with this invader so close, she simply stood tensed, in wait. There was an audible sigh from the intruder. The door slowly closed.

Vieve listened acutely. She could hear the culprit go down the steps. Who?

Vieve tiptoed to the hearth and picked up the poker. She was not about to meet any aggressor defenseless. She stood close to her bedroom door, listening for any sound, for several minutes. She had left a light in the front sitting room for Tyson. Perhaps it was a thief, gone downstairs to look for valuables.

She heard the front door open and close loudly. No thief in the night would make such noise. She quietly opened her bedroom door and peered down the stairs. There was no light at the bottom. Someone had extinguished her candle. "Tyson?" she called.

"Vieve?" he returned.

"Tyson, there is someone in the house. The sitting room."

Silence surrounded her. "Lock your door," he instructed.

She followed his orders immediately, slamming and locking the door, but the poker did not leave her hand. Only seconds passed before she heard the crashing of glass, the loud banging of a door, and the blast of a gun. She heard Tyson's angry shout and a shuffling below. With a wild cry, she snatched open her door, but stopped abruptly at the top, for the way was dark. She ran to her bedside to retrieve the candle.

She found Tyson leaning against the sitting room door, clutching his arm. Over his hand ran a stream of bright red blood. He had a dazed look in his eyes, shaking his head.

"Tyson." She dropped the poker, put down the candle and ran to him, but he pushed her aside quickly to go down the foyer toward the cookery and coach house in pursuit. She followed him through the doors left open by the fleeing assailant. Gone.

Tyson ended his search in the coach house, where he found Bevis lying just inside the door that connected the attached room to the house. Tyson bent his cheek next to his servant's nose. He felt the pulse at his neck.

Vieve trembled violently and had no idea what to do, so she frantically searched for a flint to light candles.

"Vieve, cool water. Quickly."

She dropped the flint, ran to the cookery, and grabbed a whole pail of drinking water. A sound behind her caused her to turn, spying Harriet sleepily making her way through the foyer to the back of the house. "Mum?" she questioned in confusion.

Vieve did not stop to explain but struggled on with her bucket. Tyson quickly splashed water in Bevis's face, but the poor man was slow to rouse. He moaned in pain as Tyson lifted his head and held the ladle to his mouth. A few sputters followed, but Bevis came around.

"Lord Almighty," Harriet exclaimed from behind them. "What's happening in this house?"

Bevis, sitting up on the floor by this time, held the back of his head with one hand and with the other sought a large, thick board. "Blimey," he said, lifting the board. "Got me from be'ind, 'e did." He looked at Tyson. "I 'eard a bit o' movin' about, an' before I could do aught, wopped me on the 'ead, 'e did. Sorry, Cap'n."

"You did your best, Bevis."

He shook his head. "That's twice now, Cap. The fire in the cargo 'old on me Lady Lilly...an' this. I won't be lettin' ye down again. Cap'n."

"Come on, Bevis, no grudges held. You couldn't help it either time."

Tyson began to help Bevis to his feet when Vieve intervened. "Tyson, don't... your arm. Let me." She went to the servant's side to pull him up, turning her gaze toward her husband. "Who was it?"

"I couldn't tell. It was dark, and the pistol shot blinded me."

"Andrew? Charles?"

"Probably a hired man, for I did hear the departure...and Charles is not so light of foot. If it was Andrew, our problems are just beginning, for I put Doré to the task of following him."

"Is that where he is? Good heavens... is he in danger?"

"I hope not," Tyson returned, grasping his arm.

"Come along," she said sternly. "We can't do anything about him now, and we have some wounds to tend." She took Bevis's arm, and as she helped him into the house, she snapped orders at

Harriet. "Get me rags, salve, water, brandy... a scissors, needle and thread...Hurry up, Harriet."

In the foyer there sat straight-backed chairs on each side of a table, a perfect place for her to administer to both men at once. She seated Bevis and tore the shirt back from Tyson's wound.

"The ball has only grazed you, thank goodness, but the flesh is badly torn." She turned to Bevis. "Well, your hair is not in the way of this wound. It looks to need only compresses." And back to Tyson. "There are powder burns which I must clean and snip away, Tyson, or it will fester. It will be painful." And then she ran to the end of the foyer and shouted, "Harriet, come now."

Vieve went about her ministrations with Harriet's help. Tyson's upper arm was badly torn and bled profusely. It was difficult for Vieve to work with the steady crimson flow, and many times she sighed in frustration. Finally, she was satisfied that there was no powder to infect the wound and passed the decanter of brandy to Tyson, picking up her threaded needle. "Do without a glass, Tyson. I suppose the only way to stop the bleeding is to sew it."

Watching her concentration, he smiled to himself as he tipped the fancy crystal decanter and took a hearty swallow. "I would not have thought you capable of this, madam. I commend you."

"You are my husband. I cannot have you maimed."

He chuckled lightly. "Are you sure you think of me and not yourself?"

Though a light flush marked her cheeks for this teasing in front of the servants, she looked into his eyes and smiled warmly. "Can you be still, Tyson?"

"Still as a rock, if you ask it of me."

She gave him a light kiss on his sweating brow, marveling at the way he withstood this painful tending without flinching or complaints. And though his jaw tensed and pulsed and perspiration stood out damp on his cheeks and brow, he never uttered a word. She was finished when the front door opened and Doré entered, stopping in astonishment when he sighted the infirmary in the foyer.

"Well, monsieur, at last," Tyson said, his voice slightly subdued.

"What is it? What has happened here?"

"An unknown intruder," Vieve quickly explained. "Bevis was struck in the head, and Tyson was shot before he got away. Did you watch Andrew all night?"

"I left him several hours ago, but I can assure you, it was not him. He had to be carried to his rooms, he was so drunk. Charles?"

Tyson shook his head. "Whoever, he was not a large man, but moderate in size, perhaps small, and light of foot and swift. It was very dark. I didn't see anything, but the departure was not that of a large or drunken man."

"Lenore?" Doré asked.

Tyson again shook his head. "I was with her all evening. She forced my presence to discuss a certain anonymous buyer she has found for me."

Doré took a step closer. "Everyone is all right?"

"We will mend," Tyson assured him.

Doré looked at Vieve. "Petite? You are all right?"

She nodded, her chin beginning to quiver slightly now that the emergency was past and real fear settled in.

"Tyson," Doré said. "We must consider that Lenore means to assure herself of your devotion...by doing away with your wife."

Tyson nodded, as if the thought had already crossed his mind. "There is very little left of the night, and from now on, we will be forced to give much attention to detail. Let's get a little sleep now, for sleepless nights will surely come." He turned to Bevis. "Enjoy your last night with the horses, mate. After tonight, your services will be required in the house."

Bevis nodded and, holding a damp rag to his head, departed. Harriet, for once stunned silent, lumbered up the stairs to her room. Doré smiled ruefully and turned only to throw the bolt on the front door. Vieve and Tyson were left alone in the foyer. Her brow was creased with concern.

"Kiss me," Tyson commanded.

First surprise, then amusement showed in her eyes as she willingly bent her lips to his. But Tyson surprised her with a deep, searing kiss, his uninjured arm going around her waist and pulling her down on his knee. Though surprised by the strength and amorous nature of his kiss, she locked her slim fingers into the hair at the back of his neck and gave herself to his emotion. She tasted his warm mouth, parting her lips willingly for him, and a long while later, when he released her lips, she was breathless.

"I mean for us to have many years together, my love," he said softly. "You need not be afraid. I won't let anything happen to you."

Twelve

Christmas passed quietly in the Gervais household while all residents stayed close to home. Tyson kept his injured arm in a sling, and Bevis complained of headaches. Doré made only quick trips to the Latimer household. He met the housemaid, Mary Earwhick, behind the kitchens, and was home again quickly. Since Tyson had been injured, Doré grew restless with all the possibilities. "I had thought Monsieur Latimer concerned only with profit, and a killer by association rather than pure intent, but now I wonder if he is not just another cold-blooded murderer."

"What do you mean, by association?" Vieve asked.

Tyson was the one to explain. "Many of the disasters that befell your father over the years resulted in death. In the warehouse fire a body was found, though I doubt the man was killed intentionally. And the ship that was lost, if it was sunk on purpose, saw all aboard killed. Your father's records even show that years ago a barn full of sheep's wool burned, cause unknown, and four men died fighting that fire."

"What I mean, *cherie*," Doré went on, "is that there are two criminals at work. A man who does not mourn the death of someone who happens to be in his way of making a fortune, and a man who will point a pistol and pull the trigger. There is a different set of mind, and while both types could be contained within Charles Latimer himself, it is also possible that two people are at work against us."

As if nature herself would assist, a crippling blizzard followed Christmas, covering the city with a snowstorm that drove every citizen inside. Tyson and Vieve met the wet cold of January with renewed strength.

Closeness intensified in the Gervais household. The weather not only kept them in, but in frequent discussion. On the other hand, in the Latimer household, the last remnants of family ties were falling apart. On the seventh day of January, while Charles was closed in his study with two hired men, Robert said good-bye to his mother. Elizabeth stood close to the door as Robert threw a few belongings into a bag. "After all there is for you to manage, you will go like this?" she asked.

"You knew I would," he said shortly.

"But, Robert, where will you go? Why do you not wait to take this fortune that your father has built?"

He turned and looked with exasperation at his mother. "I have signed on a merchant vessel, and I won't stay because Father has time for nothing but this driving bitterness. If he dies, send word and I will come back. And yes, I will do better with it." He laughed shortly, and his lips curved in an ugly sneer. "Don't you see that twenty more years will be lost to his quest against Lord Ridgley? If Uncle Boris dies before Father has what he wants, Father will only carry on, working against Paul, but he will never cease. You know what he has done. How can you stand beside him for more?"

"I won't," she lied.

"You will," he shouted back. "He has stolen and killed to get what he wants. To go along with it is the same as doing it."

"Robert, do not be so hard on me. I understand what your father wants...and in the end, you will benefit as well."

"He told you that, didn't he?" Robert laughed. "Well, I am not interested in the benefits achieved through thievery and murder."

"There is no evidence that your father committed such crimes. You must not say that."

"No evidence? There were hands who died in a fire at Chappington when I was a child. There were bones found in the warehouse ash; someone was using that place as shelter when it burned. There were shiphands on the merchantman that Lord Ridgley lost, and though we don't know their fate, none ever returned. It is said to have been lost in a mysterious storm that no other vessel reported. All those people are dead, Mother."

"What makes you think that your father would do such things? It is ill fortune for Boris... nothing more."

"It is a dire consequence that each time Father contrives a plan to undermine Uncle Boris, some dreadful event seems to occur. Father has never hidden his desires; we have all heard him.

Just days after his rage over the healthy profit Lord Ridgley was bound to make on sheep's wool, his barn burned. When Father feared that Uncle Boris would save his estate through profitable shipping, his largest merchantman sunk. Then the warehouses, owned for only two years and beginning a thriving business..." He turned away in disgust. "Do what you will. I am leaving."

"Robert..."

"You may leave him and come with me if you like."

"I cannot," she said weakly. "Where would I go?"

"You could go to Lord Ridgley and throw yourself on his mercy."

She shook her head sadly. "I must see to your sisters."

He laughed, a short, irritated sound. "And you think giving Faye to Shelby is seeing to her? Has Father finally poisoned you as well?"

"Faye is with child," Elizabeth said softly.

Robert whirled about and stared in shock at his mother.

"She thinks I do not know; she thinks no one knows. I suspect she has not been able to tell even Andrew, but it is he. I know what my foolish daughter has done."

Robert turned back to the bag he packed. He gave a sharp pull on the drawstring and hefted the thing over his shoulder. He faced his mother with tears in his eyes. "I would stay if I could help any of you. But I will leave rather than go down with you." He shook his head. "Why," he whispered. "Why did you ever marry him?"

Elizabeth's hand gently touched her firstborn's cheek. "I carried you, my love. My choices were fewer than even yours."

"Oh, Mother," he sighed, embracing her.

"Go," she said with conviction. "It is better that you go. When you return, this will surely be past. I have begged you to stay for myself, but I see you are right. I will salvage what I can so there will be something for you to return for. I love you, my dearest son. I love you."

Elizabeth was aware that no one would notice her mourning after her son, her favorite child, left her. Charles did not miss her presence at the dinner table, and Faye, with her own problems, did not look for her mother. Beth, who was too young to take deep interest in those conflicts that might absorb her parents, stayed with her governess by day and her maid at night. When

Robert had been gone for a week, Elizabeth braved her husband's study. She was not surprised to find that the newest addition to their household, a pretty young maid named Mary, was delivering him tea.

"Have you noticed anything different about our household, Charles?" Elizabeth asked brittlely.

"Say what's on your mind and be done with it," he ordered impatiently.

"Your son is gone. He has left us. He wants no part of this family."

"What is this?"

"Robert is gone. He signed onto a merchant vessel as an apprentice mate and means to get experience on the sea. He will not return."

"He turns his back on his inheritance? On the money I have worked for?" Charles said, stunned by this. "Why?"

"He knows, as I do, that none of what you want is for your family, but all pointed toward your brother's ruin. And you, Charles, are the only one who cares."

"The ungrateful whelp," Charles growled. "He'll be back."

"Just say you will give up this madness. Forget Boris and the title to the Chappington seat."

He looked at her as if he would look through her. "My son has left me. He is too childish. When he returns, he will be my heir to more than merchant concerns."

Elizabeth's head tilted back, her eyes rolling as if in a swoon, her fists so tightly clenched that her nails dug into her hands. He would not cease until he had won.

Her chin slowly fell forward, and her eyes opened and shone with a blazing light that her husband did not notice, for he still shuffled papers around his desk.

She took a deep breath to prepare herself for more trauma. "If you have not yet sealed an agreement with Andrew Shelby, you had best do so. Faye carries his child. This cannot wait."

She refused to wait for any reply, but fled from his study, letting the stunned silence from within answer her. Charles was completely unaware of what happened in his own house with his own family, but he knew every step taken by Captain Gervais and Lord Ridgley.

As the month of January moved slowly to its end, the level of the warehouse slowly heightened. Work was tedious, for the winter months made construction difficult. But ships from America in the spring would bring cargo, and there could be no delay, even though the cost of hiring workers was higher than in summer months.

The first week of February came softly to the land in warmer temperatures, allowing more freedom of travel and an increase in the building, and commerce in the city was strong again. As Vieve stepped into her bedroom in midafternoon, she found her husband preening before the mirror, inspecting his reflection. She smiled to herself and leaned against the door. He turned her way and raised a brow in question.

"No, my love," she said. "I am not going to tell you how handsome you look."

"Come, wench. I perceive this as my last visit with Lenore. Today I will tell her that if she cannot provide the money, I will leave London without her. Do I look good enough for the part?"

She opened her arms to him. "Kiss me in a way that will assure me I need feel no jealousy toward her."

A short time later he was climbing the stairs to Lenore's second-floor apartments. Thinking this business with her nearly over, his mind was drawn sharply to his life before all this had begun. He had thought his existence in Virginia to have been so plentiful, so full. But that was before Vieve, who had been the missing link. A long and happy marriage with her was all he wished for now. He was sorry that his mother had never known her, sorry that she had died worrying that he would foolishly wed someone like Lenore.

A maid allowed him to come in, and he sat in Lenore's sitting room for a long time while Lenore primped to receive him. She swept into the room with her usual confidence and aplomb. "Tyson, darling, I wasn't expecting you."

"I hope I don't put you at some disadvantage," he apologized. "I thought I had better come and tell you that I can wait no longer. Lord Ridgley is pressuring me for more money and actively looking for weaknesses in my character. I have been followed. Should he find out I killed an Englishman, his influence here could put me away...or see me hang. If you cannot bring an investor to me soon, I shall have to leave England. Alone."

She smiled shrewdly. "Why, Tyson, that sounds so desperate."

"Oh, it is that, my dear," he said with a smile of his own. "I can assure you, I am willing to sign over my warehouse shares for a mere portion of my original investment, but if you sell me out too cheaply, I shall be hard put once home. I'm afraid I committed a very large portion of my wealth."

"What about us?" she asked coyly.

Tyson stepped toward her and put his arm around her waist, drawing her close. "If you can help me retrieve some money, the voyage home will be more pleasant than your trip over."

"Oh, you tease. You know that isn't enough."

"What is it you want? Remember, you are dealing with a desperate man."

"Marriage," she replied easily.

He chuckled. "That might be a little difficult for me, as I am already married."

"You can get an annulment, can't you?"

"I could try," he suggested. "But can't we talk about that later...after you've..."

"No, we cannot," she said, wiggling out of his embrace. "I have suffered your change of mood before, Tyson, and I have no intention of helping you only to have you throw me over once we are home."

He lifted both brows in surprise. "Lenore, you amaze me. You offer help without my asking, then you hold out for a higher price. Just when I thought we finally understood each other, I have this terrible feeling that you want my blood."

She turned her back on him in frustration. "You know what I wish to hear from you. You played on my affection for a good many years, but when it finally met your mood to marry, you looked hard for another."

"So did you find another, Lenore."

She whirled back to face him. "And you killed him," she said, tears sparkling in her eyes. "Oh, Tyson, all I have ever wanted is your love. Why don't you see that?"

"I suppose it is because you have such a strange way of showing it. If you were concerned about having my love, why didn't you stop Everly from goading me into that duel?"

"Because," she said, sniffing back her tears, "I didn't think you would hurt him, and I thought once you fought for me you would claim me."

He stepped toward her again. "That leaves me fleeing his death and begging for your help. Well, Lenore? Where is your great love?"

"I will help you," she said. "I am bound to help you no matter how cruelly you abuse me. I will get the money you need so that we can both flee from here. But I will need a little time."

"How much time?"

"I don't know. He...the man who is interested...is away."

"What is his name?" Tyson pressed.

"He asked that I keep that to myself until after the contracts are signed and the money exchanged."

"Well, I warn you, I don't have much time."

"You'll have to wait until I can reach him," she snapped. "I will do what I can. And then do we leave together?"

He touched her cheek. "Without even bothering to pack our clothes, my dear," he said slyly.

Her green eyes sparkled. "If you lie to me, Tyson, I don't know what I'll do."

"That is dangerous talk, Lenore," he warned. "Send word when you have secured the money for me."

"You will have to... the man wants you to sign before..."

"No," he said sternly. "To give over my shares before I see money would be foolish. We will send the contracts to him by messenger."

"What if I can't convince him to do that?"

Tyson laughed. "You? Come now, my dear, you pride yourself in convincing men. You will think of something. I will await your message."

"I am to send word to your house?" she asked.

"Certainly. Once you have the money in your hands, I will book passage. On the day we depart, you may bring it to me, and I will take you to the wharves myself."

Her tongue moistened her lips, and her eyes twinkled. "I shall enjoy the expression on your darling wife's face when you bid her adieu."

"You are entertained in very strange ways, Lenore. Don't you worry about her broken heart? She is so young."

"I don't care about her at all. I only want you...and you want me. What else matters?"

"One would almost think you wish Madam Gervais harm."

She laughed in genuine amusement. "I assure you, I couldn't be bothered. But if she dares follow us to Virginia, I shall claw out her eyes. You may warn her...never mind, I will do so myself."

"Then...I await word that you have the money. And don't be long. The baron is getting impatient for more wealth."

"I will hurry, Tyson."

She smiled happily and embraced him, lifting her chin for a deep kiss. "There is time enough for that, my dear," he said. "I should be going."

One week later, Lenore's message arrived. Tyson sent Doré to dockside to book passage on the next merchantman that could take passengers. A frigate bound for France was due to leave in two days, which seemed good enough. He sent word to Lenore to be at his home by early morning, with the money and contracts, on the day the ship was to sail.

Vieve had barely slept, but was up before dawn, dressed for their visitor. She met Doré in the foyer, and he smiled and ran a gentle finger under her eyes. "Do not be afraid, ma belle. Mademoiselle will bear her vicious claws for only a moment before she flees."

Tyson came down the stairs. He was still fastening his cuff links, his shirt open, and his coat draped over his arm. "Are we ready? In the sitting room, then."

The minutes dragged as the sun slowly rose. The sound of a coach clattering up the street interrupted the early morning silence. Tyson rose and looked at Doré and Vieve. "This will be over shortly."

The sitting room doors were closed, and Tyson stood alone in the foyer. He opened the front door upon Lenore's first light rapping. She smiled her greeting instantly, excitement shining in her green eyes. She wore rich traveling clothes, no doubt hastily sewn by some abused clothier. In her hand was a rolled parchment.

"You have the money?" he asked.

"In a chest in the coach. It was difficult for the man to put his hands on so much, Tyson, and he was reluctant to let me have it. I had to purchase a voucher for passage for two to America leaving in a fortnight. It was the only way to convince the man that we will be here long enough for him to retrieve his contracts if you are of a mind to cheat him."

"I knew you would be successful. Bring the chest inside."

"Whatever for? Can't we leave at once?"

"I'm going to count the money first."

"I've counted...." Her voice trailed off as she noticed the hard set of his eyes. She shook the rolled parchment. "Very well." She left the house abruptly, and Tyson watched her from the open door. The driver of her hired coach was needed to bring the leather chest. Tyson took it from the driver and went into the sitting room, Lenore close behind.

Lenore stopped in astonishment when she spied Doré and Vieve. Doré stood and bowed in her presence. "Ah, mademoiselle, did I not tell you that we could help Tyson?"

Lenore laughed uncomfortably, looking at Tyson's back as he opened the chest and picked through the money.

"Tyson, how brazen. A farewell party?"

Tyson slowly turned, taking two steps toward her, and pulled the rolled paper from her hand. Her eyes were wide with confusion, but she did not resist. He unrolled the parchment and looked at it, a smile growing on his lips. "Charles Latimer, of course." His eyes rose to Lenore's face. "Please have a seat, my dear. This shouldn't take long."

"Tyson, really, I'd rather we be—"

"Sit down, Lenore. Now."

She clamped her mouth shut and whirled angrily to the only available settee, looking suspiciously at Vieve and Doré over her shoulder.

"The farewell party is only for you, my dear. Since Charles was generous to pay your passage to London and provide your income while you were here, I doubt he will be terribly upset that you have helped yourself to this little pot of money for your trip out of England."

"But the contracts..."

"My investment is not for sale. It never was."

"You tricked me?" she asked in astonishment. "Why?"

Tyson laughed as if in genuine amusement. "You're not used to having the bad end of the joke, are you, Lenore? Well, at least you don't have to endure the hardship of thinking you'd actually killed someone. Michael, the actor? His 'widow' is in my employ. I know how you tricked me."

Lenore was stunned speechless for a moment. Then her eyes slowly took on the fury of a woman used, and her mouth was pinched with rage. "What the hell is happening here?"

"You're leaving the country, compliments of Charles Latimer. I have committed no murder. If Charles finds out that there is nothing you can do to convict me of any crime, he will cut you loose, penniless in a foreign country." Tyson slowly walked toward his wife, leisurely took his place beside her, draping an arm around her shoulders, and smiled at Lenore. "I am doing you a great favor, Lenore. In letting you go, I am saving your life. Latimer is a desperate man...he might have killed you for your lies."

"Tyson...I don't know what you're talking about. Charles is the man with the money, but..."

"Don't bother," he said sharply. "It is over. I know that he brought you here, that you were setting me up for a hanging, and that Latimer had no intention of letting me simply leave the country unscathed. That was your reason for purchasing another voucher, wasn't it? Was he planning to meet me at dockside to arrest me?"

Much to Tyson's surprise, Lenore's eyes misted. "I wouldn't have let anything happen to you."

"How very compassionate of you. When did you tell him these contracts would be delivered to him?"

"By this afternoon," she said weakly.

Tyson looked at Doré. "I'm quite sure Charles will have agents at the wharves."

Doré slowly nodded. "Mademoiselle will be uncomfortable, but a whale boat will deliver her to her ship. We do not go to a docked vessel." He looked at Lenore. "For your safety, *cherie*."

"You bastard," she hissed. "You planned this out from the beginning. There were no letters sent to me in Richmond; Tyson had never changed his mind about marrying me."

Doré grinned. "Oui, madame."

"Just be sure she is aboard when they leave port. Even if you have to tie her."

"Do not worry, Tyson." Doré rose. "Mademoiselle? Shall we take your coach?"

Lenore rose to her feet and moved toward the chest, sneering at Tyson as she moved.

"One moment, my dear. I don't think you'll be needing all of this."

"What?" she questioned, whirling. "But you said..."

"I said your departure was compliments of Charles. I see thirty thousand pounds here; the voyage is not nearly as costly as that."

"You intend to keep it?"

Tyson chuckled, rising, and pulled some pound notes out of the chest, counting it quickly. "I have had quite a few expenses myself, my dear. Everly's wife, for instance, was also active in the theatre. And there is the damage that Latimer did, the cost of remaining in London to watch him..."

"But I did not even bring all my possessions with me."

He held out a few rolled-up pound notes. "There is enough to get you back to Richmond, and a little extra. Do be sure that you only collect your things from your home. Didn't I hear you mention an aunt in Boston?"

"What? You mean to say—"

"I mean that I will not be here forever, and when I return to Richmond, if you are living there, I will expose your crimes. The penalty, whatever it is, will be most unpleasant."

She lifted her chin indignantly. "You would have to find Everly. Otherwise, I can deny it."

"An empty grave and an actor looking for work? Do you doubt I can do it? You amaze me, Lenore; the man has already been paid by you. How do you rely on his future silence?" He laughed and shook his head. "Unless you actually bedded the fool and suppose that there is some loyalty bound to you."

"I wonder, Tyson, where there is loyalty," she angrily flung at him. "Had you accorded me the slightest amount, none of this would have ever happened. Had you married me after becoming my lover, I would not have become desperate. I did ask you to make right your affection...long before I tried trickery."

"Is that how you justify all the pain you've caused?" Tyson tilted his head in the direction of the door, holding the money out to her. Doré took her elbow in a firm grip, and with a last hateful glance, she snatched the money from Tyson's hand and moved toward the door.

"The most terrifying thing is," Tyson began, causing her to turn back and look at him. "Had you convinced me that you had the slightest bit of honor, decency, or morals, I might have married you long ago." He bowed elaborately. "I thank you, madam. That would have been a horrible trick, indeed."

Lenore whirled away from him and preceded Doré to the door. Tyson heard it slam.

Vieve was on her feet and in his arms instantly. She trembled as he embraced her tightly. He lifted her chin with a finger. "It is better that you witnessed that for yourself. That was Lenore at her worst."

"How did she hold you for so long?"

"She did not hold me, my love. I had nothing at all before you. I worked, cared for my family, amassed money, and did not know how lonely I was. They all tried to tell me there was more for me... but until I found you, I did not know what anyone meant."

"I wonder if Andrew Shelby knows what a great help he is?" Tyson mumbled as he paged through the bound ledger that Mary Earwhick brought him.

"He had a terrible argument with Mr. Latimer," Mary explained. "He left the house in a temper, young Faye was crying, Mr. Latimer was yelling, and Mrs. Latimer was trying to quiet both of them. Then Shelby came back just after dinner when the house was quiet and forced his way in, tearing through every cupboard and drawer in Mr. Latimer's study. When Mr. Latimer and his men were busy restraining him, I could not see a better chance to pick up the book and leave the house." She sighed heavily. "I would have had to leave soon, Captain. It was becoming too much. The trouble worsens every day."

"What happened to Andrew?"

She dropped her gaze. "They beat him and threw him into the street. He was badly done."

Tyson slowly looked through the ledger. Mary sat on the chair in front of his desk, and Doré stood behind Tyson, looking over his shoulder.

"Is it what you want, Captain?"

"You're certain there is not another?"

"No, sir. I had plenty of time to look through his things, and this is the only ledger he guarded."

Tyson looked over his shoulder at Doré. "It does not give evidence of crimes, but every entry here describes his purchase of Lord Ridgley's property through agents. They are not only named, but Charles was even audacious enough to label the book with Chappington. I imagine he was going to present this to his brother when he was convinced the estate was poor enough." Tyson snorted derisively. "Charles's records are as meticulous as the baron's."

"Is it enough to put him away?" Doré asked.

"Probably not, but it may be enough to convince him that he could be locked away if Lord Ridgley chose. If Lord Ridgley is forced to use this record alone to stop Charles, it should raise some very interesting questions. If Charles was acting within the law in his acquisitions, why was there a need for secrecy? In almost every instance he had established another to act as owner of these properties under the baron. I am certain that each entry will coincide with the baron's disasters."

"Will you confront him now? Lenore has only been gone for two days."

"If Charles has noticed his account missing, he will be hysterical by now." Tyson raised a brow. "A good mood, I think, in which to see him."

Tyson went alone to the Latimer house. The housekeeper did not wish to admit him, but he was insistent. From the foyer he heard a loud thump and Charles's shouting. "What do you mean you can't find him. You will find him, you imbecile. I pay you to find people."

Tyson watched in amusement as the hired man fled through the hall and out the door. Tyson walked in the direction of the bellowing, past the disgruntled housekeeper, finding Charles red-faced and furious, pacing behind his desk.

Charles stopped suddenly. He was stunned speechless as he was left to stare at the large, imposing figure of Captain Gervais.

"Good afternoon, Charles," Tyson said evenly. "I assume you have lost Andrew Shelby?"

"What do you want?"

"I came to give you these," he said, entering and tossing the documents Charles had drawn on his desk. "They are unsigned, of course. And Lenore has fled the country with your money. She lied to you, Charles. There was no death. The duel was a hoax."

Charles stared at Tyson, disbelief showing all over his face.

"Andrew is not the thief you seek. I am the man who has your ledger and papers." Tyson chuckled at Charles's expression of surprise. "That's right, I have them. They are not where you can easily find them, of course, for I know you to be well schooled in having fires set, so I will save you the trouble. You will not succeed in destroying the evidence against you by burning down my house. Lord Moresay has the ledger in safekeeping."

"What the hell are you talking about?" Charles blustered.

"I thought you were seeking Andrew to find your ledger, the one labeled Chappington."

Charles's color heightened, and he hastily opened a desk drawer, lifting out several ledgers, papers, and paraphernalia.

"You hadn't even noticed it was missing? Well, I have it. I can't help you find Andrew, however. That you will have to do on your own."

Charles leaned on his desk. "I have no idea what you're talking about. I am looking for Shelby because he is the father of my daughter's child, and she is well along. She will not deliver a bastard."

Tyson shook his head. "You do have your troubles, don't you. Well, they are only beginning."

"So you have my ledger? So what?"

Tyson shrugged. "Your records of purchases and payments to agents seem to coincide perfectly with all of Lord Ridgley's problems. Fires, destruction of property, and death. Your detail is so perfect that I think the courts will be convinced that you have gone to illegal lengths to ruin your brother."

"I have used only my own wit and success to lay my hands on the title I deserve," Charles shouted. "Boris has had bad luck that has been my good fortune, and there is nothing in it that can hurt me."

"Do you think anyone will believe that, Latimer? Lord Ridgley has suffered more ill fortune than anyone in this precious little kingdom. Anyone would agree that there had to be foul play." Tyson paused a moment and looked hard into the merchant's eyes. "Ironically, there was a fire on my ship just after I invested with the baron. A lantern was dropped into the cargo hold. Had we failed to save her, the cost would have wiped out my investment. There happens to be a payment to a hired man named Will Tetcher on that very day."

"I have paid Tetcher for services on my behalf for many years. I know nothing of fires or ships...."

Tyson's eyes burned angrily. "I have had enough of this acting, Latimer. Here are your choices: you may take your chances on your professed innocence, or you may make restitution with Lord Ridgley. He will settle for your sworn statement, money for damages, and a document, signed and witnessed, promising that neither you nor your heirs will ever seek the Chappington seat. Your ledger will remain a property of the court for future evidence."

"I have done nothing but succeed," he shouted. "I will not crawl before Boris. Never. Never in a hundred years."

"Think about it quickly, Charles. The baron is tired of your tactics, and you have lost quite a lot of money lately. If you wait, you will have nothing left."

Tyson turned and left the study. The house was quiet as he departed, but he felt the presence of many invisible eavesdroppers. When he reached his house again, Doré and Vieve were waiting for him.

"It is time to send for Lord Ridgley. Get a courier, Doré, and let's hope the weather is on our side. The baron should inform Paul, leave his property well guarded, and come to London ready to fight."

Thirteen

Charles stood at the foot of the steps and called his daughter to come downstairs. With each passing day, Faye's ripening form became more evident. She was naturally plump and so hid her pregnancy for a long while, but as she approached six months it was painfully obvious. As she came down the stairs he winced with discomfort. Her expression was sad; she seemed to feel great pain.

He reached for her hand to guide her down the last step. "Are you well, dear?" he asked.

"No, Papa. I am ill every day."

Charles sighed. "I should kill him, but that would do you no good. Come and sit down. He should be here shortly."

"There is no way you can change his mind. He does not wish to marry me."

"Your father will change his mind, dear," Elizabeth said from the stair. She had taken to wearing dark clothing, and it made her face seem all the more pale. As Charles looked up at her, he noticed that she had grayed considerably in the past few weeks. He reasoned Faye's pregnancy and Robert's flight had most likely done this to her.

It had all gotten away from him somehow. He meant to best his brother, but he had not meant to hurt his own family. He nudged Faye gently ahead of him into the parlor and met his wife at the foot of the stairs.

"I had entrusted their welfare to you. You have done poorly by them," he said.

"How dare you ask me to carry any blame." She narrowed her eyes in fierce hatred. "It is all because of you, Charles. Long ago you could have found a way to feel success without any envy of what your brother has. This is all your doing."

"I will see Faye settled, and Robert will return..."

Elizabeth laughed loudly, shrilly, showing an even row of small teeth. "Robert swears to return when you are dead, and if you think this action you plan to take will settle Faye, you are so mistaken. She will be committed to a selfish man who does not love her, just as I have been these twenty years." Elizabeth walked past him into the parlor, where her daughter waited. "Then she will know what I have been through...because of you," she said over her shoulder.

Charles grabbed her arm, looking into her eyes. "Did Robert really say that? That he would only return when I was dead?"

Her lips curved in a mocking smile. She pulled her arm out of his grasp, leaving him to stand in the parlor doorframe.

Charles was about to join the women when the front door opened and two of his men brought in Andrew Shelby. He met the feral gleam in the young man's eyes. Andrew had been cleaned up as much as possible. When Charles's hired men had finally found him, Andrew had been lost in a drunken stupor for days.

"Is that the best you could do with him?" Charles asked.

One of the men shrugged. "We shaved him up, sir. Clean clothes."

Andrew smirked. "Does my appearance not please you, Mr. Latimer?"

Charles frowned. "I gave you credit for better sense. But by God, if I have to put a gun to your head, you will give my daughter a wedded name. Get in here," he said, going ahead of Andrew into the parlor.

Once inside, Charles turned to watch Andrew enter. He took some small satisfaction in Andrew's reaction to Faye, for the young man had not seen her since her pregnancy had begun to show. He grimaced in discomfort at the sight of her round belly. But Faye could not raise her eyes. She looked at her hands.

"Sit down, Shelby," Charles demanded hotly. "I don't intend to spend much time on this."

Andrew took his eyes off Faye and sauntered toward a chair, sitting with one leg outstretched in obvious insolence.

"I have contracts drawn for my daughter's marriage to you, and you will sign them. I cannot force you to be a decent husband to her, but I can force you to marry her. And if you abuse her further, I will kill you."

"Abuse her. My God, Latimer, you have more gall than anyone I've ever met." He laughed suddenly. "She begged me to take her; she waited for me each time I left your study."

Faye's shoulders began to tremble with the weight of her sobs.

"That's enough," Charles shouted. "She carries your child, and there is no necessity to shame her further. No matter what she might have done, she is a child herself and you are a man. Or are you?"

"You thought I was man enough to seduce and conquer Vieve," Andrew snidely returned. Faye looked up. "Doesn't your daughter know that you were paying me to claim Vieve's virginity? I see she doesn't." He looked at Faye. "Paid, bribed, and finally he threatened. He took the debt off my family lands, gave me loans against a contract that they would be removed if I could marry her, and then threatened to leave me with nothing if I could not at least rape her. Why the hell do you think I was in your household so much of the time? Because we were friends?"

Faye looked in astonishment at her father. "Papa? You paid him to court Vieve?" Suddenly she smiled. "I thought... I always thought you wanted her."

"I did want her," Andrew said sullenly. "I wanted her so badly that I did everything your father asked of me."

"Oh, Papa," she said, tears springing to her eyes again.

"It was not meant to harm you, Faye," Charles said with unusual calm. "I had no idea that you were interested in Andrew."

"But who was it meant to harm?"

"Your Uncle Boris," Elizabeth said with sharp clarity. "Charles wished to have Vieve marry at least as poorly as Paul, isn't that right, Charles?"

"That is of no concern now—"

"It concerns me," Andrew said. "You used me, lied to me, and gave me instructions to act as though I burned so with passion that I was out of control." Andrew laughed sharply. "The irony is that I was so damned worked up trying to win her that when your own daughter teased me and begged me, I had no control."

Charles looked at Elizabeth and almost jumped at the piercing look in her eyes and the superior smile on her lips.

"Charles knows a good deal about that," she said sarcastically. "That's exactly how it was for us, wasn't it, my love? You were so overwrought with desire that you could not control yourself. Until you had my dowry, that is. Since that time, control has been your most charming quality."

"Elizabeth..."

"Andrew," she said, turning to him. "You will marry my daughter immediately. Charles will provide a dowry in addition to those lands which will be given back to you. I will consider no argument. It is marriage, or I will personally see you arrested and stripped of your useless title."

"You needn't go so far, madam," Andrew said. "I will marry her to get my property back, if she swears the child is mine."

The color drained from Faye's face as she looked at him. "Andrew, do you...still... love her?"

"Vieve? That is over. She won't have me." He glared at Charles. "Your father's advice was bad."

Faye rose slowly from her chair. As she looked at Andrew, tears began to stream down her cheeks. "The child is yours, Andrew. There was never anyone else. I am not as pretty as Vieve."

Faye looked at her father. "I wish you had not done all that, Papa. I might never have had a marriage proposal... but I think I would have been better off than this." She turned slowly and left the room, softly closing the door behind her.

Elizabeth turned her blazing eyes on Andrew. "Sign the contracts of marriage. You will be our guest until you wed her."

"Do you worry that I will flee, madam? With what, pray? Your kindly husband has already stripped me bare. I have nothing." He laughed a little wildly. "Nothing but Faye." Again he laughed, a sound so hysterical that it verged on sobs and Charles could not bear it. He stomped toward Andrew and lifted him by the lapels on his coat, drawing him up and shaking him furiously.

"God damn you, stop it. Stop it. It's not my fault, do you hear me? It is not my fault that you didn't get the precious little bitch. Had I known what you would do to my own daughter, I would have—"

He dropped Andrew abruptly, letting him fall back into the chair. The pressure inside Charles's head felt strong enough to explode. His mouth was dry, his eyes moist. He looked at his wife. She smiled at the rage, but had not moved even slightly. Her hands were still folded in her lap, her eyes gleaming as she watched.

Andrew's angry eyes were focused on Charles's face. "You need remember only one thing, Charles. I did to your daughter what you paid me to do to Vieve. But your daughter was easier."

Charles's hand came out and slapped Andrew's face. Blood trickled from his hp. Elizabeth rose slowly to her feet and glared at the young man. Although her posture was restrained, Charles thought she looked as if she could kill. As she slowly turned toward Charles, her expression remained unchanged.

"Charles, get the papers signed. If you wish to beat him later, you may."

Elizabeth slowly moved toward the parlor door. As her hand touched the latch there came a wild scream from upstairs. She threw the door open and rushed to the steps, catching Beth at the bottom.

"Faye," Beth cried. "Out her window... to the courtyard. She...she...jumped. Mama."

Elizabeth threw a crazed look over her shoulder at Charles and then flew to the back of the house, her husband and daughter close on her heels. Elizabeth stopped so abruptly when she saw Faye's lifeless form that Charles nearly ran into her. His hands grasped her shoulders for only a second to move her out of the way.

Charles rushed to Faye, kneeling to roll over her twisted form. His arms shook as he lifted her head. Blood spilled from her crushed skull; her eyes were open and lifeless. He stared at her for a long moment; the shock of finding her dead by her own will immobilized him. When he looked up at his wife, tears wet his cheeks.

Elizabeth was still and ashen. Over her shoulder Andrew quickly peered at Faye, his eyes rounding slightly in disbelief, before he turned and ran back into the house with great speed. His running steps through the house and out the front were the only sound.

"Is she...dead?" Elizabeth asked, her voice firm but soft.

Charles stared at his wife for a long moment. How was she so controlled? He had thought of her as frail, dependent.

The full force of what had happened hit him. He knew he was not the best husband and a less than perfect father, but he had not, until this very moment, thought that his actions would wreak such havoc on his own family. It was only the estate of Chappington he had ever wished to weaken...and he had been more than willing to build that up again once Lord Ridgley gave him his due.

He looked back at Faye's stricken face. "Oh, my God," he wailed. He let his head fall over hers and was racked with shattering, uncontrollable sobs. Distantly he heard the rustle of his wife's dark dress as she turned away and left him alone with his daughter.

When Lord Ridgley arrived in London, he was stunned by the news. He had never figured Andrew or Faye doomed to such disaster. Upon hearing the details of his niece's suicide and Andrew's disappearance, he embraced his daughter so tightly that he nearly crushed her, and his old arms trembled.

"You must believe that I did not intend Charles even the equal amount of harm as he's caused me."

Tyson intervened with a hand on the baron's shoulder. "You have not been the cause of this. It was not my confrontation with Charles that caused Robert to leave, Faye to die, and Andrew to flee into hiding. The source of this misfortune has taken years to develop."

Vieve was amazed that her father insisted they attend the funeral. Not the burial, he said specifically, nor the wake, but the funeral only. And so, donned in black, Lord Ridgley and Captain and Madam Gervais were latecomers to the church, seated behind twenty or thirty others in the back. They sat tense and alert through the words of the Anglican priest.

Vieve watched her uncle's back. She had never before seen him humbled, his shoulders rounded and trembling with emotion. Beside him, Elizabeth's shoulders were straight and square, her chin held level in dignity, her posture erect. She did not weep, nor did she comfort Beth. The three nursed their pain individually, through the difficult words of mourning.

When the priest had finished, Charles slowly rose, his back bent and his head down. He took his wife's arm and brought her down the aisle of the small church. Lord Ridgley stepped into the aisle to block their passage, and the two men met eyes.

"I am sorry, Charles, for your loss," Lord Ridgley said softly.

Charles's eyes flared slightly, but they were red-rimmed and full of pain. Elizabeth was pale, but her eyes were clear. She looked past the men at Vieve.

"Why do you come?" Charles asked. "For my daughter?"

"No, Charles. I came to end this feud. We know all about each other now. I will stay in London until you are recovered enough to speak to me. Please."

Vieve looked at her aunt, and the piercing point of Elizabeth's eyes caused her heart to sink and her stomach to jump in a fearful spasm. She had never seen such hate and loathing. Elizabeth did not even blink. Nor did she regard the conversation of the men.

"There is nothing to discuss."

"Charles, think about talking to me. I do not wish to harm you. Please don't force me to defend myself any further."

Charles stared at his brother for a moment, then pulled his wife with him past Lord Ridgley and out of the church.

They lingered in the back of the church until the others in attendance had departed and the coffin was removed to the waiting cart. When the hall was empty, Boris gave a long, heavy sigh.

"I will give him a little time. Perhaps it can be over soon."

"His pain is obvious," Tyson said. "Somehow, I did not think he valued his family as much as other men. I almost feel sorry for him."

"Elizabeth," Vieve said in a breath. "The way she looked at me..." She gave a shudder. "It is almost as if she blames me."

Boris put an arm around his daughter. "She will come around, once her grieving is done. Of them all, Elizabeth has always been the only one with any compassion."

The first of March came, and Lord Ridgley was becoming frustrated with his idleness in the captain's London house. Then the note came. Charles wished for a conference.

"Your mood toward him has softened," Tyson said bluntly.

"I will be as easy on him as possible," the baron returned.

"I have worked and put myself in danger for these months on behalf of..."

"I will not let him go," Lord Ridgley said tiredly. "I never wished to control Charles. That I must to protect my own family does not make me happy. But I will show him that he will not ruin me. He will have to pay."

Vieve was in a near panic at the idea of the conference, but she was determined to stand beside her husband and father in a show of strength, nonetheless. Doré and Lord Moresay were to witness Charles's confession, so Vieve's presence there was unnecessary, but she wore black to convey her grief and intended at least to show support for her family by being there when Charles arrived at their home.

She was tucking her hair in a tight bun at the base of her neck when Tyson came up behind her and gently squeezed her upper arms. He met her eyes in the mirror. "Are you frightened?"

"No," she whispered, turning to him. "But it all seems wrong. Charles has spent twenty years or more trying to harm my father... and now he can simply come here, have a meeting, and it is over?"

"Well, not quite as simply as that, my love. Charles will have to admit guilt and bear restitution. And he will be watched, but by officials rather than your father's distant suspicions. Yet it is what we hoped for, that he could be stopped before any more harm is done."

She shook her head and her eyes were worried. "Do you think he will admit to his indiscretions?"

"It doesn't matter," Tyson said.

She embraced him suddenly. "Oh, Tyson...I feel as if I'm in the midst of a black, vicious cloud. I feel terrible, and I should feel relieved."

He caressed her back and lent the strength of his arms. "You will when it's over. Come, he will be here soon."

Vieve thought she would face Charles briefly and then simply await his departure, but to her astonishment, Elizabeth joined him. Vieve's mouth actually hung open when she sighted her. Elizabeth's eyes were glassy, her hands held together under a thick black shawl.

Lord Ridgley was quite discomfited by Elizabeth's presence. He faltered slightly and embraced her to kiss her cheek, but

Elizabeth did not raise her arms, and she turned her cheek away. The baron withdrew clumsily. "Well, ahem, I don't see why you need witness our discussion, Elizabeth. We can handle this without the women, can't we, Charles?"

Charles nodded lamely. His eyes were bloodshot, his pallor unhealthy. He touched his wife's elbow. "This shouldn't take long, Elizabeth. Why don't you wait in the sitting room?" He looked at Boris. "She insisted, Boris. She wanted to come along. I thought it better than..."

"It's all right," Boris said, after clearing his throat again. "Vieve will sit with her until we're finished, won't you?"

Vieve looked at Elizabeth's strangely focused eyes, her oddly dignified bearing, and her superior half smile, and decided she was quite mad with grief. Vieve nodded lamely. "Of course."

"Come, Charles, Lord Moresay and Monsieur Gastión are waiting for us in the study. This is difficult business. Let's get it done."

Vieve watched her husband, father, and uncle go down the hall toward the study and looked back at Elizabeth. She tried to conceal the shudder of revulsion that went through her as she again witnessed that crazed look in her aunt's eye, the stiff posture, the demure fold of her hands beneath the shawl.

"Come, Aunt Elizabeth, let's wait in here," she said, opening the sitting room doors. She took a step within, followed by the small, darkly garbed woman, and gently closed the doors. She turned back to her ailing aunt with the best effort at a smile on her lips and gasped abruptly as the flesh of her chin met with the long, sleek barrel of a pistol. The shawl lay out of sight somewhere on the floor, and Elizabeth smiled victoriously as she carelessly lifted Vieve's chin with the gun.

"Don't doubt that I can use it, darling," Elizabeth crooned. "Your husband was injured by this very gun."

"You," Vieve whispered.

Elizabeth laughed lightly. "I suppose you thought that Captain Gervais was at risk. It was you I wished to kill, my dear niece. When I realized that your husband had such impressive support in the earl of Lemington, I could see that Charles would fail yet again, as he has for so many years. He would not be able to send the captain fleeing a murder charge. But I wished to have my daughter settled in marriage. You should have left London when I asked it of you."

Vieve stared at her aunt in amazement. "And so you wish my life in payment for Faye's."

Elizabeth showed her teeth in a vicious snarl. "In just a little while. Do let's sit down and be quiet for the men. My husband is about to beg for mercy from his brother; I wouldn't want to rob him of one moment of that."

Charles and Tyson sat in twin chairs while Lord Ridgley seated himself behind the desk. Doré and Lord Moresay stood in grim silence behind the baron. Two ledgers and a stack of aged parchment littered the top of the desk.

"I will be brief, Charles. It is clear from the records, deeds, and contracts contained here that you have been trying to ruin me with much malice. I offer you an opportunity to escape prison or charges of murder by an admission of guilt and a sworn statement that no member of your family will ever inherit the Chappington seat. And finally, there is the matter of restitution to the families who suffered losses as a result of your criminal actions."

Charles's hands gripped the arms of his chair, but still his shoulders were slumped. "I tried to buy you out, Boris. That is all."

Boris lifted a piece of paper. "Here is a contract for Andrew Shelby's land and loans against his marriage with my daughter. I'm sure he can be found..."

"The boldest thing I ever did," Charles said slowly, "was to pay Shelby, pushing him to marry your daughter." He sighed heavily. "You saw what that did to me. My own daughter was the one destroyed by that plan."

"Dammit, Charles, it gives me no pleasure to hurt you further than you've been hurt, but by God, you have to pay for your crimes. The only thing saving you from the courts now is that I can prevent your imprisonment because you are rich enough to make restitution. Now..."

"Boris, I committed no crimes. I tried only to best you in your own holdings. I was ruthless, but I was not criminal."

Boris's fist hit the desk. "Every time I made a small gain, I suffered some setback because of fire or theft or..."

"Weather?" Charles asked blandly. "Can you find a way to make me pay for your losses because of winter's plight and drought?" Charles sighed and held his hands together. "I will admit to what I did. I tried to buy you out. It was never so much of a secret; I wanted to share the title that was my mother's."

"If it was not a secret, why did you place puppets in those country holdings, as if they were not yours?"

"It seemed prudent," he said lifelessly. "If you found out the property was mine, it did not really matter. But if you did not find out, I could continue to compete with you unchecked. Is that against the law?"

"And Lenore Fenton?" Tyson asked.

Charles turned to him. "Your money stopped me. I hoped to find a weakness in you that I could buy. 'Twas my simple intent to threaten you, replace your investment with mine, and own my brother. I sent a man on my behalf to investigate you, and Lenore Fenton lied to him." Charles shrugged. "I would not have used her against you any further unless you resisted my offer, but I did not really expect you to suffer much."

"Do you deny that you would have tried to see me punished for murder?" Tyson demanded.

"I would have tried," Charles admitted, "because I thought you were a murderer. Even so," he said, glancing at Lord Moresay, "I did not expect you to pay."

"The warehouse fire?" Tyson asked. "The fire on my ship, the armed intruder in my house who tried to kill me?"

Charles looked almost amused. "Apparently you have many enemies, Captain. I only wished to assault your purse."

"Fifty men could have died, had my ship burned."

"I know nothing of fires. I cannot explain the ill fortune of you or my brother. I delighted in both, of course. I thought I was winning."

Tyson's jaw tensed. "You hired agents."

"I will name them all for you unless you already know who they are. Spies, errand boys, agents to question and buy people on my behalf. None are in hiding, none were ever paid to commit crimes."

Charles looked at Lord Ridgley. "I pushed you as hard as I could. I have nothing left. I will sign your promise, and Chappington will finally belong to only you...from your parents."

"That is not enough, Charles. The matter of deaths as a result of—"

"I realize you can buy false evidence against me...but I am too tired to fight you now. My son has left me, my daughter is dead, Elizabeth seems undone in grief, and I have no ready money. I sold several properties to pay Shelby and Lenore Fenton. I have only houses and land in the country."

"You will not admit what you've done?"

Charles shook his head. "You seemed never to understand, Boris. The way everyone looked at me while I was growing up, as if I was some bad seed. The way you doled out money, but denied every petition I made for your help in getting some noble recognition. I meant to prove to you that I could get it, somehow. I did everything in my power to get ahead of you. With every small disadvantage you suffered, I stepped in and bought up the spoils. I planned it so well: I would go to you one day with the proof that I owned you...and then you would finally see that I was made of the stuff of leaders." Charles hung his head. "Do you think I attempt to escape Newgate or hanging? You have beaten me. It doesn't matter what you do to me now. I have lost my family and I don't care anymore."

"That you're sorry doesn't—"

"Sorry?" Charles questioned. He gave a short laugh that sounded more like a sob. "I am sorry, Boris, that I failed. If it is not enough that I did not best you as I should have, though Elizabeth tried to warn me, I did not see the cost to myself. But I am mostly sorry that no one, not even you, understood why. I needed to beat you. I wanted to feel I was your equal... if only for one shining moment."

There was a tense moment of silence as Charles put his face in his hands and tried to collect himself. "We will accomplish nothing here," Lord Moresay finally said. "Lord Ridgley, you will be forced to turn your evidence over to the—"

"A moment, my lord," Doré interrupted. "Mr. Latimer, did Andrew Shelby know your reasons for aiding him in this quest for the baron's daughter?"

Charles's eyes seemed blank as he gave a rueful chuckle. "He actually thought I liked him. Yes, when I was pushing him, giving him money, taking debt off his property, he thought I was trying to help my brother...but in the end he knew the truth."

"Until Captain Gervais married Vieve, Andrew did not know your purpose?" Doré pressed.

"I never openly admitted to him that my whole intent was focused on her estate. He thought he lost her on his own account and blamed me. All the while, he was using my daughter."

"Who did know of your goal?"

"A few of my closest workers, my family. Robert left my house because of it; he has left England. I tried to find him, but I was too late and his ship had sailed. Faye died because of it, though she did not learn how Andrew came to be our frequent houseguest until the day she took her own life. There is only Beth left unscathed, for Elizabeth no longer bothers to conceal her hatred for me. She begged me to cease in my attempts, to give attention to my family, but I cast pleas aside with the promise that when I had finally succeeded and stood in line to the title, there would be time for family. She waited twenty years for me to accomplish my single objective."

"Elizabeth is a strong woman," Lord Ridgley said. "She will..."

Tyson's eyes met Doré's over the baron's head. He thought of the fires, the attempt on him in his own house, Elizabeth's strange request for them to leave England. The crimes were all committed with cowardly stealth, none requiring great strength. He remembered Elizabeth's hateful focus on Vieve's face, her strange reaction to meeting the earl of Lemington.

He rose abruptly to his feet and moved quickly out of the study, leaving the door ajar. Doré moved quickly from behind the baron in pursuit, leaving the others to stare in wonder at their flight.

Tyson burst into the sitting room, stopping short at what he saw. Elizabeth sat most calmly on the settee beside Vieve, but the fingers of one of the aunt's hands were locked into the hair at the base of Vieve's neck, pulling her head back. In her other hand was the pistol, its barrel pressing into Vieve's cheek.

"Do be cautious, Captain. It is cocked."

Elizabeth gave Vieve's hair a sharp tug, and Tyson read the terror in her eyes. He stood stock-still in the sitting room doorway, Doré peeking in over his shoulder.

"Tyson, it was Elizabeth...all the time," Vieve whispered.

Elizabeth tugged her hair again. "Be still," she ordered, her lips a white line of rage. "One little step, Captain, and before your very eyes, all this beauty shall disappear." She chuckled. "All this magnificent beauty."

"Why do you wish to hurt Vieve?" he quietly asked. "Is it not the title for your husband that you wish?"

"Bah, I have never cared for that 'twas what Charles wanted, well enough, but all I wished was for a good life for my family. And it always seemed that I could not keep my family in order, for I had no husband and my children had no father."

"Then it is Charles you wish to hurt," Tyson said easily.

"I don't care about Charles anymore," she said evenly. "This is all her fault. Prancing about and teasing the men, flaunting her success over my girls, holding onto Andrew 'til the very end...Had it not been for her, my delicate little niece, Charles would have his coveted title, Faye would have married decently, Robert would be with me...Beth..."

"You must think of Beth," Vieve said softly.

There was a slight commotion in the foyer outside the sitting room, and Vieve knew that the men were all there, though she could only see Tyson. Then Charles came into view behind him, and after a shocked gasp, he tried to push into the room. Tyson spread his hands to hid him back.

"Elizabeth. My God."

"Don't you come near me," she sneered. "You may stand where you are and watch, but don't you ever come near me again."

"Elizabeth, don't..."

She began to laugh suddenly, her light eyes gleaming. "You arrogant bungler, you idiot. Fool. Bastard. All these years spent on property, bribes, loans. It would have never been over. You couldn't get your hands on it, and while you blustered and fumbled, the rest of us were left to rot. Oh, how I hate you."

"You? Did you—"

"Robert understood. He knew that Boris would die and you would commit another twenty years to your ritual of buying property, selling, loaning, bribing...all directed at the next baron. Another twenty years...every day saying that by summer it would be finished, by winter, by summer, by winter . .."

Her voice had become a singsong of anger mixed with despair.

"Elizabeth," Charles pleaded. "For God's sake, don't hurt anyone!"

She gave Vieve's hair a sharp tug. Tyson stiffened and nearly took a step.

"You are an unmitigated ass," she hissed. "I've already hurt people, you fool. When you whined that but for the ships you would have Boris, I paid a pirate to sink his largest. It cost me everything I had managed to save. When you raged that but for the warehouses you could win, I burned them for you. And then it was the captain you wished to remove." She jammed the barrel into Vieve's cheek. "I should have seen all along that the simplest way for you to get your damned title was to do away with his children. I could have done it years ago."

"You cannot escape, Elizabeth. Put down the gun."

"Why would I wish to escape? To what? You will either hang me or my husband...it is all the same. Tell him, Charles. Tell him that you are the only thing I have. You have told me often enough that I will have nothing without you. There will be no money, my children leave one by one, my own family is gone."

"Beth," Vieve said again. "Think of Beth."

"I do think of Beth," she ground out. "I think of how much happier she will be when she no longer has to be compared to her beautiful cousin. Faye's last words before she died were 'I am not as pretty as Vieve.'"

Vieve slowly closed her eyes, tears running unheeded down her cheeks.

Charles cautiously stepped a bit farther into the room, standing beside Tyson. "It is me you should kill, Elizabeth. I did not see what I was doing to you."

Elizabeth smiled. "I think it is better that you live, Charles. And may every day be a living hell."

"Kill me," he said, taking another step to the right of Tyson. "No one will blame you. You may tell them how I've driven you, abused you, deserted you."

"I never even went to childbed with a husband near enough to hear my screams," she said to him, her voice full of venom. Doré was in the frame of the door, Lords Ridgley and Moresay still without, listening. Tyson glanced over his shoulder and met Doré's eyes. Charles moved farther right, engaging his wife.

"They will not harm you for killing me. You will convince them it was my fault. Kill me."

"Ha. You should live to face your son's hatred. You thought it was difficult growing up under your older brother's scorn, you should end your life enduring your son's unforgiving—"

"Shoot me and receive him home, Elizabeth. It is my doing; no one else stands responsible."

Tyson cautiously edged his way left, taking advantage of Charles's distraction. Doré stood where Tyson had been in the doorframe, lest Elizabeth take her eyes off Charles and look for a figure in that place.

"God knows you deserve it, Charles, but it is better for me, I think, if you watch your niece's beauty die." She cackled almost joyously. "Then you can watch your wife hang, comfort your daughter, and explain to your son—"

Tyson took two quick steps to the right while Elizabeth was shouting and then leapt suddenly, hitting the pistol arm from behind, swinging the bore off Vieve's face. The only direction it could go was toward Charles, and the report sounded along with Elizabeth's gasp of surprise. Without looking at the damage the shot had rendered, he grasped Elizabeth's arms, holding her in an iron vise. Despite her frailty, he had to struggle to hold her, wrestling her off the settee and to the floor.

Charles reeled back with the force of the lead ball and fell with a crash, his hand clutching at his chest, his face distorted with pain. The moment the gun had moved, Vieve had turned her face. In the fire blast of powder, her hands went to her face, shielding her eyes.

Doré ran to Vieve, and the room instantly filled. Boris saw the effects of the shot first and his daughter second. Doré pulled Vieve's hands from her face. Her cheek and chin were pinkened and sore from the powder, and her eyes watered profusely from the stinging blast, but she was harmed no further.

Doré quickly bent to clasp Elizabeth's hands, replacing Tyson, and jerked the growling woman to her feet. She was a slight, wiry form, kicking, cursing, and wriggling frantically. He pulled her away from the commotion over Charles and Vieve, holding her wrestling form still by brutally pinning her wrists behind her back.

Vieve went to Tyson, sobbing against his chest as he held her close. "It was Elizabeth," she wept, distraught and trembling. "Oh, Tyson, that night that you were shot, it was me she had come to kill."

As Tyson held her, he looked down as Boris lifted his brother's head.

"Be still now, Charles," he said. "You'll be—"

"Don't..." Charles attempted. Blood poured from his chest. He coughed, and a spittle of blood came from his mouth. He looked into Boris's eyes. "Don't hurt her," he rasped. "It wasn't her..."

His voice trailed off, his eyes focused on Boris's face, and he became still. The hand that had gripped his chest slowly fell away. Boris turned and looked up at Tyson. Then, turning back to his brother, he gently closed Charles's eyes and laid his head softly on the floor.

Boris slowly rose and stood before Vieve. She turned from Tyson and sought comfort in her father's arms, her frightened tears now buried in Lord Ridgley's breast. The baron stroked her back. "God Almighty, forgive us all our ambition. This never should have gone so far."

"Turn your prayers on them, my lord," Tyson said softly. "Yours was not the sin of ambition, but survival. You cannot accept the blame for this."

Vieve's head rested against him, and he gently squeezed her shoulders. "Perhaps if I had been more generous when Charles was young..."

"...Or if your father had not died, your mother had not been lonely, your brother never born," Tyson went on for him. He shook his head. "If there had been anything you could have done better, my lord, you would have done it." He placed a firm hand on the baron's shoulder. "Let it be."

Lord Ridgley held his daughter's face in his hands. "Perhaps I should have made him my heir," he said, seeking some answer from Vieve.

She smiled shakily through her tears. "And I should have been born an ugly maid...Papa, we did not know how deeply they all hated us. How jealous, how driven. What could any of us have done? Could you have passed over your own son to give Charles your title? Could I have given my cousins good looks?" She shook her head. "Tyson is right; your only blame comes in trying to survive their envy and hate. You could have done nothing more."

Lord Moresay and Doré were busily making use of a bell cord to tie Elizabeth Latimer to a small straight-backed chair. Oddly she did not resist, but stared ahead blankly with a mad, twisted smile on her face. It was in the midst of this that Harriet came to the doorway, having just returned to the house from some errand. She looked into the room, her eyes passing over the form of Charles to Elizabeth being bound, and then slowly her eyes rolled back and her bulky form sank backward with a thump on the floor.

"Blimey," Bevis gasped from behind. He came into view as the parcels he carried for Harriet fell to the floor and he stooped to her. He looked into the room, slowly taking account of the scene. "Blimey," he uttered again, not understanding in the least what had transpired.

"It will take a while to explain, Bevis. In the meantime, see to Harriet," Tyson instructed.

Tyson pulled Vieve closer to him, putting an arm around her shoulders. They looked at Elizabeth.

"I can't move my hands, Captain," Elizabeth said. "Vieve, tell him that I can't move my hands anymore. You must leave London with your Yankee, my dear. You must do so at once, for Faye is to be married and you interfere. Tell Charles that I am ready to go now."

Vieve shook her head in sadness. "Oh, Elizabeth," she sighed.

"I should have guessed," Tyson said. "The fire setting, the intruder after the ball... it always required that the person be small and fleet and quiet. I simply never imagined that a woman..."

"You must remember to wear your gloves, my dear," Elizabeth crooned, her eyes glassy and unfocused. "And by all means, take small steps. And do appear shy; you must always stay behind your husband, do not interfere with his progress. If you find yourself getting excited about some small matter, simply retire to privacy until it passes."

Vieve looked at Tyson. "All the while that you were in conference and she held the pistol to my face, when she wasn't threatening me, she gave me lessons in etiquette." She shuddered slightly. "I may never follow another social rule."

"I will see to her now," Boris said. "She will have to be kept quite closely. Robert can be found and will take care of Beth and what is left of Charles's holdings."

"Whatever can you do with her, Papa?"

"Not much more than keep her, guard her. There is no point in sending her to Newgate, mad as she is. I will try somehow to work things out with what is left of Charles's family. Perhaps Robert will take control of them now, though it will be hard for him. I will bury my brother. Come out of this room. It is too grim in here."

Boris walked with them to the foyer, where each had to step around Harriet's generous mound. The woman was softly moaning, slowly rousing.

"Please," Boris said, his voice catching. "Leave the house, the two of you. Tyson, take my daughter for a long ride. There is very little left to be done here. Let me do it alone."

"I have come this far, my lord..."

Boris held up his hand to stop Tyson. "I have detained you long enough, and what remains of this grievous business is mine to bear alone. Leave. Walk, ride, take your leisure in the park. Talk about a long sea voyage to America."

"Papa, Tyson and I will assist you to the end...."

"My sweet child," Boris said softly. "This is the end. Thank God." He gently kissed her cheek. "Go with your man."

Vieve watched as her father stepped back into the sitting room and quietly shut the doors. She looked uncertainly at Tyson.

"Come, love," he said gently, taking her arm. "The death of a brother, even one such as Charles, is a painful thing to bear. Let us do as he bids us and leave him be."

"He may need us..."

"He is not shy of voicing his needs, Vieve. Let him finish this as it suits him."

Fourteen

June 6, 1795

Vieve halted Tristan in front of the old keep. Before dismounting, she glanced out toward the coast, noting that the smudge on the horizon would be the Lady Lillian anchored just offshore, ready for two passengers.

She jumped down from Tristan's back, her heart jumping in sentimental wonder as she approached the ruined old building. She faintly heard Tyson's horse approach behind her, but she did not turn. Instead she gazed at the crumbling rock. It appeared as any fairy castle to her.

She marveled at the strange mixture of fate and chance that comprised life. She never would have met her husband, she reasoned, had he not been tricked into a duel. And had Charles Latimer not worked for so many years to ruin Lord Ridgley, there would have been no burned warehouses, no need for her father to seek a rich business partner.

Elizabeth Latimer's last violent act had been the end of her strength. She sat, now, in a bolted bedchamber, depleted of energy, weak and listless. Though she seemed finally harmless, her son guarded her dubiously, determined to proceed with the care of what remained of his family responsibly. Though the relationship was strained, Lord Ridgley and Robert seemed to have a common goal in ending the bitterness even if they could not develop a great deal of warmth. The many years of hostilities had left their mark on the young man as well as the old.

Vieve looked around the inside of the keep. She could not help but think of Andrew. He had been given back his deeds, but still he caroused London in search of a rich bride, rather than working the land his family had left him. Some things, she thought with a heavy sigh, even fate could not change.

She was ready to say good-bye to her father and begin another life for herself in Virginia. Leaving Lord Ridgley was difficult, but he was a hearty soul and promised to visit. Now he busied himself with the long-overdue refurbishing of Chappington Hall and waited impatiently for the birth of Paul's heir. It was a glad time for her family, their troubles past and hope on the horizon. She would miss them.

She felt Tyson's arms come around her from behind, and she leaned back against him. "It did not really begin here," he said.

"Mmmm," she sighed. She closed her eyes and hugged his arms tightly under her bosom. "Perhaps it began before we even met."

"Perhaps."

He turned her around and gently touched her lips with his. Her arms went around his neck. "I love you, Tyson," she whispered against his lips.

"Come away with me now," he murmured. "Are you ready?"

"Take me home, Tyson."

Robyn Carr is a RITA Award-winning, #1 *New York Times* bestselling author of fifty novels, including the critically acclaimed Virgin River series. Her new series, Thunder Point, made its debut as a #1 NYT bestseller in March 2013. Robyn and her husband live in Las Vegas, Nevada. You can visit Robyn Carr's website at www.RobynCarr.com or follow her on Twitter at @RCarrWriter.

Here's a sneak peek at Robyn's contemporary romance:

Tempted

Chapter One

Bev brushed her short brown hair, looked closely at herself in the mirror and decided to add some color to her cheeks. Going out. A big evening. It should make her feel better about herself. When a widow was going out it should buoy her spirits. It should mean progress. Bev felt like she was sliding back. Way back.

"I sure hope I look as good as you when I'm thirty-five," Terry, her youngest sister, said. She was pretty, twenty, and in love.

"I'm not thirty-five."

"Almost."

"Not almost. I'm not even thirty-four."

"Almost."

"Okay, almost to that, but don't rush me."

Terry smiled. "Steve's coming over. You don't mind, do you?"

"Not as long as you behave yourself."

Terry looked indignant. "Bev..." she said in a warning tone. Bev was closer to Terry than to her other sisters, and it sure was nice that Terry appreciated an opportunity to baby-sit.

"Sorry. Sure, Steve can come over. But watch yourselves. I have two little boys to think about."

"Bev!"

Beverly softened. Terry was a sweet girl. She smiled at the little sister who was not so little anymore.

Coming home was one of the hardest things Beverly had ever done. At first, she had thought it wise and strong to go on living in the house she and Bob had built. There were good friends in Dallas, the neighborhood was familiar, and the house was large and comfortable. Yet, their friends were couple friends, and Bev had learned quickly what that meant. They were good people, one and all, thoughtful and kind down to the very last Christmas card, but no matter how you looked at it, Bev was on her own.

And there were the boys. They needed a father figure of some kind. That meant one set of grandparents or the other. Bev didn't think there were fatherly role models in her family for Mark and Chuck, but moving near Bob's parents so the boys could pattern themselves after their grandfather seemed cruel... or bizarre. Bob's parents would have felt obligated to take care of her; she would have felt obligated to be wonderful all the time. Impossible all the way around.

Bev's dad was a fine man and she loved him, but he was in his late fifties now and wasn't up to much beyond talking to the boys about their sports. He wouldn't roughhouse with them the way their father had. Coming home had shattered the final illusions. They had no father. They had no father figure. They were on their own. And they weren't really home; they had only moved.

But the boys had each other. She was a little grateful now for that horrifying accident she had had when Mark was only three months old. She had wanted to kill herself at the time, when she found out that breastfeeding wasn't the only reason she didn't have her period. And that it was only one of the reasons she was so tired. Not long after she decided not to kill herself, Chuckie was born. And then she knew tired.

In the fall Bev watched Mark and Chuckie both go off to public school for the first time. The old pro, Mark, came home and told her about it.

"I'm the only kid in my class whose dad is dead," he said.

Bev shuddered. "Swell." They must have interrogated him.

"There's a bunch without dads though. Divorce, y'know."

"I know."

"What's the difference?"

"The difference is that in divorce the mother and father stop living together because they stop loving each other. Daddy loved us very much and I would give anything to have him back. Anything."

"Me too," Mark said meekly.

"I'm sorry, Mark. Sometimes I miss him so much."

"Me too."

She had clutched her little boy, the image of Bob as a child, close to her chest, hugging him fiercely as if begging for something secure, something to claim, some reason to live, anything...

"Will Bonnie have a man all lined up for you tonight?" Terry asked.

"Oh, sure. It's her duty as a friend to see if she can't rescue me from my loneliness with a stray bachelor. We're in good shape if it's a real bachelor. Some of these acquaintances neglect to mention their marriages.

But by accepting the invitation I've given silent permission to let myself be set up."

"Is it that bad?"

Bad. But Terry wouldn't understand. And she wouldn't really want to hear it either. Since Bob's death Bev had been the victim of her friends' good intentions many times. It usually was some unattached bachelor who worked with a friend, or a cousin, or a "fella from the club." And she would feel obligated to be charming for the sake of some well-meaning matchmaker. "No, honey. It's just not usually much fun, that's all."

"It's good you're going out, Bev. Bob's been gone for... well, it'll be two years...."

"A little over a year. One year and five months. Seventeen months. I wonder how many days that is." Same as the number of nights, Bev.

"You seem to have lost interest in that guy from work you were going out with. What was his name? That beautiful blond hunk..."

"Chet?"

"Yeah. What happened to him?"

"He's around. We're only friends."

"Oh, boy, I'd try to improve on that friendship. He's beautiful. Really nice too."

Beverly looked at her sister and grinned. "Yep. Heck of a nice guy."

"So? I had really high hopes when I met him. Something wrong with him?"

"Nothing at all," Bev said, her eyes twinkling. "I got a little excited myself—for about two hours."

"Well? He isn't married, is he?"

"Not exactly. He's gay."

"Oh." Terry sighed. "Oh, nuts."

Beverly giggled. She couldn't help herself. Actually, Chet was about the nicest man she had dated.

"That's really too bad," Terry said.

Yes, Bev thought. But for her, not him. She had been terribly disappointed, hurt, in fact, when he told her. She had let herself become optimistic for the first time. Chet was the marketing director for one of the department stores where she had worked. They had had several entertaining conversations at the store when he asked her to join him for a bite to eat. Later, they made plans to go out to dinner and she was frankly charmed. He must have noticed that she was beginning to feel romantic toward him. It was a very clumsy moment. Instead of graciously and quickly accepting the friendship he offered, she had delayed, feeling resentment well up in direct ratio to how her high expectations were crushed. "C'est la vie," she said at last to Terry.

"Maybe this will be 'it,'" Terry said.

"'It' what?"

"The man. Maybe this time you'll meet someone you really like."

"Maybe." But highly doubtful, Bev thought, mostly because she didn't have much interest. It was everyone else's interest that kept her going out. Like the coming-home party at her mother's.

Beverly had relented and allowed her mother to have a fall picnic at her house to welcome her home. Stephanie and Barbara, her two sisters from out-of-state, came with their husbands and babies and everyone was together. Delores didn't mention that on her daughter's behalf there would also be old high school friends and half the congregation from her church.

There were questions like: "Is it nice to be home?" that sounded to Bev like: "Had enough of being strong?" And introductions like, "I'd like you to meet John Smith," that sounded more like: "I'd like you to meet someone available." And Bonnie had been there, looking only ten pounds overweight when Bev knew it was a solid forty, who had asked if she would like to go with the whole gang to Lindy's, a new restaurant near their subdivision.

"Oh? I've heard of that place."

"There's this guy—"

No way. "I think I'd better pass. Maybe some other time."

Bev couldn't help feeling that some of those people had come to the picnic to see how much Bob's death showed on her. She had always been pretty, lively, and enthusiastic. She knew the sparkle was gone. It hadn't aged her face or packed twenty pounds on her hips, but it was there. If she could feel the weight of it, others could see it in her expression. And she didn't much want to bear scrutiny.

"How's work going?" Terry asked.

"Going, that's about all. I haven't had many calls."

"It's a bad time of the year."

"It's fine with me." She thought her job was ridiculous. She had been shopping one day, when a buyer from the store asked her if she modeled. She had never even considered such a thing. The woman encouraged her to try it by working in a luncheon fashion show. They needed more women in their mid-thirties to add a dash of maturity to their in-store shows. They hired her to walk around the store next. Then they pushed her toward an agency so they could hire her for some pictures for advertising for a sale. The whole silly thing had turned into a part-time job for which she was paid fifty dollars an hour, plus she received a twenty percent discount on clothes. Since she wasn't doing any-thing else, she modeled. She could choose her schedule, her jobs. But it did seem silly... meaningless.

"I'm thinking about going back to school," Beverly said. "I just can't decide what I want." You wanted to be a wife and mother. So you're a mother.

"I hope you have a good time tonight, Bev."

"Thanks, honey. It's a night away from the kids and they can use the breathing space as much as I."

"Bev, you don't think... I mean, you haven't given up on the idea that you could fall in love again, have you?"

She already had been in love again, that was one of the problems. Oh, it wasn't like it had been with Bob, but then, love came in all sizes. Guy was an old friend of Bob's from army days. Bev had known him for years. He was attractive and funny and Bev let him fall right into a routine. He was welcome in her home. He was a man in the house and that had come to mean a lot. When she saw his true colors, though, she ended it easily by moving away. He didn't cry while she packed. He didn't even say, "Awww nuts." She had come to think of it as her second bout with losing someone dear. "No, Terry, I haven't given up on the idea." Just disregarding it for a while. "Want to have a drink with me before I go?"

"A little wine maybe."

Bev poured scotch over ice for herself and a small glass of wine for Terry. She didn't really drink more now that Bob was gone; it was just one of those things she really enjoyed. A good drink. A good scotch. Her mother thought if you ever indulged it was a problem worthy of prayer. Mother might be right tonight, Bev thought, because she needed this scotch to get herself up enough to go to the party.

The "unattached male" lined up for Bev was a good-looking man about forty years old and he didn't seem to be disappointed in his albatross for the evening. He put her at ease at once.

"Do you know any of these people?" he asked.

"No, do you?"

"Most of them. I'm the only unmarried man here. I imagine it's a coincidence that you're the only unmarried woman."

"Coincidence, my eye."

"That's what I say. What should we do now? Have a drink?"

"Please, and listen, don't feel obligated—"

"I don't. For once Bonnie did me a favor."

About that time Bonnie shot a few careful glances in Bev's direction, apparently to make sure she wasn't mad, and when she was finally convinced, she came over and owned up to having played Good Samaritan. Bev learned she had told Bob Stanly that Beverly was a "nice" woman, mid-thirties, and widowed, with two little boys. Bev winced at how her vital statistics had been offered—about five-foot-six, a slim size ten with a nice—there was that word again—figure and short brown hair. It couldn't have sounded very exciting... just average, boring, dull average. She could have turned out to be a real dog. And that was exactly what Bob Stanly had said, Bonnie told her, but her husband, Phil, had quickly assured Bob that Beverly was a real looker. So good old Bob had decided to bite.

Bob was headed back, drinks in hand, and Bonnie faded away... fast. After some small talk, Bev confessed, "My husband's name was Bob."

"My wife's name was Susan. Want to tell me about yours and I'll tell you about mine?"

"Are you a widower?"

"Divorced."

"Then we don't have as much in common as I thought."

"Maybe. Susan died last year. I have the girls."

"Oh, that's rich. I have boys. I'll bet Bonnie has started sending out the invitations already."

They laughed. This was at least unique: the very first time Bev had laughed with a man over a blind date. It was a comfortable change. She was beginning to think they could be friends, talk about things. She liked his manner, his easy style. He was fun. She had a flicker of an emotion she scarcely recognized and had learned to greatly fear—optimism.

It was the little bit of snow at the temples and the tired look around his eyes that relaxed her. "I wonder if I could ask... no, never mind."

"Go ahead," he said.

"Well, I hope you don't misunderstand, but I wonder... was it so bad, losing your wife when you were already divorced?"

"I guess not," he said. He seemed to know about the gray and the tired eyes. He blessed her with a very sympathetic look that said he wasn't in love with his wife when she died. "I'm mourning my gain more than my loss, Bev. It isn't easy."

"I know," she said in a way that sounded more like a breath than words. They quickly went for another drink. A change of subject and some more anesthetic for them both.

Bob Stanly seemed safe, sober, and kind. Beverly actually had a good time. The fact that he was from Richmond and regularly drove to Columbus on business was even better. She could think about this possibility for a while. It eased some of the pressure.

The hours slipped away. It was past midnight and she didn't want to be the last to leave. Everything was very nice, she told Bonnie. Yes, Bob Stanly was a lot of fun. No, he wasn't taking her home, she drove her own car over. No, he didn't ask her out again. Yes, if he did ask, she thought she might see him again. God, but she hated the way these things ended. She genuinely hoped Bonnie would have the good sense to leave Bob alone.

"You're sure I can't drive you home?" he asked.

"No, I drove over. It's only a few blocks."

"I'll walk you out to your car and take off myself."

"Where are you staying?"

"Downtown. The Hilton."

"Wow. Expense account?"

"Believe me, I wouldn't be staying there out of my own pocket. I'm doing all right, but I'm not rich. Why don't you invite me over for a drink, Bev?"

"Sorry, maybe some other time. My sister is babysitting and she's staying the night."

"I can take you downtown, buy you a drink at the Hilton."

"Thanks, anyway, but it's late. I have to take the kids to church in the morning."

She stopped when she unlocked the car door and he held it open for her while she climbed in. She would have expected some nice, friendly farewell just before closing the door, but that was not his style. "Move over."

She wondered for a long time after why she so quickly obliged him. She moved over. "What are you doing?"

"I don't want to stand in the street and make out like a schoolboy. You can spare a kiss good night, can't you?"

She could. It wasn't obligation or conscience. She liked him. Her lips trembled. It seemed so false on a thirty-some-year-old woman. It was hardly her first kiss.

His hands slid under her coat and around her waist to pull her closer. Her lips no longer trembled. She fit to his mouth and they kissed and kissed and kissed. It felt good. She couldn't remember when she had been kissed last. Probably Guy, since Chet certainly did not like to kiss women. It was delicious, weakening.

Her arms went around his neck to hold him close. His hands were gliding along her back, caressingly, pressing her chest more firmly against his. She loved it. He leaned back and she leaned forward, enjoying the feel of his nice, lean body. It's the kind of thing you can get used to, learn to love, and find terribly hard to resist, she thought. She no longer thought of Bob or Guy or anyone. She thought only of Beverly and how good she felt, how comfortable and natural and sensual.

She kept reminding herself that she must stop him and send him on his way, but something in her went totally deaf. While he made no more demands, she couldn't bring herself to break the magic moment. Then his hand slid over her breast and she gasped in delight. She mustn't let him go further for his own good.

"No, Bob. Stop now. No more."

"Am I hurting you?" he asked courteously.

"No, of course not. Please, let's not get ourselves any more worked up. I have to go home now."

"Don't," he muttered, kissing her ear, her neck, her shoulder. The night was no longer cold. She could feel the warm blood surging through her and she wanted everything. And she couldn't.

"Stop, Bob. It's going to be harder if you don't stop now."

"Too late," he whispered, drawing her hand to his already erect member. "Come with me, Bev. You won't be sorry."

"No, Bob. Now, stop. I'm not going with you." She added a dash of firmness to her voice. It didn't register. His hands were moving and soon would find that secret place that was so vulnerable. "No. Now stop that!"

"Come on, Bev. You want this as much as I do. Come on."

"Bob, if you don't stop at once, I'm going to have to get ugly. Now, stop that."

"Bev, baby, let's just finish it here. Come on, Bev, you're a big girl. If you won't go with me, then let's just finish it here. Anyway you say."

"Nooooooo!" She shoved him against the door and slid farther toward her own side. She took a deep breath. "I don't want to battle this out. The answer is no. No, no, no! I don't want to!"

"Well, that's just fine. Why the hell did you let me go as far as I did? You ought to know better than that. What kind of frigid bitch are you?"

"I'm not frigid. And I'm not a whore either. And I don't just jump in the sack with every guy I meet and hardly know and certainly don't love."

"What's love got to do with anything? We're two adults and we could both use some relief. Grow up, Bev!"

"Oh, I'm grown-up and I can see an excuse a mile away. You can go get your relief someplace else, big boy. It's not going to do you any good to call me names and shame me into finishing you off."

"Somebody oughta teach you a lesson, lady. You're ice."

"Get out of my car."

"What does it take, Bev? You can't make me believe you wouldn't do it. What's your price? Do I have to say 'I love you'? Offer you money, marriage—"

"You bastard! Get out of my car!"

"Come on, beautiful. Let's see what it takes to thaw that ice."

He grabbed her by the arms and jerked her so that her mouth hit his hard. The gentle and courteous kissing was gone, replaced by vulgar slobbering and rapidly moving hands. He pressed her down and she squirmed under him helplessly. His aggression revolted her. He was more than ready and it didn't take an expert to figure that out. She doubted that he would actually rape her and was a little tempted to see what his next move would be.

But she was repulsed beyond that point. She fought.

She fought him wildly and he couldn't be bothered with that much resistance.

"Okay, baby, you win. You win."

It was at this point, and she had been at this point before, that she was always tempted to apologize! She held her lips in a tight line and sat still as stone while he pole-vaulted out of the car. She locked the door. She cried.

Actually, Beverly cried a lot. She just never wanted anyone to know she cried, except those select few who were allowed to know she was not made of cast iron. She had a good imagination too. Well, maybe not good, but certainly developed. She envisioned this salesman from Richmond as an ax murderer who would be sore over her reluctance and follow her home and chop her up. When she finally did drive off, she watched the rearview mirror and relaxed to see empty streets behind her. He was merely a jackass, not an ax murderer.

So this was what life had to offer widows. Loneliness, friendly homosexuals, married and unmarried sex maniacs who needed a woman and would give her a break by diving into bed with her. The dating game was definitely over. There was no such thing as a stable single man who wanted to be with her, enjoy her company. Everyone wanted her to put out... something.

Chet wanted a friend, though Beverly wasn't sure why. Guy wanted a home away from home, a woman who would make him look good and feel good. The handsome, big-time airline pilot on the make. A married or divorced woman was usually better in bed and safer than a young girl. And what did Bob Stanly want? Relief. Well, sorry, chum.

So nobody wanted Bev. Sensible, lonely, strong Bev.

How many times had she faced this? Plenty, that's how many. A lot of evenings had ended badly. A few had culminated with near rape, degradation when she wouldn't, or disappointment if she had. Well, then Bev was through. Through with matchmaking parties, most of all. Through with it all. Bev would go it alone, thank you. Alone.

Her eyes were only a little red when she got home. Terry was watching the late movie and Steve was asleep on the couch.

"Exciting evening, hon?" she asked Terry.

"Wild. Yours?"

"Wild!"

Terry made a move to wake up Steve and send him home. His apartment was near the campus, a long drive. It was nearly one A.M. "Let him sleep, Terry. I'll give you a blanket for him."

"Here?"

"Who would be waiting up for him?"

"Well, no one, but..."

"So let him sleep. I'm not worried about you. Why should I be?"

"What's the matter, Bev?"

"Nothing. Nothing, baby." She brushed the hair from her younger sister's pretty brow. She looked at the sleeping stud. Yes, he was terrific-looking. A nice, strong, lean body, plenty of coarse black hair, clean-shaven and dark-skinned. Terry had good taste. Not only that, but he was a nice guy. He was much as she remembered Bob at that age. So what happened to all the nice guys when they hit thirty-five? Were they all either happily married or sex maniacs?

"You don't look very good, Bev. Are you sure you're all right?"

"Just tired. I'm going to bed. Will Steve take you to church in the morning or do I have to get you there?"

"We usually go together. We can leave from here. Want to tag along?"

"I think I'll just send the boys to Sunday school and stay here and rest for an hour. I don't think I can handle any lessons in moral fortitude. I'm not in the mood for righteousness."

"Sure. Good night, Bev. Sleep tight."

I already am tight, she thought wryly. "Good night, sweetie. Stay in your own bed."

Bev checked Chuck and Mark, and then retreated into her bedroom, closing the door behind her. She usually left it open to listen for the boys, but with the sleeping prince on the couch she didn't want to risk the lack of privacy. She removed her pantsuit, the latest Davana design. It was good-looking. She was good-looking. She removed the very necessary bra. So what if they sagged a little? They weren't all that small. And what if she did have stretch marks? There were worse things. She had a pretty good body for someone "almost thirty-five."

She pulled on her nightgown. She hadn't worn one when Bob was alive. He liked to reach for her, touch her sometimes in the night and feel her natural cover. So why, if a guy was going to die, why did he have to give you so many lovely things to remember first? Why did he have to give you not one, but two little boys who looked just like him? So why did he have to die anyway? Why couldn't he have just stayed around a little bit longer, loved you just a little bit more?

Bob, can you see this? Can you see what's happening down here? Do you know that I still miss you, still love you? Please, I can't make it alone. Please... please come back. I can't do it, Bob. I thought I could but I can't. I can't make the hurt go away... can't make it stop... oh, please... tell God. I can't even talk to Him anymore. If He wants to make up with me, He's going to have to do something about this pain. It's getting worse. I hurt all over. Oh, Bob, I still love you, baby. I want you back... please... help me... oh, please.

End of Sample

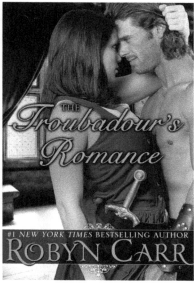
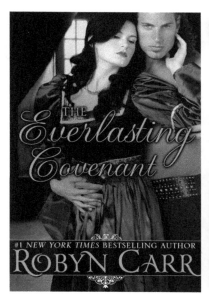

"She has done it again. Robyn Carr is absolutely marvelous."
—Danielle Steel

"Adventure, danger, derring-do, as well as doings at the glittering anything-goes court of Charles II...Carr tells an entertaining yarn." —Publishers Weekly

CPSIA information can be obtained
at www.ICGtesting.com
Printed in the USA
BVHW04s0221081018
529564BV00015B/243/P